Restraining Order

Ca$h & Coffee

Lock Down Publications
Presents
Restraining Order
A Novel by
Ca$h & Coffee

Acknowledgment

We want to thank everyone who has supported Lock Down Publications. We are a movement because of the readers, reviewers, referrers, promoters, editors, graphic designers, bloggers and more. In an effort to show our gratitude, our promise, as a company, is to deliver our creative best. You all deserve nothing less than that.

Sincerely,
Ca$h & Coffee

Dedication

Our book is dedicated to all women who have endured abuse of any kind, whether she survived and escaped with eternal scars or her life was stolen.

Authors' Note

This book does not glorify or condone abuse of any kind. It was written with the intent to shed light on a very detrimental situation through a fictional aspect.
If you are in a domestic situation and need help, please call the National Domestic Violence Hotline at **1-800-799-7233** or visit
www.thehotline.org

Lock Down Publications/Ca$h Presents
P.O. Box 1482
Pine Lake, Ga 30072-1482

Visit our website at **www.lockdownpublications.com**

First Edition February 2016
Printed in the United States of America
This is a work of fiction. Names, characters, places, and incidents either are products of the author's imagination or are used fictitiously. Any similarity to actual events or locales or persons, living or dead, is entirely coincidental.

Cover design and layout by: Dynasty's Cover Me
Book interior design by: Shawn Walker
Edited by: Shawn Walker

Stay Connected with Us!

Text **LOCKDOWN** to 22828 to stay up-to-date with new releases, sneak peaks, contests and more…

Thank you!

Submission Guideline.

Submit the first three chapters of your completed manuscript to ldpsubmissions@gmail.com, subject line: Your book's title. The manuscript must be in a .doc file and sent as an attachment. Document should be in Times New Roman, double spaced and in size 12 font. Also, provide your synopsis and full contact information. If sending multiple submissions, they must each be in a separate email.

Have a story but no way to send it electronically? You can still submit to LDP/Ca$h Presents. Send in the first three chapters, written or typed, of your completed manuscript to:

LDP: Submissions Dept
Po Box 1482
Pine Lake, Ga 30072

DO NOT send original manuscript. Must be a duplicate.

Provide your synopsis and a cover letter containing your full contact information.

Thanks for considering LDP and Ca$h Presents.

Ca$h & Coffee

Prologue

The BMW came to a sudden stop at the curb of an eerie, dark road. He yanked the gear in park and stared straight ahead. The vein on the side of his temple pulsated with hot anger that terrified me to no end. In the passenger seat, I was shaking frenziedly as I looked out of the window, too afraid to look at him. The sky was as dark as his mood and even though the heater was on full blast, inside of the car felt as cold as that muthafucka's heart.

Raindrops drummed on the windshield in an ominous symphony that matched the tears cascading down my battered face dripping onto my torn, bloodied blouse.

The fact that he wasn't talking didn't bode well for me at all. I could somewhat gauge the level of his anger when he was going off, spewing deathly threats and unfounded accusations. But when he was quiet like this, I had no idea what he would do. The only thing I was absolutely certain of was that he was going to punish me severely—death was not out of the question.

Out of the corner of my eye, I saw him pull his gun out of his waist and place it in his lap. At the sight of it, I became terrified. My heart pounded hard in my chest and pee ran down my leg.

He's going to kill me this time, I feared. How could he claim to love me so much yet treat me so foul?

Filled with fright, I began rocking back and forth.

Lord, if you get me out of this safely tonight, I promise to move far away from him, I silently prayed as my body trembled all over.

I jumped when I felt him touch my face. "Baby gurl, look at me," he said with a gentleness that belied the cruel monster he could become in the blink of an eye.

I didn't want to look at that bastard but I knew better than to defy him. Slowly, I turned my head in his direction. He cut the dome light on in the car and locked eyes with me. Stroking my face with the back of his hand, he asked, "Why you trembling? Are you afraid of me?"

I didn't know whether to answer honestly or lie. Either response could incur his wrath, so I decided to just keep quiet. But that was a mistake. "Fuck you gon' do, ignore me?" he growled.

"No," I replied meekly, casting my eyes downward.
"Answer me, then," he demanded. "Are you afraid of me?"
"Yes," I admitted in a voice barely above a whisper.
His response came with lightning quickness.
Whap!
I hadn't even seen him raise his hand but the stinging sensation on the side of my face and the taste of fresh blood in my mouth confirmed why my ears were now ringing.
"Bitch, you ain't scared of me," he spat. "Because if you were, you wouldn't keep tryin' a nigga like you be doing. Would you?"
"No. And I'm sorry," I apologized, though I hadn't done a damn thing but try to get far away from his crazy, jealous and controlling ass. Lord, he was nothing like the man I had fell in love with.
He smiled triumphantly. "Give your nigga a kiss and tell me that you belong to me."
I leaned over and offered him my lips. He covered my mouth with his and slid his tongue inside.
I couldn't help recalling a time not long ago when his kiss ignited a fire in my body that only his insatiable sexual appetite could quench, but now it felt like a serpent was slithering around in my mouth.
I forced the bile back down my throat and pretended to enjoy our lip lock. I didn't dare break the kiss until he pulled back first. "I belong to you," I said perfunctorily.
He lifted the gun from his lap and placed the tip of the cold steel against my forehead. "Say that shit like you mean it or I'll blow your brains outta ya muthafuckin' head!" he threatened.
His tone was as menacing as the weapon he held to my head. "Baby, I belong to you. Forever," I said.
"That's my gurl," he smiled. "Damn, I love you, bae. So much that I'll murder your ass if you ever try to leave me again. You understand me?" He lowered the gun from my forehead to my mouth and forced it inside. I gagged as he shoved it to the back of my throat. "You know, a few years ago I killed a bitch who looked just like you," he taunted.
I didn't know if it was true but I didn't doubt it. He was crazy beyond definition.

10

"Bitch tried to cut me off. Don't ever try that shit. Because if I can't have you, nobody will. On my life, ya feel me?" His sincerity rang loudly in my ears.

"Yes," I cried.

He removed the gun from inside of my mouth and then leaned in and placed a soft kiss on my tear stained cheek. I prayed his anger had subsided and that I would live to see my son again, but the next words out of his mouth caused me to shiver all over.

"Nah, bitch, you don't really feel me," he said. "But you're about to. Get out the car. I'm 'bout to bury your ass right next to that other ho."

Ca$h & Coffee

Chapter 1
Choppa

I pulled up in the apartment complex and parked outside of my man Cardale's unit. As soon as I hopped out of my silver BMW 4 Series and my J's touched the pavement, the sun's intense ray burned on the back of my neck and glistened off of my thick platinum chain. After adjusting my dark shades over my eyes, I slung the backpack I was carrying over my shoulder and looked toward Cardale's door. Before I could step up on the curb, a white Camry with tinted windows pulled up next to my truck.

Immediately, my paranoia and street instincts kicked in. My free hand shot to my waist where my Glock .50 was tucked in my jeans concealed by the hem of the crisp white T-shirt that hung loosely on my frame. I had known all along that this day would come, sooner or later, because, although I flew under the radar, I was starting to stack mad paper and nigga's had taken notice.

My mind was already made up. Wasn't nobody taking a mutha-fuckin' thing from me unless they took my life with it. I refused to go out like a bitch.

"They're about to find out today," I whispered to myself.

My hand gripped the butt of the gun as I eased it off of my waist and held it down at my side. My heart beat hard in my chest and adren-aline surged through my body like live currents of electricity. I tight-ened my grip on my tool and accepted my fate. I was about to go see my homies, either the one's in Thug Heaven or those in the peniten-tiary.

Let's do this muthafuckin' shit! I was ready to do or die.

The driver's door of the Camry opened slowly. I lifted my banger waist high while keeping my eyes trained on the driver. My trigger fin-ger was poised to apply the two pounds of pressure that it would take to turn the parking lot into a cemetery.

Almost in slow motion, the driver's legs swung out of the vehicle. I tensed up.

Kill or be killed. Bitch niggas, let's make this shit pop!

I was 'bout to show them that wasn't a goddam thing sweet over this way.

However, when the driver's feet touched the asphalt, they were adorned in a pair of cute pink, white and blue Nike's. And when the owner of those small feet straightened up and stood to her full 5'1" height, I couldn't help but shake my head and crack a smile. The jackboys I expected turned out to be a beautiful dime piece. A straight up stunner.

Chuckling to myself, I tucked the banger back in place and flashed baby girl an apologetic smile. Shorty looked at me with mad suspicion.

"My bad, ma," I quickly apologized.

She stood staring at me as if she couldn't decide whether to trust me or not. Slowly, I removed my shades, allowing her to see the sincerity in my eyes. My soft, dark browns seemed to relax her a bit and she returned my smile with one of acceptance.

Only three or four feet in distance separated us. I could smell the enticing fragrance of her perfume. Unconsciously, I found myself licking my lips as I absorbed all of her delicate beauty.

Baby girl was cute and very petite, but I could tell that underneath the loose fitting sweats that she wore was a whole lot of pleasure inside of her small, soft package.

Her jet black hair was pulled back into a ponytail that hung past her shoulders. She rocked oversized shades that added an irresistible sexiness to her beauty. For the first time in years, a nigga was stuck. I decided right then and there that shorty was gonna be mine.

Before I could open my mouth to speak a word, pretty mama shut the driver's door and walked around to the other side of the car. I watched as she hoisted a sleeping child onto her hip and then her struggle to retrieve groceries out of the back seat.

One of the bags slipped out of her hand and fell to the ground, spilling a few items. So I chased down a runaway can of corn and brought it back to her.

"Thank you," she said. Her voice was as soft as the flap of a butterfly's wings. I'd almost had to read her lips to make out what she'd said.

"No problem. Why don't you let me get your bags and you just carry little man?" I offered.

She seemed ready to decline, but I had already gathered up her grocery bags. With my foot, I closed the rear door and followed her to her apartment, inconspicuously admiring the twist of her hips and the bounce of her little heart shaped ass as she led the way.

I need this lil' bad muthafucka on my arm. Damn, she got a sexy ass walk.

Outside of her door she thanked me for my kindness.

"It was nothin'." I waved off her remark, then waited to see if she would invite me inside.

Quickly, she dashed out my hope. "You can sit the bags right here, I'll come back and get them," she said politely.

"A'ight." A slight frown forced its way onto my face. I was a little disappointed that she had dismissed me, but I didn't want to press up on her. I figured she must've had a man.

Shorty, if you was my girl, I would never make you carry groceries or nothin' heavier than five carats on your finger. And the only time you would ever have to break a sweat would be between the sheets.

Just as she inserted the door key in the lock, the little boy squirmed in her arms causing her shades to fall from her face. She quickly turned her head away from me, but not before I had caught a glimpse of her black eye. I didn't want to make her anymore uncomfortable than she probably already felt, so I pretended not to notice. I sat her groceries down, picked up her shades and handed them to her without comment.

The fragile beauty accepted the sunglasses and quickly recovered her shame. After thanking me again, we stood there for an awkward moment before she turned away from me, unlocked her door and carried the child inside without uttering a word.

I didn't know if her man was inside or not, but I waited outside of the door until she returned for her groceries.

"Take care," was all that I could think of to say as I handed her the two bags and watched her, again, disappear inside, leaving behind the scent of her perfume and a vivid impression of her fragility.

Ca$h & Coffee

I stood there for a minute trying to decide if I should knock on the door and offer her more help or perhaps some protection against whoever had blacked her eye. It didn't matter that I didn't even know her name, I would be her knight in shining armor, nah mean. *Nah, I'ma stay out of that woman and her man's business before I end up having to crush a nigga over someone that's not even mine,* I decided.

Hesitantly, I turned and headed over to my man's crib. But shorty was still on my mind as I knocked on Cardale's door.

A minute or two later, Cardale let me in. We G-hugged, then headed to the kitchen where his cousin, Jared, was already seated at the table.

"What's good, Slim?" I dapped him.

"You know, same story different day," replied Jared, who was smoking a Black-N-Mild.

"I hear that shit, but I'm about to make your day better." I sat the backpack in the center of the table and took a seat. Cardale leaned against the counter. "Y'all niggas ready to get these *bands*?" I leaned forward and pulled a large freezer bag full of greenery out of the backpack.

I opened the freezer bag, allowing the strong smell of the weed to escape from inside and tantalize their noses. "That's that real *loud pack.*" I smiled. "The streets ain't ready for this. I got another hundred pounds on deck and five cases of guns, AK's, fo-fifths, Nines, and a couple of Glock .50s. What y'all know about that?"

To my surprise, neither Jared nor Cardale seemed excited. Cardale uttered what sounded like an insincere "That's what's up."

"Let's get to it," added Jared, sounding only slightly more enthused. He reached inside the Ziploc to sample the product.

My hand shot out and locked on his wrist. "Hold up, bruh, what's the problem? I'm sensing shade up in here. If y'all got a problem, spit it out." I looked from him to Cardale.

When neither of them replied, I stood up and paced back and forth in the small kitchen. Their silence spoke louder than words. Quickly analyzing their facial expressions, I could tell that there was a problem. I nodded my head because I knew what the problem was.

16

My blood boiled. Disharmony had befallen many organizations, big and small. The fuck if I was about to let it invade what I had put together. I stopped pacing and glared at my man's. "Y'all gon' clam up like some emotional ass broads or y'all gon' speak what's on your minds?"

Cardale shook his long dreads out of his face and gritted at me like a Rottweiler baring its teeth.

"Nigga, what?" I challenged him. Homie was a killa but so was I. He chuckled dismissively. "What about the coke? Did you holla at your *connect* about that?"

I chuckled too. *Who does this nigga think he is to press me about any muthafuckin' thing?* I shook my head in exasperation. "Nah, bruh, I didn't ask him about any coke," I answered truthfully. "I thought about it and I just don't think that's a smart move for us. We're eating good fuckin' with the loud. Cocaine is a much grimier game and it attracts way too much attention."

"If you're scared, get a 9 to 5," said Jared.

My head snapped in his direction. Heat rose up off my brow as I walked back over to the table and leaned down in his grill. "Fuck you say, bleed?"

"I ain't say nothin'."

"Yeah, that's what I thought."

Jared smiled. "Oh, you think you punked me?" He put his cigar out in the ashtray that sat at his elbow and clasped his hands together on the table.

"I don't have to try to punk you. Just remember who's running this shit and we'll be good," I replied, never breaking eye contact.

"I hear you, boss." Sarcasm laced Jared's words.

I stared hard at him. He was a light skinned nigga who had trouble hiding his true emotions because when he was vexed his face turned red. I cut my eyes back to Cardale. I didn't like the look on his black face either. I knew that their bond with each other outweighed either of their bond with me, but that shit didn't faze me, not one muthafuckin' bit.

I removed my banger from my waist and sat it on the table in front of us. Looking back and forth from one to the other, I said, "If y'all

17

niggas don't wanna play your positions, we might as well kill each other now because that's what it's gon' lead to in the end. I know y'all rock together, but don't underestimate how quick I'll rock both of y'all asses to sleep if y'all try me. I don't know what the fuck done got into y'all stupid ass fools, but I'm the wrong nigga to test."

"Fam, is all of that called for?" asked Jared.

"That's what I'm saying," Cardale cosigned.

I looked at him with a smirk on my face. He stood 6'3" and weighed about 255 pounds, but I knew that if anything popped off, it would be the much smaller Jared who presented the tougher battle. I also wanted Jared to know that I knew he was the real one behind the push to convert our hustle from weed to coke.

"Bruh, you a goon, a certified killa—that's your get down. When I brought you in on this, it was strictly for protection and collections. I don't need you to tell me how to run my shit."

"Nobody's trying to tell you how to run things," Jared cut back in, "we're just suggesting that you think bigger. The weed game and selling guns is cool, but you know that *white girl* is where the real cheddar is at. Niggas out here getting rich while we're playing."

"Playing?" My voice bounced off of the walls. "You call a hundred pounds of weed and five cases of yoppas *playing*?"

"Fuck a hundred pounds of weed! We need to be moving a hundred bricks."

Gritting my teeth, I placed my elbows on the table and leaned forward, within inches of his face. "You're an ungrateful muthafucka," I spat. "You're greedy and you're stupid. You want it all, don't you?"

"You gotdamn right! Fuck I'm out here throwing bricks at the penitentiary for if we're not gonna go after it all?" he fired back.

I shook my head at his stupidity and turned back to Cardale. "Is that how you feel too?"

"Yeah, bruh."

I ran a hand down my face and sighed heavily. Two years ago I was back home in Cleveland, Ohio eating good all by my goddam self until I received a call from Cardale. We had grown up together on Kinsman Ave. in the city now known as The Land. Cardale couldn't catch a grip so he moved down south. A few years later, he hit me up and persuaded me to come down to the Dirty South.

"Bleed, you can get rich in no time down here. I'm telling you, the 'A' is a hustler's paradise," he promised.

I came to check it out, and I saw that what Cardale said was indeed true. I also found out that he had beef with some dudes whose murder games couldn't be discounted. Without hesitation, I strapped up and helped eliminate that problem because money couldn't be made while looking over our shoulders 24/7.

After we put Cardale's enemies in the dirt, we slowly began to spread our product on the streets. Homie knew the people who wanted the weed, and I had the connect back home. A year later, Jared, who was Cardale's first cousin came home from doing a a short bid.

Cardale explained that ATL niggas wasn't fuckin' with Jared because he was a hot boy with a quick temper, and if he ever turned against you he was a problem you didn't want to have. "But he'll listen to me," he promised.

"I don't need him to listen to you, my nigga. He has to be willing to listen to me," I said.

"Cuz is cool. I'ma bring him by so you can chop it up with him and see for yourself. But we can't go wrong with him on the team. I'm telling you he's a straight killa."

"I feel you. But a killa ain't no good to me if he's disloyal," I argued. But after meeting Cardale and feeling him out, I had decided to give him a chance. Now I was wondering if I had made the wrong decision.

"Y'all ain't using your heads." I spoke with heavy frustration. "More money, more problems. And when the feds come scooping muthafuckas up, and giving out football numbers, niggas gon' flip. Hell no, let's just rock with what we've been doing. If it ain't broke, don't fix it!"

"Get out your feelings, bleed. If you're not ready for the big time, I understand," quipped Cardale. He grabbed and handful of *loud* out of the Ziploc and buried his nose in it. "Yeah boy, this that killa shit," he declared.

Whatever tension was in the room quickly faded away. I let Cardale's comment about me not being ready for the big time roll off my back. He wasn't saying shit. Just moving his lips.

I rolled a blunt and passed it around. Jared, who could smoke like a chimney, pulled hard on it and leaned his head back as the smoke filled his lungs.

"Fam, remember that nigga, G-Shine, who stuck us for that work last year then got locked up on a parole violation?" he asked.

"Yeah, what's up with him?"

"He touched down a week ago and I know where he's laying his head. He got a lil bitch out in Dunwoody. You wanna go see him or you just gon' take the lost and let it ride?"

"Where they do that at?" I replied. There wasn't a snow ball's chance in hell that I would overlook the $10,000 G-Shine owed me. It had been nine months but it didn't matter because I had warned him not to fuck with my money when I gave him the werk on consignment. Now he was about to find out that I didn't issue idle threats.

"So, we gonna pay him a visit?" asked Cardale, hyping up. He had never cared much for G-Shine, anyway. In fact, he had warned me that the kid wasn't trustworthy.

"Is fish pussy waterproof?" I said.

"Say no more," replied Cardale.

"We can get at them tonight if you want to. I got the info and everything. Fuck putting it off. Niggas need to understand that street justice is swift," said Jared.

"Fam, you already know the business," I replied.

When Jared passed the blunt to me I waved it off. The last thing on my mind was getting high. I knew that when we kicked in G-Shine's door we wouldn't leave out of that house without leaving carnage behind. Killing was a necessary element of the game but I didn't particularly enjoy it. I always worried that one day we would leave behind evidence that would get us all cased up for a long time.

"What's on your mind, homie?" asked Cardale.

"Nothing much."

"If you got other shit to do, me and Jared can handle G-Shine," he offered.

20

I started to agree to that but I didn't want them to think that I was losing my killa's mentality. Any sign of weakness invited predators even in your own camp. "I'm good," I assured him, and then drifted off into my own thoughts.

Jared and Cardale was discussing coke deals that they could make if I would agree to move in that direction. Jared was talking about flipping some bricks and copping the new Phantom and a whole bunch of shit. Cardale was dreaming of getting overnight millions and buying a mansion.

I shook my head at their stupidity. "Y'all fools wanna hustle to be seen. I'm hustling to disappear," I said.

"You could disappear a lot sooner if--" started Jared.

"I already gave y'all thirsty ass niggas my answer so dead that." I shut him down.

This time my response quieted all of their talk about fuckin' with yayo. Before long, the kitchen was smoked out and our disagreements were forgotten for the time being. But I knew that I hadn't heard the last of their desire to move up to the coke game. I would hold them off for as long as possible then do whatever had to be done. No matter what, I was not allowing them to bring me down.

I shifted the conversation back to G-Shine. The three of us agreed that I had to make the punishment fit the crime.

"I'ma do him myself. I want my face to be the last image he sees before he depart this muthafucka," I said.

"You sure, bleed?" asked Cardale.

"Absolutely." I looked at Jared, letting him know that I was still a killa, just in case he had forgotten.

Jared acknowledged my pledge with a respectful head nod. But the look in his eyes told me that it was just a matter of time before he made a move to test my gangsta. I told myself to stay ready and to begin distancing myself from him and Cardale.

Once we agreed on a time and a strategy to get at G-Shine, the three of us began discussing other business. With a new shipment in we had drops to make and people to see. "But let's handle this murder shit first. It's been a long time coming," I said.

"Facts," said Cardale.

Jared just nodded his head. I tried to read his mind but couldn't. *It's all good,* I told myself, *they make caskets for friends too.*

Before I left, I gave my niggas the same fake dap they gave me. When I stepped outside the sun had faded from the sky like a smokers dreams disappears soon after they blaze that first rock.

I saw that baby girl's car was still in its parking space. An image of her ran through my mind as I recalled how beautiful she was. I wanted to go knock on her door and ask her out, but I decided to wait until I could find out what was up with her.

"I'll be back for you, shorty," I said as I climbed behind the wheel of my Beamer and drove off.

Chapter 2
Julz

I stood with my back against the door, clamping my eyes shut, shaking my head and cursing below my breath. *"Shit!"*

I turned around and looked through the peephole only to see him lingering a moment. For the second he stood there, it looked as if he waited for me to change my mind and follow up on his advances. But it was only a few seconds more that passed before he left and went about his business.

"Shit!" I cursed again.

There was something alluring about that man that drew me in instantly. It wasn't just his bow-legged stance or his muscular frame gift-wrapped in dark Hershey coating that made me raise an eyebrow. It was his presence that screamed *boss*. A powerful sumthin' sumthin' that said *hello* before the thickness of his lips parted or the smile in his eyes greeted me.

But I didn't feel as desirable as his deep browns said I was, so I clammed up. The horrid blue-black tint that roofed my eye had me feeling mad unpretty. God only knew what went through his mind after seeing that.

But, oh, how I wished I would have returned the flirty vibe he was giving a sista instead of camouflaging my usual brash and sexiness under such a fragile front.

I shook my head and sighed as I eased over to my front window, peeking out of the blinds. I saw no sign of him in the parking lot but I did notice his car still parked downstairs from mine.

I should have hollered, but it was all good.

I enjoyed the feeling of being desired our brief interaction brought me, even though my shyness said otherwise. It was probably for the best that I let him go his way in the long run. After all, I needed to concentrate on getting my life together and a making a new friend in the midst of still going through the *up but mostly down* relationship I had with my son's father, Marcel, would just make things more complicated.

Besides, it had been hard trusting men after him. And even as lonely as it was not having a man stroke my ego by day and my pussy come night, I figured it was best I remained single and focused on getting my life back on track.

It had taken me an excruciatingly long time to regain what footing I had. I finally had normalcy after all of the trifling bullshit Marcel took me through, shit that left me broken and insecure. And I wasn't ready to risk letting a man tear me down like that ever again. Hell no! I would take loneliness over heartbreak any fuckin' day of the week.

That damn Marcel, I rolled my eyes. I found my self-doubt deplorable because I had no real reason to be. It was factual that men had always found me attractive but Marcel left me questioning my looks and everything else.

How could the same love that built me up, break me down? I questioned, then I answered myself. *Gurl, love didn't do shit! You allowed him to break your ass down to the least common denominator. Get it right!*

The shit was too pitiful to laugh at, so I just stood there shaking my head as I reflected on our time together.

Marcel had taken so much from me I was surprised to still be standing.

Snapping out of my thoughts, I walked through my naked living room and down the short length of hallway that led into the bedroom that me and my four-year-old shared.

I told myself I would move into a larger apartment when I could afford it, but daycare was doing a fine job of kicking my ass and keeping me in what was supposed to be my starter place when I made my move from the N.O. to the ATL a year ago.

I headed over to my queen sized bed, where he lay sleeping as wild as he wanted. I slid his Jordan's off of his feet and gently shook him.

"Justus! Wake up, prince. Go to the bathroom before you go to bed."

"No, Mama, I'm sleepy." He frowned something terrible, making the ugliest/cutest faces that made me laugh out loud.

Look at my handsome little man, I gushed. He was the spitting image of his daddy but that was where the similarities ended, and I was determined to keep it that way. If Justus was going to grow up to dog women out like his father, it would have to be over my dead body. "Come on. Let's go." I stiffened my voice so it would register my seriousness.

Subsequently, he sat up and wrapped his little arms around my neck reminding me that he loved me like his father never did. I placed a soft kiss on his forehead and tried to coax him fully awake. After a minute or so, he finally stood up on his own but not without pouting.

"Mama," he whined, rubbing his eyes.

"Don't *Mama* me. Let's go to the bathroom."

Justus stood up on unsteady legs and wobbled out of the bedroom and down the hall like a drunk on a Saturday night. Laughing, I followed him into the bathroom.

My boy stood at the toilet whizzing pee all over the seat and the floor. "Oh, my God. Justus!" I cried but that didn't improve his aim.

After he was done, I pulled up his underwear and picked him up, carrying him back to bed. He was too tired to do anything but sleep, so I'd give him a bath first thing in the morning.

As soon as I pulled the covers over his slender frame, I heard my cell phone ringing from inside of my purse, up front.

I made my way into the kitchen and over to the counter where it sat and dug into the side pocket. Pulling out my iPhone, I saw it was Marcel. *Think of the devil and his no good ass will appear.*

I shook my head and declined his call. "Ain't nobody tryna hear yo sheyit!" I rolled my neck as I talked mad junk, walking back into my room.

Lawd, it felt good being free of him, rejecting his calls when the feeling struck. I was definitely feeling myself because for way too long I was putty in that man's hands. No matter his transgression, as soon as I heard his ringtone, I used to fly to the phone like a genie on a magic carpet. "Not anymore, bruh," I said with pride and then began humming Angie Stone.

My sunshine has come/And I'm all cried out/And there's no more rain in this cloud...

Gathering my pajama shorts and tank, I headed into the bathroom to run me a hot bubble bath, but not before I cleaned up after Justus.

After doing both, I stood in the mirror for a time and examined my eye before I removed the Vitamin C bottle from the medicine cabinet. According to my research on Google, it was supposed to help with the discoloration.

I hoped so. I didn't want to return to work on Monday with my customers looking at me pitifully. Or me feeling the need to tell those that pried that the balls pitched during our annual Chase Employee's Soft Ball Tournament weren't soft at all.

Throwing the pills to the back of my throat, I dipped my head toward the running faucet and pursed my lips to swig down a gulp of water.

I stood erect and glanced in the mirror again. Tiredness registered across my face. Today had been exhausting and it was time to turn down. So I began setting a relaxing mood. I lit the candles I kept around my garden-style tub, turned on the Heather Hedley station on my Pandora before I clicked the light switch off.

Ahhh, this is sexy. I looked at the ambiance I created. All I was missing was a glass of White Zinfandel and a man to wash my back, preferably a bad boy who was rough in the streets but gentle with his woman.

A small giggle escaped my lips. I had never dated a thug, but I often fantasized about them. And let a couple of my friends tell it, thug loving was the best.

Whew! I fanned myself as the thought of a certain stranger's lips on my honey dew sent a whole heat wave coursing through my body.

Stop it, girl. You don't even know that man, might not ever see his ass again, I admonished myself for not getting his number.

The tingling between my thighs subsided and I regained a sense of my normal self. I stepped out of my clothes and covered my hair with a shower cap so it wouldn't get wet. Cautiously, I slid my foot into the aquatic bubbles.

"Ouch! Ouch! Ouch!" I always overdid it with the hot water, but it never stopped me from getting in.

Once immersed in my heated abyss, I sat still for an eternity filled minute to acclimate to its temperature.

Just then, Heather's beautiful voice faded into the soulful sound of Anita Baker. After a while, I loosened up some and began to move about, swaying to the lady of soul.

"Sing it, girl!" I testified as *Good Love* played.

I wanna know what good love feels like/Good love, good love/I want a love that's sure to stand the test of time…

Morning, noon and night/Forever all my life…

I started humming as The Queen belted what I had been in search for, *good goddamn love*. Slippery little bastard was always butter in my hands, though.

One day, I giggled.

I closed my eyes and submerged myself neck deep as I started to mellow all the way out, that was until my music was paused and my ringer started blaring.

I sat back up and grabbed my phone from off of the toilet, staring at the Caller ID.

"What the hell do you want, Marcel?" I grimaced before I silenced it, sitting it back down.

Nothing right came from him. That last thing we had good between us was Justus and that was no exaggeration.

I rolled my eyes as I pondered what he could possibly want that would make him call twice but then I dismissed it because I had been overwhelmed enough as it was. Between my job, school and bills, I definitely didn't have time to add him and his shit to the list.

Not tonight, I thought before I shimmied back into my watery sanctuary.

Seconds later, my phone rang again. I didn't bother looking at the screen this time. I simply slid the green button to the right and let it rip.

"What goddamit? Why are you calling me *again*?" The bass in my voice carried like that of a man.

"'Cuse you? Who pissed in yo water and called it lemonade?" Essence, my co-worker slash just like a sister from New Orleans, matched the tone of my ratchetness.

I simmered to a cool after hearing her voice. "Gurrllll, my bad, that wasn't for you. I thought you were my BD. What's up?"

"I was 'bout to say. I know we not beefin'," she chuckled, then cleared her throat. "Well, I was hittin' you up because I needed to get an official head count for ladies' night next Friday for dinner and a movie."

Shit! I had canceled on the last two outings and I really didn't want to come off broker than a joke, so against the advice of my bank balance, I agreed. "Count me in."

"We're going to Papadeaux afterwards. You cool with that?"

Goddamn! Their prices were horrendous. Didn't Essence know that I had to ball on a budget? *Humph! I guess not.*

For some odd reason, my mind shifted to the boss looking dude who had helped me with my groceries. I bet his woman didn't have a worry in the world.

I never sweated a man for his pockets because I was no gold digger. My 9 to 5, five days a week job could attest to that, but I couldn't help but notice he screamed *cha-ching*. From the clean ride he slid out of to the expensive jewels that adorned him told me money wasn't a thing. And if I was his woman, I imagined a hundred dollars being a small drop in a bucket. Hell, he probably wiped his butt with a stack or two.

"Ummm, bitch! What's taking yo ass so long to answer?" said Essence, bringing me out of my daydream.

I smacked my lips. "Don't do me, bitch! I was thinking. Damn!"

"About?"

I rested my phone against my shoulder and began washing myself. "My business. Thank you!"

"Is it money?" Essence was insistent.

"If it was?"

"Then, you know I got you."

That eased a smile onto my face and dissolved the snap in my 'tude. "It crossed my mind but I kinda drifted off into this man I met just a little while ago."

"What? Get the fuck outta here. Alright, give it to me." Essence was always down for the juice or tea.

"Don't get all excited. I have no Tropicana to pour outside of me meeting this tasty looking chocolate dip. Picture damn perfect. Deep, circular brush waves. Strong chin. Straight, bone white teeth. Complexion the color of the last drop of coffee in the bottom of the cup, and the most amazing smile."

"Mmhmm. Give me more," she egged on.

"Let's see, he stood 5'9", 5'10" maybe, lickable lips and if the urban legends are correct, his big feet can only mean one thing." I paused to capture a visual of him.

"Aaahhhhhh! It means he workin' with something. Baby gotta big dick!"

"He probably do." I closed my eyes, rolled my neck and unconsciously moaned. She called me on my shit, too.

"Are you over there lusting? Let me find out," she laughed before she continued. "Anyway. Where did you meet him? What's his name and when y'all supposed to be hookin' up again. And oh, see if he got a friend for me when y'all talk next time."

"Damn! You're a little thirsty, don't you think?" I kidded.

"Dehydrated!" she cracked, and we both laughed. "Seriously, though, give me the goods."

I took a deep breath, calming the tingles that came with thinking about him. I let it out slowly and then replied, "I met him inside my apartment complex about a half an hour ago but I don't know his name and I didn't get his number." I was low-key disappointed as I said the words out loud. I may not have needed a man but I couldn't front like I didn't want one.

"You trippin'. Why the hell not?" My girl took offense like I was playing her to the left.

"My eye. Hellooo?" I stressed.

"Damn that eye. You should have told him what was up instead of feeling all insecure about it. Maybe you could have had some dick up in your revirginized ass."

"Puh-leeze. I want to be dicked down like the next bitch but everything isn't about sex. Besides, if a man wants to maintenance what lies between my thighs, then he's gonna have to win what's seated in my chest. In the meantime, I'll just fantasize."

"For real?" She questioned me like she wasn't buying it. "Don't get all on your throne with me. Ain't nothing wrong with thottin' it up from time to time. I mean, shit, you single and it's been a minute. Fuck around and grow cobwebs up in there." Essence laughed. "The way you described him I'm surprised you didn't panty drop right then and there, though."

"Awww, shut the hell up. You don't know me like that." I began laughing with her. Truth is, she did know me like that. She wasn't exactly right about him getting my thongs on sight but he was definitely fine enough to get them in two weeks. Hell, maybe one, if I intended to keep it real with myself.

"Real talk, Julz, see if he's down there still and leave your number on his windshield. It's been a minute since you blushed and gushed over a man. You might be on to something with this one."

By now, I had stepped out of the tub and begun drying off. The long, soothing soak I intended to have was thrown out of the window with the constant interruptions.

"I don't know about all that."

She sucked her teeth and went in.

While Essence ran my track record with men down to me. I got dressed, applied Baby Magic lotion to my skin and sprayed body perfume on my neck and wrists before I wrapped up in the bathroom and headed into my room.

It was too early to go to sleep, plus I had to put the few groceries I made in the cabinets. But I climbed into bed anyway, cutting my TV on to get off of my feet a second.

After she told me all of the reasons I was crazy for not hollerin' at ol' boy, she told me again to leave him with my digits.

I shook my head *no*, although she couldn't see it, as I gently brushed the waves of Justus' hair with my fingertips. I stared at him, adoringly. I swear to God I loved my little prince, so I couldn't dictate my moves based on the pulse of my pussy. I had to make better choices than the ones I'd made in the past.

But, God, he was fine, though.

"Nah, I'm good on it." I concluded, as I channel surfed.

"Have it your way. All I'm saying is you gotta stop overthinking shit because every dude ain't Marcel. Keep thinking that way and the only man in your life will be Justus."

"Bye, bitch!" I hung up on her. She hit a nerve with that one, possibly, because deep down I knew she was right.

As I was flicking from one station to another, something caught my attention, so I turned it back. It was a commercial for a new online dating website. That, in itself, didn't pique my interest. I did a double take because the man on my television set looked just like the one that had invaded my thoughts.

You tweakin' over a brief holla, Julz. Now just imagine if you got the dick! You would be looking for that man both night and day, I checked myself but that didn't stop me from imagining.

However, I did believe in signs and maybe the universe was telling me to go ahead and do as Essence suggested.

With a little more thought, I turned on the lamp, rummaged through the drawer of my nightstand and found a pen and paper. I scribbled my number down along with my name and a brief note that read: *Met you earlier. My name is Julz, Call me.* My digits were underneath that in a pretty little scrawl.

At the last moment, I decided to spray a dab of perfume on the note. Hoping I wasn't going overboard, I swung my feet out of the bed and stepped into a pair of house slippers. I felt a little nervous but I willed myself to press forward.

What if he found this desperate and unlady like? I worried.

I pushed the hesitancy to the back of my mind and unlocked my front door. Once I stepped outside, it took me every bit of three seconds to step back in. His car wasn't out there. He was gone.

No lie, an air of regret washed over me. But like I said, I believed in signs and clearly it wasn't meant for me to know him beyond hello.

"Baby boy, perhaps you're better off left in my dreams," I mumbled to myself.

Ca$h & Coffee

Chapter 3
Choppa

After making a few drops and collecting about twenty racks, I drove out to Smyrna, Georgia to one of my stash houses. About three blocks away, I hit Kim Marie up to let her know I would be pulling up soon.

"Sup, ma?" I said as soon as she picked up.

"Hey, Choppa, what's up? You got something good for me, baby?" As always, she sounded sexy as a muthafucka.

"You already know. I'll be at you in a blink so open the door. How's everything looking?"

"Hold up, man. I just got out of the shower. Let me look out of the window and check it out."

I heard some rustling in the background. "You got company or something?" I asked.

I heard her smack her lips. "Boy, don't play. You know I would never have anybody around your stuff."

"What's that I hear in the background? It sounded like I interrupted something. I mean, if you're in the middle of getting your tonsils checked I can get up with you another time," I said with an undertone of laughter in my voice.

"Never that, boo, unless you're the one sticking it down my throat. But wait," she paused, "you're scared of this, ain't you?"

"Nah, but business and pleasure go together like two dicks and no chick. It'll end up causing nothing but a whole bunch of shit," I said as I drew near the subdivision where she lived.

Kim Marie continued trying to entice me into fucking with her, but I wouldn't consider it. She was a cutie with a phat donkey donk, and she had displayed mad loyalty so far, but I was serious about not mixing business and pleasure. Shorty kept product and money for me. The last thing I needed was to start fucking with her in an intimate way and something go wrong. Then, she might start sticking her hand in the cookie jar, and that shit would prove fatal.

"Choppa, quit being scared and let me hit that. We don't have to do it but one time," she pleaded.

"Nah, I'm good," I stood firm. "Anyway, I'm about to roll up. Open the door."

"Okay."

A minute and a half later, I parked in Kim Marie's driveway, hopped out of my whip, and headed toward the side door with a backpack full of money slung over my shoulders.

My eyes darted left and right. At twenty-seven years old, I was already a vet in the game. I had been hustling since middle school and I had learned that you could never let your guards down. One mistake and a nigga was face down in the dirt.

I was always wary of jackboys. Those muthafuckas were more of a concern than the police. See, if the po po's caught a nigga slippin', he was going to jail. But when those ski mask niggas caught you down bad, you was going to the morgue.

With that in mind, my hand was only inches from my waist, where my heat was tucked, locked and loaded. I didn't encounter any trouble until I got to the door. Kim Marie swung it open and stood there with nothing but bare titties and bald pussy staring me in the face.

"Shorty, why you gotta disrespect me?" I slid past her and headed to the couch without giving her a second glance.

She closed the door then came over and sat across from me in a chair with her coochie on full display.

My mind flashed back to memories that I had buried deep in the dark coroners of my mind. "Yo, stop acting like a ho and go put some goddam clothes on!" I snapped.

Kim Marie's chin fell to her chest. She had heard me go off before but this was the first time my harsh words were aimed at her. "Excuse the fuck out of me for trying to give your mean ass some pussy," she shot back with teary eyes.

"You're excused. Now go cover your ass. Act like you got some class even if you don't."

As I watched her get up and head upstairs, I suddenly developed a pounding headache. I sat the backpacks on the floor between my feet and leaned back, massaging my temples.

It took a good five minutes for my headache to pass but Kim Marie hadn't returned yet. I figured she was in her feelings. That was the shit I was talking about!

I climbed the stairs and found her up in her bedroom, sitting on her bed, in pajamas, watching *Love and Hip Hop*. Gently, I sat down beside her.

"You a'ight, baby girl?" I asked in a soft tone.

"I'm fine," she replied, but her response rang hollow.

I took her hand in mine and lifted her chin with a finger, forcing eye contact. "Shorty, you know I fucks with you, and you know you're fine and all that. But you're trying to take things between us to a place I don't want them to go. What, you want me to fuck you and you end up becoming just another conquest? Or you wanna remain my friend and have the best friendship you've ever had?"

"Both." Her bottom lip was poked out like a spoiled brat.

I couldn't do nothing but laugh. I understood her attraction to me. She was only nineteen years old, pussy probably still smelled like baby powder. Of course, she wanted me to be her man. Those young boys she was used to couldn't compare.

I had met Kim Marie through her mama, who used to sell weed for me. Mama turned out to have sticky fingers, but Kim Marie had always struck me as honest. Besides, I wanted to get shorty out from under her mom's roof because it was just too much going on over there. I also felt more comfortable with someone living in the stash house to keep an eye on my shit.

So, I offered Kim Marie a free pass out of the hood and she eagerly accepted. Obviously, the hood wasn't all of the way out of her though.

I chuckled at her response. "You can't have both, lil' mama. And never choose dick over stability. Besides, the last thing you need or should want in your life is a street nigga. Find you a nice little college dude with legitimate aspirations."

"*Boring!*" she sang, sucking her teeth for extra effect.

"Maybe so. But at least you want have to make weekend visits to him in prison or put flowers on his grave at an early age. It's that what you want? You wanna be a teenage widow?"

"What—ever," she whined and scrunched up her face.

I released her hands and smiled at her in a brotherly manner. "Stop pouting and let's go put this money away."

"I guess."

"Oh, you not gonna give your big bruh a smile back?"

"You are not my brother. And I don't care what you say, I'ma get that dick sooner or later." A confident smile spread across her cute face.

I didn't challenge Kim Marie's vow, but I knew that she would never get me to surrender to it.

Sometime later and after bouncing from Kim Marie's spot, I made one last pickup then drove out to Covington where I had another stash spot. This was also the place I laid my head when I wanted to get away and chill.

When I stepped inside the fully furnished condo, the cool air kissed my face. I locked the door behind me then carried the bag into one of the spare bedrooms and placed its contents inside the hidden safe that was built into the floor of the walk-in closet.

Staring down at what was over $450,000 at last count, I felt proud of my accomplishments because I had come from the dirt. Shit hadn't always been gravy but I had weathered the storms, and now a nigga was sitting on close to a half mil plus I had stupid werk on deck. And the sweetest thing about my hustle was that my name wasn't ringing.

I lifted my right arm and stared at the tat on my forearm. It was the image of a man with a finger to his lips, indicating *Shhh!* Stacks of cheddar was beneath his head, and underneath the loot were the words *Silent Money.* I could see a million dollars in my near future. After that, I was gonna get ghost, leaving nothing behind but my legend.

Yeah, I liked the sound of that!

I smiled inwardly as I closed and locked up the safe then put the floorboards securely back in place. Carefully, I realigned the dozens of pairs of sneakers in their usually spots. Emerging from the closet, I felt ten feet tall.

I walked over to the ceiling to floor mirror that took up half of the adjoining wall. *Nigga, you're about to be rich!* I said to my reflection. *Fuck that dumb shit Jared and Cardale talking. I ain't gotta fuck with coke to get paid.*

Restraining Order

As usual, I chilled at the stash spot for a few just so it wouldn't look peculiar to neighbors if I came and left quickly. While there, I took a shower, changed into some fresh gear and fixed myself something to eat. My phone was blowing up with a familiar ringtone, but I ignored the calls because I knew who it was, and I didn't want to deal with that person yet.

After finishing my meal, I placed the dishes in the dishwasher then sat in the living room playing 2K14 until I began to doze off. Visions of baby girl whose groceries I had helped carry from her car ran through my mind.

Ma was sexy as fuck, and kinda classy with that thang. Not bougie or nothin' like that, but she appeared to be way more than a basic bitch. I was tired of fucking with those types: hoes that didn't aspire for shit but a stripper's pole in their bedroom and a baller's dick in their mouths. Or ratchet females who did nothing all day but broadcast their business on Facebook.

Shorty, I hope you're what you appear to be. Because I promise we'll meet again, and next time I'm gonna get to know you real good.

The long hours spent grinding finally caught up to me and I drifted off to sleep thinking about that beautiful queen with the long brown hair and the sweetest voice to ever caress my ears.

***

The constant ringing of my cell phone awakened me from a deep sleep and a pornographic dream. I woke up with a dick that was harder than prison bars.

"Fuck!" I spat as I reached for my phone on the table. Baby girl had been riding me backwards. Agitated, I answered the call without looking at the screen. "Bruh, you'll fuck up a wet dream."

The voice in the other end wasn't Jared's or Cardale's. "You better be dreaming about me. And why do I have to call you from a private number in order for you to answer. Are you ignoring my call, Choppa?" she asked in an accusatory tone.

"Don't start your shit," I warned.

"Don't you start yours! I wanna know when—"

"Hold up! Lower your voice. And fix your attitude."

"For real? You're asking me to fix my attitude? Nigga, you need to fix my living arrangements."

I was about to jump in her shit when a call came in from Jared. "Let me hit you back. I need to handle something."

"Fuck you, Choppa!"

I heard a little beep confirming that she had hung up. Normally, I would've been heated but this wasn't the time for her drama. I clicked over to the other line. "Speak."

"Bleed, I need that werk. My mans out in Doraville need five pounds. They already got the money on deck."

"Fool, is you crazy? How many times I gotta tell you about talking reckless on the phone," I snapped. I had warned him at least a dozen times not to do that shit.

"My bad. But for real, I need you to get at me ASAP," he said.

Sighing heavily, I looked at the clock on the screen. It was 10:35 p.m. Damn, I hadn't realized I had slept for almost two hours.

"Yo, what you gon' do?" Jared pressed.

"Dude, pump your breaks. Let me wake up and get myself situated. I'ma fuck with you in a few."

"A'ight, fam. You know I got mouths to feed."

"Say no more."

I ended the call and got up to get myself together. In less than a half hour, I was out the door and pulling up to the other stash spot where I kept the werk. I had left the BMW at the rest crib so I was rolling in my Expedition.

I didn't like riding dirty, but I preferred that to letting Jared or Cardale know where my stash spots were. I figured, as long as they didn't know where I kept the product, and they had no way of knowing who my connect was, I was good. Murking me would be biting off the hand that fed them.

Growing up in The Land, I had seen people cross their on flesh and blood when it came down to money. I fucked with Jared and Cardale the long way, but I didn't have complete trust in nobody but myself. Because for all the shit niggas in the street talked about loyalty, the truth was niggas was only loyal to the dough. Seldom were they loyal to one another. Fuck what you heard!

Anyway, while hitting Jared up with some werk, I went ahead and gave Cardale what he would need for the week too. Before leaving them we talked more about getting at G-Shine.

"You can't let him wag with a violation like that or every nigga in the city will see you as a free pick," Jared added, like I needed extra incentive to handle my business.

"Fam, you ever known me to give a guilty muthafucka a pardon?" I asked, feeling somewhat disrespected.

"I'm just saying, my nigga. Don't let the money turn you soft."

I didn't even respond to that fuck shit. Because the only thing soft about me was that beautiful woman that kept running through my mind.

I had to have ma.

Ca$h & Coffee

Chapter 4
Julz
The next day

Before I could open my eyes, I heard my television blaring cartoons and that only meant one thing, my prince was up and I needed to be as well. But I was sooo exhausted. I stayed up late last night doing a paper for my English class.

I was studying to get my bachelor's in business so I could move up in the company and make more money to better provide for us. School overwhelmed my schedule at times but I had to do what I had to do.

I looked at the clock and saw it was after ten. I felt horrible, for real. I always made my baby breakfast by eight o'clock on the weekends.

Twenty minutes later, I was standing over the stove preparing our breakfast. Justus was sitting on the counter watching me work. Usually, I'd let him help but not today.

"Turn over your meat, Mama." He pointed to the smoked sausage, sizzling in the pan furthest away from him.

Although the meat was fine without being flipped, I did it anyway. I made a face of relief and over exaggerated my grateful expression, so he could know how much mommy needed her little helper. "Thank you, my prince. Ooh, what would I do without you?"

He shrugged his shoulders and smiled as bright as the high noon sun. "I'on know."

"And I'm not gonna find out either." I gave him some kisses and went back to whipping my eggs.

The way he watched me intrigued me. He'd always paid special attention to the things I did or the people I came into contact with. He was a godsend, my protector, my joy.

Essence always said I spoiled him too much. She said, *"Showering him with so much attention gon' keep him on yo damn tittie."*

I didn't believe that because I wasn't raising a mama's boy. He knew I would bust his butt if he ever got out of pocket. But if I didn't have to discipline him, I was most definitely loving him up.

I recalled the very first time I held him in my arms, I knew we would be inseparable. I also knew I was going to be the only one of his parents he could consistently count on because Marcel's insatiable appetite for stray pussy had driven a wedge between us, and he was not the kind of man who would handle his responsibilities to his child if we were no longer together.

That was some straight bullshit but I had come to accept it even before I gave birth to our son. Over the nine months I carried Justus, his father's true colors had begun to show or maybe I just took off my blinders and finally faced the truth that Marcel wasn't worth the nut his daddy used to create him.

One of his prominent *ain't shit* moments was the night I delivered my baby, I did it alone because Marcel was nowhere to be found.

If that shit didn't hurt, I don't know what did.

That was the last straw and I'd had enough of him. I was ready to be done with his trifling ass.

So, when the nurse asked me what name I selected for my child, I stared at my baby and then off to my side where Marcel should have been and said *Justus* because I knew without a doubt it would be *just us*!

A few weeks after going through a very painful labor to bring Marcel's son into this world, I found out the reason he was not there to hold my hand. The reason was because that muthafucka was laying between one of our neighbor's thighs.

When it all came out, the woman's husband threatened to burn our house down. I was so hurt and embarrassed, not to mention afraid. And all because Marcel couldn't keep his dick in his pants!

Well, that was it for me. For real, for real.

I time traveled to the day I confronted him with my promise to leave his ass.

"It's over, Marcel. I'm leaving!" I raged.

"Baby, you're going to leave me over something that never happened? Is that fair? C'mon now, we're a family. Can't nothing come between us. Don't do this, Julz." A tear ran down his face, as he watched me sling clothes into a suitcase.

42

I stopped what I was doing and stared at him. "Marcel, are you crying?"

"I can't help it, baby. I don't want you to walk out of my life. Especially over a lie." Now the tears came in floods.

I walked across the room and Marcel opened his arms for me to step into them. But this time he had it twisted.

Whap!

I slapped the black off of his face.

He stood there stunned.

"Why you—"

Whap!

I didn't allow him to get the question out of his mouth before I slapped it back down his throat. "You lying bastard!" I screeched as I began pummeling him with both fists.

I wasn't a fighter but he had pushed me over the edge. I tried to lodge my fist in his goddam esophagus. "Nigga, you have told your last fucking lie!" My voice sounded like it belonged to a psycho.

Marcel kept right on lying and I kept right on punching him in his shit. His denials meant nothing and his crocodile tears meant even less. In fact, it was those fake tears that confirmed that he was lying.

At this point, we had been together almost four years and not once before had he ever shed a single tear. Not even when a close family member or friend of his died. His lack of emotions was one of the things that drove me insane.

Finally, Marcel grabbed my arms and pinned them to my sides to keep me from hitting him again. "Okay, Julz, I messed up," he half confessed. "But what I did with her was nothing. You were in pain and unable to—"

"In pain because I was carrying your child!" I screamed, cutting him off. "So don't you dare try to lay your filth at my feet!"

"Baby, you don't understand. For some men sex is an addiction, we need it every day. What I did doesn't mean I don't love you."

If I was a hood bitch I would've spit dead in that muthafucka's face for trying me with that lame ass shit. Instead, I took a deep breath and calmed myself down before I caught a case.

Justus' sudden wails reminded me that I had too much to lose to let Marcel's whorishness cause me to do something dumb. I gave Marcel an ice cold stare before spinning on my heels and hurrying into the nursery to check on my precious little man.

As I sat rocking Justus in my arms and crying my eyes out, Marcel came and wrapped his arms around us both. "Julz, don't say anything. Just let me hold y'all." His voice sounded so full of regret.

***

I didn't leave Marcel that night but I wouldn't let him in my bed. But as days turned into weeks, foolishly I allowed my anger to subside.

For his part, Marcel was very patient with me. And I absolutely loved watching him with Justus. I wanted us to remain a family so bad. The last thing I wanted was to be somebody's baby mama. I wanted to be my son's father's wife.

After a few months, Marcel moved us into a new house because I would not have been able to remain living across the street from the woman he betrayed me with without losing my cool one day and snapping out.

A new place seemed to lessen my pain. And on most days, I was successful at forgiving Marcel. But on others, I failed miserably because I couldn't forget what that fucker did.

Still I pressed on. I convinced myself that things between us could get better, since he was adamant about us remaining a family and overly apologetic for the misuse of his dick. Plus, deep down I needed to know he wasn't a bad man, that instead, he just made very bad decisions.

For a short period of time, he actually shaped up and returned to the man I once knew. But he taught me a valuable lesson and the note I made to self was: *Once a ho, always a ho.*

A year after promising me that he would never cheat on me again, I stumbled upon an unfamiliar cell phone in the trunk of his car. Going through the text messages, it didn't take long for me to realize that his no good ass had more flings going on than I had fingers and toes.

When I confronted Marcel, he had the audacity to try to convince me that the phone belonged to his brother. But the evidence in the texts was indisputable.

This time, I didn't shed a fucking tear.

"You know what, Marcel? You just lost a good woman," I said with dry eyes and finality in my voice.

I left him and got a place of my own but I should have known that as long as I stayed in the city, I would never be rid of him.

Every time I would try to get him to leave me alone, he would finesse his way back into my life and ultimately my bed, using Justus as the key to unlock both vaults. Then when he would leave, I felt stupid and weak for giving in to him.

After a while, I started to feel like the side bitch and pretty soon Marcel didn't even try to hide the shit he was doing. He would be riding around town with different women in the passenger seat of his car and then he'd want to come by and play house with me.

One day, after Marcel spent the night and left me feeling inadequate because his worn out dick wouldn't get hard, I looked in the mirror at myself and shook my head.

Are you really that desperate, bitch? My girl Essence would've asked had she known every sordid little detail of what I was putting up with from Marcel.

Well, I didn't need Essence to ask the question for me to answer it.

"Hell to the no!" I said aloud. But little did I know, I was not quite ready to move on. Besides, whenever Marcel felt me slipping away he began to use threats of violence to intimidate me.

"When you get tired of being tired, you'll leave his trifling ass alone," many of my friends used to say.

The back and forth carried on for two years, longer than I cared for it to, but I had to save up enough money to take care of Justus and to fund our move to Atlanta, where I had several friends.

So I played Marcel's game, allowing him to hoe hop all around the city and then come by my house sometimes at night, until I had all of my ducks lined up in a row. And then one night, I took my baby and vanished into thin air.

The only thing I brought along with me was my baby and our clothes. The furniture and the other household things were remnants of my past with Marcel, and I refused to carry any of that into my future.

"Poof! Muthafucka, I'm gone," I said as I put New Orleans and Marcel in my rear view.

Chapter 5
Julz

Adjusting to a new city wasn't easy and the job I thought I had secured before moving hadn't worked out. For a good while I was living off of credit cards, robbing Peter to pay Paul. So, when I did begin working, I was in so much debt I could hardly breathe.

A homeboy of mine named Tyriq had moved to Atlanta a year or so before me. He was doing good for himself although his occupation was far from legal. He always made it his business to call and check on me and Justus. I knew that I could ask Tyriq for help if I needed it but I seldom did.

Whenever the struggle became too real, I would become upset with Marcel. If he had just been the man I thought he was when we first got together, me and my son wouldn't have been catching hell. But what hurt me more than anything was when Justus began asking about his daddy.

"He don't love us no more?" he asked with tears in his throat.

"Yes, honey, your daddy still loves you." It was me that he never loved.

After too many times of having such heartbreaking conversations with him and for my son's sake, I got in touch with Marcel for the first time since moving away a year ago. I was still very bitter over the way he did me but I loved my prince more than myself and couldn't deny him his right to have his father in his life.

Besides, I had heard through the grapevine that Marcel had a woman whom he was very much in love with, so I had hoped we could talk without him trying to push back up on me. And I prayed that whatever anger we held against each other could be held in check for the sake of our child.

But that was not to be. I still remembered that conversation like it was just yesterday.

The phone rang a few times and then the reminder of my worst days came flooding back to me when I heard Marcel's voice, "Hello," he answered.

I hesitated a moment. I almost hung up but I remembered that I was doing this for Justus. I swallowed the lump in my throat and forced a kind tone into my voice.

"Hello, Marcel. This is Julz."

"Julz!" He spoke my name like it was shit in his mouth. That didn't surprise me one bit. I had already prepared myself for the unleashing of his demons. His voice then faded off into the distance, as if he had pulled the phone away from his mouth. "No this bitch didn't?"

"Marcel, let me tell you why I'm calling, please." I wanted to take a calm approach to counter the rowdy in him before it had a chance to fully start.

"You really got me fucked up, calling me after all this time. Where my fuckin' son at?" He got straight to it.

I didn't bother trying to correct his tone. I just answered him. "He's playing in the room."

"Put him on the phone 'cause I don't have shit to say to yo ass."

I didn't want to talk to him as much as he didn't want to hear from me but we had to reach some sort of peace agreement before I handed the phone over to Justus.

"Listen, Marcel, we need to talk first. I don't want you bringing that same negative energy to my son that you're bringing to me."

"Your son? That's your fuckin' problem. You got ghost with our fuckin' son, not yours! And then you told yo funky ass people not to tell me where you took him."

"You left me no choice. I did what I had to do."

"What you had to do? For real, Julz, there is nothing you can say to justify why you ran away with my seed and fell off the map."

"I'm sorry but you had begun threatening me. And it was you who said if you couldn't have me, you wanted nothing to do with Justus either." My voice was low and my hand was cupped over the phone so Justus couldn't hear what I was saying.

"Julz, you should've known I was just talking. I've never laid a hand on you unless it was to make love to you, and I would never neglect my seed, ya heard me."

"Yeah, I hear you. But anyway—"

"Anyway what? You stole my seed."

48

"Well, you stole my happiness!" I fired back.

"I should've stole your life, and I would've had I known you was just as ratchet as the next bitch."

My mouth flew open but nothing came out. Marcel had disrespected me in many ways when we were together but this was a whole different level of contempt spewing from his mouth. I may have put up with it back then but those days were over. Finished. Done. Finito!

"I knew it was a mistake calling you. Bye, Marcel." My nerves got the best of me. I hung up but when I stared in the direction where my child was waiting impatiently for good news, I called him back.

"What!" he answered.

"Marcel, I get it you're pissed but can you stop with all the disrespect and listen? If you want me to admit I was wrong for leaving the way I did, all right. I was wrong. All I'm trying to do now is make it right for our son. Can I do that?"

He said nothing but I could hear him breathing. No doubt he was biting down on his bottom lip. He did that anytime he was at a loss for words. So, I waited patiently on his reply.

A few uneasy seconds went by before he spoke. "The stunt you pulled had me messed up. You fucked with my heart when you dipped. You knew I loved you and you knew I loved him."

I didn't want to argue with him by explaining the definition of real love so for peace to abide, I swallowed my words and attempted to see it from his point of view.

"Marcel, I can't change what I did but for what it's worth, I'm really sorry that I removed Justus from your life like that."

"And what about you? You're sorry for walking out of my life, too?"

Hell no! I could never be sorry for that, I thought.

"This isn't about me but I could have handled things differently before I bounced and even after I left. I could have called and allowed you contact with us but I was in a bad place. Look, we don't have the best communication skills but our son is getting older and he needs you. Can we co-parent without all the extra stuff, for him?"

I knew he'd say yes before he responded because something told me this was going to be the doorway he used to get me back despite whatever fool was currently in his life.

"I can't front. I missed the hell out of y'all. So I'll do whatever to make it work. But I have two conditions."

I knew it. "I'm listening."

"One, ain't no disappearing this time and two, I don't want to talk to him, I want to see him."

We'd been talking since that day, by phone only. I insisted the importance of easing him back into Justus' life, but Marcel was becoming impatient and I knew I couldn't keep him at arm's length forever.

"It smells good, Mama."

Justus switched me out of auto pilot and into the now.

"It does, huh?" I started fixing our plates.

He took his seat and waited for me to serve him in the dining room. Just then I heard my cell phone ringing.

"I'll go get it, Mama. I got it." Justus jubilantly shouted as he ran into the bedroom to grab it for me.

"It's on the nightstand." I called out behind him.

"It's Daddy, Mama. It's Daddy!" He must have read *Dad* on the screen to know. Excitement could be heard through his shrills. But before I was able to tell him to let the phone ring, Justus already answered it. "Hey, Daddy! What'chu doing?"

I marbeled my eyes but stopped them in mid-roll once I saw Justus looking at me with strange curiosity.

Then he went about his conversation. I gathered Marcel was asking him twenty-one questions because everything that came out of his mouth was a response.

"About to have breakfast with mama—Pancakes—No, it's just us here—Yeaaa!" I shot him a quick glance when I saw his demeanor turn up. I wondered what the hell he said to illicit that from him. "Yea—Yea—Right here—Okay, love you, Daddy." Then Justus reached me the phone. "Daddy want you."

I took the phone from him. I was annoyed but Justus would never know that.

"Thank you, baby. Now sit down and eat your food before it gets cold. I'm going to step on the porch and talk to daddy, okay?"

He bobbed his head and started going in on his cheese omelet. I headed for the front door, placed the phone to my ear and spoke once on the other side of my closed door.

"Hey." Marcel had a way of making my nerves ball my stomach into terrible knots. The love and hate was real.

"Hey, beautiful. What you doing?" he asked, all sugary.

"I was having breakfast with Justus. What's up?"

"I'm in your city and I want to see y'all, *today.*"

What? How the hell he knows where I stay? Impossible!

"Quit lyin'." I seriously doubted he was in Atlanta. He was probably pulling a stunt to get the information out of me by using reverse psychology or some shit.

"I bullshit you not," he said.

"How do you know where we live?"

"My son told me. Too bad he didn't know y'all address because I would have just showed up at your door." Marcel laughed, but I wasn't amused.

I wanted to be mad at Justus but how could I? He wasn't aware that he did anything wrong by telling his father where he stayed. But I would still have a talk with him about volunteering our business to anyone, ASAP.

"Uh—Marcel, don't you think you should've waited until I was ready to tell you where we lived instead of interrogating a four-year-old?"

"Yea, whatever." He blew me off. "Well, I got in town yesterday and I'll only be here 'til tonight, so what's your address? I'll come to y'all."

My address? Oh, hell no!

"You're not invited to my place. I don't want you getting any ideas."

"You with all that playin'. Ain't nobody tryna do shit to you. I just want to see my child. After all, it has been a year since I saw him and the few months we've been talking by phone is enough time. This is overdue."

You not tryna do nothing, huh? Yea, right. That's what his mouth said, but I knew better than to believe him. He always tried to do something.

We went back and forth for a time before I discovered he really wasn't lying about being in my city. That's when the butterflies in my stomach started flapping their wings.

I wanted Justus to see his dad. I just didn't want to see Marcel and fall weak for his sweet promises and dimpled smile all over again. I had come too far for that.

I thought about making an excuse not to see Marcel, but it was time to find out if I was really done with him. "All right. Let's meet at Chuck E. Cheese on Cumberland. We can be there for two o'clock."

"Okay, Tasty Lips. I can't wait to see you and my little man," he said before getting off of the line.

I recalled a time when his calling me *tasty lips* brightened my day. I was barely seventeen years old back then and madly in love with him.

That was then, I told myself.

But I was no fool. The true test of my will would come when we stood face to face again. Could I truly resist him?

Envisioning seeing him again gave me the weirdest yet familiar feeling.

What's up with these damn butterflies? Jesus, please be a fence!

Chapter 6
Julz

I looked up into the clear blue sky as I felt the cool breeze of summer wash over the wetness accumulating in my eyes. I was not ready to see him, but ready or not, here he was.

Heaven, help me!

I opened my door and peered my head inside to check on my prince. "You okay in there? Is breakfast good?"

He couldn't respond because his cheeks were ballooned with food. I told him about stuffing his face. He shook his head up and down and that was good enough for me.

I closed the door and scrolled through my contacts, stopping at the T's. I had to call Tyriq and tell him what was going on. He knew my situation to the letter and he'd be able to tell me what to do.

His phone rang—and rang and then after a torturous twenty seconds, it went to voicemail.

Damn, Riq! I wanted to call right back, but he must've been busy.

No sooner than I turned around to head back inside, my phone lit up with his call.

I answered in a rush. "Riq!"

"Whooa, what's up, love?" he spoke with the usual calm in his heavy, New Orleans' accent.

I cut straight to the point. "Marcel is in town and he wants to see me. Well, me and Justus but you know what I'm saying."

"Why you sound all nervous?"

"I don't know." That was the truth.

"You not goin', right?"

"Wrong. I agreed to meet up with him for two, today."

"What'chu did that fah? Dude, don't deserve to lay eyes on you after all the foul shit he put you through." His words carried a bit of consternation with them.

"I know." I blew out hard. "It's just that Justus told him we lived in Atlanta, so he made it a point to pop up on us. Now I'm cornered into seeing him." A slight panic registered through my words. "What am I gonna do? I don't know where his head is. I haven't seen this man in a year. And I ran off with his son."

"Fuck where his head is at, Julz. Where is yours? You still got a thing for him or nah? 'Cause if you do, you do. But if you're worried about that nigga tripping on you, I'll go with you. Believe me, Marcel ain't built to go up against me."

I knew he was right, Marcel was a straight laced man with a college degree, while Tyriq had been born and bred in New Orleans' Magnolia projects.

"Nooo! No, no, no." I shook my head. "That wouldn't be a good idea. If he is on the up and up but sees you, given y'all's history, then that would set him off. I don't want no drama in front of my son."

It had been several years since Tyriq publically shamed Marcel's ass for misreading a coincidental encounter between friends when he saw us at a gas station, laughing. He rolled up on us and went off on me, thinking I was up to the same no good as he, but it was his guilty conscious.

"Slow ya roll, bruh. You don't have to talk to her like that, ain't nothin' foul going on. Me and Julz been rounds fah years," Tyriq intervened.

"Nigga, when I say something to you, that's when you say something to me. Otherwise, stay out of my business with my woman," replied Marcel.

Instantly, I grew nervous because niggas just didn't come out of their mouths to Riq like that and not get smashed.

I think, on the strength of me, Riq was going to let Marcel's slight disrespect slide because he just clenched his fist and took a deep breath. But Marcel misread Riq's reaction for weakness.

"Julz, you better tell this fake thug to push on before I put him on his ass," Marcel threatened.

"Naw, tell me that shit yourself, pussy!" The vein pulsating in Riq's temple told me he was a heartbeat away from flipping out.

"Please y'all, don't do this. Marcel, let's go, baby." I pleaded as I placed myself between them.

But now Marcel was feeling himself, obviously out to prove to me that he wasn't soft. He reached out and moved me aside.

54

Grilling Tyriq, he spat, *"I'm telling you for the last time— get the fuck on!" He reached out to push him but his hands never made contact because Riq's carnal instinct was to meet aggression with even stronger aggression.*

Then it happened. Riq's fists moved so fast across Marcel's face they looked blurry in motion.

Whop! Whop! Whop! Whop!

Marcel's head snapped back, blood flew out of his mouth and he hit the ground with a thud.

I was on my knees attending to him in a flash. "Oh, Lord!" I cried. Marcel was out cold.

Tyriq was rubbing his knuckles and breathing hard. "If he wasn't your man, I would put something hot in him. Real shit."

"Tyriq, please go!" I screamed at him.

"Okay, baby girl. But if that nigga ain't learned no respect for you when he wakes up, give me a call." He hopped in his ride and mashed out.

Marcel regained his consciousness seconds later and I immediately began apologizing. He was mad as hell, spewing all kinds of baseless accusations.

"Baby, that was Tyriq. I been told you about him," I said as we both climbed to our feet.

Marcel said nothing. He just stumbled to his car and drove off.

We never discussed that day again, and although he never admitted it, I knew Marcel felt a piece of his manhood left in Tyriq's pocket that day. And because of that, Marcel would always have an axe to grind with him.

When I reminded Riq of that, he said, "Then what do you suggest because I don't think you should see him alone. He might try to take Justus back from you."

"I don't know." I whined.

"A'ight. Calm down, love. How 'bout I meet you der and I'll chill in the parking lot, ya heard me. If you shoot me a text, I'ma come in that bitch and walk y'all out. I ain't gon' cause no scene unless he bring it there and then you know I'ma act up."

"See, that's what I don't want, though."

"I feel you. But if your baby daddy be on some chill shit, he'll never know I'm there."

I remained quiet for a time because I was pondering his suggestion, but honestly, that sounded like the best strategy. And there was no denying that I felt safer with Tyriq around.

I agreed, then we ended the call with the understanding he would arrive a half an hour earlier than us.

Maybe I was putting too much stock into what Marcel would or wouldn't do but I preferred to be safe than sorry. Or maybe I just didn't trust my heart in the company of the only man that I had ever loved.

***

I wasn't sure why I had spent so much time dolling up. The date wasn't for me nor did I want it to be, but I found myself dressing and then redressing in different outfits. The first few were too sexy and then the next couple weren't sexy enough. I was even torn between make-up or not. Hair up or down.

I drove myself mad until I refocused and reminded myself that I didn't like his ass like that anymore.

Shaking my head at myself, I removed the lipstick I applied and used a simple gloss, instead.

Get it together, girl. I was confused as to whether I wanted to turn him on to salivate over what he lost out on or to see if I still had it, although I didn't want him either way.

Women! I said and then chuckled as if I wasn't one.

Finally, I settled on a sundress and some sandals. I opted to keep it basic. Anything else would have shown enormous effort and I truthfully didn't want to be misleading.

Justus stopped playing with his toys once he saw me enter the living room.

"You look good, Mama."

"Awww, thank you, baby. So do you." And he did. From the creative style of braids I had woven through his curly, long length of hair to the J's on his feet. "Are you ready to go?"

An air of uncertainty washed across his face, as if he had to seriously ponder on his response. Without a word, he reached down and picked up his favorite action figure. "You think if I gave Daddy this, he'll remember not to forget me after we leave?"

Creases in my forehead formed at the same time my lips lowered. As I weighed my response, I saw vulnerability swim in his eyes, while he waited on my answer. I could have cried a river for the twinge of pain that resulted from the stab in my heart just then.

I squatted down so I reached him at eye level, taking ahold of him. "Oh, baby, your daddy never, and I do mean *never*, forgot you. So, he doesn't need help remembering you. It's impossible. You're his twin, which means looking at himself is a reminder of the little prince he created in you. And the only reason you hadn't seen him in so long is because mommy took a job here, too far away from daddy's home." I took in a breath. "But I tell you this, today will be the first of many days you'll spend with your dad. Does that work?"

"Yea." His eyes were casted downward when he answered me. Despite his earlier excitement, he was hesitant now.

The weakness in his *yea* tore me up. My baby was too young to know heartache and had I not made a decision to leave his father, he wouldn't be second guessing his own importance to him.

I felt guilty for tearing him away from Marcel, I truly did. I was oblivious to the fact, up until now, that no matter how bad Marcel was for me, he was still good for him.

Children need their fathers.

Looking at Justus confirmed I was doing the right thing. I stood up, smoothed down my dress and glanced at my watch. It was 1:33 p.m. Grabbing my purse, keys and his hand, we headed to the door. "All right, let's go see daddy, then."

***

Forty minutes later, I sat in the parking lot for a few minutes, collecting myself. I had no idea what to expect out of him or out of me.

Can I still keep my resistance up?

I sucked my teeth and shook my damn head. I hadn't even laid eyes on him and already I felt myself buckling.

Don't play ya'self, girl. He ain't what you want, I reminded myself.

After I straightened my backbone, I shot Riq a text message, letting him know the deal.

2:05 p.m. Julz: *We're here. Bout to go in.*

2:06 p.m. Tyriq: *A'ight. I'm outchea.*

Spot checking myself in the visor's mirror, I then turned around in my seat to face an eager Justus.

"You're excited?"

He supplied me with the goofiest grin before he shouted. "Yeaaa!"

"Yeaaa?" I mimicked him. "Well, let's go."

Getting out of my car, I opened the back door for him. Taking ahold of my hand, he virtually led the way.

As soon as we entered, I probed as much of the building from by the cashier's register, looking for Marcel. Standing at 6'4", he wouldn't be that hard to find. However, after a thorough scan, I couldn't locate him.

I reached for my phone inside of my purse but was startled by the lay of a masculine grip around my waist from behind.

"What tha…" I was ready to give someone the business but I stopped myself short when I saw it was him. The man who took everything from me. My virginity, my heart, my dignity. You name it, he claimed it. "Marcel." I said his name breathlessly. His attractiveness caught me off guard, but I hoped he didn't read into that.

Marcel had buffed up from the last time I saw him and the extra weight on his athletic body looked like a blessing. He grew out his full beard, something he never did before but it looked good on him. So much so that it was turning me on. Then his grey eyes sparkled against his reddish brown skin. Those damn eyes could sell fire to the devil. I had to look away.

"Julz." He called out sweetly. The way my name rolled off of his lips, mesmerized me.

He attempted to reach for me but I dropped down to a squatting level and retied Justus' shoestrings, needlessly.

"Ha." I heard his chuckle of disbelief. He swooped his young prince into his arms. "I missed you, man. You know that?" A slight cry could be heard through the pronunciation of each of his words.

Justus shook his head up and down before he buried his face into the crook of Marcel's neck as he gripped him with urgency. Their reunion was sentimental. I wanted to join in but I stood back. Instead, I subconsciously rested my hand over my chest as I felt the speed of my beating heart, regretting everything that led to our separation in the first place.

Marcel glanced in my direction and if I could still read him correctly, he looked genuinely remorseful. It was as if his eyes apologized a thousand times for us having to meet under these estranged terms.

A tear waterfalled as I watched painful emotions of longing etch across Marcel's face. It was evident that he never stopped loving Justus and he truly missed him.

I knew I shouldn't have cared but I wondered, *was any of that for me, too?*

There was a little bit of resistance on Justus' part when Marcel began to pull their bear hug apart. My baby needed this moment. I could tell.

Placing him on his feet, Marcel looked back to me but I had no idea what to do exactly. That was until Justus invited me into his dad's arms.

"Give Daddy a hug, too, Mama." Justus nudged me.

Snapping my head at my son, I reactively grimaced and didn't change the scowl on my face until his eyebrows drew inward, conveying his confusion.

Fixing my look, I released my reluctance and walked over to Marcel. I didn't want to show unwillingness to Justus' gesture because after all, it was just a brief embrace to be had.

An uncomfortable smile lined my lips as I opened my arms and walked into his. As I angled my body to give a *church hug*, he pulled me into him fully and held me tightly, like he missed me.

Did he miss me? Dammit, Julz! Does it matter?

"You smell good." He complimented, allowing his soft lips to brush up against my lobe.

I closed my eyes for a split second and inhaled him, too. He smelled of Gucci Guilty, my favorite cologne. *Damn!*

Moving backwards, I headed over to the register to pay for our tokens but Marcel stopped me.

"You trippin'. I got this." He pulled out his wallet and paid the young lady. Moments later, he handed me the token-filled bucket and motioned for me to lead the way.

I knew he wanted to watch me from behind and there was a tiny part of me that wanted him to. He needed to see what he'd never get again.

Just then, Justus grabbed both of our hands as I set out to locate a table. I smiled at him but when I noticed Marcel smiling at me, I quickly rolled my eyes and straightened my face.

Shortly after, I found us a spot. I sat down. Marcel was seconds away from sitting down next to me until Justus shrieked his anticipation. "Come on, Daddy, let's go play."

I wasn't too sure about how I would feel with Marcel scampering about the place without me being in close proximity but that initial feeling that he'd run off with Justus dissipated. My gut told me I was overthinking his reaction to the hurt our disappearance caused. But just in case there was a chance he'd prove me wrong, Tyriq was on the ready.

"Yea, go 'head, Daddy." I shoo'd him off. I didn't need him under me, weakening my defenses. I needed some alone time, to regroup. I told myself I didn't want him and I meant that, but he was looking good and his sex was the best I'd ever had.

Shake it off!

Once I saw they made their way to the Skee Ball game, I pulled out my phone. I had to call Essence. I needed her to coach me out of my feelings before something bad happened.

She answered on the first ring. "Did you crumble like a cookie, already?"

"Damn! You think it's that easy?" That made me not want to tell her shit 'cause she pinned me effortlessly.

"It ain't that. I just know the effect he *has* on you."

"*Had* on me."

"Whatever you say. What's up, Cookie?" Essence laughed, but she was playing at the wrong time.

"Bitch, you ain't funny, no. Matter of fact, I'ma just call you back."

"Nooo! I was only joking. Seriously, what's up?"

I blew out hard. "I ain't breaking, for the record. But I need you to remind me of all the reasons why Marcel ain't shit. I'm getting all nostalgic, reminiscing over the good ole days. *Tsss.* I haven't even had a conversation with this man but already I want to commit to us being a family." I paused briefly as I glanced over at them. "I'm watching how he's interacting with his son and I'm feeling a way about raising him on my own."

"I understand that, baby girl. It's only natural that you'd want your team back together again, but you don't have to be his woman to do that. I just need you to focus because I'm sure he's looking all fine but it's fool's gold. He looks authentic but the shit ain't real. Don't fall for it."

"You're so righ—Wait. Hold on a sec." I had a message coming through. It was Tyriq. I shuffled through my purse in search of my Bluetooth. Once I powered it on, I gave Essence the green light to finish running it down to me as I responded to Riq.

2:40 p.m. Tyriq: *You a'ight in there?*

2:41 p.m. Julz: *Yes. I'm good. Are you straight? Want something to eat?*

2:43 p.m. Tyriq: *I'm gucci on everything.*

2:44 p.m. Julz: *It's looking like you can go home. Marcel won't try anything.*

2:45 p.m. Tyriq: *He probably won't but I'ma stay in place just in case.*

2:47 p.m. Julz: *Thankx. XoXo*

"...just remember, you've heard it all before." Essence concluded.

"You're right and thanks for the kick to the head."

"As many times as you saved me from stupidity, no problem. Holla if you need me."

"Will do." I hung up feeling like myself. I didn't have shit to worry about now that I got my mind right.

I got up from our table and headed over to them. I wanted them to have some alone time but it was also important for Justus to see us all getting along, and we did just that.

An hour later and a few side eyes telling Marcel to keep his wandering hands to himself, we sat down to a large cheese pizza.

"Doesn't this feel like old times? When we got along so good. Tell me you don't miss this." Marcel petitioned my truth.

"I do." I couldn't lie. "I just don't miss the not so good that came attached to it."

Justus jumped in, stopping my trip down Memory Lane. "Ooh, Daddy, after we get finished eating, you wanna play basketball?"

"You got energy fa days, huh bruh?" Marcel discovered just how rambunctious his little one was. "But I'ma hafta pass on that one. I have a long drive back home ahead of me."

Justus frowned a bit before he gleamed possibility. "You don't have to drive. You can stay with us."

"Justus." I gave him crazy eyes.

"Nah, your mama's man might not like that."

"She don't have no man." He offered up my business.

"Justus!" This time I used that stern motherly tone that made children cower inside of their skin. "Stay in a child's place! Your dad *will* leave today but you'll see him again."

Displeasure resonated across Justus' face but I didn't let that sway my stance. My answer was hell no!

Marcel leaned over beside me, whispering in my ear. "You know I *can* stay the night."

Just then his phone rang. He pulled out his cell and across it read: *Wifey.*

My eyes held contempt for his despicableness. "And *you* know you can kiss my ass, right? Matter of fact, sit on the other side, by your son." I pointed my finger and dared him to buck.

He declined the call naturally and I felt a twinge of disgust for it, imagining myself in her shoes so many times before.

The next half hour, I remained silent with the exception of small talk to Justus. I didn't utter another word to his father until it was time to leave. God forbad I ruin what was a good couple of hours for us with the brutal lashing of my tongue.

Marcel saw us to my car and went about the task of telling his son good bye.

"Give me some, lil' man." Justus ran up to him and dapped him up before they hugged it out. "Look here, me and ya mama gon' plan something for us real soon, a'ight? I love you, son."

"Love you, too, Daddy."

I watched him strap him up in the backseat, closing the door afterwards. My next statement to him would be brief and my exit swift.

"All right. I'll call you some other—" my next few words were imprisoned in my throat as Marcel grabbed me from out of nowhere and slid his tongue into my mouth. I fought it for a second but then I stopped contesting it and allowed it to happen, foolishly so. For a moment, I got caught up in what I used to feel for him instead of what he had driven me to feel now.

It was in that moment that I knew I done fucked up. I still loved him as much as I hated him. *Ain't that a bitch?*

Still engaged in his persuasive kiss, I reopened my eyes and shifted them inside of my car only to see Justus' hopeful eyes glued on our every move.

Then reality hit and I pushed Marcel back, playfully, but I was serious than muthafucka. With my lips pursed, I spoke evenly. "Why the hell you did that?"

He bent down to look at Justus through the window and then stood up as he pushed my hair behind my ear. "Because like him, I'm your daddy, too."

He walked off like a boss, leaving me susceptible to the thought. *I'll be damned.*

Ca$h & Coffee

Chapter 7
Choppa

Over the next week and a half, we hustled hard. The weed was diesel so niggas was hitting us up 24/7 ordering weight. We was going through those shipments faster than ever, and my connect back home was loving it. As for the guns, we had a steady clientele for them. With the growth of gangs in and around the city, and several out of state customers, weaponry was always in high demand.

Days and nights flew by in the blink of an eye, and my bank got fatter. The moment business slowed down a little, my thoughts returned to the cute honey I'd met outside of Cardale's apartment. When I asked him about her, all he could tell me was that shorty basically stayed to herself.

"I see her coming and going with her son, but I ain't never seen a man over there and she don't socialize with anybody in the building. Maybe her dude is on lock or something," he took a wild guess.

"Maybe so," I allowed.

I found myself driving through there several times in hopes of running in to shorty again, but so far lady luck was not on my side. Each time I drove through there I didn't see her car parked outside.

Feeling slightly disappointed, I turned my attention to G-Shine. I watched him for a few days to get a read on him and his girl's routine. I noted that she went to work at a strip club at night and stayed inside most of the day. G-Shine, on the other hand, seemed to job hunt all day then return home in the early evening and not go out again.

Knowing that his feet had just recently touched the ground, I figured that he must've been on papers and his P.O. had him on strict guidelines. But his parole officer should've been his least worry.

Later in the week, my mans and me were in the kitchen of Jared's crib strapping up. Because we knew G-Shine always packed heat, we each put on a lightweight bpv and covered it with black shirts. Jared was leaned against the sink counter, saying nothing, which meant he was in killa mode. In contrast, Cardale sat at the table across from me.

He was running his mouth, as always, but that didn't mean jack—when it was time to bust his gun, homie could be counted on.

I finished loading my clip, slammed it home, and cocked and locked my German Luger. Standing up from the table, I placed the banger on my waist. "A'ight, peep the move," I began. "When we get to G-Shine's baby mama's crib, if his car is there we're going in on some Commando shit. We're not asking no questions. We're smashing everything moving but the baby. If he's not there, we gon' snatch his girl up and wait for him to come through. Jared, you gon' a stay outside in the car. Me and Cardale going in."

"See, that's the fuck shit I be talkin' 'bout," protested Jared.

"Why're you so anxious to kill?" I questioned him.

"'Cause that's what killas do." He click-clacked his Nine and stared at it fondly.

"You'sa sick muthafucka," I remarked.

"Says the man whose body count is higher than mine."

That was up for debate. True, I had sent my share of niggas to the grave, but Jared wasn't averse to killing either. In fact, he seemed to love pulling the trigger. While I never hesitated to do what I had to do, I tried to keep the violence to a minimum because bodies brought mad heat.

"Fam, why you always gotta challenge me? That's the dumb shit that cause problems. Too many chiefs and not enough Indians." I was growing tired of having to wrestle with him over everything.

"Get out of your feelings, dawg. You need a hug or something?" He stood up and held out his arms.

I aimed the banger at him playfully. "Don't get ya cabbage cooked."

Jared chuckled. "Nigga, you frontin'. Remember, it's family over everything."

"That's why you need to sit your light skin ass down and follow orders. Before family be standing over your casket." I was joking but not for real. Before all was said and done, I was gon' cook his shit.

"Let him go in. I'm good," said Cardale.

"Cool. It's you and me." I looked at Jared and nodded my head.

"Say no more," he replied. The look in his eyes told me that he was chomping at the bit. And in spite of the fact that he was becoming unruly I couldn't deny that it gave me comfort knowing that he would be watching my back.

What separated Jared from every other killa I knew was that he never missed. Not one person ever got away when I sent Jared after them.

Returning to the plan, we went over different scenarios. I kept telling Jared to keep his voice down because his girl, Taj, was upstairs. Shorty was good folk, but I didn't want her to overhear us plotting murder. The fuck if I wanted to place my freedom in the hands of a female.

I walked through the living room and went and stood at the bottom of the stairs, trying to listen for any movement upstairs.

Satisfied that Taj was asleep, I returned to the kitchen where my niggas were still debating which way would be best to get at G-Shine. Jared was doing most of the talking. "All we gotta do is lay outside until he comes home. When he drives up, we jump out and light that ass up and be gone," he reasoned.

"True. But I wanna get up close and personal on his bitch ass. I want him to look in my face and carry that image to the afterlife with him," I said.

"I feel you." He smiled.

I smiled back. One killa to another.

"What about his baby mother?" asked Jared.

"She shouldn't be there." I reached for the bottle of Hennessey that was on the table and turned it up. "Ahhhh!" The burn in my throat felt good as hell. I sat the half empty bottle back down on the table and wiped my mouth with the back of my hand. "Time to catch another body," I said. "One day these Georgia clowns are gonna learn not to fuck with a nigga from *The Land*."

Ca$h & Coffee

Chapter 8
Choppa

Sitting outside of G-Shine's baby mother's house, strapped up and ready to kill, I thought back to my first body. I was just a young jit, fifteen years old, and still up in Cleveland, Ohio, a city where you had to say *be safe* after every conversation. A dude named Santana had robbed me for my trap money, a gold chain and my brand new Jordan's.

I had been hunting Santana for almost a year when I finally caught up with him outside an apartment complex in East Cleveland. Homie had jacked so many niggas, he didn't even recognize my face as I walked right up to him.

Although the sun had vanished from the sky and nightfall had washed over the city, a sliver of light that came from a nearby hallway illuminated Santana's face. I could tell from the glazed look in his eyes that he was geeked. His cheeks were sunken and his teeth were jacked up. He barely resembled the feared stickup kid who had shoved a gun in my face and ordered me to *break yaself.*

"What up, youngster? What you tryna cop? I got that hard white and some of that sticky icky."' He licked his chapped lips and bounced from foot to foot. Crack had done the muthafucka to him in less than a year.

Obviously, he was out there hustling flex sacks. "You don't even know who I am, do you?" I asked his pitiful ass.

Alarmed by my tone and the sudden appearance of a gun in my hand, Santana began slowly backing away. "I don't even know you, Bleed," he said in a frightened tone.

"93rd and Kinsman. It was in the middle of the day. You robbed me for my trap, my chain and my Jordan's. Made me run down the street barefoot. Remember me now, homie?"

"Youngster, you got the wrong man."

"Your name is Dave, ain't it?" It was the first name that came to mind.

"Nawl, youngster. My name ain't no Dave. My name Santana." The fool fell right into my trap.

"Yeah, that's what I thought." I raised the gun so that it was leveled at his chest. *"They call me Santana. Ask around."* I repeated the words he'd said to me that night.

Recognition flashed in his eyes. "Young blood, I wasn't in my right mind. Crack had me feenin'. Look at me now, I'm all fucked up. You don't have to kill me, I'm killing myself."

"Nah, old skool, you killed yourself that night you stuck that banger in my face and didn't pull the trigger."

Pow! Pow!

I hit him twice in the chest. Santana stumbled back against a car.

Pow!

A head shot busted his melon and he slid to the ground with blood leaking from his cranium. Mercilessly, I stood over him and turned his lights completely out.

Pow!

I blew his whole forehead out.

Bending over, I snatched his raggedy Adidas off his feet. "Do unto others as you want them to do unto you!" I said.

Thinking back on it now, I was a reckless lil' nigga. They say, God protects old people, kids and fools, and I was two out of the three. How I made it away from the crime scene without any witnesses seeing me could only be attributed to His mercy. What surprised me more was that I never had nightmares about killing Santana. That's when I knew I was about that life. And from that day on I never hesitated to put in work when a nigga tested my get down.

G-Shine was about find out what dudes back home already knew: fuckin' with me was the #1 cause of death.

I screwed the silencer onto the end of my gun and disengaged the safety lock. "It's Show Time, bleed," I said to Jared.

"I'm with you, my G. Just give me a sec' to get this on."

I turned around to see him in the backseat attaching a silencer to his gun. Since G-Shine's car was parked outside we concluded that he was inside. Loud gunshots would alarm the neighbors and we wouldn't want that.

"You ready?" I asked Jared.

"Let's do it," he replied.

Cardale remained in the car while me and Jared eased out. Our all black gear, which consisted of black jeans and shirt, black ski mask, black boots and black gloves, allowed us to easily blend into the night.

As we were about to go around to the back of the apartment, I noticed G-Shine's baby mama's apartment door open up. I could see them standing in the doorway hugging. G-Shine's back was to us and his woman's face was buried in his chest. I reached out and grabbed Jared's arm, turning him so he could see what I saw.

"Damn, shorty ain't supposed to be home." I sighed.

"Fuck it. She 'bout to die with her man. Ain't no mercy. Let's move!" He began trotting toward the door before I could reply.

G-Shine must've heard our hurried footsteps, because he turned around as if he was startled. He took a step out the door and Jared's hand clenched around his throat.

"Fuck you think you're going!" He forced him back inside at gun point.

His chick started to scream, but I cold-cocked her and she went crashing to the floor on her ass. I quickly pulled the door shut behind us and shoved my gun in her mug. "Make another sound and I'ma part your weave."

Shorty squeaked like a mouse. I shoved my banger in her man's face daring him to buck while Jared duct taped the girl, silencing her with a wide strip.

"I know you wanna reach for your heat. Go ahead, so I can pop your muthafuckin top," I threatened G-Shine.

"Man, why y'all fuckin with me?" he whined.

"Cause you fucked with me first." I pressed the gun deeper into his forehead, breaking the skin

"Bruh, I don't even know who you are." He sounded like he was about to cry.

"You're about to find out!" I snatched his gun off his waist.

G-Shine broke for the backdoor, but his legs weren't faster than Jared's trigger finger. *Boc! Boc!* He chopped that ass down before he reached the hallway.

"Ahhhh!" yelped G-Shine. He crashed to the tiled floor on his face.

In a flash, I was standing over him like I stood over Santana eleven years ago. I pointed the gun down at him. Then, I pulled off my ski mask.

"Remember me!" I said.

"Choppa!" G-Shine squeaked like a rusty door. And his eyes were wide with shock.

"Yeah, nigga, it's me. You know you gotta pay for running off with my money."

"Man, I got locked up."

"Yeah, I know all dat but you had plenty time to pay me before you did. Now your time has run out." I taunted.

"I got this lil' pussy ass nigga, dawg." Jared cut in. I stepped back and let him take over because the boy was in his true element.

Jared dragged G-Shine back into the living room next to his broad. I took a seat on the couch and leaned back like I was chilling, watching a movie or something. Jared slapped G-Shine in the mouth with the barrel of his gun.

"Choppa, please get your people. I promise I'ma pay you every dollar I owe. Y'all ain't gotta do this," he cried.

"Fuck you, bitch ass nigga. You put those $10,000 over your life now it's collection time." I looked at Jared. "Bleed, show this lil punk muthafucka how we rock!"

Jared didn't hesitate. He put his tool right up against G-Shine's dome and turned it into a drop top. "Lights out, bitch ass nigga!" he muttered as he stepped over the body headed to where the girl lie whimpering.

For a brief second I thought about sparing shorty's life but she had seen my face and heard her man call my name. *No witnesses. Not ever.* I reminded myself.

My goon wasn't having any reservations, apparently. In a cold, rehearsed manner, he unsheathed a knife that he wore strapped to his side. The terror I saw on G-Shine's girl's face was indescribable. Her mouth was covered but she screamed with her eyes.

Jared showed her no mercy. He covered her face with the couch pillow then plunged the knife in her chest, down to the handle. Blood shot three feet in the air, splattering all over his ski mask.

I jerked my head away from the heinous sight and my eyes fell upon G-Shine's corpse. His dome was crooked and blown out, and a puddle of blood had formed on the floor beneath his head.

"Her blood is on *your* hands," I said.

When I looked back up at Jared, he was smoking a *Black and Mild*. His knife was embedded in shorty's chest. I couldn't help but feel sorry for her now.

The cry of a small baby came from one of the back rooms. Jared's head snapped in the direction of the sound. I quickly moved towards him in case he was thinking of doing the unthinkable.

"Let's go, fam. We done what we came to do," I said.

He hesitated to move but I was blocking his path if he planned on going into the back room where the sounds came from.

"We gotta check it out. Somebody else could be back there," he wisely stated.

"Cool, but we're not killing no babies, and I'm dead ass. Don't test me or one of us ain't leaving out of here," I said.

"It won't be me," he mumbled.

"We're about to find out," I said as we moved down the hall in step.

Ca$h & Coffee

Chapter 9
Choppa

It turned out that no one was in the back room but a cute little infant girl. I didn't know if the baby was G-Shine's and his girl's or not, but we left her unharmed.

That night I slept fitfully. In my dreams I had several gun battles with Jared and in each one I came out on the losing end. Was that a premonition or a warning to cut ties before it came to gunplay? I wondered.

The truth was, I needed Jared and Cardale just as much as they needed me. No one man is an army by himself. The problem was those niggas were forgetting I was the General, and they were the soldiers.

By the time I rolled out of bed I was no closer to deciding how I was going to deal with the discord than I had been before I closed my eyes last night. I decided to just go with the flow and let the cards fall where they may.

Last night's murders were forgotten as if they hadn't even occurred. As far as I was concerned, G-Shine had murked himself and his broad. Because in the game justice comes right to your front door. That's why I tried to keep me and mines a well-kept secret. And sometimes even that didn't assure that muthafuckas wouldn't find out where I laid my head and come gunning.

I was reminded of that as I stepped into the shower and turned on the water, and I recalled that I had an appointment today with my real estate agent. I had put my main crib on the market after some niggas tried to kick in my door a few months ago. My shit was reinforced with steel so their attempt was futile but it didn't feel safe there anymore.

I hadn't said anything to anyone about the failed home invasion, not even Jared or Cardale. Everyone was a suspect in my eyes until I weeded out the culprit. I was just low-key studying my whole circle: the people I hustled with as well as those I served. Maybe one of them had followed me home.

Anyway, living at the condo wasn't an option. I crashed out there on the regular, for appearances sake, but it was not home.

Standing under the hot jet spray, the water relaxed my muscles as well as my mind. I lathered my body and tried to wash away the stress of the lifestyle that I had chosen. My thoughts drifted to shorty again and my dick swelled in my hand. I stroked it slowly up and down imagining her hands on me. It felt good but since she wasn't actually there I didn't want to waste a nut.

Nah, I'ma save that for the real thing, I decided as I adjusted the water temperature to cold to help my hard on go away. I thought about hitting up one of the many groupie hoes that was on my dick but decided against it. I wanted the nut but not the clingy shit that came with it.

"Down boy," I commanded my wood. Then, I finished my shower and got dressed to go house hunting.

***

The real estate agent showed me several properties. One in particular caught my eye. It was a 4 bedroom, 3 1/2 bath, 2,800 square foot colonial style home in McDonough, Georgia, a good distance away from the dirt and grime of metro Atlanta.

"I'm very interested in this one. I'm going to have my people look at it in a couple of weeks. We'll be in touch by then," I explained to the agent.

"Okay, have her give me a call," she responded with a pleasant smile.

When we shook hands, I could've sworn I felt her rub my palm with her finger. I ignored it, though. Because I didn't fuck with pink toes like that. She smiled and used a perfectly manicured hand to remove her long, blond hair out of her face.

If she had any fantasies of me banging that white pussy on the hardwood floor, they disintegrated when I turned and headed out to my ride.

Before I pulled off I checked my phone and saw that I had several missed calls, all from the same person. I dreaded calling her back because I knew she was gonna be on that fuck shit. But it was best to hit her up or she would blow my phone up.

I pressed *call back* and she answered on the first ring.

"Tavares, what the fuck are you going to do? Are you sending for me or do I gotta get back home on my own. You're starting to piss me the fuck off!"

"KiKi, haven't I told you not to call me by my government?" I said calmly.

"Fuck what you told me, *Tavares!*" she yelled.

"See, I was just about to hit you up with some good news but since you don't know how to act, fuck it." I started the engine of my car and drove away from the property I had just looked at.

I heard KiKi sigh. "Okay, I'm sorry. What's the good news?" she asked.

"I found a new crib so I'll be up there to get you soon."

"About fuckin time."

"See, you're ungrateful as hell, but it's cool. You and I both know the end is right in front of us. I'ma let you keep running your greasy mouth, time will take care of everything else." I meant that, and if it wasn't for her pops I would've been stopped dealing with her in any way.

"Oh, you don't love me at all anymore?" I heard pain in her voice, but I refused to waver. Whatever we had had run its course.

"Like I said, the end is near. I'm doing this on the strength of what we had—nothing less, nothing more."

"Oh, yeah? Well, you remember that whenever my end comes yours will too, boo," she threatened.

"Keep underestimating me and watch me prove you wrong."

I ended the call without allowing her a response.

Later that night, I hooked up with Jared and Cardale to hit the club and knock down a few drinks to ease the tension of the last few days. We chilled in VIP checking out throngs of bad bitches. I knew that most of them was looking for a quick come up off a nigga who was stacking paper. When they approached me popping pussy, I chased them away like the nasty rats they were.

Cardale and Jared loved easy ass, but not me. I had a pathological disdain for females that carried themselves like hoes. So, I leaned back on the couch and got in my own zone, just me and a bottle of Ciroc.

A while later, I got up to go to the men's room and to my surprise I bumped into the woman who had been invading my dreams since we met. I smiled like a little lame ass nigga with a school boy crush on the prettiest girl in class.

I couldn't do shit but laugh. That's the crazy effect shorty had on me. In a club full of women, she was the only one I saw. She was the brightest star amongst a crowd of them and I was thoroughly attracted to her understated beauty.

Quickly regaining my smoothness, I licked my lips and gave her a thuggish smile.

"Hey, beautiful," I said as our eyes met.

Chapter 10
Julz
A few hours earlier

"It's about time you made it." Essence kissed me on the cheek as she ushered me into her three bedroom flat. "The others are in the back gettin' ready, gettin' ready, gettin' ready ready." She broke out in a slight bounce to an old Dj Jubilee hit.

I looked at my watch. "It ain't nothing but nine o'clock. I don't know why you were so insistent that I come so early, anyway."

"We both know if I would have told you to meet us there for eleven, you wouldn't have gotten out of your bed, with yo lazy ass."

I bobbed my head a little because she was right. "You just don't understand. Between work, school and Justus, I be dog tired."

"I know, and that's why I had to get you before the Sandman came calling. Anyway, to hell with all that." She fanned her hand downward, as if to dismiss what she was talking about. "You lookin' hella cute. You bound to meet you a balla tonight, wearing that hot lil' number."

"I am not interested in finding no dude up in there. All they'll be looking for is some love in the club."

"Shid, I'm all right with that. My shit needs maintenance." She rubbed her hand down the side of her body.

We high-fived each other and chorused, "Okayyyyy!" Then we broke out in laughter. I was overdue for a tune-up myself.

"Come on, I gotta finish getting' ready." She locked her door and we walked to the back of her house, where the other girls were.

I watched Essence lead the way as I admired her strapless styled, jumpsuit romper. She was thicker than most but that bitch was beautiful. She had just as much stomach as she did ass but she was still a show stopper and every bit of a diva and I loved that about her. Her confidence stayed on one million despite what some lame broads and bullshit men said about her size.

Although my Tootsie was single, any man who could match her heart would be lucky to have her. But until then, she spoiled herself.

She walked me into the bedroom she had converted into one huge dressing room.

One wall housed four individual wooded framed mirrors that were six feet in length, guaranteed to capture the best selfies. The other wall was lined with cubicles that showcased her expensive shoe game and then there were the racks of clothes that catered to her seasonal wear. If I was able to fit her gear, she'd be as good as got because I would have helped myself.

In the middle of the room was a circular 360° seating area, which allowed for her to have a view of her things from any angle. For her budget, she could rival Mariah Carey's closet, hands down.

I walked over to my girl, Precious, who was sitting at the vanity, applying too much make-up to her eyes, as usual. She was our clique's Sour Patch because she was sweet but that trick was bitter as hell. The only thing that saved her from getting that ass beat on multiple occasions, courtesy of Essence, was me, the referee between the two.

"What's up, boo?" I gave her a phantom kiss to the cheek. I didn't want to risk her caked up foundation getting on me.

"What's up, bittttcccchhh?" She smiled at me through her reflection in the mirror before she wiped the smear of tropical blue lipstick off of her front tooth.

I threw my forearms in the air and Bankhead bounced. "We 'bout to turn up, ya heard me."

"Who you telling? I got my good bra on so my girls are at attention." She pushed her double D's closer together, forcing them to protrude out of her cleavage.

"Girl, put those things away." I pushed her butter pecan colored melons down into her skin-tight dress. She gave me an evil glare before she proudly readjusted her bountiful bosoms back underneath her chin.

I threw my hands up. It was hard convincing her that *that* shit wasn't cute but if she liked it, I loved it.

Seconds later, I turned around only to bump into my baby, Fat-Fat, who was coming out of the bathroom. Hate her or love her, but my chick was bad. She was a slim beauty, whose face stayed beat and hair was always slayed to the gods.

Baby got in many unnecessary fights because jealous bitches thought she thought she was too much but truth was, *they did*. Fat-Fat was humble with her fly. It was just easier to target her to mask their own insecurities.

"What's up, Diamond Girl? Aren't you looking all good and shit?" Fat-Fat spun me around to get a better look at my curve hugging dress. "And them shoes? Gurl, you doing that!" She complimented my five inch sandals that wrapped all the way up my calves.

"That bitch know she winning, you don't have to gas her ass up. So ease off her clit. Damn!" Sour Precious arched her upper lip at Fat-Fat.

"Damn, I didn't know there would be shade in today's forecast." I looked at Precious roll her eyes, fluttering those god-awful, beauty store lashes.

"You know you fly, too, so shut the hell up." Fat-Fat threw her a bone as she walked over to Precious and began styling the back of her hair with her fingers.

Essence then came over and pushed the back of Precious' head. "Hoe, you'sa compliment whore. Can't stand for nobody else to get shine. That shit ain't cute, no."

"I ain't no damn hater. I was just saying." Precious protested, as she popped her lips and blew herself a kiss in the mirror, feeling herself.

"Well, can you say that shit over there?" Essence pointed across the room, so she could take her place in the chair and apply her make-up.

Precious feathered her hair before she slowly got up. "I guess I'm done."

"I guess I'm done." Essence rolled her neck, mocking her snootily before she iffed at her.

When Precious stood up, she had to pull her dress down because it crept so far up her ass all of her ba-donka-donk was exposed.

"I hope yo big booty ass have on drawers, sitting on my seat. Don't nobody wanna sit on yo damn juices." Essence grabbed a towel from the bathroom and laid it down before sitting.

Precious whipped her head over her shoulder. "Fuck you, E. Fuck you, Fat-Fat. And fuck you, Julz!" She gave each of us the bird before she walked and stood in front one of the mirrors, admiring herself.

Essence waved her off and went about the task of putting on her mascara.

"What I do?" Fat-Fat looked toward me for answers.

I shrugged. "Who knows but, also, who gives a fuck? You know she bi-polar." I walked up behind Precious and hugged her around the waist, pumping her ass once with the thrust of my pelvis. "She just need some dick and then she'll be all right."

"Ain't that the truth?" Essence said rhetorically.

"Shid, I do. I can't lie. So, yo ass betta get up off of me before we get it on." Precious burst out into laughter.

I released her, ASAP. I wanted no parts of that. I stepped off to the side and caught a mirror of my own. I opened my clutch and pulled out my Ruby Woo Mac lipstick and reapplied a fresh red coating. I then smoothed down my hair that I flat ironed earlier tonight as well as my little black halter dress.

"Who's watching my little boyfriend?" I heard Fat-Fat ask, standing next to me.

"Baby boy is with Tyriq."

"You ever thought that maybe y'all should be together?"

I turned to face Fat-Fat. "How did you get that question from my response?"

She nudged up against me. "Because he is always looking out for you and Justus."

"First of all, he has a lil' dip."

"But she ain't you, though," she cut in.

I smirked. "True but me and Tyriq are friends, *only*. Point blank period. That's how it's been for the last ten years and that's what it will continue to be. Besides, he asked for my son to stay the night and keep his lil' one company, which is why I was even able to get out tonight."

"Well, I like Riq for you and if you paid him half a mind, then maybe you wouldn't be thinking twice about Marcel, who by the way doesn't deserve a tenth chance from you." Fat-Fat over exaggerated the number of times I took him back but like Essence, she was right.

"I promise I won't give Marcel no holla. I'm aware that these last two weeks is just him being on his best behavior. But more importantly, I remember his slick ass has a wifey, even if he doesn't."

"Glad you know it but if you don't slow his roll, you gon' find yourself underneath him." Essence chimed in.

"Damn, when did I take center stage?" I kinda felt like I was under attack by my ladies. All I needed was Precious' two unwanted cents.

"I was only saying, friend. Be careful, is all." Fat-Fat offered solace.

"Or get you some *dick*traction." Ahh, there was the unsolicited advice I expected from Precious' ole *hot in the pants* tail.

"Bye, Felicia." I waved them all off.

"That ain't a bad idea, ya know?" Essence spoke over her shoulder.

Fat-Fat cut back in. "Julz, I do agree with my girls when they say you need a gentleman who'll give you something to look forward to so you don't go backwards but I don't think it should be a random man."

"Let me guess, you're about to campaign for Tyriq, *again*."

"Yea, I am. Come on, sis. We both know his lil' girlfriend would be yesterday's news if you gave him the time of day."

"I'm not booting another woman out of the picture just so I can be in the frame. No. Hell no!"

"I don't know how you could be so strong. Yea, he's a D-boy and you'd prefer him with a regular job, but he's a family man, a provider. He's an overall catch." Fat-Fat counted off some of the reasons he should be pulled out of the friend zone.

"Don't forget that muthafucka fine as hell, too." Precious added.

"Let the church say, Amen!" Essence said as she stood over my shoulder.

"Amen," they each chorused on command.

I looked from my left to my right, laughing at them drooling over my boy. I shook my head at them heifers. "Y'all a mess."

They went on for about five minutes, preaching the gospel of Tyriq and all his sexual glory but I couldn't join in because although he was sexy, I didn't see him like that, at all.

"A'ight, y'all ready?" Essence checked her cell phone. "It's a quarter to ten."

Fat-Fat slid into her pumps and grabbed her purse. "I'm ready."

"Born ready." I raised my hand, then I looked over at Precious.

She sniffed under each arm and then looked at me when she saw I was looking at her. "What?"

"Is you ready, trick?"

"Gurllll, I stay ready." She turned to the side and tried sucking in her stomach. "A few more sit-ups and I'll be snatched."

"More like a few hundred million." Essence burst her bubble.

"Bitch, I know you ain't talkin' with your booty-do having ass."

Essence uglied her face and I braced myself. "Oooh, one day, bitch, you ain't gon' have no reason for edge control because I'm gon' snatch yo shit out yo scalp." Essence threatened and me and Fat-Fat laughed.

"Let her make it, E. Don't hurt her." I managed to say through my chuckles. Essence was burnt up at her comment.

They stayed getting at each other's neck. I was often surprised Essence allowed Precious to sit with us but then again, Precious was the life of the party.

"Whatever, bitch! Let's roll out." Precious twirled Essence around so she could walk out of the room.

"Mmmhmmm." Essence didn't hide her annoyance as she grabbed her purse.

Minutes later, we all congregated outside, waiting for Essence to set her alarm in her house. Once she walked out, she hit the button on her keypad to unlock the doors of her truck and we all jumped in, leaving our cars at her place.

No sooner than we all got in, Essence handed me her cell.

"We're gonna need some get buck music to ride to. Julz, connect my phone to the auxiliary and put on Q93's Social Shakedown." Essence then threw her truck in reverse, so she could pull out of her driveway.

"Don't nobody wanna hear that bounce bullshit." Precious volunteered, as if she spoke for us all.

"I don't recall nobody asking you shit, Precious. If this is how you're gonna be tonight, you can get out, yea. I'm more than certain nobody wants to hear *your* shit!" I had to check her because she was working my damn nerves now.

"Are you kidding me? Chris will be in the building tonight and I ain't missing my chance to be with him."

"Well, shut the hell up 'fo you find yourself outside the club." Essence threw her weight, being she was the one with the reservations for VIP.

Precious waved her hand to the sky, as if to testify. "Let me shut up before things go left."

"Right!" I finally had something to co-sign that came from out of her mouth.

"Just chill, P. We gon' have a good time and you gon' Mrs. Brown for the night." Fat-Fat softened the look on Precious' face with a reminder of her mission for the night: *Bed Breezy*.

"You right." I saw her bob her head at Fat-Fat.

Now with Precious' mouth on mute, we hiked the volume up to the bounce remix of John Legends' *Get Higher* and headed to Downtown Atlanta.

Ca$h & Coffee

Chapter 11
Julz
The Mansion

"Ayyyeee! We in da house!" Precious yelled out ignorantly as she flailed her arms in the air, drawing the upward lips of some sadity females nearby.

"Can you forget everything you learned from ratchet reality and be classy just once in your life? Damn!" Essence scolded.

"Here's some class for you." Precious started popping her bubble butt up against Essence's pelvis.

"Come on, P. We can have a good time without being a spectacle." I locked my arm in the crook of hers, standing her up to walk with me.

"Y'all some prissy bitches. I keep forgetting that shit. I'm gon' hafta find me some new friends," said Precious.

"No you're not. You love us." Fat-Fat linked her other arm with hers.

Precious gave off a stank face until she could no longer front. "I do love y'all but damn y'all bougie as hell."

"Whatever." I laughed her off.

Moments later, we made it up to our VIP section. There was a bottle chilling on ice and next to it a fruit, cracker and cheese tray. I felt all presidential sitting pretty amongst my ladies while looking lovely doing it.

"This is nice." I complimented the scenery as I swayed to a Drake cut.

"It is." Fat-Fat agreed.

Another minute or so passed and that one song that made everyone who was sitting stand to their feet came on.

"Ooh, this our song." Essence announced right as we all started to dance to Rae Sremmurd's *Throw Some Mo.*

"Ass fat? Yeah, I know..." We all started singing Nicki Minaj's part while we dipped, bounced and snapped our fingers to the beat.

After that, it was one song after the other. One laugh after another and one drink after the other. We were having a good time, for real.

Then the effect of the liquor hit my bladder. I pulled Fat-Fat toward me and spoke in her ear. "I'm going to the ladies' room. Be right back."

She gave me the thumbs up and I headed out and down the steps to the restroom.

A few minutes later, I sighed relief as I wiggled the remaining trickles into the toilet. "Whew!"

I headed over to the sink, washed my hands and onced myself over in the mirror.

As I was walking out, a lady accidently bumped into me, stepping on my foot.

"Oh, I'm sorry. Excuse me." She apologized.

"It's okay," I told her.

I stepped out of the way and into the club, leaning against the wall as I squatted down to wipe my shoe. Then when I stood to my feet to go back to where my ladies were, I heard a man, who stood not too far away from me, direct a compliment my way.

"Hey, beautiful," he said as our eyes met.

Yessss! I screamed inwardly.

I was face to face with Mr. Thuggalicious and he was looking better than he did the first time I saw him at my apartment. He was modestly dressed but he looked good in what he wore. He had on all-black everything, from the V-neck T-shirt tucked slightly above the Gucci belt that held up his Levi's, finished off with some hi-top Gucci boots that gave his casual dress a little rugged appeal. The only thing that sparkled color on him were his pearl whites displayed between his lips, the jewelry in his ears, two chains that hung around his neck and the diamond bezzeled big face on his wrist.

I didn't want to come off as being too eager, so I played it cool. "Heyyy." I sung my one word response as I smiled with both my eyes and the smirky crook of my lips.

My, my! Fate had put us in the same space again and this time I looked good, and that was on my mama.

"Damn, ma, you're looking so good I can hardly breathe." He reached for my hand.

"You don't know me like that." I placed my hand in his, letting him know that I was only teasing.

His bushy eyebrows raised up until he caught on that I was kidding and then they relaxed and he flashed that smile that made every other nigga invisible. "I don't know you like that *yet* but you gotta give me a little time. Let's start with your last name. Because I already know your first name is Beautiful."

"I give you a 9 1/2." I rated his line. "But you're a long way off, my name is Julz and yours?" I stared into his eyes. They had a *bish* hypnotized.

He thumbed the top of my hand, feeling the softness of my skin and smiled. "Choppa."

"*Choppa?*" I repeated it back to him as if I couldn't believe it. "How did you earn that name?"

He chuckled. I supposed he must have been asked that a lot. "Remind me on our third date. I'll tell you, then."

I played it off like I didn't hear him not only imply we'd kick it but it would happen multiple times.

A shot caller. Check!

Clearing my throat, I managed to look around before focusing my attention back to him. "Sooo, you come here often?" *Oh, God! That shit sounds so cliché, Julz!* I reprimanded myself the moment the final word left my tongue.

"Nah, not really, but I've been putting in so much work lately that me and my mans needed a break and ended up here." Now he looked around a bit before he asked me a question of his own. "Where your girls at?"

I giggled at him. "That's pretty presumptuous. Don't you think? Assuming I'm here with women and not a man?"

"I ain't making no assumption, shorty. I simply observe. And what I see is a Queen who is too fine to be away from her man, if she had one. After all, we been talking for," he checked the time on his watch and the diamonds sparkled brightly, "five minutes. Too much time to be away from me, if you were mine."

This man made me blush.

"Is that right?"

"Facts. I'm just hoping you're here with your ladies. I wouldn't wanna have to crush a nigga when you leave the club with me. Nah mean?"

That elicited a full-fledged laugh. "I'm leaving? With you? Is that another one of your observations?"

I continued laughing but I stopped short when he unequivocally answered *yes*. He leaned in and sang in my ear, "I wanna be your N.I.G.G.A./ you need a thug in your life/them bustas ain't loving you right."

Under my dress, my pussy damn near jumped out of my panties and right into his hands. I squeezed my thighs together and prayed that my face wasn't hot with the undisguised desire. But apparently it was.

"Yeah, luv, you're leaving with me tonight," he repeated real cocky-like.

What he was saying wasn't so far-fetched that I didn't believe him. A woman always knew how far a man could go upon sight. I was just shocked that he felt so sure of himself and what *I* would allow.

"Oh—kayyy." I didn't know no other response than that.

"Julz, I need to go to the bathroom right quick. Don't go anywhere. I'll be back out to get you. And if some clown try to push up on you, ask him if his life insurance is paid up."

"You're so silly," I giggled.

"I'm dead ass, ma. So handle it like that, a'ight? He reached out and stroked my cheek, sending a bolt of lust straight to my epicenter.

I nodded my head. He smiled and I smiled back.

I watched him disappear behind the push of the door and I broke out in a two-step. It didn't seem out of place for me to bust a move being that I was in a club. However, that was no ordinary jig I did. That was a little victory dance because the hottest thing on the scene was checking for me!

Precious said I was winning and she wasn't lying.

As I waited, I blindly patted my hair down to ensure it was in place. Afterwards, I wiped the slight mist that formed across my forehead. It was either getting hot or it was just me. Either way, I wanted to look flawless.

After five or so minutes passed, Choppa returned. He silently stood next to me before he placed his hand on the small of my back, guiding my walk with him to wherever.

He paused for a moment and leaned into me. "You like to dance?"

I nodded my head *yes*. "It's the N. O. in me."

Choppa bobbed his head and led me through the crowd and onto the dance floor.

As soon as we found us a spot, Rich Homie Quan's song went off and a classic came on. I threw my arms up and snapped my fingers as I rhythmically moved to one of my favorite jams.

Choppa watched me for a second before he half circled around me, stopping at my rear to wrap his hands around my waist as we danced, or rather I danced and he rocked in unison to Biggie's *One More Chance.*

I suspected he would try to get his grind on since he had nothing but ass against him but he did just the opposite. I could tell he was a shotta but instead of over sexualizing the moment, he simply enjoyed the sway of my hips to the beat of the music without warranting a slap to the face.

Maybe I would just shove him a little if he tried it, I snickered at the thought. I mean, what woman didn't want something as fine as him all over her?

Nevertheless, I was impressed because most men would try to fuck me on the floor and the only time the hoe in me came out was behind closed doors with a nigga that was mine.

A minute or so passed and I felt him lean down and into my ear. I felt the slight brush of his lips and warmth of his breath wisp against my lobe as he said, "I wanna know you away from here."

I turned my head to the side, allowing it to rest against his face for a second.

"What are you suggesting?"

He spun me around to face him and grabbed my hand, leading me off of the floor and up the stairs.

We reached his VIP section, which wasn't too far from where me, Essence, Fat-Fat and Precious were sitting. Two men were waving money in the air, holding champagne bottles up and talking smack over the music.

"Them my boys, they ain't never been nowhere," cracked Choppa.

"Leave them alone." I laughed and play punched his arm.

We stopped in front of the table and they looked up at me curiously. One of them looked very familiar.

"What's wrong with y'all? Don't y'all know to stand up and pay respect in the presence of a queen," Choppa said.

The one whose face I recognized rose to his feet. "My bad, Miss Lady," he apologized.

"No, it's okay," I said.

"No, it's not," Choppa spoke over me. He gave the other one a hard stare and he stood up, somewhat reluctantly. I didn't take it as an affront to me. It seemed more like a man thing. Like the type of unspoken conflict that could sometimes exist between two alpha males in the same circle.

When Choppa formerly introduced us, it finally registered with me that Cardale lived in my apartments. We never spoke to one another. I doubted he noticed me or anyone for that matter because he always appeared distracted the few times I saw him.

Jared, the second friend, seemed to wear a natural scowl but his voice was welcoming when he spoke to me. And his eyes were even friendlier. The thought came to my mind that Choppa should watch him.

Taking a seat next to Choppa, he lifted bottles from out of a chilled, ice bucket and read labels.

"Would you like a drink? Coconut Ciroc? Ace of Spades..." He began offering.

"I'm not a big drinker but we have bottle service where I'm sitting." I pointed in the direction my girls were.

"Those your peoples? Tell 'em come over." Jared stretched his neck like an ostrich, looking to see where I directed my finger.

"Don't be a thirsty mu'fucka all your life." Choppa placed a hand on his shoulder and laughed at his eagerness.

"Ain't nobody thirsty but ain't nobody came to a club just to stare at yo ugly ass either."

It was clear that underneath the envy I detected in Jared, there was a friendship in place. I understood that because the same thing existed between Precious and Essence. "It's all good. I'm sure they'd be cool with coming over. I'll be right back."

As I stood to get up, I felt Choppa grab my hand. "Don't get lost on your way. I'm watching you, shorty."

I leaned into his ear so no one else could hear. "Enjoy the view as you do." I pulled away to see him smile as he sat back and folded one leg on top of the other.

In a matter of seconds, I was amongst my ladies and was accosted by E the moment I set foot in front of her.

"Umm, 'bout time. I thought I was gonna hafta search for you. Where have you been?" Essence folded her arms.

"Sorry, Mother, but I was dancing with that guy I told you I met at my apartment a couple of weeks back, whose number I didn't get."

She looked puzzled for a second and then she smiled a smile of remembrance. "Ooh, you talkin' 'bout the thug of your dreams?"

I slowly motioned my head up and down, twice. "That be him."

"Girrrlll, where he at and do he have any fine ass friends with him?" Precious bogarted our conversation.

"He's here with two of his potnas and it just so happens they inquired about my dime divas. Y'all wanna go over there?"

"Fuckin' right. All right! I'm 'bout it." Precious stood to her feet first, looked behind herself and started booty bouncing.

I looked at her stiffly until she calmed her ass down.

Damn, her perfume of desperation was loud.

"What? I'm supposed to be sophisticated and shit? We in a club, bitch. I'm supposed to be turnt." Precious addressed the stank look I gave her.

"I guess." I then looked to Essence. "You coming?"

"If they not cute, I'm turning my happy ass back around." Essence stood up next.

I then looked over at Fat-Fat, who remained seated. "You not coming, sis?"

"No, I'ma chill here." She waved my offer off.

I sat beside her. "Why, baby?"

Precious answered for her. "She waiting for this ole ugly ass Kermit the Frog lookin' ass nigga to pass back." She turned up her lips as if she had room to talk. Coincidentally, most men found her to look like Ms. Piggy.

Fat-Fat smacked her lips and rolled her eyes at Precious before smiling back at me. "Kermit's name is Lydell and yes I'm waiting for him to come back and holla at a sista, so go ahead. I'm good."

"Question. Is he ugly?" I asked out of curiosity when I saw Precious stick a finger in her mouth and display gag faces.

"I like his conversation."

Yep, he was.

I brought her to her feet and pointed to the section I was bringing the others. "We're over there if you need us, but I'll be back to check on you."

She bobbed her head and reclaimed her seat as we headed out.

When Choppa saw me, he stood up and reached for my hand. I looked over my shoulder and gave my girls a *bitch whatttt* look because his gentlemanly ways were worth the brag.

"Have a seat, ladies." Choppa invited them to sit.

"These are my friends, Essence and Precious." I pointed them out as I called their names. "This is Choppa." I placed my hand on his knee as I took a seat next to him before pointing out the others. "And his friends, Jared and Cardale."

"Ooh, I like you, Jared. Mind if I sit by you?" Precious called first dibs, just in case Essence may had wanted him.

I couldn't tell if Jared was okay or not with her forwardness but if he wasn't, he didn't show it.

I shook my head and pinched the bridge of my nose. *Please don't let this bitch give us all a bad name.*

Essence turned her nose up. I could read from her facial expression that she would have pushed up on Jared, too, but we never competed for a man's attention, so it was either Cardale or no one at all.

In no time at all, Precious was all over Jared, admiring his jewels and giving off the smell of a bitch in heat. Light skin niggas had a stronger effect on her than a case of gin. And it didn't hurt that he had balla written all over him. I hoped Choppa didn't think birds of a feather flocked together.

Cardale was a big black guy but he wasn't hard on the eyes. And from overhearing snatches of his conversation he seemed to be pretty interesting, but I could tell that Essence wasn't feeling him in a sexual way. She didn't like men with dreads and he was a bit too boastful for her taste.

Oh well, that was her bad luck. I was more than good. Choppa had me talking a mile a minute, telling him all of my lil' business and laughing at everything he said. I felt like a giddy school girl who'd been kissed at recess.

My eyes closed as I listened to Choppa whisper in my ear. His breath on my skin was giving a bish little tiny heart attacks and his strong hand on my leg was causing massive contractions in my *ooh la la*. He placed a soft kiss on my cheek and I swear I died for about ten seconds.

When I came back to life, my eyes fluttered open just in time to see Jared leading Precious toward the men's room. I knew her get down so I wasn't surprised. I just hoped the dick wouldn't cause her to catch feelings for a nigga that was probably out to just fuck tonight.

Awhile later, they returned with the evidence of their bathroom adventure written all over their faces. Me and Essence looked at each other knowingly. I had to cover my mouth with a hand to stifle a giggle.

"What's up?" asked Choppa.

"Nothing," I said.

Two hours had elapsed but I couldn't tell. It felt like we just arrived but from the constant yawns escaping Essence's mouth, I knew we'd hit her three hour alarm. She loved hitting the streets but she was the first to tap out.

Essence stood to her feet. I didn't want to give her eye contact but I couldn't avoid what I knew would proceed. "Are you ready, chick? It's almost two-thirty and a bitch tired."

I had to stop myself from pouting. I was far from ready but I was never one to abandon my ship, so quite naturally I didn't put up a fuss. "Yea, we can go."

"Hold on. I'm not ready for you to leave, so if it's all the same, I'll take you home." Choppa sat up, looking between me and Essence.

"Aren't you and your people riding together?" I was feeling him but not enough to feel comfortable alone amongst the three of them.

"Nah, we met up. I'm in my own whip."

Well, in that case. "Okay, give me a minute," I smiled at Choppa and then escorted Essence outside of the VIP.

"Mmmhmm." She wasted no time, giving me the eye as she reached into her purse and discreetly pulled out a condom, passing it to me.

"For real?" I looked at it like it was shit in my hand.

"Bih, it's Sweet Pwussy Satday," she impersonated Plies. "I know you gon' let him hit, so protect that pussy."

"Girl, no, I'm not!" I bucked my eyes at her. I don't think he saw what she did but I felt uncomfortable clutching the gold wrapper.

Essence looked over my shoulder and no doubt over at him before she looked at me again. "He's fine as fuck. Treat yo'self. Besides, I saw how y'all were all cozy on one another. So stop being stingy, throw caution to the wind and throw that pussy on his dick." She slid her messy tongue out of her mouth like a lizard and walked back into their VIP.

I followed behind her, shaking my head. She was no spokesperson for my sex but she was right. He was fine as hell and if I slipped up, he could get it.

I took my seat back next to Choppa and cooly slid the rubber into my clutch as Essence went about the task of collecting Precious.

"Let's roll, P." Essence tugged her by the arm, peeling her off of an uninterested Jared.

"Hold the hell on!" Precious snatched her arm back. She rolled her eyes hard at Essence before giving googlies to Jared. "This bitch bossy but she drove, so I am about to go. But what's your number before I leave? We can hook up and do this again."

Jared wasted no time rejecting her. "Nah, I'm good, but get home safe."

"You're what? You're good?" She instantly felt played and I felt embarrassed for her, too, but she played herself when she threw herself on him so quickly.

He smirked before standing to his feet, ignoring her and dapping off Choppa. "I'll get up with you, boy." He then nudged Cardale and waved him to follow. "Let's be out, fam."

Cardale downed the rest of whatever he was drinking, dapped off Choppa and said his goodbyes to us all.

Precious was looking as stupid as she probably felt. She watched Jared leave and then looked to Choppa. "Your boy is lame for that."

Choppa threw his hands up. "Aye, I can't tell another man how to handle his. Chalk it as a lesson, shorty."

"Whatever!" She stood up and exited without saying another word.

"She's salty. Don't worry 'bout her." Essence brushed Precious' attitude off, speaking to Choppa. Then she bent down and kissed me on my cheek. "I'm 'bout to peel Fat-Fat away from her little friend and head home. And you better call me. No matter the time or I'ma show up with the squad."

I laughed at her because there was no squad, but I respected why she said that.

Choppa picked up on it, too. "She's gonna be safe with me."

"Trust me, she better be. Matter of fact, text me a picture of his license plate, Julz." Essence was so protective over me, been that way since childhood. I swear she was my bitch!

"Shorty ain't playing." Choppa laughed at her brazenness.

"Not at all. That's best friend, right there. But for real, y'all be good. Talk to you later, girl." Essence looked at her phone and then back to me to wordlessly remind me that she wanted his plates, for real.

I nodded my head and waved her bye.

Choppa and I talked a few minutes more before he stood up and looked at the thinning crowd. "Maybe we should get up out of here, too. Breakfast and chill?" He suggested, reaching for my hand.

I blushed and then tucked my head into my shoulder to hide the ongoing smiles his charm kept me with.

Then after I was able to get the giddy look off of my face, I obliged. "Yea. Breakfast and chill."

Ca$h & Coffee

Chapter 12
Julz

After leaving the club, we stopped over at a Waffle House. We had breakfast and did a lot of chitchatting before we headed to my place.

I sat in the plush recline of his leather seat as I rested my head back, listening to the low volume of *Miguel*. Our conversation had simmered a bit but the silence was comfortable.

Fifteen minutes passed and I was at home. Time moved entirely too fast for my liking.

I removed my seatbelt once he threw his car in park and turned toward him, slightly. "I had so much fun with you. I just wish this night could go on and on."

He nodded his head without responding at first. From there, he simply cut off his ignition. "Let me walk you inside."

I agreed, stepped out and waited for him to reach my side before I walked to my apartment with him, arms connected.

Stopping at my door, I looked up and into his inviting eyes. "Well, here's where the night ends, I suppose."

If I looked disappointed, it was because I was.

"Not necessarily. It doesn't have to if you allow me to come in." He suavely leaned against the sill of my door, with one foot crossed on top of the other.

He caught me by surprise with that. I didn't want him to leave but I wasn't ready for the night to continue indoors, just us. Alone.

"Nah, I don't think that's a good idea." I shook my head *no*.

It really wasn't. God only knew what unspeakable things I would do if I lowered my hoe-conscience. And as bad as I wanted to, I couldn't have that.

"Why? Ya dude inside?" he asked but the tone of his voice conveyed nonchalance.

"No. I told you I don't have one of those."

"So, why you won't let me inside? I thought you didn't want tonight to end."

I dropped my head somewhat. I had to talk to my throb below. *Girl, I know he's sexy but I don't care what you say. I'm not letting him in.*

No! You not winning this one. He's not coming in and you're not cumming, at all.

Then the wind wafted his cologne up my nostrils, *He smells so damn good. Lorrrddd Geezus!*

Suddenly, I felt his finger lift under my chin to unite my eyes with his. Then my voice became audible. "Come in." I caved.

Once inside, I cut on the light switch, exposing the bareness of my place and a stitch of embarrassment glazed over me. I nervously found myself explaining the condition of my living space before he had the chance to label me a scrub.

"Excuse my home. I haven't been able to furniture shop like I want but it will happen soon."

Choppa didn't seem fazed one bit by the two bean bags that served as me and Justus' seating area. Instead, he squatted low and took a seat. "Feels comfy to me. I grew up with way less."

That knocked a little of the edge off, actually a lot of it.

"Well, make yourself at home." I removed my shoes.

He looked at me like he was studying me. I wasn't sure what was running through his mind but whatever it was, he gave an approving smile.

"Before I disappear off into the back, do you want a bottle of water, orange or apple juice?"

"Nah, I'm good. I'm content staring at your pretty little feet."

"You're sweet." I blushed.

"That's real talk. Gon' handle yo business," he said. And when he licked his lips, it was like he licked mine, too.

Move with caution, girl. This nigga will end up being an addiction, I told myself.

"Okay, I'm gonna change. I'll be right back."

"A'ight, shorty. I ain't going nowhere. I promise you that."

I left him up front as I scrambled, behind closed doors, to find something that screamed *sex me* but then again, *not tonight*. I didn't want to throw mixed signals but I wanted to still come across desirable even in my lounge clothes.

Finally, I settled on a pair of jogging capris and a baby tee. It showed off my curves but conservatively so—my camel toe wasn't on display. After I dressed, I danced over to the cheval mirror and leaned in close to get a good glimpse of myself. I checked my teeth and fluffed my hair before I stepped back up front.

"I hope I didn't keep you waiting too long." I walked toward him. He chuckled. "Not at all."

I stopped in front of him and eased down to an Indian-style seating position.

Staring at him gave me butterflies. For a moment, I felt like I was in middle school, crushing on a boy. He'd been giving me that feeling all night.

I started chewing the inside of my lip as I fought the urge to throw myself on him. I knew if I felt the magnetism, he did too. So, it was necessary for me to open the floor of discussion. I needed dialogue to distract me from undressing him or him wanting to undress me.

"Soooo, tell me something I should know about you." *Other than the fact that you're a panty whisperer. On God, he is too damn sexy!*

Choppa ran his hand over his goatee and shifted his eyes off to the corner. Looking back at me, he answered. "I don't beat any corners. When I want something, I get that something. No matter the time it takes."

Knows what he wants and goes after it. Check. "I like that. I'm a go-getter myself. Tell me more."

"I don't like being the center of attention." He lifted his arm and pointed to a tat on the opposite forearm that read *Silent Money.*

I questioned him with my eyes.

He must've felt I was putting him on the spot. "I know you're curious but you'll know everything you need to know about me because when I'm really feeling a woman there are no secrets. Besides, I'm a man of action. So now, pretty lady, how about you answer my questions?" He touched my knee but it felt like he reached my soul.

Sparks were definitely flying.

"All right. What do you want to know?"

"The most prevalent question is *why don't you have a man?*"

Marcel! Was the quick answer but I'd never have an Oprah moment with a man of interest. That shit was a turn off, so I heard. So, I gave him the secondary, yet, very valid reason next to it.

"I'm too busy trying to get my life and career together and love *or* lust have a way of making a woman lose focus. I mean, don't get me wrong, I want a relationship, I just can't afford the consequences of one."

"I like that you're striving and have a head on your shoulders but you don't want to wait to you get to the finish line of your financial dreams and then begin your search. You'll never trust the man's intent for your heart once you feel you have more to lose."

"True."

"Now tell me the *real* reason you're single." He delved a little further.

"What?" I feigned cluelessness as I stared at him.

I wanted to question how he could possible know there was more to it but I suppose he detected the politics in my answer and knew there was a more emotional motive behind my *table for one* mentality in my love arena.

"C'mon, shorty, I'm from the streets. It's essential that I'm able to see beyond the surface of a person's answers or deeds. I'm not saying your response isn't legit but my instincts tell me there's more to it. Am I wrong?"

I thought about it for a second. I felt like I could be transparent with him, but my first mind told me not to divulge so much on the first night. "It's a bit of a conundrum—relationships, I mean?"

He put his hand up to stop me. "Hold up. What kinda drum did you say—a Congo drum?"

"No, silly," I laughed, "I said a *conundrum.*" Then, it occurred to me that he really might not know the definition of the word. But just as quickly as the thought came to my mind, Choppa extinguished it.

"How are relationships a riddle or something that puzzles you?" His question showed that he indeed knew what conundrum meant.

"I see you paid attention in class," I complimented him. *Damn, an intelligent thug. This man is coming up all spades.*

"Class was never a problem. I was a sponge for knowledge. Any trouble that found me came after the last bell. But I digress, beautiful, please finish explaining your conundrum." He folded his hands on top of his knee.

102

"Really, my story is no different than the next woman's when it relate to how she's been hurt."

"It may not be different but I'm interested in your story." He sounded so sincere.

"How about we save that conversation for a different day?"

Choppa didn't push, instead, he asked me something less tension-filled.

"A'ight. Well, tell me your plans, Julz. What is it you want more than anything?" He reached for my hand, guiding me to his lap so that I sat facing him with my legs straddled on both sides of his.

Oh, God! There it is. I felt it—his print! It was as impressive as his conversation and as big as my dreams. All types of sin ran through my mind and settled between my legs.

After what I assumed was him mistaking the pleasure on my face for slight discomfort, he moved me a little, readjusting my position on top of him.

I wasn't mad at the feel of his hardened log, but the shift off of it gave me a brief reprieve from the pulsation in my panties.

I glanced at my watch and then at him, oddly. It was after four in the morning and we were *really* talking. Not that I had a problem with that. Having a connection with people was so devalued these days. And what we were doing was uncommon, making it very much welcomed.

Only thing was that I was in the compromising position to ride him 'til my fountain erupted, but he didn't want to explore my body. Uhn uhn, he wanted to discover my mind.

If that wasn't the sexiest shit ever.

I felt turned on and most desired, more so than I would have had he took his hands and ran them up my shirt and over my breasts.

He's a winner.

With a nervous chuckle, I replied, "My plans are huge and my passion runs deep. There is no short answer to your question."

I then felt the clasp of his hands around my back, faintly above my ass, fortifying his hold on me. "Lucky for me, I have all night."

He was talking real close to my ear, but I swear it felt like my pussy was the first to hear him.

All night, huh? Forgive me, Jesus, for I'm about to sin.

Chapter 13
Julz
Four days later

"I'm sprung." I verbalized the feeling that replayed itself like a broken record anytime I thought of Choppa.

Over the last couple of days, we were inseparable as if we had nothing to do other than each other. We talked, we listened, we laughed, we connected for hours on end.

Yea, I'm feelin' him.

"What? Wait a minute. Let me take you off of speaker. I'm not sure I heard you right. Come again. You're what?" All the *E*'s in Essence's name stood for *Extra.* She knew she heard me.

"Sprung, girl. S-p-r-u-n-g. Sprung! Choppa is something else. I can't even explain it. Nah, I can. It would just take me all day to sum up how sexy his mind is."

"Be honest, you let him hit, huh? That's why you all goo-goo gaa-gaa and shit."

"No! I did not fuc—" I cut myself short and looked up in the rear-view mirror to ensure Justus had his headphones on as he watched cartoons on his tablet. I called his name just to be sure he couldn't hear my conversation. "Justus? Justus?" He didn't respond, so I went back to Essence. "No, I did not fuck him, although I wanted to."

"Oooh, chile, then you better beware of a man like that. You remember Naughty, right? The trade I was with for a few weeks?" I hummed *yes* because I recalled him. "Well, he mind-fucked the shit out of me, which was why I had to let him go."

I laughed because she knew how to take things to the bridge. "You sure did drop him and for no good reason, too."

"It was good reason, sis. That boy was dangerous. And any man that can whip a pussy into submission that he ain't lickin' or stickin', is not to be fucked with. I'll let the next bitch have those problems. I'm good!"

"Ha! Ha! Ha! I wouldn't go that far but baby is mental dope."

"I hear ya. You just think long and hard before you let him hit you with that hammer because if his dick game is as strong as his mouthpiece, you through."

She was probably right. No doubt I'd be head over heels but if I was gonna attach myself to anybody, why not someone of his caliber?

"Moving on. Next." I changed records. It was time to get on her and off of me.

Just like that, her tuned changed. "Giiirrrlll, I almost forgot to tell you about…"

We continued chopping it up as we both navigated through evening traffic, bouncing from one topic to another until I pulled up to my apartments, twenty minutes later.

"Well, girl, I pulled into my apartments. Let me do my usual and I'll talk with you before bed."

"Don't forget to call me, no." Essence warned. I had a bad tendency of falling asleep after I wrapped up my domestic, school and mommy duties.

"I got you. Now, get off my phone."

"Bye, bitch!" Essence disconnected.

I dropped my phone into my purse as I cursed under my breath at the large van that was occupying all of the parking space in front of my place. It forced me to park further away from my door but oh well!

Reaching into the backseat, I removed Justus' headphones. "Come on, Prince. We're home. Unbuckle your seatbelt."

I stepped out, opening the back door and assisting Justus to his feet, grabbing his backpack, as well.

"Why we parked right here? Is it because of that van?" He pointed.

"That's correct. You are so perceptive. Always pay attention to what's happening around you. It will keep that mind of yours sharp." I tapped his temple.

"Okay." He grabbed my hand and we walked to our humble abode.

As I was going up the flight of steps leading to my door, I was stopped by a service man.

"Aye, Miss. Do you live in apartment," he looked at his clipboard, "24B?"

It was clear he worked for Haverty's. The truck he got out of gave that away but what wasn't clear was why he was questioning me.

"Yes. Why?"

"I have a delivery for you."

"Oh, you're mistaken. I didn't order anything from you all."

I turned away and continued walking when he called out after me.

"Your name is Julia Kidd, right?"

What the hell?

I turned around at the sound of my name. "It is but I didn't buy anything. I think I would know if I had."

"Well, I have a paid order for a six piece living, five piece dining and a Queen bedroom set for a Ms. Julia Kidd and I need to unload this delivery so I can drop off my last load, ma'am."

My mouth moved but I was speechless. However, it wasn't long before a smile formed at each corner of my lips, blooming a full blown grin.

Choppa!

"Bring it in, sir." I waved for him to begin as I hurriedly unlocked my door and ushered Justus inside.

I bolted into the kitchen in a nervous rush, grabbing a lunchable out of the fridge. "Come here, baby. Have a seat on the floor and snack on this. Mama needs you out of the way while these men work, okay?"

He reached for it after I peeled back the plastic and sat on the back of his legs as he stacked a cracker with cheese and meat.

I had the goofiest look on my face but I couldn't help it. *Oh, my word! No, he didn't.* I marched back up front and looked out of my door to see the two men coming my way with their first item. *Oh, yes, he did!*

The men handled their business and in under an hour, they had moved my old bedroom set out and placed the new furniture where I had specified.

My eyes darted from one side of my apartment to the other and then I became misty eyed. Because in the snap of a finger, my house felt like home.

"Sign here, ma'am. This shows you are in receipt of each piece we show listed."

I took the pen from his hand and signed on the dotted line. My signature looked a bit like scribble because of my exultant nerves.

"Thank you," I told the man as I dotted the *I's* in my name.

"My pleasure. Here's your invoice and this as well." He handed me a small envelope.

"What's this?"

He hunched his shoulders. "I don't know, Miss. I was only instructed to give it to you once you signed."

I took the packet from him along with the copy of my receipt and thanked him again.

"Have a good one." He and his co-worker trotted down the steps.

"You too." I doubt he heard me because my voice faded behind the quick close of my door. I was all but too anxious to fully admire what Choppa had done for me.

Without opening the envelope, I grabbed my phone and called him up. I had talked to him earlier today but that man didn't hint to this, at all. Not one peep. Oh, he was slick.

He didn't answer, so I called again. I wanted to call a third time but I didn't want to be a bug-a-boo. He'd see that I called and would dial me back, I'm sure.

"Can I come out now?"

"Yea, baby. Come out. Come see the new furniture."

Justus gently rubbed his hand against the microfiber texture of the sofa once he entered the living room. "It's soft, Mama. Is it mine?" His eyes sparkled with possession.

I laughed a little. Ever since he was a toddler, he felt the need to claim everything as his. It was cute for now but I'd have to nip it in the bud if I didn't want that *me* syndrome to escalate to that of his father's.

"Not exactly. It's a gift for mommy but it's yours to sit on. Hop up."

He climbed up and we both took a seat. It felt like heaven. It was precisely what I would have picked out if I bought it myself.

I zoned out for a moment, thinking how this really just happened *for me*. I started to tear up and began fanning myself with the envelope. *The envelope!* Remembering it was in my hand, I broke the seal and pulled out the content.

I read it and then dropped my hand into my lap as my mouth flung open. *Is he serious?* I lifted it back up to re-read it and the words didn't change. It read: *You'll never hit bottom with me as your rock. Choppa.* That broke me down and all I could do was cry into my hands.

As instantly as my sobs poured from my mouth, Justus scooted closer to me and pulled at my fingers to lower my hand. "Why you crying? You sad?"

I looked at him and noticed a frown forming in his eyes.

I wiped my face and shook my head *no.* "Not at all. Mama is crying because she is happy."

He wiped my tears away tenderly. "If you happy, Mama, smile."

I gave my prince what he wanted to see and he matched my shine.

Although, it had only been a meager amount of time since Choppa and I had been talking, it appeared that God sent me a King to bring completion into my life.

Later that night...

By eight thirty, I had Justus washed and in bed. I was wrapping up in the kitchen, listening to Pandora as I cleaned up and put away tonight's dinner when I heard a knock at my door.

Without a second thought, I knew it was Choppa. He was the only one who would come by unannounced.

I virtually ran to the door but I counted to ten before I answered because I didn't want to seem too anxious, which I was.

When I looked through the peephole, I saw him standing there with a bouquet of roses in one hand and a bottle of wine in the other.

He is too much!

Taking a deep breath to regulate the speeding beat of my heart, I opened the door.

"What's good, shorty?"

I wore the cheesiest grin on my face when he handed the arrangements to me. I sniffed them. They smelled as delightful as the feeling brewing at the base of my belly.

He made an attempt to step inside but I extended my hand, teasingly. "This is beautiful and all but you can't just show up impromptu. Who's to say I didn't have company?"

He shook his head nonchalantly and the *yea right* look he gave me told me he knew my ass was just talking junk.

Choppa pecked me on the lips and walked past me. "You know better," was his solid reply.

If that didn't make a bitch gush. The way he said that shit made me believe I ought to know better than to have someone at my crib, ever!

No sooner than I closed the door, he pulled me into the strength of his hold and stared into my eyes, lowering his lips to mine. My eyelids lowered lazily and my kissables pooched out just enough to welcome the kiss that never came.

Stopping an inch away from my face, he asked. "So, how you like your new furniture?"

I shoved him at the shoulder friskily and pulled his face back to mine. "I love it this much." I gently allowed my lips to press against his before I seductively glided my tongue inside of his mouth.

Kissing that man took my breath away.

My eyes were still closed when we separated. They opened sweetly at the sound of his deep voice. "You like it that much, huh?"

Like it was too weak of a phrase. I loved the heart behind what he did for me. In my twenty-six years of living, I never had a man drop over fifteen bands on me, at one time.

Whoever his mama was, I needed to meet her and thank her for raising such an extraordinary man.

"You blew me away. I spent all of tonight thinking of the words to express myself and I still couldn't find the right ones."

"Repeat after me, then. *I deserve to be treated like a Queen.*"

"Choppa!" For some odd reason, I couldn't echo him although I believed I deserved to be treated with the spoils of a man's choosing.

"Say it." The authority in his voice pushed my hesitation to the side.

"*I deserve to be treated like a Queen.*" I became bashful after I said it and he found it amusing.

"Why you acting all shy, huh?" He stooped down and shifted from one side to the other to follow the movement of my eyes.

"I'm grateful. Really, I am. I just never seen generosity like this." I pondered a little more and I felt bad for thinking my thoughts but I had to ask. "What do you want in return? You have to know I can't pay this back."

"This wasn't no loan, and I don't need your money. Besides, I already got what I want from you, so what's left for you to give me?"

"Huh?" That stumped me, for real.

"You wanna act like you don't know? A'ight. I got *you*, shorty."

Oh, talk that talk!

"You got me?" I asked incredulously. "What makes you so sure?"

He didn't answer me, at least not verbally. He allowed the thought to linger before he double pecked my lips, pushing his tongue into my mouth.

That made my knees weak but what caught me off guard was the feel of his hand cupping the center of my pussy through my leggings. I wanted to move it so I didn't come off too easy *or* like I wanted it, which I did, but I couldn't. I was stuck.

Then I felt his smile against my lips before he spoke. "The heat from both set of lips already told me I got you sewed up, so don't front, ma. Matter of fact, let me hear you tell me who you belong to."

I could have answered almost immediately but I allowed the thought to swirl in my mind for a few seconds. A girl should play hard to get sometimes.

He pulled me in closer to him, as if there was any room for that to be possible. "Say it, Julz. Tell me you belong to me."

I almost came when he demanded my obedience. The certainty in his voice convinced me, even if I wasn't sure. There was no need to play the game, so I stopped fronting.

"I'm yours." I spoke demurely, as my eyes held a gentle gaze into his.

He shook his head leisurely. "Nah, say that shit like you mean it, goddamit."

That's it! I had fallen for a man I barely knew and crazy as it all seemed to me, I didn't care.

"Choppa, I'm yours," I said it with the same assertiveness he delivered his demand.

"Again." He smirked.

I guessed he loved hearing me submit.

"Choppa, I'm yours! I'm your jewel. I belong to you," I said it from my soul.

"You damn right." He wore a satisfied smile before he devoured my face, smothering me with strong, passionate kisses.

His hands moved about my body with purpose, as mine held his face steady for the thrust of my tongue against his. Then, I clamped my arms around his neck as if to silently tell him I was ready for lift off. He read my body and hoisted me up.

I curled my legs around his god-chiseled waist, securing my position with the lock of my ankles.

"Mmmm. Mmmm." The sounds of our lip lock was better music than the swooning sounds playing from my Pandora in the kitchen. Damn! I hadn't felt so caught up since—well, never!

If it ain't about the money, you can miss me with it... was the ringtone coming from his phone.

Don't answer it. Don't answer it, I repeated to myself and it was as if he obliged my quiet request because he ignored it. *Yasss!*

His phone went mute and the humming sounds from the enjoyment of our make-out session increased, that was until his cell rang again.

He pulled away from my lips, this time, but not without pecking it once more. He walked me to the sofa and sat me down before he asked for a minute.

He answered. "What up?"

That was all he said before his eyebrows drew inward. Seconds later, his head bobbed in an agreeing manner.

Whatever conversation he and the unknown caller were having had to be of a serious nature because his energy changed. I then looked down and began playing with my fingertips, so I wouldn't stare at him. I didn't want to be intrusive.

Then after a minute or so passed, I heard him say, "Stay there."

I looked up and saw him hanging up his phone. I stood to my feet and placed a comforting hand on his forearm. "Is everything okay?"

He softened under my touch. I could tell by the way his shoulders relaxed. "How can it not be when I'm here with you?" He lifted my chin with the crook of his finger, gesturing for me to give him some of my luscious.

After a few pecks, he said, "Baby, I don't want to, but I'ma have to leave. I got some business to handle."

Really? You're gonna leave me wanting you like this? Goddammit! I thought to myself but like the good girl I was, all I said was, "Okay."

I hoped he would pick up on the displeasure in my reply and change his mind but he didn't. So, I pouted the moment I saw him reach in his pockets for his keys. He chuckled at me when he glanced over his shoulder to see my droopy bottom lip.

"Come send yo man off properly."

I put off being a baby and replied, "I can do that." Then I kissed him like I'd never see him again. I made it even sweeter than the last one so he'd remember what he walked away from, hoping that would be incentive for his quick return.

"Damn, baby. You make it hard for a man to leave."

"Then don't." I sugared my voice and the allure in my eyes.

He shook his head at me and I smiled deviously as he patted me on my ass.

Choppa kissed me once more, shaking his head at what he was stepping away from. "Be good and lock up."

He waited for me to close the door. So, I waved him goodbye and did as my man told me.

"Shit!" I echoed the disappointing thought from my mind.

I felt a bit let down that he had to go but the thing that turned the small frown of my lips into an upward curve was the fact that he'd return.

After all, and like he said, I was his and now he was mine.

Ca$h & Coffee

Chapter 14
Choppa

I was hotter than fish grease as I drove with the pedal to the metal all the way out to the airport. Man, just when the mood was right for me to love Julz down, this shit had to pop up. I should've known not to even answer the call.

By the time I arrived at Hartsfield-Maynard International, my forehead had more deep wrinkles in it than a Chinese Shar-Pei dog.

"This hardheaded trick just couldn't wait," I cussed out loud as I headed inside the terminal. "I should've made her ass catch a taxi."

Fuming, I walked in the direction of where she told me she would be. I was looking around for her with a scowl etched on my face. *Now, where the fuck is she at!*

"Choppa, over here! Over here!" I heard her call out.

I turned to see KiKi heading towards me with a porter on her heels pulling her luggage behind him on a cart. Her Red Bottoms clacked with each step. I didn't have to read the name on the labels inside of her clothes to know that she was wearing designer labels down to the feet. That was how she always rocked.

Her long weave had a luxuriant shine to it. Her makeup was flawless and her diamond earrings were mad sparkling. Her waist-length jacket stopped above hips that flared out curvaceously. And she had a walk that caused niggas to drool. Even chicks had to stop and take notice.

When I first met her a few years ago, I was mesmerized by her beauty and sex appeal, but not anymore. What I knew about her now erased every bit of desire and respect I'd ever had for her. If her pops wasn't my plug, I would've been kicked her to the curb.

For the time being, I pushed my distaste aside and prepared myself to deal with her just enough to keep the peace until I no longer needed her father. And that time was right on the horizon. *On my life, your days with me are numbered.*

If KiKi could read the scorn on my face, she damn sho' wasn't affected by it. When she got within a few feet of me she flew in my arms.

"Hey, daddy, I missed you." She threw her arms around my neck, stood up on her tippy toes and tried to kiss me on the mouth.

I turned my head and her kiss landed on my cheek. "What up? What you doing here." I removed her arms from around my neck and stepped back, putting an arm length between us.

"I was ready to come home," she said with sass.

"Didn't I tell you I was flying up there next week? We could've came back together. I don't even have the house yet." The agitation in my voice was thicker than ol' skool Welfare cheese.

"*Humph*! I would've been old and gray by the time you came for me, and I was bored up there."

"I'm sure you had no problem finding something to get into, probably some nigga's bed," I spat as I turned and led the way to the car.

"Tavares, did you really just say that foul shit to me?" She caught up to me and grabbed ahold of my arm tryna force a confrontation. But I didn't feed into it. "You know what, you're a disrespectful ass nigga."

"Fuck you know about respect?" I spat without slowing down.

"A lot more than you do, muthafucka!" KiKi followed behind me spewing cuss word after cuss word.

Inside I was boiling but I held my steam in. Whenever I unleashed it on her it was gonna be in a grand finale that ended it all.

When we reached the truck and the porter began loading KiKi's luggage in the back, he gave me a look that said *Ain't no way I would put up with a woman like that!*

KiKi didn't miss it though. She stuck her finger in his face and shook it. "Mind your business old man before you get clapped at!"

In spite of the acrimony between us I couldn't help but laugh inwardly, she was definitely her father's daughter. Gangsta to the core.

"Pay her no mind, she ain't got no home training, Unc," I apologized.

The only reason KiKi didn't come back with something fly is because she was busy applying gloss to her lips. I tipped the porter and sent him off with a pat on the back.

KiKi dropped the tube of gloss back in her Michael Kors bag and turned to me. "You not going to give me a hug, for real?" Months ago

I would've. The pouty look on her face would've been an aphrodisiac, but not now.

"Save that shit, shorty. You already know the business, ain't nothing changed."

She gave me the evil eye before walking around to the passenger side of the truck and climbing in. I eased behind the wheel and started the engine.

"That other bitch must got your head fucked up," she accused. I turned on some music to block her out but that didn't work, she just talked louder. "How long are we going to play this fucking game, Tavares? Really, it's getting old."

I didn't respond to her question. Instead, I asked, "Where do you plan on staying until I close on the house I found?"

"I'm staying wherever you are."

"Nah, I been staying with Cardale. You not staying there. We'll just get a room," I said.

"Okay." She reached over and placed her hand on my knee, affectionately.

I let it remain there but her touch had no effect on me at all. There was only one woman who I wanted to give my affection to, and it damn sho' wasn't KiKi.

***

The second we stepped inside the hotel room and KiKi saw that it contained double beds, she went slap the fuck off!

"I don't know what the fuck your problem is but you're going to quit treating me like a basic bitch. If you're still tripping over what I think you are, you need to grow the fuck up. What happened or did not happen before we were together has nothing to do with you. Damn, man, I can't win for losing with your bipolar ass. Fuck it! I'ma take a shower, play in my pussy and go to bed."

"Do you, ma," I said nonchalantly.

I kicked off my shoes and pulled the cover back on the bed before stepping out of my jeans and laying down. KiKi stripped down to her birthday suit and disappeared into the bathroom. When I heard the water come on I grabbed my cell phone and made a quick call to Julz.

"Hey, baby," she answered.

"Hey. I just wanted to tell you good night."

"Is everything all right?" she asked.

"Yeah, everything is gucci. I had to handle something but it's all good."

"Are you sure? You don't sound like yourself."

"We'll talk about it. Get you some rest and don't forget to clear your weekend and get a babysitter. I'm taking you away so we can finish what we started tonight."

"I would love that. You had me so turned on," she said.

"Did I?"

"Yes, baby." I heard her breath hard.

Instantly, I rocked up.

"Touch it for me, shorty." I whispered.

"You're late, bae, I started doing that the minute I heard your voice. Umm. I'm so wet. I need you to put this fire out, Choppa."

I closed my eyes and imagined her lying with her legs spread wide, stroking her petals. "Damn, shorty, the visual I just got! I'm telling you, once I get inside of you I'm never coming out."

"You promise?"

"Fuck yeah! Now, dip your finger inside that pussy and pretend it's my tongue."

"Oooh, boo," she moaned.

"What?" My voice was thick with passion.

"I'm soaking wet." Her voice was thick with desire.

"Put the phone down there and let me hear it." I pulled the cover up to my waist and stroked myself.

The sound of Julz fingering herself was erotic as fuck. I wished she could reach her fingers through the phone so I could taste her womanly juices. I could hear her breathing increase, which caused my balls to fill and my dick to grow even harder than it had been.

I was torn between wanting to hear her cum and wanting her to reserve it for the weekend when she could bust all over the 8 thick inches I had been blessed with. It became a battle of wills but waiting won out.

"Okay, shorty, that's enough. Save the rest for me," I forced myself to say.

"Whatever, you want, my king," she replied. "But you be leaving a sista in a bad situation."

"I know, and it's my bad, but I promise you the wait will be well worth it."

She didn't doubt that. We passed a few more tender words back and forth, and then said our goodbyes for the night. When I disconnected, I looked down at the bedspread that covered me and it was tented up like a teepee.

Damn, baby girl got a nigga feenin'.

When I looked up, KiKi was reentering the room with nothing but a towel covering herself. Before she could formulate the idea of climbing in bed with me, I reached over and turned off the lamp.

Bitch, I wouldn't make love to you if it would cure world hunger.

Chapter 15
Choppa

Things hadn't always been that way between me and KiKi. At one time I thought the world of her. She was beautiful, sexy, intelligent in a street type of way, and she knew how to ride for a nigga. And most importantly she understood the importance of keeping her mouth shut.

I knew this because I had kicked it with her for almost a year before I found out that her pops was Cross, one of the most infamous hustlas in Cleveland, Ohio. I had been hearing his name in the streets all of my life, but I had never laid eyes on the man. He was like a phantom. Niggas in Cleveland talked about Cross like they used to talk about Preacher, *The Black Hand of Harlem,* up in New York, whose gangsterism was documented all over *YouTube.* And like Preacher, Cross had a reputation for ruthlessness that resonated throughout the city. He was rumored to have his hand in everything from drugs to murder, to extortion.

It was said that drug dealers had to pay Cross a percentage of their earnings if they wanted to operate their businesses anywhere in the areas of Superior Ave, St. Clair, Hough and Euclid Avenue, which were all major drug zones in the city.

I wasn't clocking enough dough to draw the attention of Cross and his crew of killers, mainly because I didn't fuck with coke or heroin. Weed was a quiet hustle. I was stacking my chips pretty good until a string of bad luck depleted my bank. My connect, at the time, got popped returning from a run to Texas. So, my shit was all out of wack, to the point that I was stressing. When I told KiKi about my situation, she said, "I'm going to speak with my daddy and see if he will help you."

I was like, "Who is your father? What does he do? Because I'm not interested in no 9 to 5."

"My daddy is Cross. I'm sure you've heard about him. Some people call him Cutthroat," she said.

I had heard people call him that before. "Get the fuck out of here, Cross ain't your pops," I disputed.

"Yes, he is. I just don't broadcast it because my father has a lot of enemies and you could've been using me to get to him," KiKi explained.

That made a lot of sense but I still didn't believe that the notorious Cross was her pops until she took me to his house to meet him a few days later.

Long story short, Cross turned out to be as imposing as his reputation. In stature, he was a big man with intimidating features and he had the eyes of a cold blooded killa. One look at him confirmed that the stories I'd heard about him was probably true. But I wasn't one to tremble in my boots at the sight of a certified body slayer. Because when it came to that murder shit I wasn't a slouch myself.

Cross had already done his homework on me before KiKi ever took me to meet him. So, when we talked, it was man to man. I made it clear that I wasn't coming to him for a handout, and that it was, in fact, his daughter's idea that she speak to him on my behalf.

"Yes, she told me that," he said. "And since my daughter knows not to bring no lazy or lame muthafucka to me, I'll extend whatever help you need."

We chopped it up for a while. He asked what I needed to get back on me feet—money, coke, weed or I could get down with his crew and eat from the huge platter that was theirs.

"I prefer to do my own thing. And if it's all the same with you, I'll fuck with the *green*," I said.

He gave me a short speech about loyalty and the importance of a man's word. I listened but I already lived by that code so none of what he said caused me to stutter when he asked if I understood what the penalty for disloyalty would be.

"The penalty will be street justice, cold and merciless, as it should be. Cutthroat," I replied.

He flashed what was for him a smile, which meant his face kinda cracked a little, and then he said, "I'll have twenty-five pounds delivered to your door tomorrow morning?"

"Do you know where I rest at?" I asked.

He gave me a look that said he knew everything about me. I nodded in admiration for his thoroughness and then we agreed on a price for the weed he was fronting me.

We shook hands and he escorted me back into the living room where KiKi and her mother sat on the couch talking. Her moms was a stunna, the kinda trophy that came with a man's ascent to the top.

Speaking almost in a whisper, Cross said, "You see those two women right there? They're the only two people in this world that I have a softness for."

Nothing else needed to be said, I understood the thinly veiled warning. At that time it wasn't necessary, though, because KiKi seemed to be everything I needed.

Shit was gravy. With Cross supplying me, I bounced back in no time at all and KiKi was holding me down. When Cardale suggested I come to Atlanta where the money was sweeter, it surprised me that KiKi nor her pops had a problem with me making the move. Of course, KiKi demanded that I take her with me. And I think it gave Cross peace of mind that his daughter would be a good distance away from the enemies he had who might try to touch her to get back at him.

In the A, I had the perfect situation and I thought I had the perfect rider in KiKi. A pretty muthafucka who hadn't been with every nigga in the game. But that turned out to be an illusion.

A few months ago, we went back home to attend the birthday party of a nigga named Jasari, who I had mad respect for. At the party one of Jasari's man's pulled me to the side.

"Yo, Choppa, let me put something in your ear," he said.

As he led me outside I wondered what he wanted to talk to me about in private. We knew each other in passing but we had never did more than speak to one another.

"What's the business, bleed?" I asked as we sat in his Escalade blazing purp.

"Fam, what does KiKi mean to you?" he asked in a cautious tone.

"That's wifey, son. Why?" I took the blunt from my mouth and stared at him hard.

"Look, bruh, I probably shouldn't even tell you this, but if I was rocking that bitch on my arm in public I would want a nigga to pull my coat, ya dig?" he said.

"Peep this, my nigga, I'm not into solving riddles and shit. If you got something to say spit it out. But don't bring no rumors to me. If you can't prove what you're about to say just gone swallow it. Real talk." I checked him.

"Cool. I tell you what," he said. "I'ma get at you tomorrow and show you what you really have in ol' girl. What you do from there is on you," he replied.

"Bet that."

Out of pure curiosity I gave him my number then slid out of his ride and returned to the party wondering what the fuck he could show me that would change what I felt for KiKi.

The second I stepped back in the club, KiKi began bombarding me with questions.

"What were you talking to Bop about? Did that bitch ass nigga say anything about me? Where do you know him from?"

"I know him through Jasari. Why?" I questioned her.

"Nothing," she deflected.

I could see that she was worried. I didn't want to alert her and give her time to concoct an alibi for whatever dirt Bop had on her, so I played it off like me and Bop were just talking business. "Your name never came up," I lied.

"Oh. Well, don't fuck with him like that. I don't trust him," she said.

"Relax, babe, I'm not fuckin' with him." I kissed her on the lips and poured us both a glass of Patron. "To the most beautiful woman I know." I lifted my glass in the air.

"I'll toast to that." KiKi clinked her glass against mine.

She smiled so sexy the straw in my drink got hard! It wasn't until the next day that I found out that her smile hid a whole lot of ugly truth.

The DVD Bop gave me rocked my world! Six niggas, including himself, ran a train on KiKi. The bitch smiled into the camera as she took dick in every hole. Niggas took turns skeeting down her throat, on her face, on her ass—every muthafuckin' where.

And this is the ho I'm claiming as mine?

I felt played! The only consolation was the video was filmed a few months before I hooked up with the skunk bitch. But that didn't excuse the fact that she was a ho.

When I confronted KiKi with the tape she seemed to think it shouldn't matter since she made it before we were together. But like I told her that day, once a ho forever a ho, in my eyes.

There was no fuckin way I was kissing a bitch who had sucked six different dicks at once and swallowed cum like that shit was whip cream. Fuck that!

I hadn't left her yet but I hadn't sexed her since the video surfaced. It brought back memories of shit that I wanted to keep buried. And I wanted to know what Bop's true reason was for exposing KiKi. But that was a question that might forever go unanswered because a week after I showed KiKi the video, Bop's bullet riddled body was found in his truck.

He had paid the ultimate price for putting KiKi on blast. And his demise reminded me that Cross had no problem at all assassinating a nigga for shitting on his daughter.

So whenever I left KiKi, if it wasn't on good terms, I would have to leave her pops face down in a ditch.

Chapter 16
Choppa

I slept fitfully because while KiKi was in a bed next to mine, Julz was on a nigga's mind. It felt like betrayal even though I wasn't doing anything with her anymore. I knew that one day soon I would have to tell Julz about her, but the time wasn't now.

Nah, we were clicking too good to throw suspicion into the mix. So, I decided to wait until I distanced myself from KiKi completely. The last thing I wanted to do was give Julz a reason to pull away from me. Shorty was gonna be my other half. I had already tabbed her for that.

But first things first, I was gonna play my hand close to the vest and when KiKi and her pops least expected it, I was gon' erase them both. Fuck looking over my shoulder all of my life.

As soon as I was out of bed and showered, I placed a call to the real estate agent so she could show the property I was interested in to KiKi.

"If you like it, go ahead and sign the papers. The money is already on deck," I said to KiKi.

I wasn't purchasing the house with cash because I was always careful not to draw the attention of the IRS. We were going to make a down payment and assume the mortgage from the previous owner.

"Where is this place, again?" asked KiKi as she fussed in the mirror with her hair and makeup.

I had to admit that she was still a sexy muthafucka. "It's in Mc Donough, Georgia, tucked off on a nice community where you'll feel safe," I said.

"I hope so."

"You will," I promised.

After niggas tried to kick in the door of our other place, KiKi had refused to live there, which was the reason she had been up in Ohio the last few months. She hadn't told Cross about the failed home invasion because he would've probably made her come back home, and KiKi didn't want that. She absolutely loved Atlanta.

As I was pulling on my t-shirt, she walked over to me and ran her manicure nails down my chest. "Boo, I need you. Please give me some loving. It's been a long time." She made puppy dog eyes at me.

But my feelings toward her was concrete. "You gotta give me time to get my mind right." I played it off.

"Whatever, boy!" She popped her lips.

We both continued dressing and then I dropped her off at the storage where I had kept her car.

After we parted ways, I stopped by Kim Marie's and checked the trap. Shorty wasn't home but everything was in order. I hit Cardale and Jared up to make sure they were gucci. Both of them needed to re-up. That was music to my ears because it meant the product was moving. In a week or so, I would have to get a new shipment.

When business calmed down a little, I stopped at Wendy's to grab something to eat. Sitting in the drive-thru, I checked my phone and saw I had a text from Julz. Immediately, I hit her up. Fuck texting back.

"Hey, baby." Her voice was angelic. I could easily tell she was missing a nigga. Shit, I was missing her pretty ass, too.

"What's good, baby girl?"

"Now that I'm hearing your voice, everything!" I didn't need to see her face to know she was smiling but now I needed to see it in person.

"I need to see you now. Get a babysitter." I didn't ask because I didn't want to hear *no*.

A soft giggle could be heard before she spoke again. "Aren't we demanding? But I think I can manage a babysitter for a few hours. I just need to make sure I don't pick him up too late because my peoples, well I, have work in the morning."

"Call off. And we're gonna need a few days for what I got in mind." I didn't have any concrete plans as of yet but I knew once I laid my eyes and hands on her again, I was going to need more than one night.

She laughed but I was staid. "I can't do that, baby. I wish I could but I can't." Julz immediately declined.

"You can and you will. Look, shorty, I'll never put you in a position to lose—trust dat. Just listen to your man. Go 'head and make that call, I got you."

"But, bae—"

128

"Shorty, dead that and do as your man asked, please." I cut her off before she had the chance to ruin what was cooking up in my mind. "If it's lost pay you're worried about, you ain't gotta sweat that. Your nigga bank on fleek."

"I can't stand your cocky ass," she laughed.

"The devil is a lie. You know you're loving on you some Choppa, don't even front."

"Guilty as charged, sir." She giggled.

"And I'm loving on you, too. Now gon' handle your end and I'll be there in two hours. Be ready to leave when I pull up, a'ight?"

"Okay, baby." She said that shit so sweet. I wanted to tongue her down through the phone, but my lips would taste that honey soon enough.

We disconnected the line and I pulled my car out of the drive-thru. Fuck the meal! Thoughts of my jewel overwhelmed my urge for food. The only thing I wanted to eat was shorty.

***

Julz

As soon as I hung up the phone with my boss, I celebrated my A-1 performance by doing a little pirouette. My exuberance was sky high. Instead of sitting at a desk all day, I would be chilling with boo.

Standing in the middle of my living room, I bit down on my bottom lip as my eyes swept from side to side, pondering what this man had up his sleeve. I then slid my hand over my mouth to cover my wide smile when I determined I couldn't figure him out.

"Damn, Choppa. You something else." I loved surprises and it was clear there was no shortage of them up his sleeve.

Suddenly, I felt overwhelmed with happiness and became weak in the knees. I had to take a seat on my sofa. *My sofa! Yassss!* I still couldn't believe this man laced my entire apartment.

Lowering my head into my hand, I allowed tears of joy to cascade down my cheeks. If Choppa's plan was to make me fall in love with him, then he was well on his way to doing so.

After I collected my emotions, I made what I hoped to be my only call.

"What it do, boo?" Essence answered on the third ring.

I exhaled. "Girlll, I need to ask you a huge favor?"

"You all right? What is it?" Concern resonated in her voice.

"I'm more than all right. I'm actually in the clouds right now. I called because I needed to know if you'd watch Justus for—"

"Girlll…" she stepped right into my question and answered, "…that ain't no big favor. Yea, I'll watch lil' man."

"You didn't let me finish. Umm, the *big* in favor is me needing you to watch him for a few days." I literally held my breath as I waited for her to curse me out.

I knew, hands down, my request was an imposition. I was asking her to drive all over tarnation to drop and pick my son up at daycare, which was on the opposite side of town from where she lived and we worked. But I trusted her with my life and Justus was indeed *my life*.

"Julz! Bitch! Are you serious?"

I felt deflated at her tone and question but I wasn't going to trip on her. "I know, it was a lot to ask of you, especially at the last minute. It's just that Choppa sprung the idea of getting a babysitter for a few days on me so we could do God knows what, but it's cool. I'll ask Fat-Fat for the solid."

"Like the hell you will. That's *my* son, boo boo."

A smile unexpectedly appeared on my face the same way the sun sneaks from behind the gloom of a dark cloud. "So, you'll watch him?"

"I can't believe you even had to ask in the first place. We besties, bitch, and there ain't shit I won't do for you. All you have to do is say the word."

I should have known better. She was my *ride or die* and I was hers.

"You right, sis. Well, I'm about to pack some clothes for Justus, real quick, and shoot over there. I have a little over an hour and a half to be back home and ready for when Choppa gets here."

"You know I'm gon' need the 4-1-1, right?"

"That goes without saying. I got you. See you in a minute." I hung up with Essence and headed to my bedroom, where Justus was coloring in his book on the flo or.

130

"Baby, I need you to get a few of your toys. You're going by Auntie Essence for a couple of days, okay?"

He looked up at me. "Why?"

"Because I have some adult things to do, is why."

"Like what? Sex?" His eyebrows raised in curious wonder.

"Justus!" He caught me so off guard with that. "Who taught you that word and do you even know what it means?" I asked hysterically.

"Auntie Precious," he answered calmly. "And yea, I know what it means."

I'ma slap that bitch in her loose mouth!

"Tell me, then." I was pissed but interested in knowing just how educated he was on the topic.

"It's an adult hug." His response rang of innocence and I was able to release the tension in my shoulders.

Although he didn't know the true meaning, he had an idea of what text to use it in and for that I would dig in her ass.

"You're right. It's an adult thing. Something that shouldn't come out of the mouths of children. You understand me?"

"Yes, ma'am." He closed his book and stood to his feet. "So what will you do while I'm away?"

"Boyyy, who's the parent? Me or you? Just go do what I said." I gently pushed him in the back of his head, directing him to his toy box in the closet.

Fifteen minutes later, we were packed and ready to go.

It was going to take me an hour to get there and back, not leaving me much time to spruce up but I was going to do my best to ensure that I shined bright like a diamond for that man.

I pulled onto Essence's street in Stone Mountain less than thirty minutes later. I had already called her, asking her to be outside to intercept my son so I could hustle home and get ready for whatever.

"Justus, the same rules at our house applies at this one as well. I don't want your auntie giving me a bad report. You understand me?"

"Yes, ma'am."

"Okay, I'm gonna call you every day to check on you until I pick you back up but you can call me anytime, okay, baby?"

"Okay."

As I pulled into Essence's driveway, she approached my car, stopping at the back door to open it for Justus.

"Hey, lil' man. Give auntie some sugar." She welcomed him with a hug and smothered him with kisses.

I left my engine running, but I stepped out so I could shower my baby with some love before I departed.

Squeezing him tightly, I spoke into his ear. "Remember, be good and I love you."

He shook his head *yes.* "I will. Love you, too, Mama."

"I know you in a rush but when you get a minute, call me." Essence pulled his bags from the back seat.

"I'll hit you up, ASAP, but let me go." I kissed her on the cheek and thanked her again.

Both Justus and Essence waved bye to me as I backed out of her driveway. My baby looked to be sad or maybe it was just me feeling some type of way.

It was one thing to leave him in my friend's care for a few hours. It was a different ballpark to do it days at a time. But I knew he'd have fun with Essence, so I shook it off, smiled at him, blew several air kisses and drove off.

I looked at the time on the dash. I had a half an hour to get home and only twenty minutes to get ready thereafter. So with no time to waste, I floored it. I didn't want to have my man waiting.

Chapter 17
Julz

Traveling on 285 was horrendous. An accident on the highway caused traffic to creep along at a snail's crawl.

"I'll be goddamn!" I rested my head on the steering wheel as I inched along with the rest of the drivers around me.

Looking at the time, it was now 11:50 a.m. And if Choppa was precise about two hours, he'd be at my house in ten minutes. The same time I estimated to get there myself.

I grabbed my phone and called him, but I went straight to voicemail. At the sound of the beep, I left a message. "Baby, if you get to my apartment and I'm not there, I will be soon. I'm stuck in traffic but I'll be there in a few minutes. See you in a bit."

Fifteen minutes later, I entered into my complex. I crossed my fingers that he'd be late so I had some time to shower and dress, but clearly punctuality was a strong suit of his because he was leaning against his car, waiting on me as I pulled up alongside him.

I studied him the moment I stepped out of my car. Damn, he was looking swaggy from head to toe. His fresh fade and trimmed goatee had him looking precise, off top. But then he watered my mouth with the way his clothes hung perfectly off of his body.

Looking at him closely, I noticed he was Prada down to his shoes. Now I was no label whore but it was something about a well-dressed man that made a bitch want to do cartwheels and back flips.

Glancing down at myself, I didn't compliment him at all. I mean, I wasn't busted but I wasn't looking as fly as I could have if I had the time to clean myself up.

I had on a pair of ripped blue jeans, a white tank top and opened-toe sandals. My hair was pulled into a ponytail and my lips had no shine to them. I looked like an adorable Plain Jane but I wanted to present myself to him in the correct fashion he stood before me.

However, my smile reached my eyes the moment I saw his arms open to receive me. "Hey, baby." I kissed his lips. "You're looking good."

"But I ain't got nothing on you. Face pretty, smile bright, booty on swole, titties like ba-dow!" He gassed me up.

"Only you say things like that." I smiled wider. "Umm, anyway, I know you wanted me to be ready for twelve but as you can see, I'm not. Do you think you can spare me thirty minutes to shower and change?"

He looked down at his watch and shook his head *no*. "You look beautiful. Now get in." He opened his passenger door, closing it only after he ensured my comfort.

The silliest grin plastered across my face as I leaned over the console and opened his door.

He thanked me once he got in. "Do you have your ID on you?"

That was an odd question. "I do. Why? Where are we going?"

"Can I surprise you?"

You can do anything you want, is what I thought but I answered sarcastically. "Do I truly have a choice?"

"Nah, you don't." He smirked. "Matter of fact, I got this for you."

He opened his glove compartment and pulled out a blindfold.

Oh, my! What have I gotten myself into? I smiled cheesily.

He leaned over to my side, eased my seatbelt over me, stealing a kiss as he did and then advised that I put the covering on.

I obliged, securing its position so I couldn't see a thing.

"You know I'm super anxious to know where we're going since you're doing all this." I rubbed my palms together. "Can I have one small hint, pleaseee?"

He placed a hand on my thigh and double patted it before he allowed it to rest there. "You'll know soon enough. Patience, baby. Just chill and let ya man do what he do."

***

Choppa

I stared at Julz for a brief moment, admiring the attractiveness of her smile before throwing my car in reverse and heading out to Airport Rd.

With KiKi being back home, pressing a nigga for some dick that I had no intentions on giving her, the urge to get away with my lady was stronger than the desire to flip werk.

"I'm fishing here but if we're going to some nice place for lunch, am I dressed appropriately? Can you at least tell me that?"

Julz was dying to find out something but I refused her. "You can ask a million ways, shorty, and I still won't give it up, so you might as well relax."

"Humph!" She folded her arms across her chest but I could tell from her body language that she wasn't talkin' 'bout nothing!

"I gotchu, big baby. All your questions will be answered in a minute. Just enjoy the ride." I smiled as I thumbed the smooth skin of her thigh protruding from the rips in her jeans.

Thirty minutes later and minutes away from our destination, I pulled out an iPod and headphones and placed them in Julz' hands.

"What's this for?" She asked the moment she felt the weight of it in her palms.

"I need you to place these buds in your ears and listen to the short playlist."

"Wh—" I could tell from the curve of her lips that she was going to ask another question but she stopped herself this time. "All right, but just know you're killing me." She blindly wagged her finger at me.

After she placed them in her ears, I turned the player on. I needed the music to drown out the sound of our upcoming surroundings.

A few minutes later, we were pulling into the parking lot of the Dekalb Peachtree Airport, where I had a private jet waiting on us.

I could have chosen to fly Southwest or some shit but it was nothing to drop $4,800.00 on a round-trip flight to ride the skies in style. Besides, she was worth it and the way me, Jared and Cardale was moving that werk, five racks wasn't shit. As it stood, I was gonna make close to a hundred bands, profit, off of this last shipment.

As I looked over at Julz, I noticed her nervous energy. Based on the way she chewed on her bottom lip, I could tell she was becoming impatient but nevertheless, she kept quiet.

Checking the time, I had an half an hour to check in and verify my last minute phone reservations. But before doing so, I removed her buds from her ears.

"We're here, boo." I announced.

"Good. I was dying." She let out an exasperated breath and then touched her blindfold. "Is it cool to take this off?"

There was no need for anymore suspense. I doubted she'd be able to finger my exact plans still. "Yea, it's cool."

She ripped it away from her eyes and patted her hair as she looked about. Then she smiled at me. "I know where we are *and* why we're here."

I was curious for her thoughts. "A'ight, spill it."

"We're here to see the airshow. Am I right?"

I bobbed my head and smirked. She grinned back but she couldn't be more wrong.

"Aye, let me take care of something real quick. Sit tight and I'll be back for ya."

"Okay, cool. I'ma call Essence."

"A'ight. Do that." I leaned over to get a kiss. The taste of her tongue was as sweet as the look in her soft brown eyes.

Leaving the engine on, I jumped out and hurried off to check in before the one o'clock deadline.

After fifteen minutes of wrapping up at the concierge's desk, I was heading back to my car to whisk my lady off on a spontaneous trip.

The sudden sound of me tapping my knuckles against the window caused Julz to jump and snap her head my way. I obviously caught her off guard.

When she saw it was me, she put on a mean face and mouthed *boyyy* as if to let me know had I been someone else, they would have caught hell.

I opened her door. "Get the keys, ma, and let's be out."

"Essence, my man is back. I will talk to you later." She hung up, did as I asked and then chastised me as soon as she stepped out of my car. "Don't you ever scare me like that. I was fixing to give you the business."

"Shorty, you ain't 'bout dat life." I teased.

136

She put her tiny fists up and threw phantom punches. "You wanna see?"

I chuckled and put up my guard as she playfully rushed me.

"You got it. You got it." I called a timeout as I bear hugged her into submission. She giggled like a child before giving me a peck on the lips. I grabbed her hand. "Let's go, baby."

"Let's."

As we began walking toward the plane and not the crowd that typically congregated to see the fighter jets, she slowed her pace and questioned me.

"Why are we on the landing strip when we should be…" She turned her head over her shoulder, pointing away from my leading.

I didn't answer. Instead, I tugged at her hand to liven her step in my direction.

Looking at her out the corner of my eye, I noticed she was smiling. And as we grew closer to the welcoming captain, I'm pretty sure she now knew what was up.

When I walked up on him, I provided him with our itinerary. After he reviewed it, he extended his hand. "Right this way, sir. Ma'am."

"Beauty before beast." I stepped aside so Julz could go before me. She looked back at me, surprisingly. "Choppa, no you didn't! Where are we going? Oh, my goodness!" She rambled off more questions under her breath as she climbed the steps to enter the cabin. Once she found a seat, she excitedly buckled up and stared at me goofily.

I smiled back. "What?"

"Are you gonna answer me?"

"Imagine that." I spoke sarcastically. "You 'bout to find out where we're going in a just a short while. Enjoy not knowing anything except you're here with me. Can you do that?" I took a seat next to her and grabbed her hand to kiss the back of it.

Julz smiled sweetly and bobbed her head. "Wherever we're going, I'm just glad to be with you."

I kissed her forehead and then her lips before I rested my head back and prided myself on making my Queen happy so far.

***

Ca$h & Coffee

LaGuardia Airport, New York
Julz

I stepped off of the plane, looking around in wonderment. I'd never been beyond the South, so being on the east coast, for me, felt like a vacation to Bora Bora or someplace exotic like that.

Spinning around to face Choppa, I leaped into his arms. "I'm in Newwww Yorrrrkkk!" I sang embarrassingly loud, sounding like Alicia *No* Keys but I didn't care.

"I take it you like where we'll be staying for the next couple of days." He wore a handsome grin.

"Yes indeed! But on the real, we could have been shacked away at my spot and I would have been just as content." That was the truth. *His* presence made my day, so New York was just a cherry. A plump, juicy cherry, to be exact, though.

"Come on, let's grab this rental and check into our hotel." He grabbed my hand and began leading me, but I pulled him to stop for a second. "What?" He looked off to his side at me.

I rested my hand against his cheek and kissed him partially on the lips. "Thank you is what."

He placed his hand on top of mine and slid it over his mouth to kiss the inside of my palm. I saw the smile from behind my hand and although he remained silent, his eyes said it all. Choppa was happy to make me happy.

With no further ado, we resumed our walk to Enterprise and from there I was sure to know the rest of the day's event but I dared not ask. He'd proven that none of my questions merited an answer, so I'd just see what I see when I see it.

He hadn't failed so far with the surprises. *Works for me*, I thought.

Thirty minutes later, we rode out of the airport and into the busy streets in a lavish 2015 black on black Range Rover.

We made small talk as we drove through the city but I was too busy taking in the sights. City life in New York was much different than city life in New Orleans or Atlanta, for that matter. Heavier foot traffic, congested driving and taller buildings than I'd ever seen were all around.

"What'chu smiling for?" He touched my chin.

"No reason aside from I'm over the moon."

"That's reason enough." He reached for my hand to hold and I swear my heart stopped beating for a full minute.

As we continued our drive I zoned out, not sure for how long, but when I snapped out of my daydream, I shrilled with giddiness because I recognized where we were. "We're crossing the Brooklyn Bridge!"

"You don't say." His tone was condescending but his flat expression and underlying humor made his sarcastic behind funny.

"Whatever, man!" I giggled and wiggled in my seat.

Just hours ago, I was sitting in my bedroom finishing an online test for class and now I was sitting on a cloud, next to my King and in New York. *Wow!*

Ca$h & Coffee

Chapter 18
Julz

"We're here. Let's roll." Choppa opened his door once he pulled up in front of The W New York Downtown Hotel. I stretched my eyes as far as they could go from where I sat, looking up at the exquisite building before me. He stuck his head back into the truck. "You coming?"

"Oh, yea, sure." I opened the door and stepped out onto the curb.

The way I eyeballed my surrounding would have made one think I never seen daylight before. I was stuck in place because I was awed and I was only outside.

"You all right?" Choppa asked.

I bobbed my head up and down *yes,* as I grabbed his extended hand and headed into the swanky building to check in.

When we reached the front desk, I stood facing opposite of them as Choppa conducted business and took in the luxurious scenery. I was in a marveled state of mind. I'd been to hotels before but never one as chic as this one.

"Mr. Lyons, we have a Whenever/Whatever service for our patrons. So if there is anything we can assist you with, let us know." She had Choppa sign a few papers, handed him his I.D. and continued. "Here are your room keys. You'll take the elevator up to the 14th floor and your corner room will be located off to the right once stepping off. Also, it is our pleasure having you here as our guest. Please enjoy your stay here at The W."

"Thank you," he said to the lady. Draping his arm around my neck, he said, "Shall we?" all proper like.

"Ooh, bae, who stole your thug," I teased.

"Oh, it's still there. You know I'm fronting a lil' bit," he whispered in my ear. "Now, shall we?"

"Yea, let's do this shit." I mimicked his usual way of talking and affectionately rubbed my face against his lips.

"No doubt." He showed some teeth and stole a quick feel of my booty, and I didn't protest one bit.

A few minutes later, we were standing in front of our room. Behind that door would be the first of many intimate memories between us, I was sure of it. I welcomed it. Hell, he earned it!

Never in my dating life had I been with someone who treated me like a storybook Queen, impressing me with his gentlemanly ways and such. I would get the dinner and the movies and possibly flowers but never *all* of this. He made me feel special already.

He pushed the door open. "After you."

"Ahhh!" was all I could say when I stepped into my very own wonderland.

We were in the Extreme WOW Suite, as the hotel named it and I saw why. I was standing in what felt like a high-end, deluxe apartment in the sky. It had panoramic views of downtown Manhattan, eleven hundred square feet of sophistication, upscale furniture and the plush cozy feel of the good life.

"Pinch me." I held out my arm and he did it. "Ouch!" I jerked my arm away, rubbing my tender spot. "I didn't think you'd really do it."

He laughed. "Neva let it be said I don't give my woman what she asks for."

"But I didn't mean literally." I pushed him, knocking him back just a little.

"Oh, that's how you feel? Bring that ass here." He charged at me.

"Unh, unh! You gotta catch me." I ran through the suite, laughing uncontrollably until I was cornered, then I tried to reason.

"Okay, wait. I was just…" A yelp left my lips when he reached for me. Once he grabbed me, he lifted me over his shoulder and I could have died from the endless giggles suffocating me. "I quit. I quit!"

"Nah, let me get me, shorty."

He dropped me onto the heavenly cloud of a bed and mounted me as we rolled around horse playing.

"Get off of me. Get off of meeeee!" I erupted joyously.

"Oh, you want me to get off of you?" He kissed me on my neck and slowed down some of my frantic movement.

"Yes." I answered sharply.

He shook his head *no* and then kissed my shoulders. "Is the answer still yes?"

I weakened a bit and my voice quaked but I held firm. "Yes."

Then he gripped the side of my thigh, clenching part of my booty within his grasp as he planted a trail of passionate kisses along my collarbone. Shit felt sensual and I couldn't fake it. I didn't want him to get off of me. I wanted him to get in me. I began sliding my hands underneath his shirt. He had me open.

"You still want me to get off of you?" He looked me squarely in my lustful eyes.

"Mmmm, no." My reply sounded like a murmur but I was certain he was able to interpret my loud body language.

He licked his lips and dropped his head and then looked back at me. "Too bad."

"What? That's how you gon' play me?" I swiped a pillow and hit him with it.

"A'ight nah, I'ma beast with a pillow, too." He picked up his own and held it over his shoulder, threatening to use it.

I dropped mine and tapped the tips of my fingers into my palm. "All right. I give up."

He smirked and then reached for my hand. "Come on, let's grab something to eat in Union Square and see what we see."

"Eat? Sight see? Nooo, bae! I can do that right here." I ran both of my hands up and down his body, emphasizing my point.

"Later fa dat. You're in the Big Apple, let's go out and take a bite."

"Bae! You're torturing me." I folded my arms across my chest and pouted. My pussy was in need.

"Sweetheart, if you can hold off a little longer, I promise I'll put that pussy on life support," said Choppa.

"Promise?" I held up my little finger out so we could pinkie swear. But instead of locking pinkies with me, Choppa put my finger in his mouth and sucked it like it was my pearl. My ass started having visions of covering his mouth with my juices. My face flushed.

He released my little digit from his mouth and looked at me with all that manliness. "You like that, ma?"

"What do you think?" I panted.

"I'ont know." His face told a different story.

I play scowled at him and pushed him in the chest with both hands. "Let's go eat before I rape your *pussy teasing* ass."

I calmed my kitty, got up off of the bed and skipped over to the nearest mirror and fixed my hair and clothes. After that, I was all set for whatever as long as the night ended with my feet on Choppa's shoulders.

***

Later that night

After hours of doing the tourist thing: eating, shopping and walking around, we returned back to our hotel.

Dropping bags at the door, I walked through the living room and into our bedroom and flung myself onto the bed. "Baeeee, I'm so tired."

Although my face was buried into the thickness of the comforter, I could sense he was standing behind me. When I flipped over, I was staring up at him, removing his shoes.

"But did you have a good time?"

I sat up on my elbows. "Baby, I had the time of my life. I've never had over-the-top treatment before. It feels so good but then again it feels so," I hesitated as I searched for the right word.

"Strange?"

"Yea, strange. How did you know?"

"Most women aren't accustomed to being treated like queens. They're used to the basic things from a nigga whose only goal is their gain. But me? I know there's no greater return than the proper investment in woman's heart."

He now sat on the bed next to me.

"You know that I appreciate every last thing you've done for me but I don't need expensive gifts and trips to see your heart is gold."

Choppa crooked his head slightly and looked at me as if I offended him. "I don't do it for that. I do it because I *can* and because I *want* to. You don't think I read the type of woman you are? I knew the moment I saw you, *you* were different from these beggin' broads expecting for a dude to finance their lifestyle. But you? You'll go without before you dig through a man's pocket, and I respect that. But I'm the type of man

144

that will give you whatever you deserve. So don't confuse this with buying your affections. Understand this is a King simply spoiling his Queen."

He stood up, removed his shirt and quietly walked out of the bedroom. I wanted to go after him and apologize if I made him feel some type of way but I didn't want to make a mountain out of a mole hill. In my mind, I was only clarifying my stance but I should have accepted his generosity with an unquestioning smile.

Moments later, bath water could be heard in the not too far distance. I didn't bother walking in there because I felt a little embarrassed from my earlier insinuation, so I laid back on the bed and stared up at the ceiling, chewing my bottom lip.

I began to fidget with my fingers until I heard my text message alert go off. I pulled my phone from out of my jean pocket to check it.

9:35 p.m. Essence: *Hey. You're probably doing the oochie coochie so I don't expect a reply. Just letting you know Justus is asleep. We had a good day and I hope you did too. Love you. P.s. Don't come home pregnant. Ha ha and ha!*

She made me laugh out loud. I swear we couldn't be tighter if we were Siamese.

"What's funny?" Choppa asked, stepping into the room standing before me just as naked as the day he was born, except sexier—wayyy sexier.

"Ummm, it was—ummm, nothing. Well, it was a Essence from text. I mean, a text from Essence." I cleared up my babble. His body had me dumbfounded. *Oh, God! I sounded like a buffoon.*

Choppa chuckled and then walked over to me, shaking his head.

He kneeled down by the bed and removed my shoes before he stood up and pulled me up with him. As he looked me over, a slight groan left his lips.

He unbuttoned my button and unzipped my jeans, dropping down to pull each pant leg off. Still perched below, he lifted his arms over his head to remove my thong, sliding them off as well. There he had a bird's eye view of my always shaven center.

Rising to his feet, he ran his hands up under my tank and pulled it over my head. I never knew that being undressed could feel like foreplay. On God, I was ready for him to take me but he didn't. He looked down at me, soundlessly, but affectionately.

I cleared my throat and then looked up at him, meeting his eyes. He spoke.

"Don't ever question me, shorty. All I want to do is love you." He paused for a second. "You should let me love you."

Oh, my God. Yes! I want to love you, too.

I stood in front of him naked, both physically and emotionally. I shook my head, blushing. His words penetrated deeper than any I'd ever heard before. "Okay, baby."

He shook his head at my compliance, took me by the hand and led me into the bathroom.

There was so much to Choppa than what met the eye. On the outside, he looked like a straight up ruthless thug but on the inside, he was a romantic sweetheart.

We stepped in the bathroom and the soft sounds of Sade could be heard coming from his phone. And for ambiance, only the soft flickering flames of the lit candles around the tub provided the light we were to utilize.

I was overwhelmed already.

"Step in."

I obliged. The water was perfect.

Choppa came in afterwards, sitting behind me. He pulled me into him so the back of my head lay against his chest as he stroked my hair and made me feel beautiful.

"Choppa, why is your heart beating so fast?" I questioned.

"That's every time I'm near you. You didn't know?"

I blushed. I swear that man had all the right answers.

We sat in the tub conversing so long the water turned cold. Stepping out of the tub and without having bathed, we entered the separate shower to wash up.

I wrapped up first. I would have stayed in the shower until he finished but he declined my company.

"Go 'head and slip into something sexy. I'll be out in a minute," he said from underneath the spray of the water.

I kissed him and dashed off into the living area to pull out the Victoria Secret number he admired so much on the mannequin. I knew before I put it on I'd give it the proper justice but I exceeded my own expectations when I looked at the red lacey piece on me.

You're hot, Julz. I was feeling myself and I couldn't wait for him to feel me, too.

As I was walking past the bathroom, I heard Choppa make an uncomfortable groan.

I stopped in my tracks to question if he was okay in there. "Baby, you all right?"

"Yeah! I'm—good." He stumbled over his words. "I'll be out in a second." He grunted again but with less vigor.

Humph. "Okay." I wrinkled my nose but I let him be as I placed my focus back on me. "Damn! He's. Gonna. Eat. You. Up!" I emphasized my words as my anticipation for him to see me grew.

This is it. Tonight is the night!

Suddenly, I felt flushed. My nerves started to kick in, like I had never been with a man before.

What the hell? I questioned as I grabbed a bottled water from the fridge. I had to settle myself.

You've been with men before, so what's your problem? I answered myself and then countered as if I were two separate people.

Yes, I have been with men but not this man. He's different. Oh, God, I hope I'm all that he expects.

Bitch, slap yo'self when you done being silly. Of course, you're good enough. Now fix your attitude and give him something he'll never forget!

I had to laugh at myself but this man had me going in circles all got damn ready.

After I calmed myself, I sat at the window seat, looking out at the Southwest view our room captured, which gave a full scope of the Hudson River and a stunning sky view of the city. I never saw a more beautiful night than the one staring back at me.

A faint image of Choppa reflected off of the window, directing my attention to him. I stood up. "Baby, you need to see the view. It's breathtaking."

"I know." He licked his lips.

"But you're not even looking at the…" I dropped my head to follow his eyes looking at me in my negligée. "I'm what's breathtaking, huh?"

He bobbed his head in agreement and removed his towel as he walked over to me.

My eyes zeroed in on the lower half of his body and I almost collapsed like a house of cards.

When he was up on me, he pulled me into him, pressing his hard body and even harder dick against my softness. Now engaged in a tongue kiss, he walked me backwards, leading me over to the bed.

I didn't see him reach for a condom, so I scooted back slightly. I smiled nervously but gave stiff instruction. "Don't cum in me, Choppa."

He frowned. "If I have to pull out, I ain't goin' in, shorty."

As I felt the weight of his body lighten off of mine, I closed my eyes for I now regretted saying a word. I didn't want to ruin the momentum of our moment but I wasn't on birth control. I very much wanted him, just not a baby. *Damn!*

When I didn't respond to his reply, he shook his head as if to say *what a shame.* "Have it your way."

Our skin peeled further apart as he lifted off of me. I panicked. "Choppa!"

He eyed me curiously, licking his lips as he answered huskily. "What?"

My mind was telling me *no!* But I was fucked because my body was telling me *yes!* My lips parted and a small breath left my mouth. "Cum inside."

He smiled devilishly as he felt the soft clutch of my hand pulling his pulsating dick toward my pussy.

Chapter 19
Choppa

I was mad anxious to feel baby girl's inner walls, but there was no way I was gonna rush the moment. We both had been waiting on it way too long to make it anything less than explosive.

I could feel her legs trembling though I hadn't even put the head in. "Relax, ma." I whispered huskily in her ear. "Let me take you to heaven."

"Yes, please," she cooed. She had told me it had been a long time since she'd been intimate with a man and her actions supported that.

I locked hands with her and held her arms above her head, pining them into the soft mattress as I kissed her deeply. My rock hard dick pressed against her moist pussy, sending an indescribable good feeling from my toes to the top of my head.

"Baby you feel and taste delicious," I said softly.

"Oooh!" she cried out as I moved my body up and down so that the head of my dick stroked her clit.

I gently sucked that spot between her shoulder blades and her neck. I could feel her body's reaction underneath me. It must've felt good because she was rolling her hips silently begging me to enter her. "Not yet," I said, barely above a whisper.

I kissed my way down to her twin mounds and teased a nipple with my tongue. It hardened instantly and Julz wrapped her legs around my waist.

"Choppa I need you inside of me," she moaned.

I didn't reply because I had no intention to honor her request. Not yet.

I freed my hands from the intense lock she had on them, and let 'em roam her beautiful body. Her skin was on fire! Her desire for me caused me to swell to the size of a cucumber.

I continued to tease her with the tip while I flicked her nipple with my tongue. She moaned louder and gripped the back of my head with both hands, imploring me to take her nipple back in my watery mouth.

I switched my attention to her other breast and made slow love to that nipple with my tongue. It hardened more under my sensuous manipulation, and I heard Julz suck in her breath.

"Bite it, bae." Her voice was heavy with pent up passion.

This time I didn't deny her the pleasure she craved. I cupped her breast with both hands and gently bit her raisin-sized nipple, drawing a deep purr from Julz.

I traced the contours of her hips and thighs as my hand traveled south until it reached its intended destination. When my fingers came in contact with the delicate petals of her flower, she lifted her ass up to greet my touch.

I used two fingers to spread her lower lips as my tongue made a slow journey in the same direction. I found her clit and gently stroked it with my thumb.

"Ssssssss!" She moaned.

I covered her sensitive bud with my thick lips and sucked it while taking ahold of her ass with two hands and holding her in place.

"Gawd!" she cried.

Her hips was rocking furiously and her hands gripped the back of my head, pulling my face all up in that wet pussy. It smelled fresh but excited. And when I pushed my tongue deep inside of her, she tasted honeyed enough to give a nigga a cavity.

"Damn, ma, your pussy is sweet as fuck," I said.

My words seemed to turn the furnace up. Julz clamped her knees to the sides of my face and grinded her pelvis in a circular motion, feeding me a mouthful of her deliciousness.

"Eat mama pussy!"

Those words made me freeze and my mind went back to a time and place that I didn't ever want to revisit. I squeezed my eyes tightly shut and forced the memories back into the dungeon of my mind. And just as quickly as they appeared, they were gone and I returned my full attention back to my girl.

"Spread your legs wide. Open all the way up for me." The bass in my voice was deeper than normal, fueled by the luscious beauty beneath me.

Julz spread her legs into a Y and I was staring at a fat, bald, pretty pussy. I slowly licked it from top to bottom, savoring her taste along the way. Stopping to suck her swollen lips, I slid a long finger inside of her hot oven.

"Ooh, baby, please stop teasing me. I need to feel you inside of me. Now!"

She grabbed me by the shoulders and tried to pull me up but I wasn't having none of that.

"Hell no. I'ma make you come in my mouth," I said.

Before she could protest, I placed my mouth back to that sweet peach and began giving her some serious neck. I tantalized her love button with my tongue and I finger fucked her gushy box.

Julz was writhing with pleasure, moaning my name and grinding her pussy upwards. When I felt her motion increase in speed and heard her breathing heighten, I began flicking my tongue across her clit rapidly.

"You gon' make me cum! You gon' make me cum! Ooh, baby, you gon' make me cummmm!" she screamed.

"Gimme it!"

"Bae, I'm a squirter!"

"Give it to me, I said!"

"Bae!" She sounded hesitant but her body was under my control.

I hadn't ever been with a woman that squirted so the idea of her doing it had me geeked. I sucked her pussy with the grand prize in mind! "Gimme those juices, shorty. Make that pussy squirt in yo nigga's mouth. I wanna taste it!"

"Oh my god, Choppa, here it comes! Here it comes, baby! Ahhhhh!"

I pulled back a little, tightened my grip on her ass, and opened my mouth. I didn't really know what to expect but I didn't have to wait long to get what Julz had for me.

A long spray off her juices squirted out like water from a garden hose. It splashed in my mouth and all over my face, in my eyes and up my nose.

"Oh, sweet Jesus!" Baby girl cried out. Her legs fell slack and I heard her fighting to control her breathing.

In the background, Adele was singing exactly what I was feeling.
The storms are raging on the rolling sea
And on the highway of regret.
The winds of change are blowing wild and free
You ain't seen nothing like me yet.

I could make you happy, make your dreams come true.
Nothing that I wouldn't do.
Go to the ends of the Earth for you,
To make you feel my love
To make you feel my love

I reached over the edge of the bed, blindly located my shirt on the floor and used it to wipe the evidence of Julz satisfaction out of my eyes. When my vision cleared, I slid up her body and pressed my mouth to hers.

She was still panting blissfully with her eyes closed, but she parted her soft lips and locked lips with mine. Our tongues tangled deliciously as she wrapped her arms around my neck and pulled me deeper into the kiss.

Her breathing was hard. Her desire was still intense. Her hunger hadn't been completely fed, and mine was sky high.

"Do you taste your sweetness on my lips?" I whispered into her mouth.

"Mmm hmm. But now I want to taste *you*." She slid a hand between our bodies and wrapped it around my throbbing manhood. I was brick hard and as thick as her wrist. "This right here is going to open me up." She sounded both excited and a little scared.

"You wanna stop?"

"Nigga, don't play! Just let me taste it, first," she whispered sexily.

"Nah, ma, tonight it's all about me pleasing you."

I sucked on her neck and used my knee to spread her willing thighs.

"Choppa, don't hurt me. It's been a very long time."

"I got you, shorty." I moved my dick up and down her split, teasing but not pushing inside.

152

"Give it to me, boo. Make love to your woman," she said softly. "Make me scream your name." She raked her nails down my back.

That shit was a mu'fuckin turn on! My dick stiffened so hard it bent. I reached down and guided it to where Julz was pleading for me to put it.

I pushed my hips forward but her precious vault was almost too tight to enter. I could believe it had been a long time since a nigga had slid up in there. Shorty was damn near re-virginized.

"Aww!" She bit into my shoulder to muffle her cry.

I touched all over her body so that her concentration wouldn't be totally focused on the pain of my entry. Gently, slowly, I eased in. Her nails dug deeper and a louder cry escaped from the corner of her mouth.

"How you begging for the dick and can't even take it?" I teased her lovingly.

"Shut up!" I felt the wetness of real tears in my shoulder.

Worried that I was hurting her too bad, I began to push up off of her. But Julz wasn't having that. She locked her legs around mine and forced me into her entrance.

Once the head slipped in the rest was easy. I laid still for a minute to allow her to get used to my size. When I felt the dig of her nails subside I slowly started grinding.

"This what you want? Huh?" I talked shit.

"Yes! Oh yes!"

"Damn, shorty, you feel so good. A nigga been dreaming about this day and it's even better than I imagined it would be," I said truthfully. I didn't care if I sounded soft. Sharing true intimacy with my woman meant more to me than the G-code. Besides, her sex was like truth serum. "I'ma love you so good, baby," I promised.

"I need you to. And I'm going to be everything you need me to be," she replied.

"You already are." I kissed her passionately as our bodies became one and our movements synced perfectly.

Our hands were all over each other and our moans blended together in an erotic melody that that pushed us both to a tempo that had the bed rocking.

"Yes, baby, go deeper," moaned Julz. "Make love to my soul."

I was only half way in but now I gave her every thick inch that I'd been blessed with. I went deep and hit her squishy bottom. My finger gripped her ass and I pulled her up to meet my thrusts. Shorty was moaning and crying, all at the same time. I could tell that her cries were of pleasure so instead of slowing down, I sped up. Her pussy gripped my rod like she never wanted our love making to end.

My body slapped against hers as I repeatedly pulled out to the tip then plunged back in with power and passion.

"Get it, bae! Get it all!" Her head whipped from side to side and those nails dug into my back once more.

Her cries had a nigga really feelin' himself. I knew my dick game was on point but our chemistry took me to a whole 'nother level. I looked deep into Julz eyes and went balls deep in her wetness. In and out. In and out.

"Choppa! Choppa! Ooh, baby, you're going to make me scream."

Encouraged by her words, I bit down on my lip and put in some serious work. The sound of her pussy popping almost made me erupt like a volcano, but I fought back the desire. Like I had told her, tonight was all about her.

In one smooth motion I locked my legs underneath hers and rolled us over so that she was now on top.

"Get your dick, ma," I said.

Julz pinched her nipples and began riding my python. She started slowly and increased her speed a little at a time. It felt like her pussy was sucking my dick.

"Ahhh!" I moaned.

"Cum with me, baby. Nut inside your woman." She was staring down in my eyes, looking sexy as fuck! I reached up to touch her but she wouldn't let me. "No, don't touch. And don't stop looking at me."

I let my hand fall back to my side she kept my eyes locked with hers. It was like we were looking into each other's soul. Her circular movements were tight and fast, and her rapid breaths worked on me like Viagra.

We both were making fuck faces as she rode my dick with every ounce of energy in her body. "I'm 'bout to nut, baby!" I groaned.

"Do it!" She grinded down on me harder.

154

"Shit!"

"Cum with me, bae. Oooh, please cum with me!"

"Argghhhhh!" I growled like a beast.

"Oooohhhhh! I'm cumming!" She cried right before she sprayed me with that water gun of hers.

Her eyes rolled up in her head and I damn near bit a hole in my lip as I exploded inside of her gushy box.

"Julz!" I shamelessly screamed her name.

"Bae! I'ma die!" she cried.

"Naw, don't die, shorty." I laughed as I tried to regain my breath. She lifted a pillow and hit me over the head.

"Shut up, boo! You get on my last nerve." Her laughter joined mine and she collapsed down in my chest with my dick still inside of her.

I planted a few soft kisses on her forehead and told her that she was the best.

"Damn, you did that shit, shorty," I said.

She mumbled something unintelligible. I closed my eyes and savored the moment. Julz felt so goddam good in my arms with her head in my chest. I could envision a lifetime with her. Fuck any other bitch.

After a minute or so, she muttered on low breath. "I think I'm in love."

"Me too."

And the fuck if I didn't mean that shit.

***

Julz

My God, knees don't fail me now. I rose feebly, bracing myself against the nearby wall as I managed my short walk to the bathroom.

I stood at the sink and stared at my reflection in the mirror. I looked a hot mess by the head.

Feeling like a school girl, I tiptoed to the doorway and peeked out at Choppa and giggled. I may had looked like I'd been in a cat fight with my hair being every which-a-way but at least I wasn't knocked out cold like someone else.

Spinning on my heels, I headed back to the sink.

Hmmm hmmm ah hmmm hmmmm mmm…

I found myself unconsciously humming that nineties' love song *Can I Stay with You* by Karyn White. A smile stretched across my face. I couldn't even be mad at that. Choppa made me feel like none other. The way my body responded to his every stroke, touch, lick and kiss amazed me.

I ran hot water over a towel and soap. The combination of our *juju* left me super sticky in the middle.

Seconds later, I gapped my legs wide enough to slide the washcloth over and between my swollen pussy lips. "Ooow!" I hissed.

That damn Choppa!

Chapter 20
Kiki

That muthafuckin' Choppa!

Like, what the fuck? How he gonna just park me in a hotel room and go missing for days, no text or phone call—nothing!

I was hotter than a kettle!

I grabbed my iPhone and once again tried to reach his inconsiderate ass. I didn't know if he was somewhere dead or in jail. I was becoming very worried because, in spite of what we were going through, I truly did love him.

For the umpteenth time, I was sent straight to voicemail. I tried to control my emotions but that wasn't one off my strong points so that battle was lost almost as soon as I heard that irritating ass recording.

"Yo, you know who you called. Unfortunately I can't be reached at the moment. At the sound of the beep, you know what to do!"

Beep!

"Answer your muthafuckin' phone, nigga!" I screamed into the phone.

I waited a few minutes to see if Choppa would call but he didn't. I didn't know if I should be worried or angry. The first thing that came to mind was that his black ass was probably laid up with a bitch, 'cause that's how street niggas rock, all of them! He was probably with the trick who had been entertaining him while I was out of town, whoever the fuck the ugly ho was!

I was seconds away from hopping in my car and going to look for him. God protect the bitch that I found him with. In my state of mind, I was going to beat the brakes off of her!

Calm down and make a few calls before you fly off the handle, I coached myself.

After taking a few deep breaths and exhaling slowly, I placed the first call.

"Hey, baby girl. What's up?" My daddy answered.

"Nothing much, Daddy. I'm looking for Choppa, have you seen or heard from him?"

"No. Is everything all right down there?" he asked.

"I'm not sure. I've been calling and texting him for three days and he won't reply." My voice cracked with emotion.

"Don't cry, sweetheart."

"I'm sorry."

"Have y'all been fighting?"

"No, Daddy. It's just—"

"Did he put his hands on you?"

"No, no, no. It's nothing like that," I quickly put that fire out because Choppa's life wouldn't be worth one cent if Daddy thought he hit me.

"You sure? Now, don't protect him if he did. You know I don't play that shit."

"Daddy, I wouldn't lie to you. Choppa hasn't laid a finger on me. I just need to know that he's not locked up or lying up in the hospital somewhere. I'm worried to death." I stood up and moved to the mirror. Damn, I looked a hot ass mess.

"Nah, Princess, he's not locked up or we would've heard from him by now. He knows the protocol."

"Yeah, you're right. I'm probably just overreacting. I'm going to call around. I'll call you back okay?"

"A'ight, baby girl. Now, dry those tears and be the soldier I taught you to be."

"Okay, Daddy." I pretended to be alright. "Tell Mommy I love her."

"I will."

The phone hung up. As usual, he never said goodbye before ending a call. He always said that the only time he wanted me to say that word to him was at his funeral.

I searched my contacts until I found Choppa's man's number. If Choppa was on that bullshit it would be easy to get it out of his boy because the grimy nigga stayed sweating a bitch. I wouldn't have to do nothing but purr in his ear and he would sing like a canary.

The phone rang twice, and then I heard his voice come on the line.

"What's poppin'?"

"Hey, baby boy. This is Kiki, Choppa's lady."

"Sup, ma. What's good in the hood? You know you don't need no introduction. How you been?"

"I'll be better when I find out where your boy at, with his sneaky ass." I walked over to the dresser and fumbled through a dozen bottles of nail polish. Choosing midnight blue to match the darkness of my mood, I carried it back over to the bed and sat down. Painting my toes would give me something to do other than pulling out my hair trying to figure out what the fuck was up with that nigga of mine.

"Oh, I can't help you with that. I spoke to him a little while ago but he didn't say where he was at. He just said he'll get up with me later. What's up though, you back in the city?"

"Yes, I am. But obviously Choppa don't give a fuck. I haven't seen or heard from him in three days." I placed the phone on the bed and put him on speaker while I got up to get some cotton balls out of my luggage.

His voice carried over to where I stood. "Fuck that nigga yo. You know the saying ... when the cat's away the mice can play. Fuck getting mad, get even."

"Yeah, I hear you." I could definitely get petty and be a tit for tat bitch, but only on my own terms.

"You do know I be knowing things, right?" he said in a tone that insinuated Choppa was off somewhere slinging dick.

"What is that supposed to mean?" I asked for clarification as I plopped back down on the bed, pulled my legs up and began placing cotton balls between each toe.

"Man, you know what the deal is. A nigga gon' be a nigga," he dropped salt.

"Are you saying Choppa is laid up with some bitch?"

"I ain't even gotta answer that. Anyway, I fucks with Choppa but I would love to fuck with you."

"Is that right?"

"You already know."

"And you're comfortable enough to say that shit to me? What if I told him you're coming at me like that?"

"Fuck I care? Just make sure you have a black dress on standby," he said.

"You know what? Y'all niggas ain't shit!"

"Maybe not, but I can fuck you real good."

159

Ca$h & Coffee

"Nigga, go fuck ya mama." I hung up on his disrespectful ass and made a mental note to tell Choppa that he needed to cut that mutha-fucka off.

I let out a frustrated sigh and abandoned my plans to paint my toe-nails. The way I was feeling I needed a goddam drink or maybe five or ten!

I removed the cotton balls from between my toes and made my way over to the fully stocked bar. Examining the bottles I decided on some-thing hard. Seagram's gin. Just what a bitch needs. No chaser.

I grabbed the bottle and a tall glass, and went back to the bed. The clock on my phone read 2:35 p.m.

By 7 o'clock I was good and fucked up, and fighting mad.

A half hour later, Choppa came bounding through the door. I sprung to my feet and met him three steps into the room.

"Where the fuck you been!" I was up in his face breathing flames.

He reached out and moved me aside. Walking toward the bath-room, he said, over his shoulder, "Hello to you too."

His sarcasm set me off! I ran behind him and started punching him in the back of the head. Whop! Whop!

"Answer me, muthafucka! Where you been for three goddam days?"

He pried me off of his back and pushed me up against the wall. Pointing a long finger in my face, he said, "KiKi, you need to chill the fuck out before you get fucked up."

"Fuck me up then nigga! I bet you won't live to tell about it! Pssshh! My daddy will have you splattered all over the ground! You better act like you know." I slapped his funky ass finger out of my face.

The look in his eyes told me that I had struck a nerve. He hated when I threatened him with my father. But I didn't give two fucks—that gin had a bitch turnt!

"Your daddy bleed too," he said.

"Oh, hell nawl, nigga. You threatening to do something to my fa-ther?" I swung at his face.

Choppa swatted my fist away, turned his back on me and went to take a piss. Before he could fix his clothes, I stalked over to him de-manding, "Let me smell your dick."

160

"Bitch, get outta my face!" he sneered. "Go smell those niggas' dicks who you let run a train on you."

"You bastard!" I tried to kick him in his balls, but in my drunken state I lost my balance and fell to the floor bumping my head on the base of the counter. "Ahhh!" I yelped, reaching up to wipe the trickle of blood that ran down the side of my face.

My head hurt like hell but what hurt worse was that Choppa stepped right over me like I wasn't shit to him.

When I got to my feet I attacked that muthafucka like I was a wild cat. My arms flailed and my mouth had no filter. I called him every cuss word in the book and tried to gouge his eyes out. I couldn't do much damage because he was too strong, he just held me back at arm's length. But I got a few good licks in and I left my nail marks down the left side of his face.

"Nah, muthafucka! I bleed you bleed!"

He stared at me with hate in his gaze. I knew that had I been any other bitch but Cross's daughter, he would've put me on my ass.

Choppa went to the mirror to examine his scars. I could see the vein on the side of his temple pulsate when he saw the three tiger stripes I left on his face. I got scared for a second but all he did was walk to the closet and began throwing the few pieces of gear he had there in a bag. It was nothing but the clothes and shoes he'd had on the night he picked me up from the airport, but it felt like he was packing up to leave me for good.

His cell phone rang just as I was about to beg him not to leave. He reached in his pocket and pulled it out, looked at the screen and ignored the call.

"Go run to the bitch!" I flipped out. Choppa didn't respond, he just smiled at me tauntingly. "You ain't shit without me, nigga. I made you! My daddy put you on! You a fuck boy!"

The second those last words left my mouth I knew I had gone too far.

"What the fuck did you call me?" He dropped the clothes that were in his hands. In a few long strides he was across the room and in my face. His hand went around my throat and he literally lifted me off of my feet and slammed me up against the nearest wall. The impact felt like I was paralyzed.

I tried to scream but I couldn't breathe.

"Choppa! I—can't—breathe!"

"Fuck your breath, bitch! If you ever come out your dick sucking mouth at me like that again I'ma cut your head off and mail it to your daddy!" His mouth was twisted in anger.

"Let me go!" I cried.

He snarled at me then dropped me to the floor. I laid they're crying and gasping for air while he went to retrieve his clothes.

When he walked pass me on his way out of the door, I grabbed ahold of his ankles and tackled him to the floor. "No, baby, don't go! I'm sorry." I cried.

"Fuck off me!"

"No!" We were making so much noise I was surprised that hotel security hadn't been called.

He tossed me off of him, climbed to his feet and attempted to bounce again. But I was desperate to keep him there.

I hopped to my feet and dashed in front of him, blocking the door with my arms outstretched across the frame.

"KiKi move!"

"No! You've been with your bitch for three days! You're not leaving here. You're going to spend some time with me."

"A'ight. You think it's a game," he said calmly.

"No, muthafucka, *you* think it's a game!" I slung back.

Choppa shook his head then reached in his bag and pulled out his gun. He pointed it at me. "Get the fuck outta the way before I pierce your forehead."

I didn't fold though. Because losing him was the same as death to me, so I called his bluff. "Go ahead and pull the trigger because the only way you're leaving this room tonight is over my dead body." I swear love mixed with gin gave a bitch way too much courage.

Choppa seemed to be seriously contemplating shooting me, but a hard knock on the door intervened. He slid the gun back in his bag and told me to answer the door.

Being a hood chick I didn't have to be instructed on what to do. I grabbed a towel off of the wall rack nearby and quickly wiped the trace of blood off my face, and then I fingered combed my hair.

By the time I answered the door, Choppa was laid across the bed feigning sleep, and I was looking drunk but not beaten.

The security man asked if everything was okay.

"Yes." I gave him my best smile and sent his ass away. Daddy taught me to never snitch.

After closing the door behind the rent-a-cop, I went and sat on the bed where Choppa lay. His eyes were closed and he refused to open them and look at me no matter how much I apologized.

Before long he drifted off to sleep. On my way to the bathroom I noticed that he had left his cell phone on the table. I slid it into my hand and carried it with me in the bathroom.

Sitting on the toilet going through his text messages I saw proof of his infidelity. Tears streaked down my face and my anger returned two-fold.

I no longer had to pee!

I pulled my clothes back up and crept back into the bedroom. Quietly I went inside his bag and eased his gun out.

I made sure it had a loaded clip in it, took a deep breath and approached the bed. The nigga had the nerve to be sleeping like a baby, underestimating a bitch.

The text messages ran through my mind in vivid recall.

Yeah, this nigga is about to die!

I bent down and whispered in his ear sweetly. "Choppa, wake up, baby?"

I had to call his name three times before he stirred awake. And now I was standing up, directly over him.

"What's up?" he asked, stretching.

I pointed the gun down at him and clacked one in the chamber like Daddy had taught me.

"Who in the fuck is Julz?"

Chapter 21
Julz

After Choppa dropped me off at home, I immediately made my way over to Essence's house. A forty minute drive from my place had me pulling up to hers a little at 6 p.m.

I parked next to Precious' Grand Prix as I looked for Fat-Fat's Charger because she should have been there too but she wasn't there yet.

Since I was stopping over and the other girls stayed close by Essence, she decided to host a mid-week dinner gathering for us ladies and my gentleman.

I grabbed my gift bag and walked up her steps, ringing the doorbell once. Moments later, I saw Justus peer through the curtain, yelling that it was me and if he could let me in.

Seconds later, Essence swung the door open but Justus came from behind it, barging his way in front of her to get to me. He opened his arms wide and I dropped down to hug him.

"Hey, Mama!" He almost burst my eardrum.

"Hey, my prince." I kissed his fat jaws as he squeezed me as tightly as he could. "You must've really missed me, huh?"

"*Humph*! I see how you do me. It was all Auntie Essence this and Auntie Essence that but as soon as your ole stankin' ass mama come home, you don't know me, right?" Essence gave him the side eye and hugged me once I stood up.

"But that's my mama." Justus shrugged his shoulders.

"Mmhmm, I'ma remember that next time." Essence warned.

I turned him around so we could walk inside. "Justus, do you sense some hateration in this dancery?"

"Ye—" He attempted to answer.

"You better not." Essence curled her lips.

"Yea." He answered darefully, smirking.

"That's it!" Essence laughed as she took off behind him, chasing him indoors.

I locked the door and shook my head as I followed them into the kitchen. While they were wrestling, I couldn't help but notice how good it smelled.

"What you got cooking, sis?" I lifted a lid off of a pot before I noticed Precious sipping on a glass of wine at the table. "What's up, P?"

She nodded her head upward once and replied dryly. "The usual."

I wasn't even about to investigate her attitude because I was feeling too good from my getaway with Choppa just to come down from my high and entertain her mess.

Essence finally let go of my son and he came running over to me. She caught her breath and then answered. "*Whew*! Justus wanted smothered chicken, so I made that along with some rice, mac n cheese, corn bread, potato salad and green beans."

I looked down at him. "You was feeling like all of that?"

He shook his head up and down. "Yep and Auntie Essence is making a chocolate cake for dessert, too."

"And you say I spoil him. What you think you do?" I questioned the feast she prepared at his request.

"Trust me, I don't compare to the royal treatment you give him. You act like he's ya boy Hakeem, Prince of Zumunda from Coming to America."

"Ha! Ha! Ha! Well, he is the prince and one day he'll be king, so respect my mind."

"It's your world. I just pay rent to stay here." She threw her hands up.

"You're such an A-S-S." I spelled out, jokingly.

"Justus, why don't you finish watching Netflix in my room, so the adults can talk."

"Okay." He took off down the hall.

Once he disappeared, I turned toward Precious. "Speaking of adult, why were you talking sex around my baby?"

"Bitch, bye! I was talking to a nigga I know and he walked in on my conversation. You know your son's ears hustle harder than a ho tryna meet her quota for her pimp."

"Mmhmm, she gotta a point. Baby, don't miss shit." Essence co-signed and laughed too hard for my liking.

"Whatever! Just watch yo mouth when he's around, is all I ask." She fanned me off and I looked to Essence, pointing over my shoulder. "What crawled up her ass?"

"It's probably who didn't get in it. She hot 'cause the new dude she met last week ain't giving her no holla. But I told that bitch to keep ahold on her drawers."

"Who? Dougie or Nick?" I asked.

"Neither. Some nigga named Te'Darrel," replied Essence.

"Funny how you speaking on my shit like I ain't here." Precious scoffed.

"At least you know I'm no different behind yo back, then." Essence pointed out. "Anyway, what you got good, Julz? You know I'm anxious to know how your time was."

I lit up like the 4th of July just thinking back on it. "Well, before I run it. I got something for you." I reached into my pocket handed her a little monetary gratitude. "Choppa said *thank you.*"

She unfolded the money and counted off three bills. "Oh, I can't accept this, sis. You know I did that on the love."

"And that's why you have to keep it. We're showing love back."

Essence pooched out her bottom lip, softened her eyes and gave me a hug. I wrapped my arms around her, too.

"I love you, mama." She kissed my cheek.

"I love you, too." I kissed her back.

"Awww. You sure y'all two hoes ain't on the licky low?" Precious took a shot at us and chased it with another glass of wine.

We ignored her because we'd be all day if we addressed every slick thing to come out of her DSL's. "Oh, but I got something for you, too." I reached into the bag I carried inside. She couldn't help but smile, then.

"Well?" Essence became impatient.

"Hold up." I grabbed my phone and shot my boo a text since he was heavy on my top.

6:21 p.m. Julz: *Can't get you or New York off of my mind.*

"All right. Where do I start?" I asked facetiously but I knew I was going to tell it all.

I told them how we shopped in Soho. Walked the Brooklyn Bridge, took pictures of passing boats at the South Street Seaport, ate at the infamous Grimaldi's and had NY's best pizza on down to the sunset stroll we had at the Brooklyn Heights Promenade. I spoke briefly on our passionate love making because no matter the cool level with women, it was a must to be stingy with those details.

"Ahhh." Essence expressed yearning for the same attention from a man of her own. "I don't see how you not with him now. I know I would be."

"Gurrrlll, I wish! A bitch almost died when I watched him drive away earlier."

"You is boocoo retarded, for real." Essence retorted.

"But I'm being hella serious. You just don't know what it feels like to be in that man's arms." I closed my eyes sweetly but popped them open after hearing the first few words to come out of Precious' unfiltered mouth.

"Let me borrow him for a night or two so I can know what you know, if it's like that." Precious teased but I didn't find that shit funny.

"You can't have him, boo, but you can get these hands." I lifted them to my face so she could get a preview of the ass whoopin' I'd lay into her.

"Chill out. I was only playing." Precious defended her inappropriate comment.

"Well, bitch, we don't joke like that." Essence set the record straight.

There goes my babyyy... My ringtone went off and my pussy thumped to the beat.

I threw up a finger to my lips, telling Precious to mute it but she was going off on E. "Shut up, bitch! My phone ringing. Damn!"

As Usher belted so clearly, it was my baby calling. I cleared my throat while my lips took the usual shape of a smile. "Hello." I waited on his reply but what I heard instead was a gruff sound I couldn't quite make out. I raised the volume on my phone and spoke again. "Hello? Choppa?" A few seconds later, I heard a double beep, letting me know my call was disconnected.

Humph! I was about to call him but another call came through as I was. It was Fat-Fat.

"Hey, glad you answered since Essence wasn't picking up. Look, let her know that I won't make it tonight. I have mandatory overtime. I hope y'all not mad."

"Mad? Hell no. It's cool. Make that fetti, baby girl." I advised before hanging up the call. "Aye, that was Fat-Fat and she's stuck at work."

Precious picked up on her rant from where she left off. Pointing both of her fingers at us, she said, "Y'all hoes are gonna stop tryna boss a bitch like she done came from either one of y'all pussies, ya feel me. I ain't the one…"

We battled with her, like normal, up to the point that I didn't even want to call my baby back. I didn't want him hearing anything less than the joy in my voice that he brought me.

After thirty minutes of P getting everything off of her chest, she finally digressed and we were able to have dinner.

'Bout fuckin' time!

***

Choppa

After waking up staring down the barrel of my own gun, I had calmly talked KiKi into pointing it away from me before her drunk ass fucked around and bodied a nigga.

As soon as she lowered the banger, I was on her like white on rice! I had gripped her wrist with both hands and squeezed it until the Nine hit the floor. Luckily, her finger hadn't been inside the trigger guard or one of us would've had a hole in them.

I had her pinned to the floor with my knees on either side of her body and she was getting real buck, tryna toss me off of her. "Fuck is your problem, pointing that muthafucka at my head!"

"Whoever your bitch, Julz, is—that ho is my muthafuckin' problem!"

I looked down at her, bewildered. How could she know about Julz? I wondered, and then I immediately suspected Cardale or Jared because the snake is always someone close.

"Girl, you listening to the next nigga. You better take that fuck shit somewhere else. And don't be coming to me with nothin' a bitch nigga told you." I unstraddled her and rose to my feet.

The gun was a few feet away but closer to where I stood than to where KiKi lied. I saw her eyeing it like she wanted to scramble for it, so I quickly scooped it up, dislodged the clip and removed the bullet from the chamber. I put the banger in one pocket and the clip and the single bullet in the other.

I looked back down at KiKi and shook my head.

"You're sad, shorty. Real talk."

"Sad? Nigga, you're the one who's sad." She used the side of the bed to pull herself up on her feet and pounced right in my face. Her attitude was on one thousand! "Yo boys ain't tell me shit, loose dick muthafucka! Everything is right here in your phone. I read the text, you black, cheating, ungrateful ass, lowdown, dirty dog!"

She pulled my cell phone out of her shirt and held it up for me to see.

Damn, I thought. Now, shit is really about to hit the fan because KiKi had her pops wrapped around her finger. It wasn't that I was afraid of his wrath, I just didn't want to get cut off. My bank wasn't in shape for that. So I lied.

"See, you're stupid as fuck. I left my phone with my nigga while I was out of town. He must've been using it and that's probably one of his friends that text the phone." That shit sounded weak even to my own ears, but it was the best I could come up with on the spot.

KiKi was too game tight and suspicious to go for that, though. "Boy, you're a whole ass lie!" she spat. "I wish I was a man, I would knock you the fuck out for playing me like that."

"Believe what you want."

"Choppa, stop with the games. You're busted, baby boy. I'm about to call this Julz bitch and let her know I will fuck her all the way up over mines. Keep fucking with the ho and she gon' come up missing.

Trust and muthafuckin' believe!" KiKi turned her back to me and dialed a number.

I couldn't let her call my baby and fuck everything up. Hell no, it wasn't going down like that.

I heard the phone ringing as I rushed up to KiKi.

"Hello." *Oh shit! That's shorty's voice.*

KiKi was about to blow my spot up and have Julz thinking it was something that it wasn't. I dove and tackled her like a linebacker, knocking her down and causing the phone to fall from her grasp.

"Aww!" she shrieked.

"Hello? Choppa?" I heard Julz repeat.

I knew better than to pick up the phone and say anything or else KiKi would have started loud talking so Julz would hear her. So I just pressed the *end* button and the screen went black.

When I turned around, KiKi had a murderous look on her face. "You goddam ho!" she hissed.

Then she attacked.

I had to rough KiKi up a little just to prevent her from fuckin' me up fa real.

All the hood came out of her as we tussled around that room. When she was all out of breath and had no more buck in her, she sat on the floor crying as I gathered up my shit and bounced.

I drove out to the condo to chill alone and gather my thoughts. A nice long shower relaxed my muscles and my mind, and a fat blunt gave me clarity on what I needed to do.

I decided that it was time for me to explain everything to Julz because I didn't want to risk losing her if she found out about KiKi some other way. What Julz and I shared felt special, fuck destroying her trust by keeping secrets. I recalled something I read somewhere: *You gain trust in drops. You lose it in buckets.*

Yeah, I had to keep it a stack with shorty.

But that conversation would have to wait until tomorrow. She was probably still in an emotional high after our three day excursion in New York, no need to ruin it tonight.

Now that that was decided I finished my blunt, fixed myself some steak burritos, and made a few calls, checking on business, while I tore into my food like there was no tomorrow.

Cardale and Jared had sold the work I left with them, and a couple of other dudes I fucked with had money on deck for me.

But this one lil' nigga named School Boy from Decatur, who I had left some work with claimed he got robbed.

"So, what you saying, fam? You tryna tell me you ain't got nothing for me?" I asked, perturbed. He started stuttering and babbling so I cut him off. "I'll just get up with you tomorrow, bleed. Say no more."

I ended the call and lit another blunt. *Niggas always on that bullshit.* I finished the blunt then carried my plate and glass into the kitchen and put it in the dishwasher. I sat the timer then made my way to the bedroom, feeling tired as hell all of a sudden. Wrestling with KiKi had my muscles sorer than a mug.

Before going to bed I went back into the living room to get my cell phone. I was expecting an angry, threatening call from Cross at any minute, but the later it got the sleepier I became. It was after midnight and he hadn't called yet, so fuck him and his spoiled ass daughter.

I kicked both of them out of mind and started thinking about Julz. Shorty was everything that KiKi wasn't. I fell asleep counting the ways I was gonna show her how deep my love for her ran.

I slept past noon, something I rarely did.

When I woke up, I checked my phone and saw that I had thirty-five missed calls from KiKi and too many texts to count. I didn't bother responding to her. She was nothing but a headache.

But a smile spread across my face when I opened up a message from my boo.

Julz: 10:13 a.m.: *Good morning, bae. I love and miss you.*

Choppa: 12:17 p.m.: *Love and miss you too. Gotta handle some things so I won't come through until tomorrow but I'll call you later.*

Julz: 12:20 a.m.: ☹ *But I understand. Talk to you later baby.*

I started to text her that there was something I needed to speak with her about but I didn't want her to be at work worrying so I put it on hold.

Restraining Order

My phone rung with back to back calls from a private number. I knew it was KiKi tryna get me to answer the phone so I pressed *ignore* and went on about my business.

An hour later, I was in the streets collecting bread and hitting Cardale and Jared off with the last of the weed I had. After leaving them, I hit these Detroit niggas I knew off with some choppas and a half dozen semi-automatic handguns.

I took all the money over to Kim Marie's spot and stashed it in my safe. Shorty wasn't home so I was in and out in no time at all.

When I stepped outside, the sun was just beginning to close its eyes. The sky was fire red, what was known as an Indian summer. KiKi was still blowing up my line but she was the last thing on my mind. As I adjusted my rearview mirror to back out of the parking space, I saw the heavy scratch marks that crazy fool had left on my face.

"Fuck you!" I said and sent her ass to voicemail for the hundredth time that day.

Her time was over. From now on it was all about my Julz.

I turned on my sound system and headed to my shorty's crib. I had told her I wouldn't fall through but I decided to surprise her with my presence.

Ca$h & Coffee

Chapter 22
Julz

Being at work today was pure agony. After having spent the best three days of my life away from the hustle and bustle of the grind made me view my return to work for the slavery it truly was.

I rubbed my temples as I studied the hands on the clock, summoning 3:30 to come so I could leave.

Several grueling hours later, I was pulling up to my apartment with Justus at my side when I noticed Tyriq getting out of his car.

"Hey, Riq. What brings you by?" I tiptoed and gave him a hug.

"I was 'round yo way and decided to drop in on you since I ain't seen you in a hot minute." He then looked to Justus and held out his fist. "Hit that rock," Justus showed all teeth as they double touched fists the way Riq taught him. "You good, lil' man?"

"Yea, I'm good."

Tyriq looked at his watch and then to me. "I thought I would have caught you home and relaxed by now. But I ain't gon' hold ya, ya heard me. Get yo Calgon on and I'll get up with ya."

It was creepin' on seven o'clock and I was tired but not enough that I couldn't catch up with my round. "Nah, you don't have to roll out so fast. Come inside. Have dinner with us."

"A'ight. Cool."

"Uncle Riq, you gonna play with me?"

"Fo'sho. You know you my favorite lil' man next to my son."

Justus got excited and rushed up the steps.

As I pushed the door to my apartment open, I heard Riq whistle from behind me.

"What lick you hit? I see you done came up." He referred to my new furniture.

"Ha ha! I ain't 'bout that life." We walked into the kitchen. I pulled the ground meat out of the fridge, a skillet from the cabinet and continued. "This wonderful man I'm seeing surprised me with what you see as well as a new bedroom set."

"Man? When dat happen and what's this cat's name?"

Justus was right in the mix when I looked off to my side. "Baby, go in the room, put on Transformers and close the door while I talk with Riq."

"But he was gonna play with meee." He pouted in high pitch and threw his back against the wall.

"And he will but…"

"Hol' up, I got it." Tyriq stopped me. "Aye, what I told you boys don't do?" His face was firm.

Justus straightened up. "Complain."

"Right. What *are* they supposed to do instead?"

"Handle it quietly."

"A'ight. Well, do what ya mama say without all that feminine shit, ya heard me. I'll rock with you in a bit."

Justus bobbed his head and turned around to do as he was told.

"Thank you." I said to Riq.

"You good. Now back to my question." He wasted no time.

"Oh, well, we only been dating for a few weeks but he's the one." I cooed as I seasoned the meat now frying in the pan.

"What's homie's name?"

"Oh, it's Choppa."

"*Choppa*? What's dude's government?"

"Tavares. Tavares Lyons. Why? You know him or something?"

His brows drew inward, as if he was searching his mental rolodex for the answer. "Nah, I don't. But you fuckin' with a nigga named Choppa don't sit well with me."

"But you don't know him, so why are you judging? He's a good man, Riq, so forget his nickname. You'd like him if you met him."

"I know with a name like *Choppa* he ain't running for mayor. No doubt he earned his moniker by splitting wigs with dem AK 47's. But fuck all that, since when you started foolin' around with street dudes? That ain't yo get down."

"Riq, he's not what you think."

"Or maybe he's not what you think. Don't be naïve, love."

I had been a fool more times than I cared to admit but I took immediate offense to the words coming out of his mouth. "I'm not a duck. I know him well enough to know I've found a winner. Trust me."

176

"A winner like Marcel? You was certain about him once upon a time, too."

Was my friend trying to stab me in the heart?

"Wow, Tyriq. You really went there." Tears began to well in my eyes. I felt ambushed by his verbal assault.

I could see he regretted his words but there was no taking them back. I dropped my head the moment the tears came spilling from my eyes.

He lifted my head up. "My bad, love. I was out of pocket fah dat, ya heard me. Don't cry. I didn't mean to get on you like dat. I know this yo life. I just don't want you thinking you done struck gold only to take that nigga to get appraised and find out he ain't worth shit."

Wiping my eyes and sniffling from my nose, I stared at him dolefully. "If I'm wrong, I'll be wrong but I really don't think I am."

He used the base of his palms to swipe away the wetness on my cheeks. "Go wash your face, love. You too pretty to be crying."

I shook my head passively, gave him the spatula and took off down the hall.

Closing the door behind me, I headed to the sink. I splashed cool water over my face and then dried it off, looking at the woman staring back at me in the mirror.

Tyriq was only being Tyriq. He cares about you. So let this be. He'll meet Choppa one day and know, for himself, the type of man he is.

That gave me a piece of mind because I knew he'd like him for me once I introduced them and he saw how loving and respectful he was.

While in the bathroom, I heard my doorbell ring. I wasn't expecting anybody so I was curious as to who was at my door.

I yelled out loud enough for Tyriq to hear. "I'll get it!"

"A'ight." I heard him shoot back to me.

As I was halfway down the hall and near the door, I heard a knock. "Coming!" I sang. I leaned against the door and looked through the peephole. It was Choppa.

My heart began racing with joy that I'm sure spread to my face. I hurriedly unlocked the door. "Hey, bae." I beamed like a 1,000 watt bulb.

As he stepped inside, I reached to hug his neck but to my utter surprise he knocked my arms down and roughly moved me aside.

"What the fuck you got going on up in here?" His tone was hard and very accusatory, and his eyebrows were a straight line as he eyed Riq stepping out of the kitchen and taking a leisurely seat on the sofa.

"Oh, baby, it's nothing like that?" I quickly explained after picking up on what he must've thought. "Tyriq is my homeboy and one of my closest friends."

"Julz, do I look stupid? What the fuck another nigga doing up in my woman's house?"

"Choppa, you're kidding, right?" I searched his face for any sign of playfulness but there was none. Flummoxed, I look from him to Tyriq. "Riq, this is my man, Choppa. Will you please tell him that we're only friends and nothing more?"

I knew that normally Riq wasn't for explaining anything to another man, but my eyes begged with him to make an exception.

He shook his head in dismay but did as I asked.

Rising to his feet, he looked at Choppa. "Son, it ain't nothing like you're thinking. Julz is like my sister, ya heard me."

I was praying that the truth sufficed because the steam coming off of Choppa's gaze was incendiary. His lips curled and his jaw twitched and then things seemed to happen in slow motion.

Choppa's hand went to his waist and up under his shirt. When it reappeared, he was holding a black gun. His arm rose as he stepped toward Riq and placed the nose of the weapon under his eye. "Nigga, did I ask you anything!" he said.

"Noooo!" I ran over and grabbed Choppa's arm. "Please, baby! Please, don't shoot him!" I screamed.

"Don't beg that nigga fah my life. Let him pull the mu'fuckin' trigger," Riq said bravely.

"You think I won't? Nigga, I'll murder your ass right muthafuckin' here!" Choppa gritted.

"No, baby! Nooo!" I was crying and pulling on his arm.

178

Choppa tried to shake me off of him but my grip was a desperately strong one. In the tussle, we both stumbled back and fell over a chair. I tried to hold him down so that he couldn't get up and shoot my round.

"Fuck off of me!" He growled menacingly.

"Run, Riq!" I shouted.

Riq's laugh reached us on the floor.

"Fuck I'ma run fah? You need to be telling your nigga that," he replied coolly.

Choppa rolled me off of him and stood up. I hopped to my feet a second later and then I saw why Riq didn't seem fazed. He was standing there with his own gun aimed at Choppa's chest.

"Riq, noooo!" I cried.

He grilled Choppa hard. "I ain't nevah ran from a nigga, ya heard me. Let's make these thangs pop."

I was shaking so bad I could hardly remain standing. I screamed for them to both put their guns down but neither of them paid me any mind.

"Make it pop then, fam," challenged Choppa.

Oh, my God! They're about to kill each other over nothing!

I half covered my crying eyes and screamed.

It was at that moment I heard my child's voice. "Mama!" He cried out for me, cautiously walking toward the brewing hurricane.

"Justus, go back in the room. Now!" I pointed to the bedroom but he didn't move. He was frozen with curiosity. I turned my attention back to Riq and Choppa. "Please, I'm beggin' y'all don't do this. Not in front my son. Please." I reached out to touch Choppa's arm to appeal to his sensible side but he stiffly jerked away from me.

"Fuck off me!" His scowl was so intimidating it forced my heart to drop to the base of my stomach. But at least, he lowered his gun. Still grimacing at me, he said, "You know what, shorty, you can have that muthafucka. I'm out!" He turned to Riq. "I'ma see you around."

"I ain't hard to find," Riq shot back.

Choppa turned back to me and I swear it looked like he wanted to spit in my face. I was hurt and mad as hell but I didn't want him to leave thinking I had tried to creep on him.

179

"Baby, please listen to me." I made one last attempt. But he shot it down cruelly.

"I'm not your baby. Ya baby is that nigga over there whose dick you probably been sucking."

My chin dropped to the floor and a fresh flood of tears that came deep from my heart poured down my face as he opened the door and walked out of my life.

***

Julz

I made my way outside to chase Choppa down. I couldn't have him leave with the wrong thought in his head.

"Choppa!" My voice cracked as I yelled out behind him, but he refused to look back as he angrily got into his car.

I attempted to run after him but I was jolted backwards. Tyriq yanked me by the arm, pulling me inside of the house and slamming my door as he jumped in my shit.

He had me hemmed up by both of my arms as he shook me slightly. "Julz! Don't go after that muthafucka. Have you lost your mind?" His tone was hard and reprimanding.

"Tyriq, let me go!" I bawled so hard my words came out in hiccups.

"Mama! Uncle Riq!" My baby pleaded as he called our names.

Our heads snapped over to Justus, who was now crying along with me. I felt immediate shame. My head dropped low when I saw the petrified look on my son's face.

Tyriq released me and I dropped down to my knees and opened my arms. "Come here, baby."

Justus ran over to me and I cried even harder than before. I couldn't believe what just happened and that my child had to witness it.

"It's all right, baby." I consoled him moments before I stood to my feet and lifted him up in my arms, cradling his head firmly against the side of my face. I then turned to face Tyriq. "I think you should go."

"I don't think I should. I don't trust that nigga."

My head was pounding. My God, I knew there was much to learn about Choppa but never would I have expected for him to jump out the bag on me. He didn't even give me a chance to explain before he flipped.

I figured he felt threatened, as I would had, walking in on us and thought the worst. *But to pull a gun out? I didn't even know he carried.*

Well, what I knew was I had to make things right and I couldn't do that with Tyriq over.

I shook my head *no* and walked over to the door. "Please, just go. I'm gonna take care of my boy and pull myself together."

"Julz." He was about to protest but I stopped him.

"Just go!" My words were sharp. I didn't want my wishes to be challenged.

He stared at me like he was losing respect for me by the second and I wanted to shrink into my shell because of it.

"A'ight, but if he come back, don't open yo door. I ain't fuckin' around, ya heard me."

I shook my head, hurriedly. I heard him talking but I wasn't paying him any attention. Choppa spazzed out and he was wrong as hell for it but I knew he wouldn't hurt me. "Okay." I walked up on him, further urging him to leave.

"Look here, I'm gon' call you. You better answer or I'ma come through and get it poppin'."

I shook my head side to side woefully but promised I would answer because what I knew was he didn't talk just to hear himself speak.

"Take care of ya moms, lil' man. I'll be back to check on y'all, so don't trip nothing."

Justus turned his head to look at him. "All right." He sounded unsure in his response, then he turned his head back to rest it in the crook of my neck.

Tyriq looked at me again and then pulled his gun from his waist and dropped it to his side as he carefully scanned the lot for Choppa.

I couldn't believe that my man and my best friend were at war over nothing!

Satisfied that there was no sign of Choppa, he headed out but not before ordering me to lock up.

I did as he asked but I quickly rushed to my phone. I sat down on my sofa with Justus straddled across my lap. Rubbing his back in a circular motion, letting him know things were all right without me explaining a word.

I then dialed Choppa's phone.

Voicemail.

I called again.

Voicemail.

Frustrated because I knew he was ignoring me, I tossed my phone to the side and buried my head into my son's shoulders, silently sobbing over how fucked up everything was.

Chapter 23
Choppa

Parked around the corner from Julz' apartment, I let the front windows of my car down to get some fresh air. That shit I walked in on had stirred something in me that had me thinking reckless as fuck. And that nigga had tested my gangsta. *That was something that couldn't be tolerated.*

As for Julz, shorty had fooled the fuck out of me, pretending to be one way but turning out to be a slut in disguise. We hadn't been home from our trip but two days and already she was about to let the next nigga run up in her! Had him sitting on the couch I bought her with money that came from doing shit that put my life and freedom at risk.

That's why you can't be good to no woman. All of them ain't shit but some grimy ass bitches who have no love and loyalty in their scandalous hearts! They'll fuck ten different niggas and suck a hundred different dicks in the same week!

A nigga could give them the world on a muthafuckin' silver platter but as soon as he turned his head, they'd lie on their back for another man. Julz was no different than all of the slimy broads I had encountered in my life, from the bitch that adopted and raised me to KiKi's trifling ass.

When I was pulling off from her spot, I saw the punk bitch tryna run after me. Had she came, perhaps it would've given her claim to be *nothing but friends* with ol' boy some validity. But, nah, she let him stop her. So, he had to be fuckin' her.

Penny ante ass bitch!

Let him close the door like he was running something up in there. And he probably was! Prolly had her in the buck at this very moment.

Visions of Ms. Tonie, my adoptive mother flashed in my mind.

"Tavares, go outside and play in the yard, baby. Me and Mr. Childs have grownup business to discuss."

As soon as I stepped outside, the door would slam behind me and I would be locked out for hours at a time.

The men's names changed daily but almost every day it would be the same routine. I was only five years old when Ms. Tonie adopted me and a short while later the routine began.

At seven years old, I became curious as to what grownup business she had to talk to all these different men was about. So I asked the lady who lived across the street.

"Baby," she said, "Tonie ain't in there talking. She's in there tricking. And she not getting paid nothing but a few dollars either! That's the worse kinda ho." She took a sip of the wine that sat on a table next to the porch swing where she sat for hours every day watching everything and everybody.

"Ms. Sharon, what's tricking?" I twiddled my thumbs.

"Boy, you sho is slow." She burst out in laughter. "Here, grab that chair right there," she pointed, "and go put it up against the house so you can stand on it and look in her bedroom window. When you come back you'll know what tricking means." Again she laughed heartily.

I took my curious lil' ass back across the street and did what Ms. Sharon said. I propped the chair up under Ms. Tonie's bedroom window, climbed up on it and pressed my face to the glass.

Ms. Tonie was on her hands and knees hollering, "Fuck me. Yes, long stroke this pussy, daddy! Beat the walls down with that big dick!"

The man had something long and black in her. At first, I thought it was, like, a policeman's billyclub, until he pulled it out and I realized that it was his johnson.

I stood on my tippy toes when Ms. Tonie took his thing in her mouth and started bobbing her head up and down. The chair titled back and I crashed to the ground on my butt.

I hurried and hopped up before they looked out of the window and busted me, but I had seen what tricking was and a few minutes later, Ms. Sharon explained to me that only hoes tricked.

"And Tonie is the biggest ho in the whole neighborhood," she said.

And all the shit that went on in our house while I was growing up proved Ms. Sharon right. I came to despise my adoptive mother with an intensity that bordered on pathological. Any chick that showed the slightest sign of being a ho repulsed me.

I had never expected anything like that from Julz, though, and that's why my head was so fucked up right now. She had played me for a mark!

My head began pounding so hard I had to rest it against the steering wheel until the pain subsided some.

Shorty and that nigga gotta pay for playing me, I decided.

I lifted my head, put my car in gear and headed back to her apartment. When I got there, I parked several units down from her door. The sky had darkened enough to allow me to blend into the shadows.

Just when I was about to get out of the car and creep toward Julz' apartment, I saw the headlights of a car coming toward me. I slid low in my seat but I was still able to see the driver when the car passed by.

There that nigga go!

A devious smile spread across my face as I started my engine, backed out of the parking space and discreetly followed him.

Like you said, homie, you ain't hard to find.

I placed my banger on my lap and maintained a safe distance behind him. As soon as the opportunity presented itself, I was gonna hop out and light his ass up. Let's see if Julz could creep with a corpse!

***

I had followed many unsuspecting dudes home and crushed them, so it was nothing for me to tail this lame without being detected. I kept my eyes on his taillights while making sure I always stayed a couple of cars back. He hopped on I-285 North and quickly maneuvered his white Corvette into the fast lane.

I increased the speed of my car and jumped into the left lane, too. There were two cars between us but the bright color of his whip made it much easier to keep track of him.

Nearing the Flat Shoals exit, he switched lanes and decreased his speed. I noticed him in time to follow without making it obvious. And when he exited just like I had anticipated, I made the move with ease but now there was no cars between us.

I was sure the nigga didn't know what type of whip I was pushing so I wasn't worried about him being alerted. Instead, I patted the banger on my lap and grinned wickedly.

As I proceeded down the exit ramp and into normal traffic, I heard my cell phone ringing in my pocket. I was tempted to answer the call to see if it was Julz but I had to keep my mind on the mission.

Ole boy made my job easier when he pulled into a drive-thru. *The only thing you gon' eat, bitch nigga is gon' be some lead*, I told myself as I turned into the same parking lot.

I pulled up behind him in the driver-thru line. Two cars were in front of him and I had that ass boxed in from behind.

As I eased my ratchet off of my lap and reached for the door, for some strange reason a verse from Shyne, my all-time favorite rapper, came to mind.

Lost my conscience somewhere in between
Watchin' niggaz die and leavin' the murder scene
Hot gun in my waist
Stockin' over my face
And I tell you niggaz this, I never miss, check it
My point of view is me or you
And I'ma burn anyway, what the fuck?
Bust seventeen shots up in your guts

I was halfway out of the car now, gun down at my side, murder on my mind but the sound of a car pulling into the lot got my attention. A quick look over my left shoulder alerted me to danger! A few seconds later, a police cruiser pulled up behind me in the drive-thru.

"Fuck!" I gritted as I hopped back inside my ride and eased the passenger door closed.

Like always, whenever *one time* got behind me, I became a little nervous. I didn't have nothing on me but a half ounce of weed and a gun, but I couldn't recall if I had ever used the toolie in a murder or not.

My palms felt sweaty but I forced myself to act normal. The car ahead of me moved up so it was my turn to place an order. I lowered my window and order the first thing that came to mind.

"Give me a chicken sandwich and some fries, and a large Coke."

The worker inside thanked me for my order and I inched closer toward the cashier's window. My phone was ringing persistently in my pocket. I knew it was Julz calling but I had nothing to say to that woman so I let each call go to voicemail.

Each time she called, I mentally heard her plead for me to answer but I just ignored her.

Up ahead, he drove off after retrieving his food. As far as I could tell, he still hadn't spotted me.

Bruh, you better thank your lucky stars 'cause that ass was mine had the rollers not showed up on the scene.

A minute or so later, I drove away from the drive-thru with my food on the seat next to me but the bastard was nowhere in sight, which had me heated.

I looked at the food with a snarl on my face. I didn't want no burgers and fries! I wanted to eat that nigga's face but Julz' lil' side piece had disappeared.

A mile or two away from Wendy's, I grabbed the bag of food and slung it out of the window. Her nigga had gotten away but somebody had to die tonight to feed the animal that raged within.

I jumped back on the interstate, headed south this time, to pay a late night visit to a fool who obviously didn't know that fucking with me was the quickest way to be reunited with his dead homies.

Ca$h & Coffee

Chapter 24
Choppa

It was after 3:00 a.m. when I made it to the hotel room where KiKi was still staying. I chose to go there instead of to the stash house because I had a change of mind about her.

Convinced by Julz' actions that all females would do some ho shit, I decided to rock with KiKi because at least her ho moment had occurred before our time. Besides, I believed if it ever came down to it, KiKi would die for me or get on the stand and lie for me. That had to count for something.

I didn't have a door key anymore so I had to knock. I waited a few minutes then I heard her soft footsteps getting closer. She disengaged the lock and opened the door. We stood looking at each other, without uttering a word, for a few brief seconds.

Tonight she was the proverbial sight for sore eyes. She had on a simple white t-shirt that showed the outlines of her 38C's, flared out with her wide hips and it stopped mid-thigh, leaving her long caramel toned legs on full display. Her hair was pinned on top of her head in a bun and her lips looked suckable. She looked inviting and if I had awakened her out of her sleep, she was doing a great job of hiding it.

"Sup, can I come in?"

"Of course. You don't have to ask that." She stepped to the side and allowed me to enter before closing and locking the door behind me.

I walked toward the bedroom area of the suite which was illuminated by the television and the bedside lamp.

When I turned around, KiKi was studying me hard. "So, what made you come back?" she asked. But before I could answer, she observed, "Choppa, there's blood all over your clothes. Oh my god! Are you alright, baby?"

"I'm good but that nigga ain't." I pulled my shirt over my head and tossed it on the floor.

"Who? Cardale or Jared?" She looked alarmed.

"Nah, it ain't either one of them. Why did you think that, you know something about them that I don't?" I pierced her eyes with mine and waited for her response.

I had a few more hours before dawn. If one of them had violated, I could easily go back out and slay another fool tonight.

"No, Choppa, neither of them has violated. I don't know why they were the first names to come to mind. But like Daddy always says, it's the ones closest to you that gets the first bullet."

"True life," I agreed as I headed to the shower to wash that chump's blood off of me. Tomorrow I would get rid of the clothes.

In the bathroom, I stripped down to nothing and stepped into the shower. I turned the water up to almost scalding to help wash away all traces of homeboy's DNA. I lathered up from head to toe, rinsed off and then repeated it twice more.

KiKi pulled back the shower curtain. "Clean under your fingernails."

"Yeah. Good looking out." I thanked her. Cross had schooled her well. When I stepped out of the shower, she handed me a towel.

"Okay, now who was it?" she asked.

"Not anyone you know. Just a lil' punk who tried me at the wrong time. It's best you don't know his name because what you don't know can't hurt you or me." I walked into the bedroom with the towel wrapped around my waist.

When I sat down on the bed, I saw that KiKi was carrying my blood stained jeans. She tossed them on top of the soiled shirt. "You better get rid of these," she said.

I nodded that I indeed planned to do that. But at the moment I needed a change of clothes to put on, I told her.

"Let me throw on something right fast and go find a Wal-Mart," she volunteered.

Normally, I wouldn't be caught dead rocking Wal-Mart gear but it was either that or leave out of the hotel butt ass naked in the morning.

While KiKi was at the store I laid back on the bed, blazed a blunt, and relived the whole day. Fuck School Boy, bodying him was nothin', the shit with Julz was what still had me heated. I had thought for sure she was wife material.

As hot as I was, I was still tempted to call her but I didn't. She had proven that she couldn't be trusted, so what was the point? I reasoned.

Restraining Order

I couldn't even lie, I was hurt because we had clicked so well. Now all of that was over. The memories we'd made in New York was erased by the dirty shit she did tonight. I didn't understand how a woman could seem so in love one minute and the next, she be climbing up on some other dude's wood.

It was all good, though. *From now on I'm a just fuck 'em and leave 'em, stack my paper and love my mu'fuckin' self,* I vowed.

By the time KiKi returned I was on my third blunt and I had been chasing the loud with Hen Dog. She came into the room with an arm full of bags and set them on the other bed.

"You wanna see what I bought you?" she asked.

"Let me do that in the morning, I'm tired as hell right now. Aye, but did you get me some boxers." I set up and put out the last of the blunt.

"Boy, you ain't even gotta ask me that. You can act like your ass don't remember but I always know what you need. There ain't a bitch in the world that can hold you down like me." She pulled several pair of boxers out of the bag for me to choose from.

"Let me get the black pair. Them shits fit my mood." I reached for the Haynes but KiKi slapped my hand away.

"No, just lay back and let me take care of you like I used to."

I was too tired to argue so I laid back and allowed her to slide my boxers on. Of course, KiKi had other shit on her mind.

I felt her soft hands rubbing all over my body. They traveled over my six pack, up to my chest and then back down to my swelling rod.

"What you doing, girl?" I put my hand on top of hers to stop her.

"I'm about to get some of *my* dick." Her voice was as sultry as sin.

"Nah, playgirl, you know we ain't rocking like that no more."

"C'mon, Choppa, quit being stingy. Fuck that other bitch, she ain't KiKi." She bent her head down and ran her tongue around the tip of my meat.

I tried to scoot up to get away from her but she just moved up with me. "Stop! You know I don't like that shit!" I reminded her.

"I 'ont give a fuck. I'm sucking this dick tonight." She covered the head with her mouth and rubbed my balls with her hand.

The shit felt good and bad, and KiKi knew why but she didn't stop. I wanted to push her off of me but, at the same time, I wanted to let her finish. A nigga needed a nut to forget about the bullshit that had popped off with Julz.

"You like how I suck your big, black dick?" she asked, taking it out of her mouth and jacking it off with her hand.

"Humph!" I grunted.

"Oh, you wanna act like that? I'm about to make you nut in my mouth. I ain't playing, you gon' give me those seeds." She dripped spit on my pole and slurped it up noisily. Her mouth felt like a dripping wet pussy and the longer she worked her oral skills on me the harder it was to resist her.

My eyes were squeezed shut and my toes were curled. Both of my hands gripped the comforter and my legs began to shake. KiKi was a real headmaster, true to her game.

A myriad of images flashed in my mind. First, the video where she did this same shit to six different niggas. Then an image of Ms. Tonie entered the frame.

I felt myself about to throw up.

"Ugh! Ugh!" I coughed.

"Nut in my mouth, daddy." KiKi coaxed. I wondered how she could speak so clearly with 8 inches of beef down her throat. "C'mon, bae, bust that nut."

My legs locked up at the sound of *bae*. That was what Julz was fond of calling me. "Stop! Get off of me." I snapped, tryna push KiKi away.

"Hell no! Not this time," she bucked.

I reached down and pried her off of me. "I told yo ass *no!*" I said, snatching my shit outta her mouth.

"Ughhhhh! What the fuck is wrong with you, dude? Let me find out you done turned homo!" She stood up and stared at me with her hands on her hips.

I laid back on the pillow with my hands behind my head and laughed. "Nah, playgirl, never dat. You know how I feel about getting head. But, anyway, you're pushing too hard. Give me some time to work this shit out in my own mind. When, and if, I can get past the images in my head we'll be a'ight, you feel me?"

"What the fuck ever, Choppa! All I know is that a bitch pussy gon' have crickets in it waiting for you to get over that dumb shit. Fuck it, I'm going to bed and play with my own stuff!" She walked over to the other side of the room in a huff.

"Turn the lights off. I don't wanna see that shit." I laughed.

"Fuck you!"

"Fa real, though, lil' mama, let's call a truce to the beefing we've been doing. I'm about to refocus on my grind and I don't need any static between us. Tomorrow we're going furniture shopping for the house. The agent hit me up the other day and said everything is ready."

"Yay," she said dryly.

"Oh, you not happy? You must like living in a hotel room?"

"Happy? If you wanna make me happy come beat this kitty up."

"Nah, I'm good. Goodnight. I'll holla in the a.m." I reached over and turned off the lamp.

"I know one thing for sure and two things for certain," KiKi's voice carried over to me, "if you ain't fucking me, your ass fucking some other ho."

Yeah, you're right and ho is the operative word. But never again, I promised myself as I closed my eyes and welcomed sleep.

Chapter 25
Julz

Two weeks had passed since the ordeal and Choppa still hadn't called, text or answered my phone calls.

In front of Justus, I put on a happy face but when I was alone in my room, all I did was hug my pillow and cry.

The only reason I went to work was because I had to or bills would pile up and suffocate me, but I was sure my performance was terrible. My co-workers could tell that there was something bothering me but when they asked I denied having any problems.

As soon as my workday ended, I picked Justus up from daycare, performed my motherly duties as best I could with a broken heart. And once Justus was in bed for the night I stayed up crying and staring at my phone praying Choppa would call.

I couldn't sleep or eat and every song that came on the radio reminded me of the love I had lost over nothing.

I couldn't concentrate long enough to do any school work so I tried to read to keep my mind off of Choppa, but that didn't work either. I found myself staring blankly at the screen of my Kindle Fire reminiscing about our first kiss, the laughs we shared and the dreams of a future with him that I had conjured in my mind during our weekend in New York.

My phone rang, startling me off of the one track I was on. I was initially hopeful it was him but I grimaced instantly when I didn't hear Usher's ringtone.

Allowing the call to go to voicemail, I then began going through the several pictures of he and I in my phone's gallery and started to crawl deeper into my depression.

Damn, I missed him so much. Didn't he know the silent treatment was killing me slowly?

Since the day he left, it felt like a dagger was lodged permanently in my chest, preventing me from breathing easy.

Please come back and take away the pain, I looked up to the ceiling with two streaming rivers flowing from each side of my eyes.

My phone started ringing again. I was really becoming irritated by the incessant calls from people I didn't want to hear from. All I wanted to do was mope in peace.

If I hadn't been so obsessed with not wanting to miss Choppa's call, that I prayed would come soon, I would had been turned my phone off.

Essence hung up but she called me *again*. I rolled my eyes, threw my head back and let out a gruff sound. I was not in the right frame of mind to be holding a conversation but I didn't want to snub her reaching out to me, so I answered.

"Hello," I spoke flatly. My broken spirit was the very first thing she detected.

"Julz, you're still over there crying?" I couldn't gauge whether she pitied me or found me pathetic but at this point, how she felt about me didn't really matter.

"Nah, I'm jumping for joy." My voice quaked and then I questioned sarcastically. "What you think?"

"I *think* you've spent enough time boo-hooing over that bi-polar muthafucka! Sure, he wooed you. Hell, he wooed me, too, but that doesn't give him a pass to click the fuck out and endanger not just your life but Tyriq's *anddd* your son's. He could have killed all of y'all that day. Think you can stop crying long enough to think about that?"

I sucked my teeth. "But he didn't."

"But he could have, is my point."

I knew she was enforcing the sister code and speaking the raw truth but like I said, the way I was feeling, nothing mattered. So, in a feeble attempt to shield some of the heat from off of Choppa, I deflected things on her.

"How many times have you, yourself, went off the deep end and did something unnecessary all over looks that were deceiving?"

"Really, Julz? A'ight. When I thought my ex was cheating on me, yea, I ransacked his house and even bust the windows out his car *but* I didn't try to take that same bat to his head. In my moment of anger, I didn't threaten his life."

"But the point is…"

"Bitch, you have no point." I could hear that she was bristling now. "You haven't known that man but a hot minute. Fuck him and the horse he rode in on. If you ask me, it's his loss," Essence tried to get me to see it her way.

"I'm not like you. I can't just let go like that. When I care about a person, I want to do everything I can to make it work. I don't like going from man to man," I explained.

"It's not that at all, your ass done got dick whipped," she said, but nothing that ever came out of her mouth was further from the truth.

I wasn't addicted to Choppa's sex. Yes, he knew how to please me in bed but it was his gentleness and his thoughtfulness that had seized my heart. I could tell that he was a hard ass in the streets but with me he was a true sweetheart.

All I had to do was look around my apartment and there was proof of his kindness in every room. In every conversation we'd ever had, I could tell that his feelings for me were sincere, and that's why I just couldn't give up.

"Mamaaaa!" Justus called out in duress. I bolted off of the sofa to go check on him.

"Let me call you back." I hung up in the middle of her talking not knowing whether she heard me or not.

I then rushed into the bedroom, cutting on the light. "You're okay, baby. Mama's right here." I sat alongside him and rested his head in my lap as I tenderly stroked the side of his face.

For the past weeks, he'd been waking up in a panic if he didn't feel me beside him.

I faked like I wasn't in withering pain just to ensure he'd feel at ease and fall back to sleep, which he did in a matter of minutes.

After easing off of the bed and kissing him on the forehead, pulling the cover up to his chin, I went back in the living room and curled up on the sofa.

I picked my phone up, hoping that just maybe Choppa had text me but the only notifications I had were from Facebook.

Dejected, I decided to send Choppa a text.

10:01 p.m. Julz: *Bae please call me. I just want to know that you're okay.*

I waited fifteen minutes for him to respond but, again, nothing.

Tears began to well up in my eyes. *Damn! Just give me a chance to explain!* I screamed silently.

Then, it felt like I was going to throw up. I ran to the bathroom and bent over the toilet, dry heaving because there was nothing in my stomach to vomit.

Not being able to talk to Choppa was driving me insane and making me physically ill. My head felt light and my stomach contracted painfully. I stood up and staggered over to the sink, where I managed to splash cold water on my face.

After a minute or so, I felt better. I brushed my teeth and rinsed my mouth and then made my way back to the living room.

I sat and pondered on a way to get Choppa to talk to me, to hear me out because I couldn't go on like this.

I called Essence back on her house phone, like I said I would but it wasn't so I could hear her snap off on my man but to get her to help me make all of this right.

She answered in half of a ring. "Why'd you hang up?"

"I didn't. I had to check on Justus. Look," I got straight to it, "I know how you feel about Choppa and I don't blame you for your concern but I need you to do me a favor and call him on three-way."

"I think not." She didn't give it a second thought.

"E, this ain't about you. It's about me and I *need* to talk to him and since he isn't answering my calls, I want to see if he'll answer yours. Now if he answers, I need you to see if he'd be willing to talk to me. Tell him how everything was a huge misunderstanding and all I want is a chance to explain it." I was desperate and willing to try anything to make the nauseous, upset feeling go away. "Please, E. Please."

"Why do you care about making it right with him? Tell me that."

The answer was simple. "I'm in love."

She went on mute for what felt like forever but then I heard her exhale exhaustedly. "All right. What's his number?"

I wasted no time calling it out to her. "It's 404…"

While E clicked over to dial Choppa's number my heart beat fast. It felt like I was close to having an anxiety attack. "Okay, it's ringing," she came back on the line. "If he answers, don't say anything. Just let me do the talking."

"All right," I replied on short breath. *Lord, please, let him answer his phone.* I put my hand to my chest and took a deep, nervous breath.

By the time the phone rang three times, I couldn't take the agony anymore. I opened my mouth to tell Essence to hang up but, then, by the grace of God, Choppa answered.

"Who is this?" His voice was penicillin for my soul. E came in on cue.

"Hi, Choppa, this is Essence, Julz' friend that you met at the club. Do you remember me?"

"Yeah, ma, I know who you are. Sup?"

"Well, um, I'm calling on my girl's behalf because you won't answer her calls."

Choppa chuckled. "I most definitely won't! I ain't got no holla fa her no more. Tell her to hit that nigga up who she was chilling wit'."

I wanted to jump in and set the record straight but I didn't want him to hang up as soon as he heard my voice, so I reached over, grabbed the throw pillow on the couch and bit down on it to keep myself from speaking.

Essence defended me well, though. "Wait a second!" she said sharply. "Tyriq and Julz are nothing more than platonic friends from way back, plus that man has a woman. Besides, I know for a fact that you're the only man my girl wants."

Again, he chuckled. "I hear you but you ain't saying nothin'. I saw what I saw. See, your people never expected me to come through her spot that day. Humph! Yeah, her ass was tryna creep."

His continued accusation broke my heart. I had never been a cheater, and I loved him too much to do anything like that to him, especially with Riq.

As if she could read my thoughts, Essence said, "Choppa, I know you don't really know me but I wouldn't lie for her. Julz is a good woman and she would never do anything like what you're suggesting. I think you should call her and give her a chance to explain."

"Naw, I'm good on shorty. You're a good friend for calling for her but ain't nothin' changed. I'ma count my losses and keep it moving.

Tell ya girl I said have a nice life." His tone sounded so final, I panicked.

"Baby, please don't do this!" I cut in. "I swear it wasn't what you think. Please, Choppa, I love you!"

For a minute the phone went quiet, causing me to think he hung up. My heart stopped and I let out a small cry, not caring if my bestie thought I was pitiful.

It was only when he spoke again that my heart restarted.

"Oh, you on the phone, huh, shorty? Y'all played a nigga." His words weren't pleasant but at least he had something to say to me. *And he still called me shorty.*

"Baby, I'm sorry but I was desperate. I've just been missing you so bad and all for what? A big misunderstanding? I can even call Tyriq up right now and let you and him talk. He can assure you there's nothing going on between us."

"What? Fuck I got to say to another nigga?"

"Okay, I'm sorry if that offended you but I just want to prove to you that I'm being honest."

"Um, why don't I get off the phone and let y'all talk," Essence interjected.

"Nah, ma, you ain't gotta get off no phone. What I'ma say ain't no secret. And you need to hear this, too, in case you ever encounter a real nigga, you'll understand the rules."

"Uh, no disrespect but there's nothing I need to hear. Maybe Julz care to hear it but I've heard enough," Essence replied with distaste, then she said to me, "Julz, I'ma set the phone down. Just call me back when you're done."

"Okay," I gave her a second to set the phone down, then I began pleading and begging for Choppa to hear me out. "If you don't want to do that, just give me the benefit of the doubt. Please," I pled.

"Julz, I'ma tell you like this—"

"Oh, it's *Julz* now, not shorty?" I cut him off, trying to appeal to the affectionate side of him.

"Julz? Shorty? It don't matter how I address you. What I'm 'bout to say still gon' be the same. Understand this: I'm a real nigga, a boss. I don't tolerate shit from a woman that involves another man. Nothing.

200

Nada! If there's any question as to who you belong to, then you belong to the next nigga. Because what's mine is never in question."

"But it's not in question, bae. I'm all yours." I lowered my voice for optimum effect. When he didn't shut me down, I pressed on. "Choppa, don't you trust me?"

"Imagine that!" He scoffed.

"Why not, baby? What have I done to lose your trust?" I was perplexed and hurt that he could see me as some grimy chick that wasn't principled. "Answer me, bae, because I would really like to know."

Choppa didn't answer my question, not directly. Instead, he stated, "Whether you were creeping or not don't really matter. See, in my world, the appearance of an impropriety is just as damning as the actual act."

"But that's not fair, bae. Suppose I saw you—"

"This ain't fuckin' about me!" He shut me down hard. "Anyway, I'm tired of talking and I got moves to make. Don't call me again!"

"Choppa, wait!" I pressed the phone to my ear to listen for his breath, hoping he didn't hang up. "Choppa? Choppppaaaa!" I held on a little longer until I was convinced he was truly gone.

I then fell lifelessly onto my sofa and balled into a fetal position, whimpering as my chest and stomach muscles rapidly jumped up and down at the pace of my cry.

If only he could see how us not being together was tearing me up, he'd know I'd never betray him. Not for Tyriq, not for Marcel, not for anybody.

As my tears stained the cushion beneath me, I felt myself slipping into an inconsolable place, where all I'd want to do was sleep and sulk.

Thankful that tomorrow was Saturday, I'd be able to do just that.

I called Essence back and told her to be at my house first thing in the morning to pick up Justus. I was no good to him like I was and I needed uninterrupted time to grieve the way things were.

She agreed without any speeches and we hung up shortly after.

I was so mentally drained. I thought to drag myself to bed but I was void of all physical energy, too, so I remained where I'd been for the last couple of hours and cried myself to sleep.

Ca$h & Coffee

Chapter 26
Choppa

"Dang, who was that? You gave her the business," remarked Kim Marie.

"Never mind who I was talking to, finish telling me about this little knucklehead who has you smiling from ear to ear every time I come over here, lately." I looked up from the safe and waited for her response.

She sat down in the wicker chair a few feet from me and folded her legs up under herself. Smiling, she said, "Well, like, his name is Pierre but everybody calls him Pop. And so, like, we used to crush on each other in the 8ᵗʰ grade but then he got sent away to juvie for shooting some guys at the basketball game and we, like, lost contact. But he just got out of prison and I ran into him at Lenox Mall two weeks ago and we been back on since."

"And now you crushing on him all over again?"

"Something like that. Why, are you jealous?" she asked facetiously.

"Hell no!" I laughed. "I just wanna know something about the nigga who has my little sister all caught up." That was true but I also wanted to check him out and make sure he wasn't a threat, tryna slick his hands on the stash I kept at her place.

"So, you wanna meet him?" she asked.

"Yeah, set it up, but I hope you haven't had him over here around my stuff. You know the rules..."

"No company," she completed my brief lecture.

"Absolutely!" I reinforced.

I finished what I had come to do and then dipped so I could hook up with Cardale and Jared.

Earlier in the week, I had gotten a new shipment of werk in, and I wanted to make sure that everything was operating smoothly. Plus, I had been hearing whispers of something I needed to question them on.

It seemed like there was always a fire of some sort to put out. At least KiKi wasn't giving me any problems. Since we had moved into the new house two weeks ago, she was content with decorating it and having me there every night.

I still hadn't boned her. Matter of fact, we slept in different rooms but she was forever tryna talk her way into my bed. And although I wouldn't smash her, KiKi wasn't being a bitch about it or causing friction between me and her pops.

My bank had jumped up to almost $400,000, so I really couldn't complain about shit, anyway. If I had to put somebody on their ass from time to time, well, that was just a day in the life of a gangsta.

No matter how it stacked up, every day above ground and not in the penitentiary was a win.

But if there was one thing that shaded my happiness, it was the situation with Julz. Though I had just rebuffed her again, I really missed her like crazy. And as time continued to go by, I wanted to believe that she hadn't been tryna creep that night. I just didn't wanna open myself up to getting played because, beyond everything else, a street nigga had to be able to stand amongst other men and hold his head up high. And I couldn't do that if my woman was fuckin' with the next dude behind my back, nah mean?

I won't front, I had been going through Julz' spot, periodically, to see if she had her so-called homeboy or any other man over there cupcaking with her. I hadn't seen anything foul and when I asked Cardale about shorty, he could only say, *"I see her coming and going with her son, that's all."*

That made me wonder if baby girl had been telling me the truth. I went back and forth with the thought but the fact remained when it came down to the woman I would claim as mine, I didn't wanna have to guess whether she was *100* or not, I needed to be able to say that shit with my chest sticking out. Real shit!

And since I wasn't a bill about Julz, I just kept my mind on my money and my money on my mind.

I pulled up at Jared's crib thirty minutes later. His girl let me in almost as soon as I rung the bell.

"Sup, Taj? How you been, ma?" I greeted her. She was a thick girl but I noticed that she had put on quite a few more pounds lately. I started to ask if she was pregnant but if she wasn't, the question would hurt her feelings and I wasn't gonna do that.

"Hey, Choppa. I'm doing fine. How about yourself?" she asked, closing the door behind me.

"Another day, another dollar."

"That's all y'all think about." She shook her head in amusement. "How's KiKi? Tell her we need to have a girl's day." She led me toward the kitchen.

"Ha! Every day is a girl's day for her."

"Shut up!" She pushed me playfully. "She deserves it for holding you down for so long. Believe me, it's not easy riding for y'all niggas." She cut her eyes at Jared who was seated at the table.

"You throwing shade now?" Jared frowned.

"Nope. Just starting facts." She looked past him and Cardale and said, "Goodnight, Choppa. Don't forget to tell KiKi what I said."

"No doubt."

When she left out of the kitchen, I dapped Jared up. "You must not be taking care of home, bleed."

"Fuck what Taj talm 'bout. Bruh, you know how women is, you can give them the earth and they gon' want Mars and Venus, too."

Cardale chuckled. I bent down and locked fists with him. "What's good, fool?" he said.

"Y'all tell me. I'm just a squirrel tryna get a nut." I pulled out a chair and took a seat.

We kicked the bobo for a minute and then jumped in to business. As we talked, I waited to see if either one of them was gonna volunteer the information I had heard from a reliable source, but neither one of them did.

Finally, I just came out and asked them. "Word on the street is that y'all got bricks of that white girl. Is that fact or fiction?" I folded my hands on the table and studied them both.

Cardale looked at Jared, and there was my answer.

"Yeah, we doing a lil' something," confirmed Jared.

I ran my hand down my face and let out a long sigh. "Y'all just wouldn't listen."

"Bruh, listen to what?" Jared pushed up from the table ready for combat. "What we're doing ain't got shit to do with you. I gave you the chance to get the werk from your plug, but you deaded it!"

I smiled. "Oh, *you* gave me the chance?" Just like I suspected, he was the driving force behind their push for us to fuck with coke. I looked from him to Cardale and just shook my head at him. *A born muthafuckin' follower.*

"Speak your mind," Cardale said.

I let his invitation linger in the air for a minute while I fired up one of the blunts they had sitting on the table. "Oh, I intend to," I finally replied as I pulled on the sticky icky.

Jared leaned back on the sink counter with his eyes trained on me. He was grilling me mad hard, like he expected a heated confrontation. But this time, I wasn't even about to take it there.

All of a sudden, Cardale stood up and opened his mouth. "What we do on the side ain't got nothin' to do with you," he said.

I looked up at him a laughed. "Nigga, sit your ass down. You ain't nothin' but a puppet and ain't nobody pulled your strings for you to talk."

"Fuck is you talking to?" His voice was loud but my eyes were on Jared.

"Bleed, where do you and your girl keep the remote? I need to turn the volume down on this nigga." I nodded my head in Cardale's direction.

Black as that nigga was, his face turned red. "If you wasn't my homie, I would smash you," Cardale threatened.

"And if my mama had a dick she would be my daddy."

"Keep playing wit' it!" He looked like a raging bull, with his nostrils flaring in and out.

"Relax, homie. I ain't even on that type of time tonight." I handed Cardale the blunt and he reluctantly put it to his lips and inhaled.

"What kinda time you on?" asked Jared.

I waited for my lungs to clear before I answered and then I said, "I believe coke is gonna be y'all downfall. I believed that when you first brought that to me, and I believe it now. But I can't stop grown niggas from doing what they wanna do. All I gotta say is don't let y'all shit end up in my toilet. Other than that, I wish you nothin' but success."

"So, what you saying?" asked Cardale.

I didn't even look in that fool's direction. Still looking at Jared, I said, "Explain it to him, fam."

I hit Jared with some dap and a gangsta hug and then I headed for the door.

***

A week later...

They say: *When one door closes another one opens.* That turned out to be the case when I severed business with Jared and Cardale.

Kim Marie introduced me to her boyfriend, Pop, and him and I instantly clicked. Being that he was young and fresh home from the joint, he was anxious to get his weight up. His track record proved that he would let the toolie cough so I just needed to teach him the ropes and I would have myself a loyal baby goon.

Pop had little more than the clothes on his back and whatever Kim Marie broke him off with, so he appreciated everything I gave him, including the street jewels. Youngin was like a sponge, sopping up everything.

I taught him how to weigh weed and how to package and move it without the loud smell giving him away. I bought him a used Tahoe so he could move around freely and I introduced him to the customers that Cardale and Jared used to serve.

Once I had him set up with all the essentials, I decided to make him earn everything else because when things came too easily, it made a nigga a bad hustla.

Pop didn't sweat that, he loved grinding. Before hooking up with me, the most money he had ever seen at one time was 10 stacks, he said.

"Well, you'll see more than that every day," I assured him.

"I promise, I won't complain, big homie," he said with excitement.

And within days I had youngin carrying duffel bags full of dough.

Toward the next weekend, I hit Cardale up to let him know I would be coming through to pick up the rest of the money he owed me from the werk of mine he had from before we cut ties with each other.

Jared had already cleared his tab.

"Come on through, I got half of it now. I'll have the rest in a couple of weeks," he promised.

I felt like he was juggling me but I didn't bitch about it. We had gotten money together for a good while so I extended him my patience.

When I went to his crib to pick up the dough he had for me, there was no beef in the air. We blazed a few blunts and chopped it up for a minute and then he gave me 60 racks—half of what he still owed and then I bounced.

"Be easy, bleed. You know it's a dirty game out here," I said as he let me out of the door.

"Same to you, bruh."

I hit him with some dap and then headed to my ride but I stopped dead in my tracks when I came face to face with the one person I didn't want to see. *Julz!*

Chapter 27
Julz

Time heals all wounds, at least that's what my mother said right before we hung up with each other.

She was probably right because as of last week, I finally accepted that me and Choppa were over and that I'd never see or hear from him again. I kind of had no choice but to believe it, really. It had been a month since the incident occurred and he'd been steadfast on not giving me the time of day.

He done probably swept another bitch up off of her feet, like he so whimsically did me.

I shook my head and then dabbed at the corners of my eyes, stopping the tears before they started.

Damn!

The thought that he was happy with someone else almost made me regress. I mean, shit still wasn't sweet but at least I was eating regularly and I gave a damn about my appearances again.

Needing to focus on something upbeat, I cut the radio in my car up and started jamming to *Milly Rock*.

Fake it 'til you make it, I reminded myself as I winded one hand in the air and guided my steering wheel with the other.

As I continued my drive home, my cell phone vibrated and lit up with a call from Tyriq. I turned my music down and answered. "What's up, Riq?"

"I'm coolin', love. Look, I'm calling to see if you want to pass over by the crib tonight. We having game night with a few of our potnas. I'ma be on that grill and my girl gon' make those drinks you like. Plus, my lil' one been asking for Justus."

Although Tyriq and Iesha knew how to throw a party, I didn't want to be around them. I didn't hate on their love, I was still just very salty over the lack of mine.

"Nah, I'ma pass on it but thanks."

"Come on, love, it'll do you good to be around fam. Besides, aren't you tired of being cooped up in the house?"

Not really, I answered mentally. "Since when is being at home jail?" I chuckled. "I'll get another opportunity to come kick it with y'all but I'm gonna spend my Friday night curled up with a glass of wine and Netflix."

"You sho it don't got nothing to do with that Choppa muthafucka, huh?" He spoke distastefully. I could imagine his lip arching, showing off his fang.

In some ways, it did have everything to do with him but I wasn't gonna tell him that. "No. I just want to be alone."

"*Humph*! Well, bounce all da way back, shaggy. The spades table ain't the same without your shit talkin' ass." He laughed, which made me laugh, too.

"I know, right? But, ummm, for real, we gon' catch up. Tell Iesha I said hello and thanks again for the invite."

"A'ight. Be easy." He ended the call.

As I slid the phone back into my purse in the passenger seat, I cut the sound back up on the radio, only to quickly turn it back down. My heart raced instantly, as I heard *There Goes My Baby* playing and I didn't need any more reminders of him than I already had.

I pushed the knob in, cutting it off altogether, opting to ride in silence the rest of the way home.

When I pulled into my apartments, I ran down a checklist of things to do once I got inside.

Email your professor, take a bath, walk around naked for a bit, order a pizza and watch TV until TV watches you.

I smiled and spoke to myself. "Not a bad plan, Julz."

After I pulled into my parking space, I gathered my belongings and stepped out. With my head down, looking at nothing in particular, I marched toward my door, that was, until something told me to look up.

When I did, it felt like I had seen a ghost. Well, technically I had because he'd disappeared like one. My mouth separated but nothing came out. We both just stood there, staring at one another.

Finally, I called out for him. "Chop—" but with a dismissive shake of the head, he opened his door, started his engine and pulled off.

I let out a light whimper and dropped my head. I was stuck where I stood, momentarily. *He really hates me*, I gathered.

A tear cascaded down my cheek as I watched his truck vanish, forcing me to relapse in the progress I made on the spot.

I picked up my face and made my way inside, placing everything in my hands on the sofa. From there, I went straight to the bathroom and braced myself against the sink as I cried for the thousandth time.

Lifting my head to face myself in the mirror, I became disgusted with myself. *Is he crying over you? No! So why do you keep crying over him?*

That was a good question but I still couldn't stop myself.

After my cries died down to light grumbles, I went ahead and ran a hot bath. Hopefully, the heat would help ease the tension my muscles now had.

I stripped out of my clothes, went into my kitchen and poured me a glass of wine. I downed the first pour like it was water but the second glass I would savor.

Walking back into the bathroom, I lit my candles, turned off the lights and stepped into the tub.

"Ssss," *hot as usual.*

I took my time getting in but once I was fully emerged, I laid my head back and closed my eyes.

Visions of Choppa then entered my mind and I both smiled and released more tears because of it.

After twenty minutes of bathing and brooding, I heard a frightening bang at my door.

"Oh, shit!" I reactively jumped at the unexpected sound, causing me to splash an excessive amount of water onto the floor.

Boom! Boom! Boom!

I heard the flood of knocks again. Quickly, I wrapped myself in a towel and threw my robe, hanging up on the door, on top of it.

I started breathing sporadically as I tiptoed through the living room. Panic took root in my chest as I moved in closer to investigating what urgency awaited me on the other side of my door. As soon as I pressed my eye to the peephole, I jumped back because the heavy thud came again.

Boom! Boom! Boom!

Gathering my nerves, I looked again, this time I was able to see it was Choppa.

"*Choppa!*" I said below my breath and quickly disengaged my locks.

He reeked of anger. "Fuck took you so long to open the door?" He invited himself in and took off to the back of my apartment.

"I was in the bathroom." I answered from behind as I followed him.

He opened every closet door, checked my bathroom and then bedroom thoroughly.

Satisfied that I was home alone, he questioned. "Why didn't you answer your phone? I called you five fuckin' times?"

I was in shock at his harshness. I'm sure he picked that up, but I dared to address it. I simply headed back up front and grabbed my phone out of my purse, waving it high for him to see. "My phone was on vibrate and I was taking a bath."

He looked less pained by my answer as he then realized I was dripping wet. But instead of an apology, he went on to further interrogate me.

"Where's your shorty? Why he not here?"

"He's over at Essence's for the weekend to give me time to myself."

"Why, you was expecting company? Tyriq?"

He's jealous, I smirked a tad. *He still cares*. "No! *Hell no!*" I bass'd up my voice.

Choppa walked over to the light switch to illuminate the room. "Look me in my face. You been creepin' on a nigga? Don't lie."

"The thought never crossed my mind. You were *and* are all I need. You gotta believe me." I beseeched with the use of my swollen eyes.

He eyeballed me intently but I didn't buckle because I was telling the God's honest truth.

Then after about a minute, his tone softened. "You been crying, shorty?"

I looked off to my side and casted my eyes downward before I looked back at him. "Every day since you've been away." Choppa grimaced and then started shaking his head from side to side, as if he was wrestling with an idea. I took the opportunity to say what I needed. "Baby, I waited all my life for someone like you and there's not a single soul who could convince me to jeopardize my once in a lifetime with you. I never cheated on you. *Would* never cheat on you. You're all the man I need."

"Is that right?"

I shook my head up and down *yes*.

"Tell me who you belong to?"

"You. It's always been you." I reiterated.

He paused for a second. "I want to believe you, but I don't know if I can." He shook his head with a look of regret and turned for the door.

"Choppa?" I sounded pathetic to my own self as I cried out his name.

I dropped my chin to my chest and groaned. I would have tried to stop him from leaving but I had no more fight in me. I just cried into my hands.

Then after some time went by and I didn't hear my door open and shut, I looked up. Choppa never left. He just stood there, watching me remorsefully with his hand on the deadbolt.

He then twisted it to the left, locking it. "Show me you belong to me," was all he said.

Chapter 28
Choppa

In my line of hustle, I've read the faces of many lying ass bitches and bitch niggas, so I knew the look of a liar when I stared in the eyes of one.

So as I stood there watching baby girl as her body vibrated through her cries, my instincts were telling me she'd been real all along. And although the Tyriq situation still needed to be handled, I would show her reprieve, for now. Besides, I missed everything about shorty. And as much as I tried to get her off of my mind, she stayed there 24/7. A nigga was sick without her, no lie.

But tonight, all of that was about to change. I looked up at her and studied her, using every street-honed instinct I'd acquired over the years. A man could tell if a woman was still *his* woman, and the look she returned confirmed that Julz was still mine.

She walked over to me with no hesitation in her stride, removing her robe and dropping the towel, revealing all of her sexiness.

I licked my lips and repeated my demand, with a little more force this time. "Show me you belong to me."

***

Julz

The instant the last word rolled off of his tongue I became infused with many emotions: *Love, lust, anxiousness, relief…* I thought this moment would never come again but it did and I was going to make sure it never slipped from between my fingers, ever.

In seconds, I was naked, standing before him with my lips pressed passionately against his. Sobs left my mouth as I was overwhelmed by the feel of his hands wrapping around my body the deeper our kiss grew. His grip was strong. I could tell he missed me just as much as I missed him.

Unable to contain the desire to have him, I began to vigorously take off his jeans as he took off his shirts.

My legs shook with impatience as he stepped out of his boxers and his mammoth man muscle sprung up and poked my belly. It looked to be bigger and fatter than I remembered. I knew that desire was altering my recall but what I saw before my eyes was almost unbelievable.

I didn't know how that big, delicious looking sausage had ever fit inside of my oven, in the first place. Yet I was already creaming to open my oven's door for it again.

My hand moved on its own and wrapped around the width of Choppa. Sticky pre-cum from the head of his dick wet my palm as I stroked him.

"I'ma show you that I belong to you and no other," I said as I began lowering my body to take him into my mouth.

A sound of confusion escaped my mouth as Choppa reached down and pulled me back to my feet before I could taste him. He didn't say a word and when I looked at him and opened my mouth to ask why, he pressed me against the wall and pinned my arms above my head, pushing his tongue deep into my mouth.

He kissed me so hard, I gasped for air when our mouths separated. "Tell me I own you," he demanded as he lifted one of my legs around his waist and entered me roughly.

Had I been in my right mind, I certainly would've questioned him on that demand, but I was already gone off the dick though he had just stuck it in.

"You own me, Choppa." I cried with lust and passion as he filled a bitch completely up.

"Tell me you'll always do as I say." He pushed deeper than I ever knew my walls went.

"Always, bae. Always!" I slung the pussy back at him.

"I missed the fuck out of you, shorty! Don't ever make me have to walk away again." He stroked my pussy almost angrily.

"I'm sorry." I bit into his shoulder to muffle my cries.

Choppa put both of my legs around his waist and pressed my ass and my back against the wall. He pushed forward with his hips and penetrated me at a new angle that hurt and felt so fuckin' good, at the same time.

216

Restraining Order

"You're mine, Julz—nobody else's. Never let another nigga touch this pussy!" He punished my walls. "Never! Do you understand me?"

"Yes, baby! Yes!" Our bodies made those smacking sounds as he tried to fuck me to death, and I tried to kill that dick in return.

I had missed him so much during our separation—had feared that I had lost him forever—and, now, all of my pent up emotions came bursting out. I screwed him back, furiously, for causing me weeks of pain and heartache.

With each roll of my hips, I tried to prove to him that there was no place better on Earth than where the fuck he was now.

"Yeah, shorty, you're mine. Give it to me! Make your pussy pledge allegiance to this dick!" groaned Choppa.

Turned the fuck on by his words and the squishy sound of his wood going in and out of my wetness like a high-powered piston, I rose up and down with a fury that was new to me.

I felt a gigantic orgasm coming and the room started spinning. "Ooh shit! Ooh shit!" I chanted like a crazed woman.

Choppa banged me harder, hurting my coochie and pleasing it in the same stroke. I tried to hold back my watery eruption but he was hitting my spot repeatedly, making me want to surrender the battle.

It was as if we were fighting to make the other one concede that they could not live without this burning love and fire we shared. His dick punched. My pussy grabbed and twisted. Sweat from our bodies dripped down to mix with the wetness of our copulation.

"I own you!" Choppa growled as he sped up his strokes.

"Yes, you do!" I agreed as he rocked my world.

Lifting me high in the air and slamming me back down on his largeness, with brutal but satisfying power, he put his mouth to my ear and growled, "You're mine, shawdy. Don't ever forget that!"

At that moment, his uttered possessiveness brought out the freak in me. "Hell yeah, Choppa! I'm yours! I'm your bitch!" I screamed and squirted a whole muthafuckin' waterfall.

A second later, he screamed my name and flooded me with his nut.

After we both climaxed, I was as limp as a Raggedy Ann doll. Choppa carried me over to the couch and laid down with me. Exhausted and satiated, I ran my finger over his hairless chest in circular motions,

217

enjoying the intimate lay in his arms. My breathing was labored and so was his.

For a minute we said nothing. He kissed me on the forehead and stroked my cheek.

Finally, he broke the silence. "I'm not gonna ruin this moment with talk of what need to happen but we gon' cross that bridge real soon. It's a must."

I knew he was referring to Tyriq because there was no other source of contention between us. My gut told me he would make me choose. I hoped to God he wouldn't, though.

"Okay," I said demurely.

"And if you got something you need to say to me, you'll get to do that then."

Although he suggested I save my questions for later, he opened the door for something that had been on my mind so I jumped right through it, preferring not to wait.

"Bae, there is something that hasn't been sitting right with me for a while."

I could tell by the exaggerated exhale he took that he wasn't too thrilled that I chose to question him now. "Yea, what is it?"

I raised off of his chest and looked at him. "Why have you never taken me to your place?"

"C'mon, shorty. You wanna do this now?" He looked at me perplexed.

I raised completely off of him and sat up. "Yes, now. Baby, when I wanted so badly to see you and talk face to face, I couldn't. And as your woman, I should have known where my man lay his head at night, period."

He laughed at me and then pulled me back down on him. "You wanna know where I be, so you can pop up on me?"

"Maybe." I kidded. "But, no, seriously, though, it shouldn't even be a debate. I should know that, unless *you* have something to hide." His smile went flat and he got up with no warning, moving me off of him. *My stupid mouth!* "Choppa, what are you doing?"

"I'm getting dressed—to leave." He slipped into his boxers and jeans.

"Baby, what did I say so wrong? I was only saying I think I should know..."

He interrupted. "As you should but don't insinuate that I'm playing off on you because I'm not!"

I did the exact thing he didn't want to do—ruin the moment. *Shit!* "Baby, please don't go. Not again."

"Nah, shorty. I'ma bounce," he bent over and grabbed his shirt from off of the arm of the sofa, "but so are you."

That caught me off guard as a silly smile stretched my face. "You're taking me to your place?"

"Yea, so pack an overnighter. You'll stay the weekend with me." He smiled my way and I didn't dillydally.

I pounced to my feet and did exactly what he said.

Fifteen minutes later, I was outfitted in a maxi dress carrying a small tote of extra clothes and daily essentials. Choppa smiled approvingly, took the bag from me and pulled me into his embrace. I giggled and then buried my head into his chest.

"Julz?"

I looked up. "Yes."

"I'll do anything for you but be your fool, understand?"

I wasn't sure why he was telling me this but my intuition told me again it was about Tyriq or any man for that matter. So, I definitely didn't want to press the topic. I'd wait for *the talk* that I knew would come sooner than later, so I simply replied, "Understood."

He kissed my temple and I closed my eyes sweetly as he did.

"A'ight, let's be out." He motioned for the door.

Ca$h & Coffee

Chapter 29
Julz

After a forty-five minute drive, we arrived at Choppa's condo.

"Welcome to my man cave." He waved me inside, theatrically.

Behind me, I heard him lock the door. My eyes widened at the masculine spender that greeted me. The furniture in the living room was all black leather, glass and stainless steel. I could tell it was expensive. But what really impressed me from first glance was the tidiness of the room. Not only was everything neat and in place, the room had a delightful smell about it.

"Do you have a housekeeper?" I asked over my shoulder as I began my tour of each room.

"You're talking to him," he called back.

"Lies!" I half-kidded as I located the master bedroom and went inside to allay my womanly suspicions.

To my surprise, Choppa remained out front. I headed straight for the closet. *If another woman has been here, she probably left evidence behind to mark her territory.*

My lips parted into a smile when I rumbled through his extensive wardrobe and couldn't find any women's apparel anywhere in sight, not a stitch.

I checked the bathroom for feminine hygiene products, nail polish, etcetera. Again, nothing. Maybe he was keeping it real with me, I started to think. But my search for the slightest evidence to the contrary wasn't over just yet.

I crossed the hall and checked the other bedroom in case there was something suspicious there. But everything was kosher.

Wait!

I retraced my steps and checked the bathroom cabinet and the dressers in the bedroom for condoms and shit like that. I mean, there would be nothing I could say about him having condoms, though he never used them with me because he could've purchased them before my time. But to find some would've raised my antenna.

Anyway, my worries were put to bed. I didn't find a single condom anywhere and, believe me, I checked everywhere, even the waste baskets.

When I returned to the living room, Choppa was sitting on the couch smiling at me. "You satisfied, with your suspicious ass?"

"What, I was just checking out your place?" I lied. But laughter gave me away.

Choppa pulled me down on his lap and planted a fat kiss on my lips. "Never doubt me, shorty. This nigga right here is all yours."

"You better be." I made it sound like a shallow threat.

"Shorty, I keep telling you, you ain't about that life." He chuckled.

"*Humph!* Just don't try me and you won't have to find out." I put him in a headlock and wrestled him down on the sofa.

In no time at all, we were kissing and touching all over each other. My pussy was hotter than July in the Sierra Desert. It only took a few nasty words whispered in Choppa's ear and a stroke or two of my hand and that nigga was rocked up and ready for Round Two.

We did it in record time, but it was the best three minutes of my life. And the next thing I knew I was out like a light.

Hours later when I woke up, one arm was hanging off of the couch and spittle ran from the corner of my mouth. "Dang, bae, you put it on me good." I felt around on the couch for Choppa but he had done a Houdini. "Bae!" I called out in my most whiny voice.

"I'm in here, baby girl."

I sat up on the couch and wiped my mouth with the back of my hand. That's when the delicious smells came wafting from the kitchen and tantalized my nose.

When I stood up, my kitty felt like it had been hit by a battering ram.

"Oooh! Ouch!" I spread my legs and walked bow-legged to help ease the soreness.

In the kitchen, I found Choppa standing over the stove. He had on long basketball shorts and a fresh t-shirt. I walked up behind him and wrapped my arms around his waist. He smelled fresh so I assumed he had showered while I napped.

"Sup, ma?" he said.

222

"You and whatever you're cooking that smells so good."

"Oh, see, good pussy will have a nigga with an apron on."

"You so damn silly." I laughed. "For real, for real, though. What you cooking?"

"Steak and shrimp Quesadillas, and I'ma hook you up a nice Caesar salad on the side."

"Ummm." I rubbed my tummy.

"Just wait and see, baby girl, ya boy got stupid, crazy chef skills."

"I believe you, bae, 'cause the smell is delicious. But, umm, do you think your shorty could take a quick shower and freshen up while you do that?"

"Yeah, make yourself at home. You should already know where everything is," he said, alluding to my snooping earlier.

"Trust and believe." I admitted without shame because just as I belonged to him, he belonged to me.

The shower felt amazing. I used the detachable nozzle to run the hot water all over my body, especially my thighs and my between my legs.

Fifteen minutes later, I was dressed in some comfy shorts and one of my favorite long t-shirts. My hair was tied back in a ponytail and I was smelling good, too.

When I walked back up front, Choppa already had the dining room table set for two. I looked at the care in which he had arranged the plates and silverware, and commented, "Bae, you're the best." I gave him a kiss.

Immediately, his hands got busy. "See, what you started?" he said, palming my booty.

I smacked his hand away and snatched a fork off of the table. Holding it like a dagger, I playfully threatened, "Touch me again and you die."

"A'ight, I'ma leave you alone for now. But later, I'ma take you down through there again. Believe dat."

I couldn't do nothing but shake my head, this man was insatiable. But his behind could cook, I tell you that. Those Quesadillas was to die for! And the salad was scrumptious, too. I washed it all down with an ice chilled Coke.

Later on, he stepped outside on the back balcony and smoked a blunt while I stood in the door, enjoying my view of him.

"Bae, I'ma go to bed if you don't mind," I said when he put a flame to a second blunt.

"A'ight, I'll be in there shortly."

I went in the bedroom, and since he had told me earlier to make myself at home, I changed the bedding, just in case.

***

I don't know what time it was when Choppa finally came to bed but we woke up in the morning spooned together. I breathed a huge sigh of relief when he didn't try to get my goodies first thing in the morning. Oh, I desired him as much as he desired me, but my stuff needed a short break from the beating he had put on it yesterday.

Returning Choppa's favor from last night, I fixed breakfast for us. I was still kind of full from dinner so I only had toast and orange juice. But I cooked Choppa an egg omelet, pancakes and hash browns, all of which he conveniently had in the refrigerator.

"Thanks, shorty, it was delicious," he complimented once his plate was clean.

"Anything for my man," I said sincerely as I stood up to clear the table.

"Baby, I'ma get dressed and make a few moves. I'll be back in a couple of hours and the rest of the day will be ours."

"Okay, bae," I said, wearing a smile that wouldn't go away.

After a short while, when it was time for Choppa to leave, he kissed me at the door. I couldn't help but dream of the day he would become my husband and that would be an everyday occurrence.

While he was out handling business, I missed him terribly but that slight disappoint evaporated when he returned later that evening with a present for me.

The next day, we made love three or four times. We took our showers together and went to a comedy show downtown with Choppa's friends, Kim Marie and Pop.

It tickled us to see how in love those two were with each other. Every time we looked up, they were rubbing on one another.

"Y'all mu'fuckas need to get a room," cracked Choppa. But we were no better. I couldn't keep my hands off of him and his hands stayed in my bra more than my titties did.

It was obvious that Kim Marie adored Choppa. He had told me their story so I wasn't the least bit worried, to him she was like a little sister. Besides, she was cool as hell.

On the other hand, Pop didn't talk much but from what I was able to pick up he had tremendous respect for Choppa. I didn't know exactly what their business was, but I concluded that Pop worked for Choppa in some capacity.

I had my idea of what type of work they were in but I didn't want to ask, just yet. I was too busy enjoying happiness to invite trouble into it.

As Saturday night turned into Sunday morning, finding me in bed, in Choppa's arms, I began to pout because I didn't want to awake from this beautiful dream and have to leave him.

"What you got your lip poked out for?" He observed.

"Because I don't want this weekend to end."

"Then, don't let it."

"Some of us have work tomorrow," I said, thinking rationally.

"That's never a problem, shorty." He didn't have to say the rest.

"No, Choppa, I am not calling off work again."

"Why not?" He pulled me on top of him.

"No!" I tried to sound firm.

"Who do you belong to? A boss nigga, right?"

"Yes, but—"

"Ssh! Ain't no *buts.*" He put a finger to my lips.

And just like that it was decided.

"So, call off work for tomorrow?" I reconfirmed.

"Tuesday, too," he said.

I shook my head in amazement. His assertiveness was so damn sexy.

"Bae?" I called his name as I looked down into his eyes.

"What's up?"

"Can you put me back to sleep?"
He responded by rolling me over and spreading my legs apart. The rest was earth shattering.

Chapter 30
Julz

"*Mmmm.*" I purred as I stretched from the Choppa induced coma I had awaken from. Recalls of our session had me giggling and covering my eyes, shyly.

Thoughts of that man make me blush, even in the company of myself.

As I got out of the bed and headed out to locate my boo, the sound of his cell phone vibrating on the nightstand curiously pulled me back.

I looked down at the screen and it read: *KiKi.*

"*KiKi?*" I said out loud. "KiKi? KiKi?" I had seen her name once or twice before. I never inquired about who she was but when she called right back, she sparked my interest to know now.

I carried the phone into the living room, where he was playing NBA 2K15 on PlayStation.

"Bae, this computer whoopin' my ass, ole cheatin' bitch. Come give me a kiss for good luck. Hurry up!" He rushed me to come over.

I peppered my step, sitting down next to him. Feeling my body next to his, he then turned his lips my way as his eyes remained glued on the 60" flat screen.

"Baby?" I called him but clearly I was distracting him.

"One second." He silenced me. "Come on, LeBron. Come on, LeBron. Woooo! Hell yea, baby show 'em we came to play." He cheered as his player made the basket. "Kiss me again, lucky charm." He stuck his neck out, giving me his cheek.

I did as he asked and decided to wait the thirty seconds remaining in the third quarter before I asked him about this KiKi person.

As soon as the buzzer sounded, I went for it. "Bae, you had two missed calls." I placed the phone in his lap. "Who's KiKi? She called twice." I gave an *I'm waiting* look, the one where my eyes were opened wide with no blinks in its future.

For a slight second, it looked like he held his breath or maybe I was looking too hard.

"Someone I do business with." His answer was a bit short.

"Well, how do you know her and what type of business does she have with you?"

He resumed his game but the joy once plastered on his face dissolved under my line of questioning.

"I've said everything you need to know about shorty, so let it go. It's nothin'." He spoke sternly.

Shorty? Why the fuck are you calling her shorty? Maybe I was in my feelings at this point but I didn't like the vibe I was getting. *I mean, he volunteered a whole story about Kim Marie, how they met and who she was to him, so why not her?*

I stared at him sideways before I halfheartedly got up to answer my phone that was now ringing in the bedroom.

After taking Essence's call, I was back up front a few minutes later but now he was on the balcony, talking on his phone. No doubt it was KiKi.

I sat down quietly and ear hustled as hard as I could. I picked up bits and pieces of what he was saying but he didn't use a name once, so I remained clueless.

A minute or so later, he walked back inside and slid his phone into his short's pocket. Something he rarely did.

I had no reason to doubt him, none at all, but something about the way he answered my questions was fucking me up. I was so puzzled that the look of confusion mixed with a bit of perturb altered my facial expression.

"Julz, you feelin' some kinda way, ma?" he asked, sitting back down.

"I'm fine."

"I can read through you, shorty. You ain't foolin' me." He pulled me to come sit on his lap. "Baby, we good. Don't let yo mind take things somewhere it doesn't belong. After all, assumptions kill relationships. I told you KiKi is nothing but business, so leave it at that, a'ight?"

I waited a few moments and then I answered. "A'ight."

I dropped it because I didn't want or need him to bring up the reason we were making up in the first place. *His assumptions on my relationship with Tyriq.*

"Now give me another kiss and watch yo nigga whoop the sleeves off of Golden State."

I kissed him and remained on his lap the rest of the fourth quarter.

Once the game was over and he thoroughly cursed out the computer for beating him by eighteen points, he tapped me on my ass to raise up.

"I'm done with this shit. What you feel like doing?" He stood to his feet, rubbing his six pack.

"Oh, shoot! I need to go home, get some clothes for myself and for Justus, as well as drop them off to Essence. She's expecting me to pass by this afternoon."

"A'ight. I'll take you and then we can catch a movie or something."

I felt awkward telling him no but I had to. "Bae, I'm gonna go alone." He looked at me strangely but I quickly answered why. "You know my son has never officially met you and given the circumstances he saw you under, it's really important to me that I introduce you two on better terms."

Choppa's jaw twitched but whatever ill thoughts rested on his tongue, he swallowed because all he said was, "Handle your business, then."

I tiptoed to kiss him. "Thanks for understanding."

"I ain't trippin' it but me and your shorty gon' hafta meet soon 'cause I ain't your cuddy buddy."

"It will happen soon. I promise." He nodded and sat back down as I headed to the bathroom.

After a quick shower, I dressed, grabbed Choppa's keys, gave him a kiss that would tide him over 'til I got back and left out.

From Choppa's condo to my spot and then over to Essence's house took me roughly two hours. I called him to let him know I made it and that I'd spend some time with my son before I came back to his crib.

I exited his truck, feeling like big shit. Never had I ever pushed anything so bossed the fuck up in my life, so it was only natural that I wanted to floss for my girl.

After I rang the doorbell, I rubbed my hands like Birdman, prepared to stunt like my daddy the moment Essence opened the door but when she did, the face she gave me made me straighten up real quick.

"What's the matter with you?" I quizzed.

"Nothing's up with me but something is up with *your* man." She welcomed me in but I didn't budge.

"Nah, close the door and let's discuss this out here away from Justus." She did as I said and I continued. "Why does it sound like you have a problem with Choppa?"

"It's because I do. The nigga no good, sis. Yesterday…"

"Pew! Pew! Pew! I childishly held my hand in the shape of a gun and shot at the air.

Essence smacked her lips. "What the fuck are you doing?"

"Demonstrating you shooting down my happiness."

"What? You rather I say nothing? Because I can, ya know?"

I rolled my eyes hard and took a deep breath. "Of course not. Go ahead." I was disinterested already.

"Like I was saying, yesterday me and Justus went to visit my friend's house in this new subdivision built out in McDonough."

"Andddd." I rushed her with the wave of my hand.

"Andddd, *bitch*, I saw Choppa. He was carrying men's clothes, boxes and other shit into what I strongly believe is his house. Did you know about that?"

"What's wrong with having a second house?" I was interested in seeing where she was going with it now.

"Did you know about it?" She repeated.

"No, I didn't." Attitude registered in my voice.

"Then, that's the muthafuckin' problem. Sis, every last one of those houses are big ass family homes. *Fa-mah-lees,*" she pronounciated retardedly slow. "Now, tell me what does one man need with four plus bedrooms when he already has a condo? I'll wait." Essence was in one of her modes where she was right even if she was wrong.

But she had me thinking. *Damn!* "Did you see a woman with him?" I held my breath.

"No, I didn't but that don't mean one isn't in the picture."

I started breathing again. "Well, it's probably nothing, sis. Besides, assumptions kill relationships." I regurgitated Choppa's words from earlier.

"*Really?* Does his dick shoot out stupidity serum in its nut?" She shook her head like she didn't recognize who I was. "You can be stupid all you want but I'm not. Look here, I'm gonna give you this address because you know I wrote it down and when you get back to being the Julz I know, ask him about it. But do it in a slick way because he's not going to tell you the truth, especially if you're somehow the side chick."

"All right, cool." I replied, coolly but on the inside I was crispy.

I knew she came from a place of love so I didn't sweat the delivery. However, the implication that he was working two separate lives like a first and second shift was blowing me.

I went to move past her to go inside to see my son, but she stopped me with a tug of the arm.

She blew out hard. "Wait, before we go inside, let me apologize. You know I didn't mean to come off so strong and I only get like that because I'm sensitive about you." She looked up to the sky and then back to me with teary eyes. "Remember when the world kept shitting on me, giving me one bad hand after the next? Well, you were the only one there for me. No judgment, just love. So I feel strongly about anyone trying to play you. But if it means anything, I do hope it's nothing. I know how happy you've been since y'all made up."

I smiled because I knew Tootsie was sincere.

I nicknamed her Tootsie, as in Tootsie Pop, back in our childhood days for this very reason. She was hard as a brick on the outside but soft as butter on the in.

"I am happy but I don't want to be a fool about it, so I respect your mind."

"That's what's up, sis. You look out for me and I look out for you, always."

We hugged it out and went inside. I spent a couple of hours with Toots and my boy.

Before I left, I told him I'd be back on Tuesday evening to get him before I headed back out to Covington, to the only place I knew of Choppa staying.

Chapter 31
Choppa

The past week had been all about Julz. Now that we were back together, it was like a nigga was walking on air. I couldn't get enough of her, every time I laid eyes on shorty I had to make love to her. It didn't matter the time or the place, those panties had to come off or get pushed to the side.

I still handled business while she was at work because making paper was a must. I wanted to always be able to give her the better things in life. Shorty wasn't looking for a sponsor, though. She just wanted to be loved and appreciated, and I had plenty of both to give. But it didn't hurt nothin' for me to be a rich nigga.

Whenever I was chilling with baby girl, my youngin, Pop, was holding down the business. He had brought in a small team of lil' jits, whom he met while locked up, and together they were making me proud. What I loved about those baby gangstas was that they weren't about that flashy shit. They had taken heed to the directive I issued through Pop. *"Real gangstas get silent money,"* I preached.

Those boys soaked that jewel up and applied it to their hustling. So far, I hadn't had a single problem out of any one of them, and Pop never came one dollar short with my bread.

Of course, life was never completely drama free with KiKi in the mix. She had started complaining that all I did was stay in the streets. To keep her from questioning what I was doing on the nights I didn't come home, I told her I was setting up spots in different parts of the state. On the surface, she seemed to accept my explanation but I knew her well enough to know she could see through my lies.

I could've given her some dick to hush her up but, on the real, I only had attraction for one woman. If she wasn't Julz, I wasn't tryna run up in it.

Still, being that I had been away from home so much lately, I spent the day with KiKi going grocery shopping and getting flowers and shit for her to plant in the yard.

She turned heads in the stores like always. But now that I no longer desired her in that way it was amusing to see men bump into poles staring at her ass when she walked by. Had they done that a few months ago, they would've been the top story on the evening news.

"You still got it. These niggas, old and young—white, black and Mexican are drooling," I complimented her.

"But *you're* not." She kept on shopping without giving those dudes a second look.

At home, we put up the grocery and when the sun cooled off a bit, KiKi went outside to plant her flowers. I took off my shirt and lounged around, making a few calls until I caught up with Pop.

***

Julz

Being back with Choppa felt like a one-way ticket to heaven, that was, until Essence gave me alarming news, a couple of days ago, that sent me crashing back down to Earth.

In these last few days, I managed to keep him in the dark regarding the little light that was shined on his sneak behavior but I couldn't fake it anymore.

The two remaining days I stayed over at his place, he'd left me for hours, stating he had business. I couldn't help but wonder if that business was KiKi and/or that second house.

Essence told me she saw his truck out there between two and four, so when I asked him in a roundabout way what he did that Saturday around that time, he said everything but that. *Red flag!*

I tried suffocating the annoying feeling that he was living a double life, but the echoes of common sense were too loud to ignore.

Thoughts of what I should do plagued me so severely I was literally sick.

"You're not looking well," my supervisor stopped by my desk and observed.

"Actually, I'm not feeling good at all." A look of agony replaced the usual pleasant smile I wore.

She looked at her watch and then back to me. "It's almost noon. You've completed most of the day anyway, so go ahead and leave. Get some rest and come back tomorrow refreshed."

Considering I just took off Monday and Tuesday this week, I was glad she offered me the option to go home today so soon after returning.

I gave a thankful nod and seconds later, she left and went about her business.

Gathering my things, I quickly called Essence's work phone in the process.

She answered on the first ring. "Thank you for calling Chase. Essence Whitaker speaking."

"E, it's me. Come stop by my desk and bring me your truck keys."

"For what?"

"E!" I stressed the call of her name, knowing she'd understand with no explanation.

"Huh? Oh—ohhhh. Okay, on my way."

A minute after we hung up she was standing in front of me.

"What are you about to do, exactly?" She passed me her keys and I gave her mine in exchange.

"I'm gonna drive out to that address you gave me for Choppa and see what's really going on."

"You're gonna knock on the door?"

"If I have to, yes!" That was no bluff. If he was domiciled there doing God knows what, I damn sure was going to investigate further.

"Don't do anything..." Essence paused as she waited for a co-worker of ours to pass before she continued. "...foolish. See what you need to see and leave."

This was advice coming from a woman who bleached and burned clothes, slashed tires and snatched plenty of weaves. Tuh!

"I can't promise but I'll keep that in mind." I stood to my feet to leave.

"Well, just in case stuff gets real, call me and I'll be there in a jiffy. And don't worry about Justus. I'll pick him up and bring him to my place."

"You're my bestie," then I whispered, "*bitttchhh!*"

We both smiled at that and then I left out of the building.

My drive over to Choppa's alleged home was excruciating, to say the least. I played out three different scenarios of what I'd do if I learned he indeed stayed there and with a secret family. *None of the outcomes were good.*

To think, I thought he was unlike any man I've ever known.

Precious believed wholeheartedly that *all* men were dogs and she preached it to us every chance she could. Maybe she was right and maybe I underestimated the size of Choppa's collar, believing men could be monogamous.

You think you would have learned your lesson after Marcel, but noooo, you're hardheaded and don't forget stupid! I scolded myself.

I went back and forth in my head until the forty minute drive from my job placed me on the street Essence gave me.

As my nerves kicked into overdrive, I slowed my speed down to a crawl. I wanted to, scratch that, I needed to know the truth but if the truth was that Choppa was fucking with my heart, then it would shatter my belief in love.

I wasn't ready for that rude awakening but I came too far to turn back now.

As I came up on the address, I unconsciously pressed the brakes, stopping directly in front of Choppa's truck when I saw it and who I assumed was the woman of the house, tending to its garden.

I'll be a son of a bitch! I was pissed off, so much so I didn't recognize her staring at me, attempting to get my attention.

It wasn't my plan to stop in front of his door like I had. I wanted to be inconspicuous, but I was frozen with fury seeing what I saw.

Eventually she walked up on me and tapped on my window, startling me into the present. I composed myself and then powered the passenger window down. "Yes."

She flicked her finger, flippantly. "Ummm, you're just sitting in front of my house. Can I help you?" The beautiful woman spoke with an ugly tone.

My house?

I looked about for a second, shamming confusion. "Ah, maybe, I'ma bit lost. I'm looking for…" I called off an address.

She studied me for a second and then diverted her eyes down the street, pointing in the direction I was to go. "This is the 2600 block so you have to go down another street."

I gave a look of relief and then thanked her for her help. Bitch didn't bother replying, just walked off.

I watched her briefly then glanced over at Choppa's truck, shaking my damn head. *Don't make a fool of yourself. He's a cheater. Just go. It's not worth it.*

I almost listened to myself but then something inside of me snapped.

As I was pulling off to head home because I knew all I needed to know, I saw a shirtless Choppa coming out through my rearview mirror and my heart broke into a million tiny fuckin' pieces on sight.

The small side of me that was a glutton for pain navigated the Suburban a few houses down, across the street from them. I now needed to see what else would unfold from this dirty discovery of mine.

***

Choppa

Everything was gucci with my young guns, so I decided to go outside and see what kinda progress KiKi had made. When I got in the yard, she was down on her knees planting something in the flower garden in front of the house.

"I told you I would've hired a professional landscaper to do that," I said, walking up to her.

"Nope. I wanted to do it myself. Nah!" She stuck her tongue out at me like a little girl.

"Put that thing in your mouth!" I scrunched up my face and feigned like I was gonna pop her in the mouth.

"You better not." She laughed and tossed a handful of dirt up at me.

"That's how you rocking?" I flexed my pecs.

"Yeah, that's how I'm rocking." She did a little shoulder wiggle like she was the shit.

"A'ight. I got that ass, believe dat."

I walked a few feet over to the water sprout and unraveled the hose. By the time KiKi looked up, I had turned on the water and I was running toward her with the hose in hand, laughing. I aimed the spray nozzle at her.

"No, Choppa! I just got my hair done!" she screamed but it was too late. I sprayed her from head to toe.

She sprung to her feet and tried to charge me, but I was backing away, wetting that ass up.

"I told you not to fuck wit' me. But you wouldn't listen. Now look at you, you stoopid fuck." I mimicked Tony Montana.

KiKi braved taking a face full of water to get to me. When she got closer, I stuck the nozzle down her shirt and squeezed the handle. She was jumping around, laughing and screaming, and finally she wrestled the hose away from me. I dipped my shoulder and broke for the door.

"Scary ass nigga!" she called out behind me.

"Yeah, but I'ma dry ass nigga, too," I said over my shoulder.

A few minutes, later KiKi came inside, dripping wet with dirt all over her knees and legs.

"Dammnnn! You look a mess," I teased.

"Go to hell!"

I laughed. "In clean and dry clothes. Can't say the same for you."

She gave me the middle finger and then headed for the stairs. "I'm going take a shower."

"Run me a bath when you're done."

"When Hell freezes over," she said, fronting. I had gotten the best of her but she wouldn't miss the opportunity to please me.

***
Julz

"Ahhhhhh!" I belted, throwing myself against the back of the driver's seat. "Why the fuck would you do this to meeeee?" I cried so hard I began choking violently. Then unexpectedly my cheeks ballooned with bile, so I hurriedly opened the door and released puke onto the street.

Once I upchucked breakfast and my belief in him, I ran my hand over my mouth to wipe away any remnants of my vomit.

"Liar! You fuckin' lied to me." I blurted my resentment.

Flashes of them frolicking outdoors turned into images of them fucking indoors and I felt my temperature rising off the charts.

Frantically, I grabbed my phone and called Essence. The moment she answered, I bawled my eyes out, ranting off every sordid detail of what I just witnessed.

"Girl, I'm so sorry you're going through this. You don't deserve to be mistreated, no woman does. Look, leave him be and deal with him another day, when you have a cooler head. Just come over to my place, I'll call the girls and we'll get through this together, like always."

My head agreed with her. It was the logical thing to do but I was thinking with my heart and it told me to check him, and her too if she got sporty, right now!

"I hear you but I can't close my eyes tonight without confronting this nigga. So, if I don't call you in an hour, that means I'm in jail. In that case, bail me out." I placed the truck in gear to drive the few yards to his door.

"Julz! No! Just leave, for real." She sounded like she was my mama and not my friend.

So like a rebellious child, I screamed on her. "Bitch, just have *my* back!"

Click!

***

Choppa

Ten minutes had passed since KiKi went to shower. I was in the kitchen, going through the fridge when the doorbell chimed. *Now, who could this be?* I wondered.

We hadn't been there but a few weeks and KiKi would know better than to give anyone our address. Maybe it was a neighbor just welcoming us to the neighborhood, I guessed as I went to answer the door.

I didn't bother to look out of the peephole, I just turned the knob and pulled the door open. When I saw who was standing there, my mouth gaped.

"Shorty, what are you doing here?" My voice was low and terse.

"No, the question is what are *you* doing here!" Her mouth was twisted in anger and her face was wet with tears.

I quickly looked over my shoulder to see if KiKi was walking up. That was the last thing I wanted to happen. I grabbed Julz by both arms. "Baby, listen to me. I can explain everything but you gotta leave. Now!" My eyes pleaded with her not to argue.

"Are you married, Choppa? Is the bitch your wife?" Julz' eyes were squinted.

"No, baby. It's nothin' like that?"

Whap!

My face stung from the sudden impact of her hand.

"Well, why the fuck are you here with your goddam shirt off!" She lifted her hand to slap me again but I grabbed her wrists and locked them at her sides.

"Shorty, you gotta believe me. Man, it ain't what you think. Please leave and go home, you're gonna fuck everything up."

"You're a liar! A liar! A liar and a cheat!" she bawled.

Fuck! I had to talk fast, before KiKi came down the stairs and all hell broke out.

Keeping my voice low, I begged her to leave. "Go home and I'll be over there in an hour. I'll explain everything then," I promised. I pulled her to me and tried to give her a quick kiss.

"Get your lips off of me!" she growled.

"Okay! Okay!" I threw my hands up in supplication. "Just go home. I promise you I'll be over there in an hour."

"No, you won't. You're just lying." She sobbed.

"Nah, shorty, you gotta trust me." I dug in my pockets and pulled out two fists full of money. "Here, hold this. If I don't show up in an hour, you can have it." As soon as that shit came out of my mouth, I knew I had fucked up.

"I don't want your muthafuckin' money!" she screamed.

I was tryna talk low, calm her down quickly, and peek over my shoulder for KiKi. If she walked up on this shit, somebody was going to the Emergency Room.

Through the mercy of The Most High, I was able to convince Julz to leave. "I'ma go! But if you're not knocking on my door in *one hour* I'll be back," she said acidly.

As soon as she turned on her heels, I closed and locked the door. I heard her engine start in the driveway just as KiKi walked up behind me.

"Who was that?" she asked, moving me aside and looking through the peephole.

"I don't know. Some lady that had the wrong address," I lied.

KiKi turned around and looked at me with doubt. "Are you sure?"

"Yeah, I'm sure." I maintained eye contact as not to reveal my dishonesty.

"Well, the bitch must me stupid because I just told her the same thing a little while ago."

I let her comment linger as I headed upstairs.

I took a bath in record time and then got dressed. Now I had to come up with a reason to leave the house without raising KiKi suspicion more than what she already held. But if push came to shove, she would just have to suspect me, because what mattered most to me was going to talk to my shorty and drying her tears.

Chapter 32
Choppa

I rolled up in front of Julz' door, with five minutes to spare and parked next to her car. I didn't know exactly what to expect from her when I knocked on her door, but I knew it wasn't gon' be pleasant. I was cool with that because I was armed with the truth and, in an odd way, I felt relieved that the cat was out of the bag. I couldn't help but wonder who had dropped dime on me but, really, I should've been told her about me and KiKi's *situationship*.

Now, there was no better time than the present to lay my cards on the table. No matter what, I wasn't about to lose her again, I would go to the depths of Hell to prevent that from happening. Things had been so good between us since we got back together, and I was determined to keep that happiness going.

Shorty makes everything I do worth doing it.

I chided myself for letting all this time pass without breaking it things down to her, and it hurt a nigga bad for her to have to find out the way that she did. The last thing I ever wanted to do was make her cry and distrust me. She could find any nigga to do that, na mean? My job was to keep a smile on her face and show her that every nigga wasn't a liar and a cheater.

As I opened the driver's door to get out, I remembered that I had picked up a little surprise for Julz the other day. I leaned over and unlocked the glove compartment and retrieved the present. I had planned to give it to her the next time we saw each other, but I hadn't expected it to be under these conditions.

Fuck it! I decided to just roll with it since the gift came from the heart.

As I walked up to her door, that same heart was beating like I was about to stand trial for murder. And in a way, I guess I was. Because if I couldn't convince shorty that there was nothin' between me and KiKi, it would certainly be the death of our relationship.

Mannn, I didn't even wanna ponder how I would react to that. *Me, without Julz again? Where the fuck they do that at?* I asked myself, because in the short time we'd been back together, baby girl had become my rib.

I slid Julz surprise in my pocket and knocked on her door. A millisecond later the door was flung open and she stood there with her arms folded across her chest.

Her eyes were puffy from crying and her hair was a bit disheveled, but she was still absolutely breathtaking to me.

"Explain! I'm listening." The heat coming off of her words and her brow was scorching.

"Baby, let me come inside," I said softly.

"No! You can say whatever you have to say *right here* and then you can go!"

"Julz, just let me step inside and speak my piece. Trust me, baby, it ain't what you think. Just hear me out."

"The same way you heard me out about Tyriq?"

I fought back the urge to snap, just the mention of that nigga's name conjured thoughts of blood. But shorty had a point. "I get it, ma. But you're a lot more reasonable than I am. Just let me come in and talk to you. I promise you'll understand."

"Is she your wife, Choppa? Just tell me that." She looked down and stared at my left hand as if expecting to see a wedding band all of a sudden.

"Nah, it's nothin' close to that. She's not even my woman. Besides, you're my wife," I tapped my chest with my fist, "right here where it counts, in my heart."

"But is she your wife by law?" Her arms were still folded over her chest, blocking my entrance.

"Shorty, let me come inside. I'm 'bout to lay everything out for you."

This time she stepped to the side and let me in. I took a seat on the couch while she locked the door. It didn't surprise me that she left much space between us when she sat down on the sofa. "You have about fifteen minutes to explain and then I'm going to bed so I can get ready for work tomorrow." Her inflection sounded so cold and dispassionate, but I knew it disguised hurt.

I slid closer to her and took her hands in mine. Julz tried to resist but I wouldn't let go of them. I looked in her eyes and spoke the absolute truth. I told her everything, leaving out nothin'.

It was way past fifteen minutes when I concluded, finishing up with, "I haven't slept with her since my homie showed me that tape. That's on everything I love," I swore.

Julz asked me a few questions about Cross and how long I planned to be in the game.

"Just let me get a mil' and some change, and I'll leave the game alone."

"And in the meantime, I'm supposed to be okay with my man living with another woman? And I'm supposed to trust you not to sleep with her?" Her voice grew louder with each word. "You can trust me, shorty." I promised.

"Well, I don't!" she finally exploded. "And even if I did try to trust you, I don't fuckin' trust her!"

"Baby, she can't make me do nothin' I don't wanna do, and I don't wanna be with her like that." My thumbs caressed the back of her hands as I continued to hold them in mine.

"No, Choppa! No! Please, just walk out of my life and leave me alone. Go to her, she's beautiful and sexy, and she's the type of woman you need. I can't offer you anything." The dam broke, and her face flooded with tears.

I tried my best to kiss them all away. "Shorty, please don't cry." I felt tears pushing at the corner of my own eyes. "Baby, you're everything to me. I don't want her. You just have to allow me to leave her the right way or it could cost me my life."

"No, Choppa! Please, stop talking to me. I don't wanna hear anything else. Just go to her." She pulled her hands away and covered her ears.

I reached up and gently held them in mine again. "Okay, baby, if you want me to I'll leave her tonight. Fuck her daddy. I'll take his ass to war before I lose you. I'll lay my life on the line," I said with sincerity.

"No, I don't want you to die for me," she cried.

"It don't matter, baby, because I would die without you." Now a tear fell from my eye.

Julz dropped her head and then slowly lifted it and looked into my eyes.

"Do you know how bad I was hurt when I saw y'all in the yard having a water fight?" she said as a fresh river of tears ran down her face. "It looked like y'all were so in love."

I kissed her and reassured her that wasn't the case at all. "I mean, I don't hate the girl but I don't love or want her, either. On my word, I love *you,* shorty—not nan other woman in this world." The conviction in my voice must've broke through to her because she wrapped her arms around my neck and laid her head on my shoulder. I then reached into my pocket. "Baby, I have something for you and before you think it—no, I had been bought this for you."

She opened the box and gasped, looking up at me. "Choppa, what does this mean?"

I took her right hand and slid the promise ring onto her ring finger. "It means that my word to you is bond and I'll love you forever."

I held her tightly and our hearts beat together until her tears dried and her sniffling stopped. She placed her soft lips against my ear and whispered, "I need you to make love to me."

I needed the same thing, so I turned my head and covered her mouth with mine, kissing her like never before. I slid her pants and panties off and when I touched her delicate flower, it was already wet. She inhaled from my touch and reached for the top button on my jeans.

"I want you now," she said.

I helped her undress me and then I gave her what we both needed.

Chapter 33
Choppa

The sex was ridiculously good, like always, but now we had to get an understanding, I thought as I sat down on the couch and watched Julz head to the bathroom.

After a short while, she returned with a soapy washcloth and a dry towel. She washed the sex off of me then dried me off.

"That's called a trick bath," I remarked.

"I guess I took a ho bath, then," she said, bending over to pick our clothes up off of the floor.

"It's all good, shorty, we're nasty like that."

"Speak for yourself." A slight grin played on her face as she handed me my clothes.

I pulled on my jeans while she stepped into her pants and pulled on her top, then she sat down on the couch and draped her leg across mine.

She was quiet and not really looking at me, so I asked, "You a'ight, shorty?"

"Yes." She played with the hair on my arm.

I could tell that the new revelations were still heavy on her mind. "Peep this, Julz. Everything I told you about KiKi is fact. You have my word, I won't let the situation linger. And if you get to the point where you can't deal with it anymore, just say the word and I'll end it. Fuck what I lose."

"I'll be okay, boo."

"A'ight, but here's what I need from you," I paused while I stroked her hair and looked into her eyes. "The friendship you have with Tyriq—that shit's dead. I mean, over with!" Her eyes saddened. "Oh, you 'bout to cry over that nigga?" I pushed her leg off of me and shot up off of the couch, heading for the door.

Julz was on my heels. She grabbed the back of my shirt and pleaded with me not to go. "I'm not crying, Choppa. It's just—"

I spun around swiftly and grabbed her by the chin. "It's just what? Say the wrong muthafuckin' thing!" I threatened.

"Oww! You're hurting me!"

Her pained cry stopped me from boiling over. I released her face and kissed her softly on the nose. "I'm sorry. I shouldn't have done that. But it's either him or me, you choose. Right here, right now." My face was tight with anger.

"Of course, I'ma choose you," she said.

I stared at her to see if her eyes watered but they didn't.

"Cool, now c'mere." I took her hand and led her over to the couch. Picking her phone up off of the table, I said, "Gon' make that call and tell that nigga not to ever contact you again."

"Choppa, please let me do it in a better way. Tyriq doesn't deserve that."

"Fuck did you just say to me? You think I give a fuck what he deserves? Julz, do it now! Don't test me, shorty, I'll walk up outta this bitch and never come back." My heat index was one million!

"Okay, Choppa, I'll do it."

I handed Julz her phone and sat with a mean unit on my face while she made the call. The phone rang three times and then the voicemail picked up, identifying it was definitely him.

"Tyriq, this is Julz. Please don't ever call me again. Thanks for everything you've ever done for me and Justus but Choppa doesn't want me to communicate with you anymore, and I'm going to respect his wishes. Take care."

When she hung up the phone, I leaned in closer and saw tears in the corners of her eyes. "You crying?" I gritted.

"I'm sorry." She put her head down.

"You bet' not let those muthafuckas fall or I'm out!"

"Choppa, I did what you asked me to do. Please don't be mean to me," she said in a child's voice that melted me like butter.

I wrapped my arms around her and held her tightly. Placing soft kisses on her lips, I said, "I'm sorry, shorty. You know a nigga love you to death. I don't wanna hurt your feelings, ma, but I need you to be all mine. Ain't no halfway, understand?"

"Yes." She nodded her head up and down.

"Good, because ain't no middle ground with loyalty. My enemies should be your enemies, too. Just like yours are mine. I don't care if you're in the wrong, let a bitch get stupid, and I'll twist that cap."

248

"I understand," she said.

Whether she meant it or not, I was about to find out.

"Call and change your phone number. I don't want that nigga to be able to contact you ever again." I was dead ass serious.

This time, she didn't put up any buck. I guess she realized it was useless to do so.

At the same time Julz was getting her number changed, my phone was ringing on the table beside me. I picked it up and answered it.

The call turned out to be from Cross. I braced myself for some bullshit, but he was just calling to check on everything.

"I'll be at you in a week or so." I estimated.

"All right." He hung up and I returned my attention to Julz.

She finished her call to the phone company and then she programmed her new number into my phone. "That's my baby." I smiled and thanked her with a kiss.

"I love you so much," she said with indisputable conviction.

"I know you do, baby girl, and I promise to make you the happiest woman in the world."

She threw her arms around my neck and rested her head in the crook of my shoulder.

I put my nose in her hair and inhaled her scent. As we remained silently cuddled, I promised myself that I would deliver on my promise to her because she was truly all the woman I'd ever need.

***

Julz
Three days later...

After what felt like the longest week of my life, the weekend was finally here and today was the day the two most important guys in my life would meet one another.

I figured the best way to do that was having a family day at Six Flags over Georgia. Hopefully, the thrills and excitement of being at the amusement park, which Justus loved, would smooth over the turbulent first impression my son remembered of Choppa.

"Mama! Mama! Mama! What are we waiting for?" He gleefully questioned, jumping in mini pulses.

I scooted forward on the sofa. "We're waiting on mommy's friend."

"Who? Uncle Riq?"

I lifted my eyes to the roof of my lids. "Justus, baby, don't do this. Not today. I already told you it's Choppa that's taking us. And we're gonna have so much fun." I grabbed at his belly but he stepped backwards and out of my reach.

"I don't want to go with him. He's a bad man." His face was straighter than an arrow.

I couldn't argue his perspective, only give him a new one.

Pulling him between my legs, I rubbed his shoulders and spoke tenderly. "The day you saw him wasn't the *real* Choppa. You know, sometimes I get mad and do things I wouldn't do on a normal day. Well, that's what happens when people get upset. And that's all that happened with Choppa."

"But you never pulled out a gun to shoot nobody." He looked away and fiddled with his fingers the same way I did when I felt at a loss.

The conversation was making me uncomfortable but I had less than five minutes to impress on Justus to give Choppa a chance.

"Baby, he was wrong and he regrets ever doing that. But what you'll learn as you get older is that people make mistakes, a lot of them, but they shouldn't be crucified for them forever. Can you please forgive him like mommy has?"

He was silent, like he didn't know I was waiting on his response, so I nudged him to answer.

"Okay," he mumbled.

Knock. Knock. Knock.

"Baby, that's him. Be respectful and be nice, okay?"

"Yes, ma'am."

I smiled generously at him before I opened the door and welcomed Choppa inside.

"Hey, baby." I ushered him in. "I have a special someone I want you to meet." I summoned Justus to stand next to me with a wave of my hand.

250

Choppa squatted down and smiled brightly. "What's up, shorty?" He extended his hand for a shake.

"It's Justus."

Oh, God! I intervened. "He knows your name." I nervously giggled. "Baby, shake his hand."

Justus looked up at me and then back to Choppa, who was still smiling. Then he curled his hand into a fist and extended it.

"Oh, okay. You're into bumping fists." Choppa went to ball his hand to touch with Justus but stopped mid-way when Justus spoke again.

"Yea, that's how me and Uncle Riq do it."

Choppa's smile flattened and then he stood to his feet without giving any daps to my son. "Well, I ain't that nig…"

"Choppa!" I bucked my eyes at him.

He ran a hand over his mouth and down his goatee. "A'ight, ya'll ready to have some fun?"

I shot a quick glare at Justus, mouthing to him: *Be nice!* "I know I am. Are you, baby?"

"Yes, ma'am." It was an unenthusiastic reply but I'd take his respect over a smart remark.

In a matter of minutes, we were all loaded up into Choppa's car and heading out to the city of Austell, which was a thirty minute drive from my apartment. Plenty of time for us to talk—or not.

"So, tell me some things you like to do, Justus?" Choppa tried to spark conversation.

"I like to be quiet."

Oye! I pinched the bridge of my nose and dropped my head slightly.

"I feel that. I'm not much of a talker either." He turned on the music and we rode in uncomfortable silence to the park.

I was itching to talk to Justus privately, so the moment we arrived and got out of the car, I pulled my son off to the side and spoke to him firmly.

"Listen to me closely. Your behavior is unacceptable and I am displeased with your attitude. You better straighten that up real quick or else. You know I don't tolerate this out of you and I will not reward your rudeness. Do you understand me?"

"Yea." He looked off to the side but I grabbed his face and made him look me squarely in the eyes.

"Do you really understand because I'm not playing with you?"

"I said yes, ma'am." He was less than pleased.

As I wrapped up with my child, Choppa came over to us. "Y'all ready to go in?"

"Oh, yea!" I spoke for myself and Justus.

In between rides, I found myself apologizing on Justus' behalf, trying to convince Choppa that in time they'd be as thick as thieves. I truly believed in my heart they would be.

"It's all good, shorty. I'm Teflon. Besides, a four year old ain't strapped with enough ammo to take me down. I'ma win him over just like I did his mama."

That removed some of the discomfort I'd been feeling since our time together began. We shared an innocent kiss and then continued riding rides.

Hours later, we were back in the car and ready to head out to another destination.

We'd been snacking in the park but now it was time for some real food. "I don't know about y'all but I'm hungry?" I rubbed my stomach.

"I'm with it." Choppa agreed. "Aye, Justus, what you feel like eating?"

He hunched his shoulders. "I don't know."

"What you in the mood for? Pizza, hamburgers, chicken..." Choppa called out a list of foods but Justus declined them all. "A'ight. Maybe we can work up an appetite once we leave the toy store."

"Oooohh," I patted my fingertips together. "That sounds like fun." I could put off eating for that.

"Wanna go and get some Leggos? Your mama said you love them." I touched Choppa's leg and smiled appreciatively.

"No, sir. I don't play with them no mo'."

My eyebrows drew inward and I turned around in my seat to face Justus. "Since when? You just asked me to buy you some last week."

"Since last week." He looked at me with thinly veiled defiance.

"What?" I was torn between wanting to beat his lil' ass for being flip at the mouth or leaving him alone because I needed to understand it was gonna take more than one day for Choppa to grow on him. I thought about a little harder and concluded that I would *beat his ass!* I was still his mama.

"I'ma deal with you when we get home. Believe that!" I was breathing fire.

"Ease up, shorty. I got this." He spoke low enough for only me to hear. Looking through the rearview at Justus, he spoke. "It's your day, so how about you tell me what you want to do next?"

Justus didn't hesitate in his answer. "I wanna go by Uncle Riq and play with Carmello and y'all can do the adult thing."

Choppa's demeanor changed. I didn't know what was going through his mind but I was sure the overuse of Tyriq's name pushed his buttons.

My mouth dropped open. I was embarrassed for myself but more so for Choppa. Justus was known to get beside himself, as all children do, but today he broke records. He was acting outside of his body, for real.

"Justus!" The reprimand could be heard in the call of his name alone.

"What? He asked what I wanted to do."

I narrowed my eyes at him because he knew what he was doing. Sure he couldn't spell *antagonize* but he knew how to provoke a situation.

I looked over to Choppa. "I'm so sorry, baby."

"Don't be." He gritted, which made believe otherwise.

We pulled out of the lot and the ride leaving the park mimicked the ride going there—quiet.

It didn't surprise me when a half an hour later, we were back at my place. But what did surprise me, was Choppa's iciness toward me.

"Are you coming?" I said with one foot out of the door. He didn't even recognize my question. I frowned at that. After I pulled Justus from the back along with the toys Choppa won for him, I asked again.

This time he looked at me. "Close my door."

I wasn't about to argue with him, so I smiled and thanked him for today and did as he said. The moment I did, he pulled off like he had somewhere to be.

Justus looked up at me. "Can we go by Uncle Riq now?"

I looked him up then down. "No. You can go upstairs and prepare for this spankin'. Now go!"

His shoulders dropped and he began to whine already but I wasn't fazed. It was one thing to not like him but it was totally different to be disrespectful.

I followed behind him, shaking my head.

Today was a damn disaster but it's still fixable—I hope.

Restraining Order

Chapter 34
Choppa

As I pulled off from Julz and her son, I was reminded why I had never before invested a lot in a female who had children. I mean, a nigga might go all out to provide 'em with food, clothes, shelter and love, but their little unappreciative assess would be quick to come outta their mouths with some *you ain't my daddy* shit or in Justus' case, *Uncle Riq!*

True enough, I hadn't done all those things for Justus yet but, still, the lil' nigga made me seriously reconsider whether I would be willing to ever. To make matters worse, he didn't throw his daddy in my face— nah, he hit me with the one nigga's name I despised.

I felt steam coming off of my forehead as I put distance between me and their crib. Thoughts that Julz had lied to me about what was really up with her and Tyriq resurfaced in my mind.

Bleed, you can't blame baby girl for what her son said. Just think back to when you was a lil' shorty, anything used to come out of your mouth.

I couldn't even deny that. So, I let out a chuckle, followed by a deep, slow exhale and blew that shit to the side. *Small thing to a giant.* Besides, on the strength of Julz, alone, it was worth my best effort to win her boy over.

When I talked to shorty later that night, she was mad apologetic about her son's behavior. I told her, "You don't owe me no apology, baby. Just give it time, I'll break through that wall lil' man got up."

"I know you will, but—"

"Kill that, ma," I cut her off. "Ain't no buts. I was a little salty earlier but that's on me. Shorty just a kid."

"Justus knows better, though," she insisted.

"It's all good. It'll go better next time," I predicted and like a prophet my prediction came true.

The next time I was around Justus he didn't suddenly act like I was his best friend, but he didn't mention that bitch nigga, Tyriq, name one single time. And as summer came to a close and we spent more and more time together, we actually started liking each other.

255

Lil' dude was smart as a whip and was mad protective of his mama. Occasionally, he would block or want her attention when I was tryna get a little attention myself. At times, it could really get under my skin but, overall, things were good with us.

In fact, things were pretty good for me all around. I had the occasional problem that came with being in the game, but that would forever be the case. I let the small shit slide because I had learned a long time ago that *elephants don't swat at flies*. However, there was one thing I couldn't overlook.

Jared and Cardale were getting money, hand over fist. Not only were they moving more bricks than a demolition team, they were tryna squeeze in on my weed customers. Something had to be done about that.

"We can either get an understanding with 'em or we can get a coupla bodies," I told Pop as we drove to a prearranged meeting with them.

Behind us, a caravan of five cars, all loaded with young guns, traveled at an even speed.

Thirty minutes later, we pulled up at the restaurant where we were to meet. I saw Jared's new silver Jag' XF parked next to Cardale's new Lincoln Nav'. I choose to park a few rows behind them and instead of pulling into the open parking space, I backed in, just in case I had to move out fast.

The little homies fanned out strategically, to keep an eye on the front window of the restaurant, just like I had instructed them. I checked my banger to make sure it was ready to cough then put it back on my waist as I climbed out of the truck. Up under my shirt I wore a lightweight bpv. Pop was rocking one, too.

Before heading inside, I glanced at Jared's and Cardale's new whips again. I was happy to see them getting paper, I just didn't understand why they had to step on my toes in the process. I was also a little rankled that, besides a new ride, Cardale also had moved into a new crib, yet he still hadn't paid me all of the money he owed me.

He don't believe shit stank.

I was flat out of patience with him and my tolerance for Jared wasn't much longer.

"When we get in here and start talking to these niggas, if anything move besides their mouths we gon' make it go still," I said as me and Pop both opened up the car doors at the same time.

"Say no more."

"Say less," I replied.

***

Sitting across the table from the two niggas I had given their start in the game, I couldn't help but look at them with a measure of contempt as they tried to justify the moves they made to poach customers from me.

"We can't make them buy our shit, we just offer them a better price," said Jared, biting into the steak in front of him.

"And you think it's okay for you to go to customers you met through me and under sale me?" I asked gravelly.

"Ain't no rules to the game," said Cardale.

I looked at him and shook my head in disgust. "I always knew you were a grimy, unappreciative nigga, but I'm just now realizing you're a fool, too."

"Oh, yeah? How is that?" He dug his fork into his lasagna and shoveled some into his mouth. His head was down, showing me no respect.

"If I gotta answer that, it proves you're a fool," I said.

"Whatever, my nigga, I'm just doing my thing, don't hate on that," he replied, still holding his head down concentrating on the mound of food on his plate.

Jared, who was much wiser than the gluttonous Cardale, sat his fork down on the table and watched me closely. He had been at my side too many times when I peeled a disrespectful nigga's cap to underestimate me.

"Bruh, I feel where you're coming from now that I think about it. How about we do this," Jared paused to chew the rest of the food in his mouth and after washing it down with Pepsi, he continued, "we'll stop selling the green to anybody we met while rocking with you, but we're not gonna stop selling it altogether."

"I thought the money from the loud was too slow fa y'all, ain't that what you said? That's why y'all wanted to do your own thing and fuck with that white girl?" I reminded him in a voice that wouldn't travel beyond our table.

"Don't nobody owe you no explanation," said Cardale. Both of his jaws were stuffed and he still hadn't looked up from his plate.

The money done went to this fool's head. He must've forgot that I put the muthafuckin' 'G' in gangsta!

Beside me, my lil' soldier must've sensed I was close to popping off. He scooted his chair back from the table at the same time I rose up out of mine.

My hand shot across the table and grabbed ahold of Cardale's shirt. I wrapped it around my fist and pulled him halfway across the table, knocking over glasses and plates that clattered to the floor noisily.

With my face inches from his, I said, "Bleed, look at me when I talk to you, pussy! You wanna eat, muthafucka? I'll give you something to chew on?" With my free hand I lifted the bottom of my shirt, giving him a glance at the heat on my waist.

"Choppa, be easy, fam. You drawing heat," said Jared. He didn't move, though, or Pop would've lit his ass up.

With Cardale's collar still held tightly in my grasp, I looked around the room and saw I had indeed attracted the attention of the few patrons that were in there.

I gave Cardale a warning stare and released his shirt. "Keep playing pussy, my nigga, you gon' get fucked," I said, easing myself back down into my seat.

"You just dug your own grave, homie," said Cardale.

Pop's hand went to his waist but stopped when I touched his arm. "Another day, youngin," I advised.

He let his arm fall back to his side but his eyes communicated to Cardale that they made graves big enough for his fat ass, too. Giving Cardale one last hard look, Pop turned his chair around and sat down, straddling it backwards.

Jared cleared his throat. "If y'all finished, let's get down to business. Time is money," he said, glancing at the icy timepiece on his wrist.

For the next twenty minutes, or so, we discussed a solution to our problem. I did most of the talking and they did the listening because when it came to them serving my customers, there was nothin' to negotiate.

"That's where I draw the line," I restated.

Jared looked from me to Cardale. "Cuz, I can respect that. What about you?"

"It's whatever with me," he said in a noncommittal tone.

"Cool. Do what you do, and I'll do what I do." I rose up out of my seat, bringing the meeting to an uncertain end.

"Bruh, you have my word, we won't sell nothin' else to your clientele," said Jared, affording himself a stay of execution.

As for Cardale, I began planning his death from that very moment. Fuck the dough he still owed me, he could take it to the grave with him.

I looked at Pop and read the look on his face, he was just itching to put in work, but this wasn't the time or place.

I rested a hand on his shoulder. "Let's be out, lil' bruh." Neither one of us had taken a bite of the food we had ordered when we first arrived.

Pop had to make a statement before leaving, though. He reached across the table and slapped Cardale's plate on the floor.

"They call me, Pop, nigga! Ask around!"

On the way out of the door, I smiled to myself. Youngin wasn't nothin' nice.

Ca$h & Coffee

Chapter 35
KiKi

I could tell Choppa had a lot on his mind lately but things between us had reached a muthafuckin' breaking point and I wasn't that bitch to keep quiet about it!

"Baby, let that man handle his business in the streets and you take care of home. Don't be another problem to him, you have to be his pillow. The one person in his life who he doesn't have to go to war with," said Mama.

I rolled my eyes to the ceiling and connected my headphones so I could get dressed while we talked on the phone. "No, Mama, I'm sorry, I can't be that sweet docile woman to him like you've been to Daddy all of these years. I'm not his *flipping* doormat!"

"Honey, what is a confrontation going to get you?"

"Some answers! And hopefully some dick. Do you realize it's September—hell, almost October—and he hasn't touched me since March?"

"Oh my!" she exclaimed. I could picture her hand over her mouth. "Well, I can see why you're so snappy lately."

"Exactly! But I tell you what," I paused to wiggle into my jeans, "I'm about to show this nigga and that bitch he been fucking with that you and Daddy didn't raise no punk."

"KiKi, don't you get yourself in trouble down there," she warned.

I laughed sarcastically. "Ha! Mama, you ever known a chick named KiKi to be afraid of trouble. When I get finished with Choppa and that bitch, they're gonna make a *Lifetime* movie out of the shit I'ma do."

"Baby, no!" she shrieked, but I didn't want to hear anymore of her rationale ass suggestions.

"Bye, Mama, I love you. Tell Daddy to call down here and contact a bail bondsman." I hung up and turned my phone off so no one could reach me.

Breathing fire, I put on a sports bra and covered it with a body-fitting workout shirt. I didn't want to leave much for Choppa's bitch to grab at when I commenced to kicking that ho's ass. Next, I put on a pair of footies and then slid on my Air Max and tied the laces super tight.

Before leaving the house, I checked to make sure my canister of pepper spray was in my purse. On the way out of the door, I leaned into the hallway closet and grabbed the Louisville Slugger I had bought.

These muthafuckas gon' learn today!

As I drove over to Choppa's bitch house with the baseball bat on the passenger seat, I programmed the system in my car to play a Kelis' song that captured exactly how the fuck I felt.

Yo, this song, yo
This song is for all the women out there
That have been lied to by their men
And I know y'all been lied to over and over again
This is for y'all

"Sing it, gurl," I said.

Yo, maybe you didn't break the way you should have broke, yo
But I break, know what I am saying, this is how it goes y'all, damn
Last year, Valentine's Day, you would spoil me, say
"Babe, I love you, love you babe I swear"
Held you when you were sick, even' sucked your dick
The whole time I think to myself, this isn't fair.

Hot, angry tears spilled down the sides of my face as those lyrics hit home. I thought about the past Valentine's Day, the heart-shaped, floating diamond ring Choppa had given me—the one I faithfully still wore on my finger, hoping we would recapture the love we shared when he gave it to me.

What is this I see (No)
You don't come home to me (Oh, no)
When you don't come home to me (Man)
Can't deal, can't bear

Kelis was edging me on with every verse.

"Bitch, you about to make me kill both of their asses," I said, as if Kelis could hear me.

Lord, please let Choppa have his ass over there when I get there. That's all I ask of you, I prayed.

His own boy had gave up the goods on him and the ho. Choppa and him was already beefing plus the nigga had been trying to get with me for months, so all it took was a little freaky talk and dude snitched him out.

I knew the bitch name, address and her work schedule. Now she was about to get introduced to a Cleveland, Ohio bitch that would fuck a country ass ho up in a New York minute! And Choppa was gonna get it, too. Lying ass muthafucka!

I hate you so much right now
I hate you so much right now
I hate you so much right now
Ahh...

I screamed right along with the song as I hoped onto I-285. Already in a murderous mood, my attitude got jacked up even more trying to deal with Atlanta's fucked up traffic! Every day there was an accident on the way to whatever the fuck I went.

Traffic crept along at a ridiculously slow pace. I might as well jumped out of my car and walked to my destination, for all the progress I was making.

An hour and a half later, I finally neared my exit but now I had to get over or I would miss it.

I looked over to my right and signaled for this white man in a pickup to let me in. He made a face at me then gave me the finger.

"Fuck you, cracker!" I mouthed.

As traffic drew dangerously closer to where I needed to get off, I saw an opportunity to switch into the proper lane. Just as I hit the turn signal some mousey looking old lady closed the gap, cutting off my chance to get over.

"Bitch! Let me in or I'ma ram your fucking ride!" I raged at her.

Panic struck her face and she came to almost a complete stop in order to let me in. I maneuvered my car into the right lane just in the nick of time to make the exit.

Kelis was still screaming *I hate you so much right now,* causing the devil in me to turn redder and redder the closer I got to the apartment complex where I was told Choppa's little side bitch, Julz, lived. I knew exactly where the complex was and what unit she lived in, because, until recently, Cardale lived there, too.

Just let Choppa be there when I roll up, I kept saying over and over again as I impatiently weaved in and out of traffic.

Ten minutes later, I pulled right in front of the bitch's door. Neither of Choppa's vehicles were in the parking lot but I saw the white Camry I was told Julz drove.

I parked right behind it, grabbed my baseball bat off of the passenger seat and got out of the car, half closing the door.

Being that it was about 6:30 in the evening, the sun was still out, meaning whoever came to the door would be able to see my face clearly. I didn't give a fuck, though.

***

Julz

It had been a long, trying day at work. I was glad to finally be at home with my shoes off. Choppa had called a short while ago to tell me he loved me and he would be over later. I was so looking forward to that. Just seeing his face always brightened my day and when he held me in his arms, all was right in my universe.

I was so pleased Justus had begun to really take to him, that meant the world to me. I wouldn't have known what to do if Choppa hadn't been able to win my boy over because Justus was my life.

Sitting across from him at the dining room table, I smiled proudly as I watched him do his homework correctly.

"When you're done, my love, we're going to have dinner. What would you like to eat?" I asked.

"Hot pockets!" he replied excitedly.

"Well, hot pockets it shall be."

I knew it wasn't the healthiest meal but he was such a good kid, I didn't mind giving him a treat from time to time.

"Yay!" he exclaimed, doing a little dance in his seat.

"Concentrate on what you're doing," I said.

"Okay, Mama. Can I have a kiss first?" He looked up at me with those puppy dog eyes just like his father. My heart fluttered for my young prince.

"Of course, you can have a kiss." *Muah.* I leaned down and planted one right on his puckered lips.

"Ummm! Your kisses taste like candy, Mama."

"Aww! That's so sweet, baby. I love you." I kissed him again.

"I love you more," he replied, smiling.

I rubbed his arm affectionately and then got up to go the refrigerator, but a hard knock on the door diverted me.

"Who is it?" I called out as I went to answer it. If it was Precious, I was going to cuss her butt out. I had told that heifer a hundred times about banging on my door like it was an emergency.

Knock! Knock! Knock!

The pounding grew louder. By the time I got to the door, I was so irritated I didn't even look out of the peephole to see who it was. Instead, I twisted the doorknob and snatched the door wide open.

"Precious! Didn't I tell your ass not..." I stopped in mid-sentence as I recognized the face that was staring back at me. *KiKi!*

"Bitch, you bold to creep with my man!" She pushed her way inside and raised a baseball bat over her head. "Ho, but I'm the muthafuckin' answer for you side bitches!"

***

KiKi

I cocked the bat back and swung at that ho's head like I was trying to hit a homerun.

Luckily for her, my aim was off and the bat connected with the inside of the door.

"Ahh!" she screamed and dashed to the other side of the living room.

"Nawl, don't run now, bitch!"

"Get out of my house!"

"I will, after I fuck you up!"

"Get out now or I'm calling the police!" she threatened.

I paused for a second, not because she threatened to call the po's but, because in that moment I got a real good look at the ho and I realized she was the same bitch that came to my house that day. *Oh, hell to the muthafuckin' naw!* Her and Choppa had played the wrong one!

She again threatened to call the po's, like that shit was gon' scare a real bitch. "Bitch, I ain't from Compton but *fuck the police!*" I said as I smashed a lamp on my way to tear into her ass.

"You're crazy! Get out of my house!" She flew across the room again.

"You muthafuckin' right! And I ain't on my meds!" I lifted the bat over my head and brought it down with all of my might, shattering a glass end table.

I looked up and saw a little boy run up to the bitch. "Mama!"

I froze in place again as I stared at the boy for a full minute or more, searching his face for the slightest feature of Choppa's, but I saw none.

"Lil' boy, you better say your prayers tonight!" I said.

"Look, bitch, if you lay a finger on him we're going to kill each other up in here!" said Julz.

"Ha! Bitch, you ain't killin' nothin'.'"

"Get out of our house!" the little boy screamed at me and grabbed a toy truck that was sitting on the nearby couch. He held it up like he was going to throw it at me.

"Go ahead," I dared him. "I fuck up little kids, too!"

Julz stepped in front of him and although she was glaring at me, she was talking to him. "Justus, go in the bedroom and lock the door. Now!"

"No, Mama, she's going to hurt you," he cried.

You goddam skippy! I thought.

"No, she's not. Just do as I say!" She pushed him to run as she dodged my incoming swing.

He ran reluctantly, eyeing me with distrust as he did as he was told. As soon as his little ass was out of sight, I looked at his mother again. The bitch was nowhere near as pretty as me. And compared to mine, her body was nothing that should've attracted Choppa's attention.

That made me hotter. *Why would he fuck with a lesser bitch than the one he had at home?* I wondered. Well, I would ask his punk ass

266

that question later, but right now I was gonna break every bone in his side chick's body.

Staring at Julz with pure hate, I said, "Ho, you gonna come and get this ass whuppin' or you want me to bring it to you?"

"Bring it, bitch!" she said.

So, that's what the fuck I did.

Ca$h & Coffee

Chapter 36
Choppa

Man, I couldn't believe this! I was in the middle of handling a deal for 130 bands when I got a frantic call from my shorty. My mouth fell open as she tearfully told me what happened.

It didn't surprise me what KiKi had done, that was the type of chick she was. In fact, I was more surprised that she had gone over to Julz' crib with a baseball bat instead of a gun. But what really had me throwed was *how did KiKi find out who shorty was and where she rested?*

Cardale!

That was the first name that came to mind. His bitch ass knew he couldn't win a war, man to man, with me, so he had done some real ho shit by telling KiKi about Julz. He knew KiKi was crazy like that gorilla glue and would act the fuck up in a heartbeat.

Cool! All that nigga did was rush the death I had planned for him.

KiKi was a whole 'notha problem I'd have to deal with. I knew that whenever I went home, she was going to be ready to fight. She had probably already cut up or burned all of my clothes, but she wouldn't be satisfied until she drawed blood.

Fuck her, tho'. I had to go check on my baby before attending to any of that other shit.

As soon as I pulled up to Julz' crib and got out of my truck, I saw the evidence of KiKi having been there. The overhead lights in the parking lot revealed it all.

Every window on Julz' car was smashed out and there were huge dents in every section of the car's body. All four tires were flat and the words *Bitch, you fucked the wrong woman's man* was spray painted on the hood.

I ran my hand down my face and let out a huge sigh. I had never intended to bring this type of drama into baby girl's life.

I stood there in a daze. KiKi had fucked Julz' Camry up. I could only imagine how things looked inside of the apartment and knowing the street fighter KiKi was, I feared Julz' face might be black and blue.

Julz didn't deny being beat up pretty badly but, at least, Justus was unharmed. Still, I dreaded facing her right now.

I shoved my hands down in my pockets and took a deep breath, exhaling slowly to relieve the tension that had built up in my chest since receiving the call from Julz an hour ago.

After finishing up the deal, I had drove straight here. I still had the 130 grand in my trunk. But money was the furthest thing from my mind as I hurried inside to inspect the damage and comfort my woman and her son.

I heard Julz disengage the lock just as I rapped my knuckles on the door. When she opened it to let me in, I expected her to go off on me for what KiKi had done. Instead, she greeted me by walking into my embrace, quietly sobbing.

"Oww. Oww. Oww. My arm." She winced and I loosened my hold around her.

"Don't cry, baby, it's gon' be a'ight." I rubbed her back gently.

We stood in the doorway for a while with her crying into my chest. I kissed the top of her head and tried to sooth her body-shaking sobs.

The harder she cried, the angrier I became at KiKi. Looking over Julz' shoulder I could see the destruction she had done to the living room. Broken glass was everywhere and furniture had been turned over.

I'ma put my foot in her ass this time! Fuck her daddy and any of his goons he wanna send after me. This is going too far!

I walked Julz in the house backwards and softly closed the door.

Getting a better look at my shorty, she looked like she'd been to war and in a sense she had. KiKi had done the muthafucka to her. Julz' look was indescribable.

Looking at how she wrecked shop on Julz, I wouldn't have been surprised if KiKi walked away untouched.

I was boiling fury but I kept my contempt for KiKi's actions hidden behind my concern for shorty.

"Baby, don't say nothin' right now. Just pack some things for you and Justus, I'm taking y'all to the condo and then I'm going to handle this shit."

Thankfully, Julz didn't put up a fight, she simply retreated to the back. I think shorty was too emotionally drained to do anything but do as I asked.

"Choppa!" I heard her cry out for me and I quickly dashed to her side.

"What's wrong?" I asked anxiously as I held my hands out in supplication.

"My arm hurts worse when I move it," she cried as she cradled it close to her body.

"Just tell me what to grab. I got it from here."

I had promised Julz that I would lay my life on the line to protect her and now it was time to do just that. Cross' daughter had to be dealt with regardless to the ramifications.

***

That night, I took Julz and Justus to the condo. I would nurse her wounds later but for now I made sure they were okay inside before I left.

Julz pleaded with me not to go and hurt KiKi but her pleas fell on deaf ears.

"A man gotta do what a man gotta do," I said as I walked out of the door.

"Bae, please!" she followed behind me crying.

I turned around and looked into her eyes. "Shorty, you've already cried enough for me. Now it's time for that bitch's family to cry." I hopped in my truck and drove off with only one thing on my mind. *KiKi ass is going down!*

God must've had other plans for her because when I got home, KiKi wasn't there. I called her phone but she wouldn't answer. Finally, I received a text from the bitch.

9:47 p.m. KiKi: *I'll hit you back later. I'm fucking your boy.*

I didn't even respond. I would deal with her ass when we saw each other.

In the meantime, I went back to the condo only to find Julz in extreme pain and Justus sitting next to her, laying his head against her.

I rushed inside without fully closing the door. "Baby, what's wrong?"

She looked up at me painfully slow. "It's my arm!" she cried loudly. It hurts so bad and I can't move it all!"

Putting pieces together, I questioned. "Did KiKi hit you with the bat?" She bobbed her head *yes*. "Why didn't you tell me that? You might have a broken arm, shorty. Real talk."

"Because I thought the pain would go away on its own but instead it got worse." She cried more tears, which made Justus look at me with a baby mug on his face.

I'ma ring that red bitch by the throat. And I meant that shit!

"Come on." I eased her off of the sofa, caringly. "We're going to the hospital."

***

Julz
Piedmont Newton

After a forty minute wait, I was seen by the intake nurse and then thirty minutes later, the ER physician. Both Choppa and Justus wanted to stay with me but the doctor thought it was best that my son not be further exposed to my situation.

I agreed. "Justus, I'm gonna go with the doctors now. Mama's gonna be okay, okay?" I tried giving him a reassuring smile but the split on my busted lip began burning, preventing me.

"No, I wanna be with you. I can help. I promise." Justus pleaded on the verge of crying.

I sucked back my emotions as best as I could and nodded my head to Choppa and then to the door, asking him to take him to the waiting area.

Choppa didn't put up a fuss. "Okay, we'll be right out here." He leaned over, kissed me on the forehead and then steered an unwilling Justus by the shoulder to turn around and leave.

My son was displeased to describe it lightly. I could read the hurt in his eyes when I sent him away.

The moment I was alone with the doctor, he began asking me what I assumed were the typical questions for a battered patient.

Was I being abused?

Was I afraid for my life?

Did I know my assailant and was it my boyfriend who hurt me?

I answered emphatically *no!*

After I put to rest the need to file a police report, he thumbed through my chart and read off my chief complaint.

"Immobility of the right arm. Tell me what caused this."

Shaking my head in disbelief, I recalled the malicious attack. "I was swung at with a bat and I used my arm to shield myself."

"Okay, I see." He hummed as he read some more and then he asked another question. "Ms. Kidd, are you pregnant?"

I shook my head *no*. "No, I don't think so. Well, I don't know."

"It's okay, we'll get a urine sample to test before taking you to Radiology. We have to be certain before exposing you to radiation if you are."

I groaned as I nodded my head slowly. The two Tylenols I took earlier did nothing for the headache I was suffering from.

We spoke for a few more minutes and then there was a faint knock at the door as it opened slowly, producing my nurse.

She stood nearby as he slid his hands into a pair of gloves and began his examination. After he surveyed the damage to my head and face, he then opened the gown I slipped into earlier and scanned me visually, checking for bruises, all the while pressing along the contour of my torso, back and stomach.

"Does this hurt?" He touched alongside the length of my side.

I told him *no*, then he did the other and I yelped. "Yess! That hurts!" Tears rolled from my eyes.

Directing his conversation to the nurse, he said, "I'm ordering a CT w/o contrast of the head and x-rays of her right arm and full right torso. While we wait on the films, give her four stitches for this gash over her eye."

"Yes, sir." The nurse nodded.

"She's going to take it from here. Once I get a read on your films, I'll be back to go over treatment with you. Do you have any questions for me?"

"Yes, what about my eye? What exactly is wrong with it and will it stay like this forever?" I referred to the pool of blood inside of my eyeball.

"The medical term for it is called subconjunctival hemorrhage also considered a broken blood vessel as a result of direct trauma. It looks worse than it really is. You'll actually notice a decrease in size after a 24 hour period but they typically heal within two to three weeks." He smiled at me and then tapped me on the knee. "I'll be back."

I nodded my head as I watched him scurry out of my room.

"All right, Ms. Kidd. I need you to take this cup and go to the third door on your right and fill it up as much as you can."

I took it from her and scooted off of the table. "Umm, Miss, do you know how long I'll be here?"

She shook her head *no*. "It's hard to determine that."

"Okay, well will it be all right if I make a quick call? I'll be one minute, only."

"Sure. I'll be back in five." She excused herself and I called Essence.

Considering it was after midnight, I already knew she would be asleep but I needed a favor.

After the fourth ring, she groggily answered. "Hello."

"E, I'm so sorry for waking you but I'm in the hospital."

At the snap of a finger, she became alert. "Julz, what happened? Which hospital?"

"The ER at Piedmont on Hospital Dr. and I'm here because I was beaten up…"

"By who?" She interrupted. "I *know* Choppa didn't put his fuckin' hands on you, did he?"

"Of course not!" *Why would she think that?* "It was that girl, KiKi, I told you about. Look, it's a long story and I have to get x-rays and stuff done. Can you please come by, pick up Justus and stop off at my place to get his uniform and backpack? I don't know how long I'll be here and he has school in the morning."

"I'm already getting dressed." I could hear her moving about. "But, umm, tell me, how bad are you hurt?"

"I'm pretty banged up, sis. Look, I promise we'll talk about everything later. Just come get my boy. He's in the waiting room with Choppa."

"All right. I'm leaving ASAP."

We both hung up. I then slid my phone back into the pocket of my jeans that were folded on the counter before I headed out into the hallway.

As I hung my head in shame away from inquisitive eyes, I silently began praying that no more drama followed my relationship with Choppa.

Ca$h & Coffee

Chapter 37
Julz

Today was Sunday, a week since the rumble with KiKi sent me to the ER. That psychotic bitch gave me a grocery list of injuries that I was slowly but surely recovering from.

My face was next to normal with the exception of a small scar and the bloodshot eye. The contusion to the ribs didn't hurt as much and the pain meds for the fractures I suffered in both my arm and wrist numbed the constant aching but it would be another five weeks before the orthopedic would consider removing the cast I was in.

"You're gonna be okay watching Justus by yourself?" I asked Choppa before stepping out of the truck.

"Come on. What type of question is that?" he asked facetiously.

"A silly one." I leaned over and gave him a kiss, then I stepped out, opened the back door and kissed Justus, too. "Be good. I'll see you two back at the condo."

"Or I can stay with you." Justus offered.

"Or you can hang with Choppa and have fun as I gather what we need from the apartment. That won't be much fun at all." I ballooned my cheeks and shook my head sadly.

"All right." Justus settled.

"You sure you don't need me to wait until your friends get here?" asked Choppa.

Just because KiKi got the better of me didn't qualify me as a scary bitch, I thought. I was low-key offended but I knew he was just being my protector.

"No, I'll be fine. Besides, they'll be here any second. Just go, bae. I'll call you when I'm on my way back. Love you, guys." I blew air kisses and walked away.

Choppa decided the night of the fight that we'd stay with him at the condo until he found us a house we could call home. I was good with that plan because I didn't like the fact that his ex could pop up anytime she damn well pleased to raise havoc all over again.

I left the door open as I entered the apartment, taking in all of the damage KiKi caused and I felt myself get mad as if it just happened.

"Knock, knock." Fat-Fat tapped on the door as she announced their presence. "It's me, E and P."

I spun around to see my girls spill in, one by one. "Hey."

"Hey, Diamond Girl, you're looking so much better." Fat-Fat walked up to hug me, careful not to crush my arm in its sling.

"Thanks. I'm feeling better." I informed her.

Essence kissed me on the cheek. "It's good to see you in better spirits."

I nodded and smiled, then I gave Precious a one arm hug. "Thanks for coming, sis."

"Girl, where else would I be?" Precious questioned.

"Nowhere but here." I replied.

Choppa advised that I only collect and pack what me and Justus absolutely needed. Everything else he'd replace. Since he felt all of this was his fault, he told me it was the very least he could do.

Being that I was temporarily handicapped, there was very little I could do by myself. So my girls were a godsend.

So I knew when I enlisted their services they would do their best to convince me of retaliation. And as much as I entertained the thought from sun up to sun down, I just wanted to put *her* behind me.

I tried to navigate the conversation away from KiKi as much as possible but the closer we came to wrapping up, Precious and Essence doubled their efforts to dig KiKi right back up.

"Bitch, you don't understand. I cried real tears when I saw you all banged up and shit." Essence pounded her fist into her palm every couple of words to highlight her frustration. "Then to see your car and place look like a tsunami done ran through it set me all the way off. Ain't no way this bitch supposed to be walkin' around like shit sweet. 'Cause newsflash, *it's not!*"

"I'm mad, too, believe me but I don't want no more drama."

"You're being for real, right now?" Precious wore her usual stank face as she addressed me. "Then she's gon' take you for a weak bitch, like she run shit at her house and *yours*."

"Thank you!" Essence said with attitude, jumping back into the conversation. "The ho need to be taught a lesson."

278

Fat-Fat remained silent but she usually faded into the background when verbal confrontations ensued. That was just her demeanor because she was far from a punk, more like a quiet storm if the right buttons got pressed.

"Fat-Fat, you're a voice of reason. Do you agree with them, too?" I turned to her.

"I have to say that I do. I mean, ol' girl needs to either respect or fear you. Right now, she has neither."

"Right, but if we go and tag that ass, she'll think twice about fuckin' with you." Precious added.

"And I don't believe in fair nothing. You come for one you best be prepared to come for all, ya heard me." Essence began getting hyped.

After hearing all of them on one accord, it really had me thinking. I had told myself to leave well enough alone but the more Essence and Precious spoke of how payback was a bitch, and *they* were those bitches, was the more I was pulled in the direction of getting on board with what they proposed.

"Y'all right. Fuck that ho! She ain't hesitate to come for me, so I don't give a damn about keeping the peace with her." And I meant every word of it.

"You remember how to get to her house?" Essence asked, heading for the door.

"Like I lived there all my life," was all I said.

***

The four of us sat in Precious' car, parked down the street from KiKi's house waiting for her ass to come out. We had been waiting for over an hour already and our legs were catching cramps from sitting there so long.

"Bruh, where this Billie Bad Ass bitch at? She need to bring her ugly ass on out of the house," said Precious. She cracked her knuckles. "I'm ready to show that ho these hands."

"But how do you know she's ugly? You ain't even seen her?" I said in a joking manner, to keep the mood light and to settle the butterflies in my stomach. Not that I was afraid but I knew this fight was going to cause some type of friction between me and Choppa.

"If the bitch ain't ugly when she walk out of that house, you can bet she'll be *tore up from the floor up* when we get through with that ass," Precious swore.

Essence and Fat-Fat agreed. But now my reservations became strong.

"Look, y'all," my voice quaked, "I ain't no weak bitch, but I don't want this to cause problems for Choppa."

"Fuck that nigga!" the three of them belted out in perfect unison.

I didn't want to tell them about his connect being KiKi's father so I just said, "It's deeper than what I can say."

Precious looked over at me in the passenger seat and made a face at me like I was retarded. "Bitch, bye! That ho getting these hands today!"

"Okayyy!" intoned Essence.

Fat-Fat, who hadn't said much at all since we got there, finally spoke. "While y'all *'bout it* hoes doing all of that popping, the bitch just came out. Unless that ain't her." She pointed up the street where KiKi was just descending the porch.

Seeing her, even from a distance, made my blood boil. "That's her!" I confirmed.

Precious didn't need to hear another word. She put the car in gear and drove up the street with purpose. When we pulled up to KiKi's house, Precious parked so that her car blocked the driveway.

KiKi had just reached her own car and she was opening the driver's door to get inside.

Essence hurried out of the backseat of our ride and called out, "Excuse me, can I ask you something?"

"Who are you?" KiKi called back.

Slouched down in the seat, but peering out of the slightly lowered tinted window, I could tell from the frowned expression on KiKi's face that she was irritated by her presence already.

"A bitch's worst nightmare."

KiKi sat her bag on top of the car and put her hands on her wide hips. "Come again."

Now, Essence was up close to her. I could see their mouths moving and Essence was becoming real animated. "Let's go, bitch!" said Precious. Her and Fat-Fat bailed out at the same time, leaving their doors wide open.

By the time I climbed out of the passenger door, Essence and KiKi was going at it. "Bitch, you put your hands on my people and now you're about to pay the cost!"

My bestie hit that ho with two quick punches, like, *Whack! Whack!*

"Whup that bitch's ass!" said Precious, running up to where they were fighting.

Fat-Fat was on her heels.

KiKi wasn't dressed to rumble, she had on high heels and a tight ass tube dress. But the hood rat ho transformed real quick. Off came her shoes, one at a time.

Essence was still punching her in the face repeatedly. But when KiKi finally stood flatfooted, she sidestepped the next punch and danced away from her car.

She held her guards up and rubbed her nose with her thumb, while bouncing up and down on her toes. "C'mon, bitch, now I'm ready to get down! I'm a Cleveland, Ohio thoroughbred! Come get some of this shit, all of y'all!" She lunged at Essence and caught her with a punch high on the forehead, knocking her back a few steps. Glancing over at me, she smiled. "You thought this was a picnic? Think again, bitch!" She punched Essence in the stomach, doubling her over for a second. But when she tried to rush in and punch her again, she had two bumblebees that were coming to sting.

Fat-Fat rushed past Precious to reach KiKi first. She grabbed her by the back of her weave and yoked her head back. "Nah, bruh, it ain't no picnic, it's a gangbang, ho!" She elbowed her in the face, busting her mouth.

"Three the hard way, son!" said Precious, stepping in to pummel her with both fists.

To her credit, KiKi didn't scream or holla. She snatched away from Fat-Fat and tried to buck on the triple team, but my bitches were way too much for one stank bitch to handle. KiKi got a few licks in but the six fists against her two was overpowering.

"Fuck her ass up!" I rooted as they knocked her to the ground and started kicking her.

KiKi tried to ball up in a tight knot to protect her exposed areas but all she accomplished was making her dress rise up around her waist, exposing her naked ass.

"Move out of the way!" Precious pushed Essence aside. "I'ma kick her in that funky ass pussy that she let six niggas run up in at one time."

I laughed because I had told them the story on the way to her house. It was funny because I was thinking, *Girl you're gonna have to throw away your shoe.*

I walked up to the beat down just as Precious stomped down on her cooch for the third time. I leaned down in her face so that she could see me up close. "It ain't all fun and games now, is it?"

"Fuck you, weak ass trick!" She hawked a glob of blood and spit up in my face. And that's when I lost it!

When I came back to myself, I had blood on my shoe and sweat poured down my face. I looked down and saw that a stream of blood ran down from KiKi's brow. "You still think I'm weak, bitch?" I stood over her taunting.

Precious held me back to stop me from stomping that ho to death. I looked up to see Fat-Fat returning from the car with a tire iron. She was twirling it in her hands singing, *"Take me out to the ballgame!"*

No doubt Fat-Fat was going to destroy her car the same way she had done mine.

The three of us laughed as KiKi struggled to her feet and wobbled around to the other side of the car. "Don't run now, Money Mayweather," Essence quipped.

KiKi stood up straight. Her weave was everywhere but on her head. Her dress was bunched around her waist and one of her titties was out and blood was all over her face.

I almost felt sorry for her until I remembered who started this and who put my arm in a sling.

"Watch out! She's going in her bag!" yelled Fat-Fat.

I looked up to see that KiKi's bag was no longer on the roof of the car.

"The bitch is going for her pepper spray!" I alerted my girls. I knew that because KiKi had threatened to spray me the day she attacked me with the baseball bat.

"Oh, she's not the only one that will spray a bitch," said Essence, who reached down in her back pocket and pulled out a small canister.

I watched as my friends stalked around the car and over to KiKi. Another round was in progress but the ho done had enough.

I stepped around the car to stop them from doing her any grave injuries. And that's when KiKi's hand came out of her bag, brandishing a gun.

Essence was just closing in on KiKi, thus she was the closest to her. *Pow! Pow!*

The gunshots made us all freeze. I watched in horror as Essence stumbled backwards, dropping the pepper spray and clutching her stomach as she fell to the ground and on to her back.

"Noooo!" I screamed, seeing the blood ooze out between her fingers.

Fat-Fat raised the tire iron shoulder high and took an angry step toward KiKi.

Pointing the gun at Fat-Fat, KiKi gritted, "Do it, and I'll blow your fuckin' face off, skinny bitch!"

That stopped Fat-Fat in her tracks.

Precious and I ran over to Essence at the same time. We both went to our knees and immediately tried to comfort her.

"Don't move, E. Please don't try to move," tears and snot ran separate trails down my face.

She was on the ground writhing in pain. "She shot me! I'm going to die," she cried.

"No, you're not." Precious used her hand to wipe the perspiration off of Essence's face.

"Precious! Call an ambulance!" I screamed.

"Drag that bitch out of my driveway!" said KiKi, callously.

"Shut the fuck up! You're going to jail for this!" My voice cracked as I yelled through my flood of tears.

Seemingly unbothered, KiKi calmly sat the gun down on the hood of her car and went in her purse. She pulled a phone out and dialed a number.

Beside me, Fat-Fat was encouraging Essence to hold on. Behind us, Precious was screaming to the 911 operator to send an ambulance. "I don't know the address, bitch!" she yelled into the phone as tears ran down into her mouth.

I reached up and hurriedly took the phone from her. I had no problem recalling the address, it was seared in my memory. Tearfully, I recited it to the operator.

"Ma'am, an ambulance is on its way," she assured me in a soothing tone. But her calm voice did nothing to help the panic rising up in my chest. So much blood was pouring out of Essence's stomach, I feared the worse.

I rushed back over to her, dropping to my knees as she looked at me fearfully. "I'm going to die," she mumbled softly.

"No, bitch! You better not!" I cried as I stretched my legs out, dropped the phone on the ground and held her head in my lap.

"I love y'all bitches." She coughed and blood spilled down the side of her face, mixing with a steady stream of tears.

"Julz, turn her head to the side. She's choking on her blood," said Fat-Fat.

I hurriedly did as she suggested. Essence coughed twice more. Her lips were caked with blood now. And her eyes fluttered open and closed.

"Please stay with us, E." I coached, praying for a miracle.

"Where is the fuckin' ambulance!" screamed Precious. She was walking around in a circle pulling out her hair.

Essence muttered, "I'm cold. I'm so cold."

I went to take off my shirt to cover her with it. "Oww!" I winced. In the excitement of the situation, I had forgotten all about my injured arm.

My shirt barely covered her but I'd take anything off of my back to give to her.

"Toots, open your eyes. I need to see those pretty brown eyes." I began rocking back and forth at this point.

"I can't. I'm too weak." Her voice was becoming faint.

"Yes, you can, E. I need you. We all need you." I looked off to my side and saw Precious squatted down with her head between her knees and then directly in front of me at Fat-Fat who looked to have animosity for me.

I hoped to God I was misreading her but if she did hate me, I couldn't blame her. I was hating myself, too.

The wail of police sirens fast approaching gave me hope. I looked up from Essence to KiKi, expecting the bitch to take off running but she remained talking on her cell phone, calmly.

"Yes, Daddy, I just shot a bitch. I'm gonna need your best lawyer." She looked at me with a smug expression on her face. "No, Daddy, Choppa ain't around. He's the one who got me in this shit."

"Bitch, I hate you!" I screamed at her.

"That ain't nobody, Daddy. Just a bitch that's about to get shot next."

The sirens were very close now.

"Hurry up!" I cried while looking back down at my girl.

Her eyes hadn't reopened but I could see that she was still breathing, though faintly.

When the police car turned onto the street, Precious took off toward them waving her arms and jumping up and down to get their attention.

The car pulled up to the curb and two white policeman got out with their weapons drawn. KiKi remained cool as a cucumber, which made me despise the bitch even more.

While one officer rushed up to us and attended to Essence, the other one watched his back. "What happened?" asked the one bending down over Essence.

"That bitch right there shot her!" I pointed my finger at an unfazed KiKi.

Chapter 38
Julz

As I was getting in the back of the ambulance, I saw one officer bag the gun KiKi used to shoot Essence and the other one handcuffing her. *That's good for that evil bitch,* I thought before I sat down and watched the EMTs work frantically to save my best friend's life.

I stared directly at Essence and the two technicians working to stabilize her but tears distorted my view and everything became a blur.

Lowering my chin into my chest, I shut my eyes tightly and visions of a much younger us, twelve years old to be exact, appeared in my mind.

October 2000

"If you don't stop following me, I'm going to kick your ass!" The chunky girl balled her fists up and raised them to her face.

I jumped back a little. "I didn't meant to scare you."

"Who said I was scared? Just stop following me!" She readjusted her backpack and continued walking down the moderately empty hallway away from me.

I didn't listen, though. "Umm, girl. I just want to be your friend. My name is Julia but everyone calls me..."

She looked over her shoulder. "I don't care. Do I look like I do?" Then she inquisitively looked at me and turned all the way around. *"Why won't you leave me alone?"*

Walking up on her so the other middle school classmates didn't hear, I whispered. "I noticed you sleep in a car and I wanted to help you."

Anger resonated on her face and she hemmed me up by my uniform collar, gritting her teeth and talking low. "I'm not homeless and I don't need you as a friend. Now leave me alone before I beat you down."

She released me and turned on her heels but I boldly called after her. "Then I guess we're gonna fight every day 'cause I'm not leaving you alone."

"Oooo!" The echoes of those standing around us bounced off of the walls.

"What did you say?"

"You heard me!"

She rushed up on me with her fist lifted alongside her face to pummel mine but my seventh grade teacher stood in front of me.

"Essence, do I need to call your mother?" Ms. Williams spoke firmly with her arms folded across her heavy chest.

Essence shook her head side to side. "No, ma'am."

"Good, then I suggest you go to class," then she turned to me, "and you, you better do the same."

I nodded my head yes and walked off in the opposite direction of the girl whose name I now knew to be Essence.

At 3:15, the bell sounded and I left, thinking nothing of the awkward encounter from earlier until she greeted me at the bus stop with her fist.

Whap!

"Oooh, Julz just got snuck by E." One girl commentated and everyone stopped to watch.

The blow to my face came from out of nowhere, knocking me down into the dirt seconds before she sat on top of me, wailing on me.

I shielded myself as I really didn't want to fight her. I doubt I would had won if I tried.

Eventually, after a few minutes, some students broke us up, well, got her off of me before truancy officers took notice of the small congregation surrounding us.

I got up clumsily, dusting off my skirt and moving my mouth in a circular motion to loosen the tightness of the hit I received, saying, "Fight you tomorrow—friend."

She eyeballed me. "You crazy!"

And I must've been but everybody needed one person to care about them. And I was prepared to be her one because it broke my heart every day, since learning of her bleak situation weeks earlier, that I was privileged to go home to a warm house with good parents and see a girl my age not as fortunate. After all, no one, not even a tough-ass like Essence, deserved to live a hard life.

The next school day I saw her and put my sets up, immediately. I didn't plan to use them but I was ready to protect my face from her heavy hitting ass.

"Put down your guard," Essence told me, shaking her head.

"Why, so you can sneak me? Nah. ain't happening."

She laughed and for the first time since I had seen her around, she looked like she wasn't mad at the world. She extended her hand. "I'm Essence."

I smiled. "I'm..."

"Julz. I know." She then fidgeted a little before she blurted. "I'm sorry 'bout yesterday."

"What happened yesterday?" I played it off like I didn't know what she was talking about.

Then we started walking under the breezeway and into the building.

"So, you really want to be my friend?" she asked distrustfully.

"I do."

"But why?"

"Because we both can use one," I said genuinely.

The answer seemed to please her because shortly after, she draped an arm around my neck. "Well, let's get to class—friend."

That day was the start of our journey as partners in crime. Tootsie could do no wrong in my eyes and I was spotless in hers.

In under a week and with little persuasion, I convinced my mama to let Essence live with us and away from her wayward mother, whom she often ran away from. She had lived with us up until she moved to Atlanta, directly after high school, on a scholarship to Clark Atlanta University.

I've had her back through everything: heartbreak, the abortion at fourteen that no one knew about except the twenty year old who impregnated her, depression from family not being family and the list continued.

And as much as I have had her back, she had mine, too. But now I was regretting it. We always said that we were *ride or dies* for one another but it had a whole new meaning to me now knowing her life was hanging in the balance and all because she was down for me.

Beep! Beep! Beeeeeppppp!

"What's going on?" I panicked hearing her machine flat lining. Attempting to stand to my feet, I was pushed back down.

"Stay back!" I was told.

"She's arresting." Another said as he reached for some awkward looking machine and belted, "Clear!"

"Essence, you're a fighter. Fight goddamit. Fight!"

"We're losing her…"

We're losing her? Hearing those words made me dizzy and then my world went black.

***

Piedmont Henry

I woke up on a gurney, disorientated. But once I identified where I was, I hopped off of it quickly.

Running up to the first person I saw in scrubs, I frantically questioned, "Where's Essence Whitaker? I need to see her."

"Who?" The male nurse was puzzled.

I didn't have time to explain, so I left him in my dust as I ran over to the nurse's station. Throwing myself against the partition, I ranted off like a mad woman. "Ma'am, my friend, Essence Whitaker, was brought in by ambulance with a gunshot wound to the stomach. Look in your computer. Is she in surgery? Is she all right? What can you tell me?"

Before the lady had a chance to answer any one of my questions, I heard my name being called from behind.

"Julz! Julz!"

I turned around and ran over to Precious, who was waving for me to come over to them. She went to hug me but I dodged her embrace. Now wasn't the time for consolation, I needed answers.

"Where is she?" I looked for Precious to give me an immediate response but she was hesitating, so I turned to Fat-Fat. "What's going on?" Shifting my eyes between them both, I shouted. "Tell me something. Fuck!"

"Julz, she's dead." Fat-Fat's reached out for me, but I staggered back, holding my hand out to stop her from coming any closer.

Closing my eyes, I took a deep breath and composed myself. In the calmest voice I could muster, I asked again. "Where is my friend? You know the one who isn't *dead!*" My voice elevated, piercing my own eardrums.

Fat-Fat didn't answer me. Instead, she plopped down in the seat next to where Precious leaned against a wall and buried her face into her hands, sobbing.

"No, no, no, Precious. She can't be. Not my sista." I pulled at the collar of a hospital shirt I was given, unable to breathe. I hopelessly looked around the waiting area, lost for words. Finally, I questioned. "Has anyone seen her to know for sure?"

Fat-Fat stood to her feet. "I need air." She headed in the direction of the automatic doors, stepping outside.

I jetted back over to the nurse's station, grabbing at my stomach. I felt myself becoming sick.

"Can I help you?" She looked up from her paperwork.

"Yes. I came in earlier with Essence Whitaker and I need to speak to the doctors who worked on her. I need to see her, period." I turned my head off to the side and began making violent gagging sounds, as I tried to repress the urge to puke my guts up. The morbid thoughts clouding my head was overwhelming on my stomach.

She stood to her feet. "Ma'am, are you okay?"

"Hell no! I need to see if my friend is—if my friend is..." *Bluh! Bluh! Aarghh!*

Vomit poured out of my mouth, creating a revolting pool of gruel at my feet.

The lady came from behind her desk and offered me a seat once I was done spilling my content but I declined her swiftly. "No! I just need to see Essence."

"Ma'am..." She attempted to sit me down anyway.

"Are you deaf? I don't want no damn seat!"

A gentleman in a white overcoat approached us and intervened. "I'll take it from here," he told the nurse. Then he looked to me. "You're here for Ms. Whitaker?"

"Yes! Yes, I am." I wiped my mouth with the back of my hand. "Will you tell me what happened? Will you take me to her now?" He bobbed his head. "Okay, hold on. Precious, let's go." I spoke ignorantly loud but I wasn't concerned with my volume.

Precious sprinted my way but not before peering her head through the sliding doors and telling Fat-Fat to come as well.

When the girls walked over to me, I reached for a hand, any hand would have been sufficient. I just didn't want to collapse on my way to see her. Precious grabbed mine and in turn, she grabbed Fat-Fat's and we walked behind the doctor, taking the longest stretch of our lives.

As we stood outside of the door I knew would confirm my worst fear, the doctor gave us each a solemn look. "I'm truly sorry for your loss. I'll give you all a moment."

He stood off to the side of the door and gave me a nod, permitting me to walk in.

Before I pushed the door open, Fat-Fat let go of Precious' hand. "I can't!" She cried, taking off down the hallway.

I watched her run away before I clutched Precious' hand tighter and leaned against the door, forcing it to open.

The moment I saw my friend lying on a cold slab I began unraveling, slowly.

"Nah, this shit ain't right! This shit ain't right!" Precious separated her hand from mine and threw a tantrum where she stood, jumping up and down, repeating the same four words.

I was too shocked to react with sound at first. It was a lot to process all at once. *That's really her?* I questioned, even though I could recognize her as effortlessly as I could myself.

Taking petrified steps toward her body, I covered my mouth once I stood next to her head. As I dropped my hand to my side, a combination of tears and snot traveled with it. "Oh, my God! Essence, this wasn't supposed to happen, not at all!" I shook my head to reiterate the truth in my words.

By this time, Precious had left. I supposed it was too much on her. It was overwhelming to me, too, but I couldn't leave her side. I needed time with her. No! I needed to rewind the hands of time for her.

"Fuck! What's life without you in it?" I used my shirt to wipe excess snot from under my nose and lips.

I stared at her, taking her in from top to bottom. *E, you was supposed to die an old lady, damn near in your hundreds after you done seen it all, surrounded by your husband, children, grand and great grands. Not at twenty-six, having barely lived!*

My face contorted into an ugly ball of pain and I wailed a long cry. "Aaaaahhhhhhhhhhhh! Wake up, E. I need to see your eyes. Hear your voice. Tell me something. Anything." I coached. "Say, *Surprise, bitch! I ain't goin' nowhere.* You gotta wake up, sis!"

I went to shake her. My hands trembled as I moved in to do so. Once we made contact, my emotional switch went from sorrow to infuriate. *"Why is she cold?"* I asked the question more so to myself before I belted out in anger. "Why is she cold? She needs a blanket!"

My voice must had echoed into the hallway because a male nurse suddenly appeared, standing close up on me. "Ma'am, it's time to go."

"Not until I get a fuckin' blanket. She's cold and she deserves better, so get one now!" I snapped.

He tried to coerce me into leaving with him but it was pointless because I wasn't hearing him, so he walked out. I presumed it was to do what the hell I asked but shortly after, I noticed he only went to get assistance.

Glaring coldly, I shouted. "If you can't get what I asked for, then at least get the fuck out. I gotta talk to my sister."

"Ma'am, we're sorry but..." The struggle began.

They went to grab at me but I dove for Essence, grabbing her arm. "Essence! No, don't touch me! Essence!" I prayed that she'd hear my cries and raise off of the table and come to my aid. After all, coming for me was like asking for her to get involved.

One nurse tried prying my hand off of her and if I could have bit that muthafucka, I would have. Finally, after much tussling, kicking and screaming, they managed to pull me away from her.

"Noooooooooo! I got to tell her I'm sorry." I put up a fight not to leave out of the room, using my feet as a barricade from exiting out of the door.

Moments later, the men managed to haul me out. Knowing my time was fading into seconds as the door was slowly closing, I cried out to

Essence, "I'm sorry! It should have been me who died! Not you! Not you! Meeeee!"

Chapter 39
Choppa

Justus was playing video games on the flat screen and munching on gummy worms and caramel popcorn. Julz would've had her panties in a bunch if she knew what I was feeding her son, but I believed you had to let a kid be a kid, especially a boy.

In her presence, lil' man was mad mannerable. He wasn't sissified or nothin' like that but he had strong traits of becoming a mama's boy, and in this dog-eat-dog world, that wasn't gon' cut it. So, whenever it was just me and him, I let him break a few rules. Because, later in life, he just might have to break a few heads. When that time came, I didn't want him waiting around for his mother's permission.

According to the time on my wrist, it had been hours since Julz left to go get more of their things. As more time went by, I began to get a funny feeling in the pit of my stomach, the way I did when I was nervously awaiting the arrival of a shipment.

I reached in my pocket for my phone but it wasn't there. *Damn! Where did I put it?* I had a bad habit of hiding that mu'fucka from myself. And since I had been keeping the ringer on *silent,* lately, dat bitch was gonna be hard to find.

Cussing myself, I retraced my movements in the crib. I struck out in the bedroom and the kitchen but I hit pay dirt in the bathroom. There that muthafucka was on the floor beside the toilet tissue.

After picking it up, I scrunched up my nose at the smell that lingered from my time on the toilet a while ago. "Grown man shit, literally!" I said out loud and then started laughing at myself.

Before leaving out, I grabbed the air freshener off of the sink and sprayed about ten squirts in the air. "Now, that's what I'm talm 'bout," I continued clowning.

I sat the air freshener back in place and turned on my phone screen. I was shocked to see that I had numerous missed calls and text messages from Julz and from Cross.

Cross had hit me from the emergency number he used when something was urgent. The only other time he had called me from that number was last year when I went up there to meet with an associate of his to purchase some mini submachine guns. At the last minute, Cross had gotten the word that the man was setting me up for a lick.

That call came just in time because I had been a mere few minutes from reaching the place where we were supposed to meet up. Had I continued there I would've been ambushed, robbed, shot, and left for dead.

Of course, a week later we crushed the dude for the betrayal he had planned. Now, seeing that rare call from that certain number, I couldn't help getting a bad premonition.

In spite of the urgency of Cross' call, I still chose to call Julz back first. Business was business but shorty was my heart, her concerns came before any of that other shit —point blank period.

I hit *call back* and listened to her phone ring as I walked back up front where Justus was. The moment Julz answered I knew that something was seriously wrong because she was sobbing uncontrollably.

Wanting to shield Justus from anymore possible drama, I detoured to my bedroom room and closed the door behind me. "Baby, what's wrong?" I sat down on the bed with worry creeping up on my face.

"Essence is dead!" She screamed through her tears.

"What?" That fucked my head up. "Baby, what happened? Were y'all in an accident?"

"No, that bitch shot and killed her!" She broke down crying harder.

"Julz, what are you saying? Try to calm down and tell me what happened. Who shot Essence?" I paced the floor.

After more sobbing, she screamed, "Your bitch! KiKi! She killed my sista."

I heard the phone drop, but I could still hear Julz crying hard in the background. *What the fuck?* I couldn't believe what she had just said. *Hell no! I had to have heard her wrong.*

"Julz! Baby, please pick up the phone. Talk to me. What's going on?" I heard *and* felt the growing excitement in my own voice. "Julz! Julz!"

After a minute, or so, someone picked up the phone and began to speak. "Choppa?" They called my name angrily.

"Yeah, who is this?"

"Precious."

"A'ight. Sup, Precious? What's going on?" I stopped pacing and impatiently waited for her reply.

When it came, it was laced with venom. "What's going on is Essence is dead and your bitch is locked up for killing her—that's what the fuck is going on!"

"Yo, hold up! Fuck you think you're talking to?" I responded like the street nigga I am. "I don't know what's going on and the shit y'all saying ain't making no sense. You need to calm yo ass down and tell me what happened."

"Fat-Fat, here, you can talk to him, I don't have shit to say to this muthafucka!" I heard her say and then Fat-Fat came on the line.

Shorty was sniffling stupid hard and I could tell it wasn't from her having a cold. "Yo, ma, what the hell is going on? Where my baby at? I need y'all to tell me something." I lowered my voice to a non-confrontational pitch, much different than I had with Precious.

"Choppa, the nurse is attending to Julz. I think she's hyperventilating, but she'll be all right."

"What happened?"

"Oh, my God!" she said. She took a deep breath then told me everything that had transpired, concluding with, "They pronounced Essence dead a short while ago."

I sat down on the bed, heavily, and ran a hand down my face. The only thing I could think to say was, "I'm sorry."

"Julz is tore up," she replied.

"What hospital are y'all at?"

"Piedmont in Henry County. In the ER."

"Okay. I'm on my way." I ended the call, sighed heavily, and stood up on leaden legs. Now I knew what the missed call from Cross' urgent number was about.

He was gonna be livid. He would find a way to place the blame on me and if I responded with any aggression, things would get ugly real fast. Because when it came to KiKi, Cross didn't play.

The real threat, though, was that when it came to Julz, I didn't muthafuckin' play, either!

Assessing the likelihood of a clash popping off if I called Cross back now, I decided to hold off on doing that until I made sure my girl was a'ight. After that, I would make the necessary calls to see what KiKi was being charged with and find out if she had a bond or not. Until then, she would be okay. The holding tank in the jail wouldn't break her down, she was trained by her pops to endure that shit.

However, my immediate dilemma was what to do with Justus. I didn't think Julz would want him exposed to what we would walk into in the Emergency Room.

***

When I reached Piedmont, Kim Marie and Pop were already there waiting for me outside of the entrance. I had called them because I didn't want to take Justus inside nor could I leave him in the car alone because it had begun to get dark outside.

I walked up to my young comrade and Kim Marie with Justus right by my side, holding my hand. On the way there, he had kept asking where we were going. I'd told him I had to go pick up a prescription from the hospital, so he wasn't curious when he saw where we were.

Justus had met Kim Marie and Pop a week earlier when me, him and Julz ran into them while at the mall. The five of us ended up spending the day together and lil' man developed a slick little crush on Kim Marie that was funny as hell. So, he didn't put up a fight when I told him to wait in the car with her and Pop while I went inside.

As soon as I walked into the ER, I looked around for my shorty. I saw her and her girls across the room talking with a nurse. As I walked briskly toward them, I held out hope that this shit really wasn't happening. But when I got close up to them, the grieving look on their faces told me that no part of this was a joke.

Julz looked up and ran into my arms crying, "She's dead, Choppa! My Tootsie is gone."

My heart broke for her. I held her against my chest and rubbed her back as she wept.

Looking over Julz' shoulder, I saw Precious mugging me awfully hard. Had it been under any other circumstances, I would've been all in her shit. But on the strength of their loss, I just let it ride.

Fat-Fat acknowledged me with her eyes but remained talking to the nurse. I led Julz over to a chair and helped her down into the seat. She was limp as a cooked noodle, and she couldn't stop crying.

I sat down beside her and wrapped an arm around her shoulder. "Baby, I'm so sorry this happened."

"Oh, my God, Choppa, she's dead! I want her to come back! I want her to come back!" Her whole body shook as she sobbed painfully loud.

All of a sudden, she sprung up out of the chair and bolted down the hall. I hurried behind her, confused. "Baby, where are you going?" I called out as I pounced up out of my seat and ran after her.

I caught up with her just as she reached a room where the door was shut. Before she could push it open and go inside, I wrapped my arms around her and held her tight. I knew what she was attempting to do.

"Baby, let's go," I said gently. If there was something left for them to do at the hospital, I was going to ask Fat-Fat to handle it. Right now, all I wanted to do was get Julz home so she could lie down.

"Let me go! I want to see my Tootsie!" She struggled to free herself from my embrace.

Her foot kicked the door open to a crack, giving me a brief look inside of the room before the door closed back on its own. "E! Get up! Please, get up!" Julz cried.

We both had caught a quick glimpse of Essence's uncovered face. I had seen death many times so even from that distance, I recognized that Julz' homegirl was deceased.

"Damn!" I said under my breath as I strengthened my hold on shorty to keep her from breaking 'loose.

Fat-Fat saw what was going on and she came over to help me comfort Julz. Her face was just as wet with tears as shorty's was, but she was holding up much better.

Precious walked up, still grilling me. "It's your goddam fault, too!" she had the muthafuckin' nerve to accuse.

"Bitch, this is the wrong time to run yo mouth." I warned.

"Okay, both of you need to chill! It's way too much going on for that," Fat-Fat jumped in to diffuse things before they reached the point of no return. "Choppa, we need to get Julz out of here right now."

"She's not going home with *him*!" Precious objected.

"P, will you shut the fuck up, please! Later for all of that, right now just be a friend to Julz," said Fat-Fat.

Precious shut up but her visage remained hard and directly trained on me.

Like I give a fuck! I shot back at her with a killer's stare.

Julz stopped wiggling against me, trying to break free. Her sobs turned into light whimpers as her body ceased rocking. "Choppa, where is my baby?" Her voice was weary.

"He's out in the car with Kim Marie and Pop." I looked and pointed in the direction of the parking lot. As I did so, I noticed two cops walking toward us.

I figured they were coming to get statements from the girls. Still I patted the front of my waistband to make sure I wasn't strapped. The last thing I needed was to get cased up on a humbug weapons charge.

I breathed a quick sigh of relief after confirming that I had, indeed, left my banger in the car. The two po's walked up to us and asked each of the girls their names. Julz was the last to reply.

"Julia Kidd." Her voice was so low, he had to ask her to repeat herself. "Julia Kidd," she said once more.

"Ms. Kidd, I'm placing you under arrest. You have the right to remain silent. Anything you say can be used...."

"What did I do?" Julz cried out.

Precious and Fat-Fat started going off until they were told they were under arrest, too.

The boys in blue explained that the three of them were being charged with assault on Kiara Webb.

"Bruh, are you fuckin' serious! Show these ladies some compassion, they just lost a friend. Fuck is wrong with y'all?" I railed to the black cop.

"Sir, step out of the way or you'll be arrested for interfering with the official duties of a police officer," warned his partner, a white boy with a pink face.

"You think I give two fucks about going to jail?" I spat. "I got bail money in my pocket and a whole team of lawyers on deck." I held out my wrist for him to clamp them with cuffs. I didn't know who the fuck he thought he was scaring. A nigga ain't street if he scared of going to the Bing.

"This is your final warning. Step out of the way, sir," said Super Nigga.

I was about to make him do what he got paid to do until Fat-Fat spoke with reason. "Choppa, don't get yourself locked up. You need to be out here to get Julz out."

I gritted my teeth and stared death at the po's. Those punk muthafuckas had no compassion for the girls.

"Don't worry, shorty, I'll bail you out as soon as they're through processing you in," I told Julz.

"Choppa, *do not* let my baby see them bring me out of here like this?" she cried.

"A'ight. Baby, don't make any statements. Tell them you want to see your attorney. I'll have one down to the jail ASAP."

I jogged ahead of them to whisk Justus away before they escorted his mother and his aunts out in handcuffs.

As I raced outside to the car, a nigga shuddered at the thought of shorty in jail. What was a thousand times worse was that in a minute, her girl would be lying up in the morgue. And that wasn't the half! KiKi was locked up for murder and Cross would be furious. So, when he sent heat my way, I was gonna have to send it back just as intense.

Which meant, shit was about to get drastic.

Ca$h & Coffee

Chapter 40
Choppa
Two days later

Julz was in the bedroom at my condo. With the help of sleeping pills, she had finally closed her eyes and was getting some much needed rest.

She had remained in jail 36 hours before a judge set her bond at $10,000 and I was allowed to bail her out.

Fat-Fat and Precious were out on $10,000 bonds as well. I had been willing to put up the dough to get them out, too, but their peeps came through for them.

Since coming home, Julz had done little besides bathe and lay in the bed and cry. I knew shorty was fucked up bad over Essence's death because she wasn't being attentive to Justus like she normally would be. She would let him lie down beside her and hold him, while whimpering, but that was the extent of the attention she was capable of showing him.

Lil' man didn't know what was going on but he knew his mother was hurting. He kept asking her what was wrong but all his questions did was make Julz cry even harder and then he would start crying too.

My head and my heart was fucked up because I did feel somewhat responsible for everything that happened. I kept thinking had I told shorty about KiKi from the jump maybe none of this would've occurred. *Or maybe I should've never stepped to baby girl, in the first place, until I had squashed things completely with KiKi.*

Straight up, I was drowning in guilt, but I had to keep my head up for shorty and Justus.

Kim Marie agreed to stay at the condo for a couple of days or longer to help with Julz who was emotionally invalid and physically weak from it all.

"Justus, come eat dinner," she called out from the kitchen.

"Okay. I have to go wash my hands first," he yelled back from the living room where me, him, and Pop we're playing video games.

Once Justus was out of earshot, Pop said, "Big homie, I hate to bring this to you at a time like this but those niggas are still selling to some of our customers. I know you have more important things going on with your girl and nem, but I thought you should know what was going on."

I took a minute to process what he'd just said before responding. *So, that's how those niggas gon' do it? They must think they're bullet-proof. But, a'ight, I'ma show 'em.*

"Way to keep your ear to the street, youngin," I commended him.

"I'm learning from the best," he tossed it right back.

I smiled through my inner misery. Pop's loyalty was the one bright spot in the darkness that came with street hustlin'. "I salute you, young nigga, because you keep it a bill. Not many other niggas do," I acknowledged.

"Always, fam. It's *100* or Nathaniel with me." *Nathaniel* meant *nothin'* in street slang, so I understood his point. "If you give me the go ahead, me and my mans can get at those niggas ASAP. Ain't nan one of 'em hard to touch, believe dat."

I folded my hands under my chin in a steeple and took a minute to weigh everything. In times of pressure a man had to be careful not to react on emotions. I hadn't always adhered to that jewel, but I was de-termined to do so now.

"Pop, I really wanna sic y'all on them right now," I said, speaking slowly and in a lowered tone so my voice didn't carry into the kitchen where Justus had gone. "But now is the wrong time to strike. If nothin' else, they'll be expecting it. So, I'ma let them do their thing like we haven't even noticed it. Allow them to get comfortable and let their guards down. Then, we'll hit 'em with everything we got.

"In the meantime," I continued, "I'ma make sure my shorty is straight."

"Aye, sir." Like a soldier, he put his hand to the side of his head and swiftly brought it down in salute.

"Thanks for holding things down these past few days. I won't for-get it."

At that moment, Kim Marie came from out of the kitchen into the living room where we sat. She was carrying a tray with two plates of food on it. She handed her man his first, bent down and gave him a kiss and then she handed me my plate.

The tilapia, wild rice and sweet peas smelled delicious and tasted even better. I hadn't really eaten since I got that call telling me that Julz' homegirl was dead and that KiKi was responsible.

"Thanks, lil' sis, this shit is good," I complimented Kim Marie, then I looked to Pop, "Youngin, you better put a ring on it."

"Oh, I plan to," he said, smiling up at lil' mama with pure affection that reminded me of how I looked at Julz.

"Aww, you're so sweet, Boonkie," she cooed, calling Pop by the pet name she had taken to calling him lately.

I couldn't do nothin' but chuckle because Pop was cheesing like a mug. The shit was a trip because around Kim Marie, that boy was softer than a baby's ass. But once his foot touched the ground outside, he was a beast.

I wondered if I was the same way around Julz. Prolly so. Love had a way of doing that to the hardest nigga, nah mean?

"Yo, I'ma go and see if shorty will eat something," I said with my baby in mind.

"I was going to do that," said Kim Marie.

"I got it, lil' sis."

"Okay, well, I'm going back in the kitchen and sit with Justus. Are you okay with that, Boonkie?" she respectfully asked.

"Yeah, but I'm feeling a little jelly," Pop teased.

With all of that affection being tossed back and forth between them, my ass was getting jealous, fa real. I wanted to rewind back to a week ago when me and Julz were kicking it like that.

Feeling heavy-hearted, I got up and carried my plate to the bedroom and tried to get Julz to eat a bite or two, but shorty was out like a light.

I sat the plate on the table by the bed and laid down beside her and fell asleep holding her close to me.

An hour later when I woke up, Justus was asleep on the other side of Julz, holding her, too.

I swung my feet over my side of the bed, sat up and grabbed my cell phone from off of the nightstand.

I checked my messages and saw the one I had been expecting. It was from Cross, he had just arrived in town, and he was summoning me to his hotel room. I felt a tightness in my chest because the conversations we'd had since KiKi was arrested hadn't been peaceful.

Cross had been dealing with some legal issues of his own, concerning a killing at a nightclub he owned, so he hadn't been able to fly down to Atlanta until now. His wife had flown in immediately after hearing about their daughter's arrest, but since KiKi was being held without bond there was little she could do besides visit her at the jail.

I had visited her, too. She had been surprisingly upbeat and unregretful, and she wasn't mad at me, at all.

"Those hoes tried the wrong bitch," was her attitude.

Normally, I would've respected her gangsta but this time it had caused Julz a whole lot of pain so I hadn't responded when she blurted it out, almost boastfully. But I did wonder if KiKi understood the severity of what she was charged with.

Daddy might not be able to get her out of this, I thought as I re-read Cross' message ordering me to his room.

Oh, I'm coming! But I ain't coming alone!

I stood up and went to the closet where I had a cache of guns. If I died tonight, I wasn't gon' die alone.

Chapter 41
Choppa

"A'ight, this is how it's going down. I'ma be in room 714. If I'm not back in forty-five minutes, come in that muthafucka blasting. Kill everything moving because the nigga up in there ain't no ho," I instructed Pop, who was in the passenger seat of my truck, strapped with enough artillery to arm a small country.

"Say no more." He slammed a banana clip in his M-16.

"Y'all follow what I just said?" I turned to look at my two young guns in the backseat.

"Forty-five minutes, not a second more," said Cha Cha, a 16-year-old head banger from Atlanta's notorious Bluff neighborhood.

"We'll be there, cuz. When we kick in the door just hit the flo' because I'ma air that bitch out," added Insane, a crazy ass Crip nigga who Pop had met in juvie.

I saw that look in my young boys' eyes that told me they were ready to back up their words. Just in case I didn't come out of Cross' room alive, I sent Julz a quick text saying *I love you*. Stuffing my cell phone back in my pocket, I climbed out of the truck and trekked inside of the hotel and caught the elevator up to the 7th floor.

Two solid knocks on the door got me inside, where Cross and two of his henchmen were seated around the suite. The third goon closed and locked the door behind me.

"What's good people?" I spoke to the group as I walked over and took a seat in a chair across from Cross. The goon who had let me in posted up by me. I turned to him. "I would appreciate it if you wouldn't stand behind me."

Immediately, a pregnant silence enveloped the room. Goon #3 didn't move. I casually stood up, facing him. My hands were close to my waist where my twin Glocks rested under my shirt.

"Sit your ass down!" said Cross.

I half turned so I could see him and the nigga behind me at the same time. "Nah, OG," I addressed him respectfully but without fear, "you might kill me up in this bitch but you not gon' punk me. Now, I know you're pissed about KiKi being locked up, and I am too, but like I told you on the phone, I didn't have shit to do with it."

He looked at me and crossed his legs at the knee and then folded his hands on top. "Were you not fuckin' one of the girls she got into it with?"

"No disrespect but what you got to do with my dick?" My response came off just as I intended.

Cross shot up outta his seat. I heard the click of guns all around me but I didn't flinch.

"You getting smart out of the mouth with me?" he snarled.

The wrong answer would get me wet up but oh well.

"Nah, I'm just letting you know that this shit right here ain't necessary." I pointed around the room at his people with their guns drawn. "I mean, do you let your wife's father question you about who you fuck?" I let that sink in for a minute and then I continued, "Real talk, Cross, you're a street nigga just like me. You know how it goes."

"I do, but I also know that my wife is in the room across the hall crying her eyes out because her baby is charged with murder."

I nodded my understanding. "What happened was unfortunate but KiKi gon' be a'ight. The lawyer I hired for her says she'll get a bond in the next day or two. And at the end of the day, the murder charge ain't gonna stick because basically it was self-defense," I thoroughly explained.

The muscles in his neck relaxed and he drummed his fingers on his leg. "She better not end up with no prison time or I'ma have those other three bitches killed," he threatened.

"I feel you," is what I said, but what I was thinking was something altogether different. If anything happened to Julz—whether she got ran over by a train or struck by a bolt of lightning—I was gonna blame every man in that room. And from there it would be war!

Cross signaled for his triad of trigger men to have a seat. They put their bangers away and did as they were told. Once they were seated where I could keep an eye on their hands, I relaxed a little and explained everything to Cross.

He tried to tell me I shouldn't have been fuckin' with Julz, but that was the pot calling the kettle black. That nigga had more bitches than his wife had shoes, and her shoe game was stupendous.

I didn't bother telling him that, in my heart, Julz was my one and only. Nah, in time the whole world would find that out. But the time to broadcast that wasn't now.

We rapped for another fifteen minutes and then I had to bounce before my young killas ran up in there and 187'd everything breathing.

Ca$h & Coffee

Chapter 42
Julz
Thursday morning, 5 a.m.

Who would have known that you had to go
So suddenly, so fast
How could it be, all the sweet memories
Would be all, all that we have left...
I softly patted my swollen eyes and blew my nose before I continued singing in broken pitch to *Missing You.*
Now that you're gone, every day I go on
But life's just not the same
I'm so empty inside and my tears I can't hide...
I sat with my knees close to my body on the floor of the bathroom, beating my chest repeatedly as if to jump start my heart. "Essence, baby, I'm tryna be strong but I don't know if I can do it. How am I supposed to get through this?"

Dialing her cell phone for the thirtieth time that morning, I listened to her voicemail.

Hiiii, if you're getting this message, it means I'm occupied with work or I'm living life and can't stop to answer. So leave me a message at the beep and I'll be sure to call you back. Byyyee!
That choked me up and threw me right back into the song.

'Cause you were my sister, my strength and my pride...
Huh? I opened my eyes, looking up once the music stopped. "Choppa! Why'd you cut it off? And turn off the lights. It's hurting my eyes." I used my hand as a visor to shield off the brightness.

"Nah, baby girl. You've been listening to that same song for hours. You're gonna drive yourself into a depression." Choppa walked over to me, slid his hands underneath my arms and lifted me to my feet, leaning me against the sink.

"But it feels my pain." I croaked as I double-tapped my breastplate.

"Baby, I feel your pain, too. C'mere." He pulled me into his arms, where I cried a fresh batch of tears.

After a minute or so, he picked me up, bridal-style, and led me into the bedroom, laying me on the bed. He stepped out and returned with a cold towel.

"Close your eyes, shorty." He placed the cool compress over my puffy eyes and then I felt the soft press of his lips against my forehead. "Pop and Kim Marie left late last night so I'ma go take care of Justus. You get some rest."

"I love you!" I felt the strong need to say it to him.

"I love you, too." I could feel him lingering nearby before I heard the lenient close of the door behind him.

An hour later…

KiKi may had shot the gun but you loaded it when you led Essence out there to fight your battle. You're lucky she stopped with her and didn't take Precious and Fat-Fat to their graves, too. E's blood will forever be on your hands, Murderer. Murderer!

"Ahhhhh!" I yelped, waking myself from a nap I didn't know I drifted off into.

Those nightmarish thoughts were the very reason I had trouble sleeping since Sunday, the day of her death. My mind made it impossible for me to sleep peacefully without my subconscious reminding me that I was culpable.

My shirt was sticky against me. Perspiration had me drenched from the scalp down.

Choppa entered, cutting on the light. "Baby, are you a'ight?"

I shook my head swiftly from side to side. "Nooooo!" I cried and he rushed over to my side to console me.

"Damn, baby, you're soaked," he said, rubbing my back. "I'm gonna run you a bath."

"Wait!" I didn't want him to let me go just yet. "Hold me, please."

"I gotchu." He held me a few minutes more and I was grateful for his comfort.

After the water was ran, Choppa gave me a soothing bath, careful not to wet my cast. After that, he also washed my hair.

His kindness made me feel extra sentimental. "I love you," I told him again.

"I know you do, shorty." He finished dressing me and then helped me back into bed. "Chill for a sec. I'll be right back."

Less than a half an hour later, I heard two sets of footsteps coming down the hall. Choppa came in first, stretched out in the bed beside me and then came Justus.

"Mama, I made you breakfast," he announced, as he carried a bowl of cereal with both hands over to me.

"You did this all by yourself?" I mustered enthusiasm.

We told Justus the kid friendly version of what happened to his Auntie Essence. He couldn't grasp the finality of her move to heaven but he knew I was upset about it. Still I wanted to bridge back as much of my pain, in front of him, as possible.

"Choppa helped me a little bit," he confessed.

I fully sat up. I wasn't hungry by a long shot but I needed to eat something.

After placing it in my lap, he ran out only to come back with a glass of orange juice.

"Thank you, baby. I don't know what I'd do without you." I tried smiling as much as my grief allowed.

"You're welcome." He climbed in the bed between us, turned my face toward his and gave me the sweetest kiss on the lips.

Choppa sat on the side of me, watching. The size of his smile decreased when he saw Justus' warm affections toward me. He told me too many times about my son kissing *his* woman the same way as him. I didn't see anything wrong with it but it rubbed Choppa wrong for some reason.

"Can I watch TV in here with y'all?" Justus asked either of us.

I looked over at the time. It was 7:10 a.m. "Ummm, no, sir, you have to leave out for school in a few minutes." I then ate my first bite of the cereal and was already full.

"Come on." Choppa helped him out of the bed. "Go get your backpack, so we can go."

"Okay." He took off for the second bedroom, where he'd been sleeping.

"Do you want to take the ride with me? Fresh air will do you good?" Choppa whisked my semi-dry hair behind my ear.

"Nah, I have calls to make to family and friends in preparation for Essence's…" I choked up, placing my hand at my throat.

He kissed my temple. "Just handle your business. I'll be back to help you with what I can, a'ight?"

I swiped a tear away. "Okay."

"I'm ready." We looked up to see Justus at the door.

"Cool!" Choppa kissed me again, grabbed his keys and wallet off of the nightstand and stood up.

"Come give me a hug before you go, mister." My boy rushed over to me and I hugged him like I didn't want to let him go, ever. Nuzzling my nose in the crease of his neck, I said, "Have a good day at school, okay?"

When I pulled away from him, my face was wet.

He looked at me strangely. "Mama, why are you crying now?"

"Because I love you and I'm going to miss you while you're away."

He thought for a second and then he hit me with a whammie of a question.

"Mama, how far is heaven?" he asked so seriously.

I looked over at Choppa who hunched his shoulders. I wondered what made him ask me this and now.

My lips trembled but I forced a smile, wiping my face dry. "Baby, it's really far from here."

His eyebrows drew inward. He looked to be processing his next question and sure enough he was. "When will we go to Auntie Essence's new house, so you don't be so sad?"

I only had enough strength to produce a one word reply. "Eventually."

"How 'bout we go later today? You can get Auntie Precious and Auntie Fat-Fat to meet us. I'll even get Auntie Essence to bake a cake. You love her cake."

That broke me, causing my tears to fall in heavy thuds against the comforter moments before I threw them back and bolted to the bathroom, shutting and locking the door behind me.

Knock! Knock! Knock!

"Mama! What I do?" I could hear Justus ask distressfully. "Mama?" My sobbing grew louder and Justus' cries for me faded beneath it. I wanted to ease his mind but I was falling apart.

I trusted Choppa would step in and make him understand for me because I couldn't do anything else in that moment but break.

***

A week later...

In the nearing days to her funeral and with the help of our families who still lived in the city, I was able to organize most of her arrangement while in Atlanta. However, there were certain things I needed to be in New Orleans to personally handle, so Choppa booked me and Justus a flight that would have us there later that evening, two days prior to her actual services.

"Baby, are you sure you can't come?" I'd grown so dependent of his support I wasn't sure if I would be able to hold up without him.

"I'm sorry, shorty. I can't." His eyes housed the remorse he felt to disappoint me.

I nodded my head dismally in acceptance. "Okay." My reply came off gloomily.

He rubbed my arms up and down simultaneously. "It isn't for a lack of sympathy, baby girl. If I could be there, I would. I just have to put out some fires before they blaze out of control on my end."

"Okay," I said once more.

He lifted my hand to his lips, kissed it and then led me into the living room.

We had a few hours until it was time to pick up Justus from school, so Choppa turned on the TV as we both crawled onto the sofa. "Anything you'd like to look at?"

I nestled myself further into the crook of his body, shaking my head *no* as I did. I'd been very blah about pretty much everything so what we watched didn't matter to me.

He put on a random movie, then he curled his arm around my waist, pulling me closer into him.

I closed my eyes sweetly as I enjoyed the strength of his embrace. "Mmm, I love you, Choppa."

He planted tender kisses along the shores of my shoulder and shortly after that, I felt the continual jump of his dick against me.

His voice became husky. "Can I show you how much I love you?"

It had been roughly two weeks since we were last intimate. He'd been patient with me but I knew he was overdue for the feel of his woman.

Choppa glided his hand over my thighs and ass, sending chill bumps up my spine, eliciting an immediate answer.

"Yes," I said above a hush. His love was probably the medicine I needed for the anxieties I'd been having.

Essence's sudden and tragic death made me realize how life could be over in the snap of a finger. Every singly iota of a moment had to be lived to the fullest. So with that thought prevalent in my mind, I pushed my grief aside for the moment and welcomed Choppa's desire.

Moving his hand to the waistband of his shorts, I felt him pull them down to his thighs. Then, I felt him run his fingers over the lips of my juice box.

"I've missed making love to you," he whispered in my ear, lustfully. "You missed feeling me inside of you?"

It was in that moment I realized I did, terribly. I wanted to reply with words but all I could do was moan. The touch of him swirling my wetness around as he teased my clit was overwhelming.

Moments later, he lifted my leg slightly while maneuvering himself past my boy shorts, wasting no time to plunge into me.

The feel of him penetrating my tight walls broke my silence. "Oh, baby!" I grinded against the slow thrusts of his pumps.

The pleasurable pain of his every stroke somehow lessoned the pangs in my heart and all I could do was succumb to feel of him.

After a few more pumps, Choppa pulled out of me. I gasped. "Why'd you stop?"

He fully stepped out of his shorts and removed his wife beater, then he pulled me up and took off what little I wore. "I need to feel your naked body against mine." He pushed his tongue into my mouth and I wrapped my arm around his neck.

Choppa lifted me off of my feet with one arm around my waist, kissing me nonstop as he walked us into the bedroom.

I already knew what to expect once my nakedness touched the sheets. He'd take me to another place and after the days and nights I'd been having, I needed this trip.

Chapter 43
Julz
Later that evening

Justus and I stood outside of the Louis Armstrong Airport in New Orleans as we waited on our ride. I pulled out my phone and sent a text to Choppa, letting him know that we had arrived safely.

7:07 p.m. Choppa: *Aight. HMU before you go to bed. Love you.*
7:09 p.m. Julz: *I will. Love you too!*

After five minutes elapsed, I saw my daddy's silver Ford F150 pull up alongside the curb. I grabbed our luggage and told Justus to keep close as we walked over to where he parked.

He stepped out and took my bags from me, placing them in the bed of his truck. "Hey, baby."

"Hey, Daddy." I gave him a kiss on the cheek and he hugged me tightly.

"How you holdin' up, baby girl?"

Shifting my eyes to Justus and then shaking my head, I plainly answered, "I'm good."

He nodded his head with the understanding that I didn't want to have any discussions surrounding our visit around my son. Daddy looked over at him. "Hey, son. Give your granddaddy a hug."

Justus walked into his lowered embrace. "Hey, Paw Paw."

Daddy ruffled his hand over the crown of his head before he lifted him up into the backseat. I climbed in the front afterwards as Daddy made his way around to his side.

"Y'all still staying by us, right?" he asked before pulling off.

"I am, but I agreed to let Marcel keep Justus for the next few days while we're here."

"What about your friends? We have room for them. Will they be coming?" He inquired about Precious and Fat-Fat.

"Yes, but they won't be here 'til Saturday, the day of." I looked over my shoulder and then out of the window.

Daddy then clutched my hand. "Wish we were seeing you under different circumstances but nevertheless, it's good to see you, honey. We've missed you."

"I've missed y'all, too." *More so now than ever.*

Once we passed Kenner and Metairie's traffic, it was smooth sailing the rest of the way to my families' Gentilly home.

Dad pulled into the driveway. "Home sweet home." He threw the gear in park and turned off the engine.

I stepped out, pushing the seat forward for Justus to jump down. Daddy grabbed our bags and we all walked up the steps of the porch.

Before I could knock, the front door swung open. Daddy had dual pipes that announced his comings and goings.

"Mam—Marcel?" I was surprised to see him answer my door instead of my mother.

"Come here." He pulled me into his embrace and rocked me.

"Dad." Justus called out to Marcel, but Daddy shushed him as he escorted Justus past were we stood partially blocking the doorway.

Marcel then walked me backwards onto the porch, pulling the door shut behind him. He hugged me tighter a few seconds more and then released me. "Hey, how you holdin' up?"

"Considering all things, I'm okay?"

"That's what's up." He looked down at my cast and attempted to ask me what I assumed was up with my arm.

"I fractured it. I'm okay with that, too." I neglected to tell him how but my statement sufficed.

"I know you wasn't expecting me until tomorrow but when your moms told me y'all be in tonight, I wanted to come through and offer my condolences ASAP and let you know that I'm here for you, in any way you need me to be."

I hoped he wasn't taking this opportunity to be a creep but even so, it was a sweet gesture of him to offer his support.

"Keeping Justus away from the emotional hoopla that this weekend will bring is more than enough." I smiled a small smile and motioned to walk inside. "I have to see my mama. I knew she's hurting just as much as I was. I mean, Essence was like her child, too."

"Yea, she pretty bent out of shape. She done pulled out boocoo photo albums, ya heard me, of y'all from junior high and up."

I shook my head because I knew it was going to be a long, tearful night but it was the bridge I had to cross. "Well, stay a while so Justus can be with my family for a minute."

"No doubt." We both went for the door until Marcel reached for my elbow.

I turned toward him. "What?"

"I meant what I said about being here for you. You're not just my baby moms. You're still the love of my life."

I allowed that to sink for a second before I nodded my head and silently walked inside to begin the home going of my friend.

***

The day of the funeral

Precious and Fat-Fat arrived around 4 a.m. We didn't do much talking when I picked them up from the airport. I could have assumed they were emotionally drained because of our loss, but I couldn't help but think it was because they faulted me, like I blamed myself, and they just didn't have words for me. *Sigh!*

Later that morning, I knocked on their door before I let myself into the bedroom. "Hey, guys. How'd y'all sleep?"

"Didn't get much." Fat-Fat responded first.

"Me neither. I'm not ready to face today. I can hardly deal, to be honest. I mean, me and E always got into it, but that was our thing, ya know?" Precious turned her back toward me so I could zip her dress up.

"I know," then I chuckled, reflecting on some of their classic arguments. "I'm gonna miss that, too. Y'all worked my nerves but cracked me up at the same time."

"Yea, that was the homie, for real." Precious smiled.

I took a seat next to Fat-Fat and she slightly moved away from me. I said nothing, just reached to pull Precious beside me. Looking to both sides of me, I spoke. "We haven't really talked about that day since it happened because we all have been grieving in our own way. Now, I'm not suggesting today or anything," turning toward Fat-Fat, I continued, "but we need to. Anyway, I just want to say that I love y'all and I don't want nothing breaking us up."

The room was silent for a minute but then Precious spoke. "Does that include Choppa? You know this is his fault."

"How is this…" I took a second to breathe. "This isn't the time, P. Just know what I said was real and we'll talk after we get through this but right now, let's be here for each other."

"All right." Precious agreed.

I looked to a quiet Fat-Fat, who I was sure felt some form of resentment toward me or Choppa. "I love you, Fat-Fat."

She looked up at me, studying me for a moment but then she spoke. "You know I love you, Diamond Girl."

I kissed her and then I kissed Precious on the cheek.

After wiping a few tears that escaped my eyes, I stood up. "The limo will be here in fifteen minutes. See you two up front." I walked out and closed the door, knowing I couldn't allow what happened to my sister happen to our friendship as well.

Service for Essence's home going presented its challenges but each of us leaned on the other and managed to remain strong throughout service.

There were those who occasionally fell out from their seats on the pew, my mother being one of them, but other than that it was everything my Tootsie deserved for an outro.

Immediately following an emotional service, we headed to cemetery where she would rest eternally. The pastor spoke his final words and then she was lowered into the ground.

I stood in so much disbelief of this day I surprisingly didn't cry. Maybe, I was all cried out or numb for the moment. But I kept reading and re-reading the scribe on the tombstone, which read: *Essence Marie Whitaker: Sunrise: November 3, 1988/ Sunset: October 4, 2015*

I can't believe this is real, but I'll see you again, sis. One sweet day!

As family and friends departed, me, Precious and Fat-Fat remained. We stared blankly at her gravesite, probably each embedding our final memory of her.

"I'm gonna miss my beautiful friend." Fat-Fat kissed her fingers and placed it tenderly on the headstone.

"That bitch slayed." Precious applauded how attractive Essence looked in her navy blue, all-in-one pant suit through a tearful voice.

I knew she was only trying to liven the moment the way Essence would had wanted it but Fat-Fat uglied her face at her comment.

Not taking any offense to what she said, I commented. "Indeed. She looked flawless, as always." I complimented how gorgeous her make-up and hair was. It looked as if she was at peace, quite the contrast to how I felt internally.

"Everything about her service was on point. The sermon, the turn-out of her people, the praise dancers and…"

Fat-Fat rudely cut Precious off. "Y'all bitches talking like it's all good or something, like we just left one of her parties and not her funeral."

Me and Precious looked to each other, confused. "Fat-Fat, you don't think this is hurtful to us?"

She bowed her head and shook it slowly, choosing not to answer. I walked over to her and threw my arm around her neck.

"This is hard on all of us, sis. But we're gonna get through—together."

Precious walked over to Fat-Fat and grabbed her hand, forging a weak smile onto her face.

We then stood there silently for a time until we collectively decided to leave, but not without giving Essence's gravesite one last look.

Chapter 44
Julz
Days later

"Bae, thanks again for the flowers and the card. They were beautiful."
I smiled at the arrangements Choppa had sent to my mother's house the
other day.

I could tell from the smile coming through his voice he was slick
blushing. "It's nothing, baby. You deserve the world."

It was my time to blush now. He knew how to make the sun appear
when my skies were gray.

We went back and forth in conversation. He said something funny,
I laughed. I said something grim and he cheered me back up.

"Aye, where's your shorty? I haven't heard lil' man in your background."

"Oh, that's because he's with his daddy." I answered innocently
enough.

"Oh yeah?" Unless I was wrong, Choppa's reply sounded accusatory.

"Yes, bae. Is there a problem with that?" I asked.

"You tell me?"

"There's nothing to tell you other than what I've already told you."

Then straight out of left field, he said. "I hear you. But you bet' not
be down there fuckin' with that nigga behind my muthafuckin' back!"

I had to take the phone away from my ear and look at the screen to
make sure I wasn't talking to a complete stranger. Sure enough, I was
talking to who I thought I was talking to. "Choppa, where did that come
from?" His needless insecurity changed the temperature between us
immediately.

"Fuck that, have you been with that nigga or not?" I could detect
anger rising in his voice and I felt high-key offended.

"Look, Choppa, don't disrespect me like that," I said tersely.

"Why you stalling?" He continued his line of senseless interroga-
tion.

"I'm not. You just shouldn't have to ask me that. However, the
answer is *no!*" Now I was hot under the collar.

"What about Tyriq? You hooked up with him down there?"

"Okay, now I'm about to hang up this phone! Don't you dare come at me like that!"

He made a gruff sound, then he spoke. "I'm gonna get you a flight to leave out tonight. It's time for you to come home."

"Choppa, I'm not ready. I haven't seen my family in a while and I'm just catching up with everyone. Get our tickets for the end of the week. We'll be home then."

"Nah, fuck that! You're coming home tonight." He was unyielding.

I smacked my lips in disgust. "I don't know what's gotten into you but this is a time where I need to be around my family. I thought you'd understand that."

"You've been around family for damn near a week now. Look, Julz, I'm not arguing with you. I said what I said. And if you're mine, you're gonna do what I said *point muthafuckin' blank!*"

I knew I was going to test him with what I would say next but he was my man, not *my daddy*. "And you heard what I said. We'll be home at the end of the week."

There was silence on the other end but I refused to break it. I didn't want to buck up more than I already had.

A solid minute passed and then he spoke. "A'ight. Bet." He hung up.

Damn, Choppa! I rolled my eyes.

I called him back but he allowed it to go to voicemail. I already knew calling him on repeat wouldn't inspire him to answer, so I sent him a text.

1:12 p.m. Julz: *Bae this visit is about family, not Marcel and not Tyriq. I know you know that so please don't be mean to me. I love you. I'll be home later in the week to prove it.*

I held the phone for ten minutes, hoping for a response but when one didn't come, I opted to leave well enough alone. Tossing my phone onto the bed in my old room, I lifted my eyes to the ceiling. *Peace be still.*

***

Choppa

I see I'ma have to show shorty the flip side of the game! That's what I told myself as soon as I hung up the phone. *How the fuck she gon' defy me?*

I figured she was down there feeling herself, probably giving what was supposed to be mine to her baby daddy. I swear a nigga couldn't trust a female further than he could pick 'em up and throw 'em. They all claimed to just wanna be loved and treated right, but when a nigga did that, they took his kindness for weakness.

Nothing could convince me that Julz wasn't down in New Orleans doing something foul. I could feel that shit in my chest! Life had taught me that women couldn't be trusted to keep their legs closed, especially when they were out of town or around their kid's father.

A nigga would think his girl was being loyal and she'd be somewhere taking dick from the next nigga, just like KiKi and the bitches I fucked with before her. And all of those hoes reminded me of Ms. Tonie.

Julz prolly like that, too.

I didn't wanna put shorty in that category but her change in attitude had me thinking that maybe it was true.

Just the thought of her possibly laying up with another nigga had me mad as fuck. If I hadn't had a coupla major moves to make I would've hopped on the highway, right then and there, went to New Orleans and turned the fuck up! But, as it already was, niggas was blowing up my phone looking for that werk.

Besides that, KiKi had been calling me all day on some fuck shit. Her pops and nem had gotten her out of jail on a $150,000 bond the other day. One of the conditions of her release was she had to go back to Ohio until her case was ready for trial.

KiKi hated that, and she was really pressing a nigga to come up there and chill with her. Of course, I couldn't do that. I had business to maintain in the 'A'.

Not wanting to argue, I let the phone ring until my voicemail picked up. After the recorded greeting and the beep, KiKi went ham.

"Nigga, I know you see me calling your muthafuckin' ass! You're down there laid up with that toothpick ass bitch while I'm the one facing life in prison over your trifling ass! I promise you, if you don't call me by tonight, I'ma go fuck the first nigga I see!"

I didn't even have the energy to call her back and address that shit. Hell, she had already fucked six niggas at the same time, one more wasn't gon' matter.

With so much shit on my mind, I hit the streets and handled my business hoping it would distract me from the uncertainties I was having about Julz.

"Big homie, you a'ight?" asked Pops, hours later, after we had finished making drops and collecting cheddar. I guess he could tell I wasn't my usual self.

"Yeah, I'm gucci. Sometimes the game gives a nigga a tight face," I played it off.

"Is it the beef with those niggas you used to hustle with, Cardale and Jared?"

"Nah, I'm not stressing those clowns. I already got bullets with their names on 'em," I said truthfully as I pulled up to Kim Marie's crib, where I was dropping him off at.

"Bet that." He held his fist out for a pound.

Bumping fists with him, I replied, "Stay solid, my nigga, and I'll give you the shirt off of my back."

"You know my get down, *100* or nothin."

"To the grave."

"To the grave," he echoed. As he was getting out of the car, Pop leaned back in. "All of that frontin', I think you just miss Julz. Shorty got you crazy." He laughed.

I laughed, too. But inside I hurting and I was mad. I couldn't get the idea out of my head that she was up to no muthafuckin' good.

"Lil' nigga, I got mine. I'm a Big Dawg. You better go in there and handle Kim Marie." I forced a chuckle out of my mouth.

"I'm just saying, homie," laughed Pop, who could obviously see through my facade.

I threw up the deuces and mashed out. Yeah, shorty was on my mind, but I was determined to push her to the side. I would deal with that ass whenever she came home.

After going to the crib to put the money in my stash, I tried to lay down and close my eyes. But sleep was a hard bitch to capture that night. When it finally came, I tossed and turned for hours. When I awoke the next day, I knew what I had to do to get a peace of mind.

Once I was showered and dressed, I grabbed my keys and my banger off of the dresser and headed out of the door. New Orleans was my destination. Julz was bringing her ass home, by choice or my force.

I was through playing games.

Chapter 45
Julz

Twenty-four hours had passed and despite me reaching out to Choppa, he hadn't reached back. It was obvious he was displeased with my defiance but his happiness couldn't be based on my sole obedience.

I sent him a text although I knew he wouldn't reply.

3:30 p.m. Julz: *At a time like this I don't want to feel alienated. Not from you. Please call me. I miss you.*

As I pressed send on the message, the doorbell rang. I got up from the sofa and looked out of the blinds to see it was Marcel and Justus.

I let them in.

"Hey, Marcel. I waved at him before I squatted in front of Justus. "Hey, baby. You had fun with your daddy?"

He hugged me around my neck. "I had so much fun. We did a lot of stuff."

Standing to my feet and walking over to the sofa, I asked, "Want to tell me what *stuff* is?"

Just then my mama walked in and got Justus riled up. "You're ready to go see Goosebumps?"

Justus jumped with his hand in the air. "Yea!"

"Hopefully, we'll make it to Elmwood Center in time for the 3:55 showing." My daddy checked his watch.

"I tried to get here earlier but my peoples was holding Justus hostage." Marcel reached in his pocket and gave Justus a twenty dollar bill. "Get'chu some popcorn at the movies."

"Thanks, Daddy." He spun around and headed to my parents.

"Well, so much for talking to mommy," I said as he walked off from me. He turned to come back but I shooed him away. "Nah, go 'head with Maw Maw and Paw Paw. I'll talk to you when you get back."

"All right, let's go!" Daddy corralled them out of the door, leaving me and Marcel alone.

He sat down next to me. "So, what you got going on for today?"

"Nothing now. I don't have a car."

"What you wanted to do?"

"Get an infinity tattoo with me and Essence's name, but I'll do it another day."

"You know, I don't have nothing on the agenda. I can take you, get you out of the house."

I scrunched my nose and shook my head. "I don't know."

"Why you actin' all spook? You wanna go, right?"

"I do."

"A'ight, then." He stood up and pulled me up as well. "Go get your purse or whatever and I'll be in the car, waiting.

I thought about it briefly. "Okay, give me a sec."

I headed to the back of the house, got my things and the extra key my peoples left me. I knew I didn't need to spend any alone time with Marcel but it was only going to be a couple of hours. *No harm. No foul.*

After leaving the tattoo shop, it was a little after seven o'clock when we pulled up in front of my mama's house. I was happy I went ahead and got the piece done. It made somehow made me feel closer to her.

I was seconds away from opening the door to get out but he stopped me. "Wait up a minute. I wanna play something for you." He smiled naughtily, while licking his lips.

He just never stops, I thought.

He turned up the volume.

You know I know it's gonna be good, girl...

Sons of Funk *Pushin' Inside of You* played from the speakers and I smiled inwardly. That was our song back in the day. And for a split moment, it felt like 2005 when we first started dating and we'd sit outside of my door, like tonight, in the Chevy Tahoe he drove back in the day. I chuckled and then turned down the stereo.

"What you laughing for?" he asked.

"You know why."

He laughed as well. "Yea, but I thought you might find it sweet, though."

"Maybe, if I was feeling you like that but I'm not, Marcel, and going down Memory Lane won't change that either. Just face it, all we have between us now is Justus, that's it."

"You sure 'bout that?" He questioned like he didn't believe me.

I didn't need to answer that. I just gave him the side eye. We talked a few minutes more on the topic until I decided I no longer wanted to entertain it, then I reached for the door handle. "Marcel will be Marcel, huh? Look, I'm 'bout to head inside."

"Hol' up." Marcel got out of the car and hurried to my side as I stepped out. "It's cool you don't want me but do you think I can have one kiss to say good night, Tasty Lips?"

"Hell no, Marcel. I can say good night without doing all of that. Besides, I have a man." I laughed.

"But ya man ain't me and he ain't here."

Thank God to both of those, I thought.

Marcel rested his hand on my hip and leaned in to kiss me anyway.

I removed his hand off of me and shook my head *no* and what I caught out of my peripheral both startled me shitless and made me glad I declined his weak advances.

The slam of the car door got Marcel's attention next.

"Do it and I'll leave both of y'all leaking right here on the ground," Choppa said on even tone as he stepped to us.

***

Choppa

I had my strap out, cocked and ready to spit. Julz' baby daddy, whose face I recognized from pics Justus had of him, froze at the sound of the bullet being housed in the chamber. When he opened his mouth to say something, I shoved my banger inside that muthafucka.

"Utter one word and I'ma pop yo top," I gritted.

Fear shone in his eyes as clearly as the red stain I would leave on his chest if he let his tongue flap.

"Choppa, what are you doing?" Julz cried out.

I bit down on my lip in anger. Slowly turning my head in her direction, I said through gritted teeth, "If you don't want me to clap this nigga, you best shut yo mouth!"

"But, bae—"

I snatched my whistle out of Marcel's mouth and turned toward her, menacingly. I held the gun down at my side but my voice sounded just as deadly as my forty-cal. "Say another word!" I dared her.

Fear and shock registered on her face and whatever she was about to say got stuck in her throat. I didn't give a fuck tho', I was on one!

Stepping back up in Marcel's grill with my toolie now aimed at his chest, I saw the bitch come out of him. The nigga was shaking so hard, all he needed was music and a pole.

"Man, please don't kill me. We wasn't doing nothing," he whined.

Every fiber in my body encouraged me to squeeze the trigger and open his chest plate, but I knew he couldn't do shit to Julz that she didn't allow. Still, I had to make him bow to my gangsta so he would know that fuckin' with mine, even with her consent, would get him obliterated.

I raised my hand and slapped him across the brow with my banger, drawing blood. He fell to the ground holding his head and whimpering like a ho. What Julz ever seen in a pussy like him dumbfounded me. And it made me even madder that she would creep on a trill nigga like myself with a chump whose clit was bigger than hers.

Glaring down at him, I pointed to Julz. "Bruh, you see shorty right there?"

"Yeah," he muttered weakly.

"Don't mumble, muthafucka! Say that shit like you respect it!" I drew my foot back and violently kicked him between the legs.

"Ahhhh!" He cried, clutching his little ass nuts.

"Do. You. See. Shorty. Right. There!" I repeated.

"Yeah!" he shouted.

"Well, she belongs to me now. I don't give a fuck if you got a child with her or not. If you ever put your lips on her again, I'ma make your mama mourn you. You understand me?"

"Yeah, man, I understand you." He cowered all the way down. But that wasn't good enough for me. I was intent on leaving an impression that he and Julz would never forget.

I lifted my foot and stomped him in the face twice. "Let this be the first and last time I gotta tell you that shorty belongs to me, nigga!

Every single part of her!" The last stomp was to his nose. A rush of blood poured down over his face.

To the side of me, Julz looked horrified. Her hand covered her mouth and tears poured down her face. Seeing pity in her eyes for him almost made me go ballistic.

I stepped toward her and snatched her hand down. "What, you crying over that fuck nigga? 'Cause I can let you be with him!" My face was a halfa centimeter from hers.

"Choppa, what's wrong with you?" She tried to back away.

I snatched her by the front of her shirt and roughly led her over to my ride. She was pulling against me but my strength overpowered hers. "Shorty, get in the truck before I hurt you."

"No!" She yelled.

"Get in the truck or else," I turned and pointed my gun at Marcel, "you're going with me or you're going to this nigga's funeral."

That got Julz' attention. "Oh, my God!" she cried.

After wiping at her tears, she opened the passenger door and climbed inside. I then closed the door because she left it wide open.

Before going around to the driver's side, I walked back over to where Marcel lie on the ground, withering in pain. As I sneered down at him, the headlights from my truck illuminated the area, allowing me to see that blood was all over my white Jordan's and the bottom of my pants leg.

I raised my foot one last time and stomped him in the chest. "Thug life, nigga!" I spat

I looked up and saw a few neighbors standing out in their yards but since the sun had already faded and darkness was forcing its way over the sky, I wasn't worried about witnesses. *Shid, I wasn't a familiar face no way.*

But, instinctively, I held my head down as I rushed back to my whip and hopped behind the wheel. "Now it's time to deal with you," I told Julz as I drove off.

Chapter 46
Choppa

Julz turned sideways in her seat, facing me with eyes that burned red with anger. "In front of my parents' house, Choppa? In the place I grew up? In front of neighbors that have known me since I was a little girl?"

"Fuck I care about that?" I spat.

"Are you fucking crazy? Why did you do that?" I drove on as if I didn't hear shit she was spewing. "Why, Choppa? Why?" She turned forward in her seat, lowered her head in her lap and balled so hard her shoulders rocked back and forth.

"That's what I should be asking you? But, nah, I already know the answer. You weren't ready to come home because you were down here fuckin' your baby daddy."

Her head shot up and I felt the heat from her gaze on the side of my face. "Do you know how crazy you sound?"

"Nah, ma, I just know what I saw."

"What the fuck did you see?" She scoffed. "No need to answer. You didn't see shit because I wasn't doing shit but telling him that I have a man!" Her tone was at a fever pitch but anger often hid lies.

"He was about to kiss you. If I hadna rolled up, y'all prolly would be fuckin' by now." My chest rose up and down.

"What did you just say?" She questioned in a voice shaking with rage. "Don't you dare disrespect me like that!"

"Disrespect *you*? Nah, you were disrespecting me," I corrected her.

"I was not!"

"The eyes don't lie," I said as I came to a stop at a traffic light.

Julz tried to gather herself and explain that, yeah, Marcel had tried to kiss her but she claimed to have told him *no*. It didn't really matter, though, because she had no business being in the car with that mutha-fucka. According to her, Justus was off somewhere with her parents, so what the fuck reason did she have to be with her son's father? I asked.

"He took me to get this," she replied, showing me a fresh tattoo with her and Essence's name off of her shoulder. "That's all it was, Choppa. Once again, you overreacted. You didn't have to do that to him."

As the light turned green and I pulled off, I weighed her explanation against the deceit I knew women were capable of. I would probably never know the truth whether she was tryna fuck with Marcel or not, but I had told her ass once before that *the appearance of an impropriety was just as damning as the actual act.*

I repeated that adage, adding, "This is the second time I caught you outta pocket. I gotta believe it's more than coincidence."

That seemed to blow Julz' stack. Her eyes turned into slits. "You didn't catch me doing nothing! And stop fucking accusing me! I'm very capable of being around Marcel or any other man without sleeping with them. I'm not KiKi!" she hurled.

"Maybe you're worse," I slung back.

"Stop the car and let me out!"

"Fuck that!" I shouted over her.

Julz started crying but her tears didn't move me. I hopped onto I-10 East, destination Georgia.

I had traveled almost ten miles when Julz realized where we were headed.

"Choppa, take me back home!" she yelled.

"That's where I'm taking you," I said.

"No, I want to go back to my parents' house."

"Why, so you can check on your pussy ass baby daddy?" That shit had me heated. "Make me find him and put two in his head."

"For what? You think that makes you more of a man? Is this what I'll have to go through with you? Because if it is, I can't do this!" She broke down crying hard as hell. Loud sobs that penetrated a nigga's steel armour, this time. But I refused to be played.

"I can't do it, either, if I can't trust you to keep your legs closed," I said between clenched teeth.

"Stop saying that shit to me!" she screamed.

"Stop giving me a reason!" I yelled back.

"Look, nigga, I haven't given you no fucking reason. You're muthafuckin' crazy!" She snapped.

We yelled back and forth until both of our voices were hoarse.

Finally, we both just stopped saying anything to each other.

In the quietness inside of the car, Julz' phone rang. She fished it out of her bag. "Hello," she answered.

"If that's that nigga, I'ma take you back to him and let you have him." I was fed up with it all.

Fuck I gotta argue over who she wanna be with? I'ma boss nigga! Bitches will disown their whole family to be with me.

Julz cut her eyes at me and continued with her conversation. It only took hearing a few words to know she was on the phone with her Mom Duke. "Okay, I'll be there in a minute. Bye." She hung up. Without looking at me, she said, "I need to go get Justus."

I took the next exit and hopped back on the interstate, going I-10W to do just that. Grab shorty and still mash the fuck out.

A short while later we pulled up at her mom's crib. Marcel's car was gone and there was no sign of the police. I put the car in park and looked out of the window for any hint of danger. I didn't think Julz would set me up but the streets had conditioned me to not take shit for granted.

Without saying a word, Julz opened the passenger door and began to get out of the truck. This was the moment of truth, I decided.

"Are you coming back?" I asked.

Her body froze halfway out of the car. One foot was on the ground and the other one was still inside of the car on the floorboard. I waited for a response but none came.

I knew she was thinking, pulling up images in her mind of the nigga I could become when consumed by jealousy and heavy suspicion. But she also had to recall that part of me that loved her like no other man ever could.

Her long silence caused a sharp pang of anxiety to shoot through my chest, like the impact of a .22 caliber bullet straight to the heart.

"Are you coming back?" I asked again, hopeful, doubtful.

This time she answered and my happiness hung in the air, suspended in time, until her response registered clearly. "Yes, Choppa, I'm coming back," she said unwavering.

I felt myself unconsciously exhale. The air that was caught in my chest released, like trapped gas from a balloon, and I leaned back in my seat breathing a sigh of relief.

"Okay. I'ma wait right here," I said.

"Sure." Her response was clipped but at least she was returning.

As I watched her hurry up the walk, I knew that even had she wanted to leave me I wouldn't have let her go.

Chapter 47
Julz

The seven hour drive back to Atlanta was going to take forever, considering me nor Choppa had much to say to each other. Justus was in the backseat asleep, so it was deathly quiet.

I was still angry over his behavior and he probably was still distrustful of mine, though he had no reason to be.

Instinctively, my hand slid over toward Choppa's leg. I just wanted him to feel my touch and know that I loved him and no other man could have what was his.

But I also needed him to understand that his violent reactions had to cease. And there was no better way to protest that than by putting a temporary cold distance between us.

I swiftly drew my hand back and rested in my lap. Absent-mindedly, I fiddled with the promise ring on my finger as I stared out of the side window at darkness and nothing.

As we proceeded up I-10, I thought about Marcel, wondering if he was okay. For a split second, I considered texting him, but I didn't want to chance starting another fight with Choppa, who I was finding out, could go from zero to a hundred very quickly.

I looked over at him and tried to gauge the man he was. His temper was a scary thing, but he had never directed it toward me, physically. But he would be a threat to any man I might have to interact with and that was not a good thing.

On the other hand, Choppa's love and desire for me was indisputable just as mine was for him. He made me laugh. He made me feel beautiful and special. He also made sweet love to my body, mind and soul, and there was nothing he wouldn't do for me.

Leaving him was not an option I wanted to consider. I just wanted him to trust me because without trust, love couldn't breathe. I had learned that with Marcel. Every time he stepped out of the house, I suspected he was with another bitch, and that shit tortured me.

But what had I done to cause Choppa to feel that way about me? I wondered.

It had to be something because he was not a mean man. I knew that many men falsely believed a woman's heart would forever belong to the man whose child she borne, but that didn't explain the way Choppa reacted to my friendship with Tyriq.

I'd just have to earn his trust, I told myself.

Bitch, you sound crazier than him. Don't go blaming yourself for his insecurities. Essence spoke to me from Heaven.

Tears welled in the corners of my eyes. Flashes of her in her casket blinked in and out of my mind. I couldn't help but let out a loud sob. My sista was gone forever.

"You okay?" asked Choppa.

"Yes. I was just thinking about Essence," I clarified, so he wouldn't think otherwise.

He reached over and placed a strong hand on my leg, and his touch comforted me. My tears dried, and I stroked the back of his hand as I forced myself to recall nothing but the good times I shared with my sista.

Before I knew it, I had fallen asleep and when I woke up, several hours later, we were pulling up in the driveway of a small but beautiful house.

"You're home," Choppa announced.

I blinked a few times to clear my vision. "Home? Where are we?"

"Out in Doraville."

"Who lives here? Is this another one of your places?" I asked.

Choppa leaned across the seat and kissed me on the lips. "Why you gotta ask so many questions?" He turned off the headlights and the ignition. Before I could ask another question, he hopped out of the truck and came around to my side and opened the door. Extending his hand out to me, he said, "Step down, Queen, and welcome to *Su Casa.*"

"Gracias, King," I played along, still wary of the house before me. "Will a servant retrieve my bags?"

"Yeah, El Choppa, in the morning."

I giggled like a school girl. "Okay, bae."

Choppa opened the back door and hoisted a drowsy Justus into his arms. The long drive had him in and out of sleep. "We're home, lil' man," he said affectionately.

342

He used his hip to shut the door, then we walked up the short pathway that led to the front door of the unfamiliar house.

"Baby, who lives here?" I asked again as we approached.

"Broads! Ain't got no patience," he said playfully.

Laughing, I punched him on the arm. "Bae, how did I go from a queen to a broad in less than thirty seconds?"

"You're always a Queen." He leaned down and gave me a loving peck on the cheek.

"And you're always my King." I reached around his back and squeezed his ass.

Choppa jumped a foot in the air. "Yo, shorty, don't do that shit."

"My bad, boo. It was just so tempting." I laughed.

"Yeah, well, next time grab the front."

"Oh, I definitely intend to," I let it be known.

Three steps led us up on the porch, which was illuminated by the porch light. Across the front door was a big, red ribbon.

Shorty's New Crib, it read.

I gasped with excitement.

"You didn't!" I cried.

"I did, Queen," he said.

Still holding a sleeping Justus across his shoulder, Choppa reached into his pocket and handed me a key. My heart raced with love and excitement as I tore the ribbon down and inserted the key into the lock.

Twisting the doorknob to the right, I held my breath as the door swung inward and I stepped inside. The soft light from a lamp not far away lit up the living room. It was decorated beautifully, and with such care, that it brought instant tears to my eyes.

This man of mines was unbelievable!

"I'ma take Justus up to his room. Go 'head and give yourself a tour. It's all yours, baby girl," he said.

As I went from room to room, I was speechless. The furnishing was so *me*. The kitchen was spacious and equipped with modern appliances. Choppa had moved all of my personal belongings from my old apartment to the new house, and he had even arranged my clothes in the closet.

343

Venturing into Justus' room, I saw that Choppa had done the same for him. That touched me even more because sometimes I sensed jealousy between the two. Nothing heavy, just a little tug-of-war for my affections.

Despite being in a brand new bed, my son was sleeping peacefully. I smiled at the innocence on his face as I walked over and placed a goodnight kiss on his forehead.

When I turned around, Choppa stood in the doorway smiling at me. How could I not love him?

"Thank you, bae, you're the best," I walked up to him and wrapped my arm around his trim waist.

He cupped my ass and pushed his tongue into my mouth. I swear, a bitch was floating.

It was almost 4 o'clock in the morning but I was full of energy. *Burning* energy that I wanted to coat Choppa's dick with.

"Why you looking at me like that?" He asked after we broke our sensual kiss.

"Dudes! Ain't got no clue." I reversed the game on him.

"I got more than a clue." He took my hand and placed it on his print. He was rocked up and all the way over in his front pocket.

My pussy controlled my tongue. "You ain't saying *Nathaniel*," I stole his slang. "Let me get that dick."

"The bedroom?"

"Nah, boo, the shower. Let's go break it in."

***

Choppa sat on the bathroom counter, admiring me as I slowly undressed. The way he stared at me made me hot. I cupped my bare titties. He licked his lips. My na na jumped.

I slid my pants down to my ankles and stepped out of them. He released his steel from his pants and stroked it. My clit throbbed.

I turned around, placed my palms against the wall and made my cheeks clap. He bit down on his bottom lip and shook his long dick at me. My juices stirred.

Looking over my shoulder, I spread my legs and grabbed my ankles. Choppa hopped off of the counter, walked up behind me and rubbed the head of his dick up and down the crotch of my panties. I was soaking wet.

Forget a shower, I wanted that pipe inside of me right now. Hard and aggressive. *Manhandle a bitch. We can make love in the morning.*

Choppa moved my hair aside and gently bit my neck. I moaned and pushed my ass against his hard on. It felt so good my knees wobbled.

"Ooh, bae!" I sucked in my breath to keep from screaming when he pinched both of my nipples.

"You wanna feel this dick inside of you, don't you?" he whispered in my ear.

His voice was deep and confident. His thuggish sex appeal resonated through my entire being. "Yes, boo, right now." I ached to feel him part my lower lips with his length and immense width.

"If you want it, tell me you're mine and you'll never even look at another nigga." His hand slid down my body and located my sensitive pearl.

His demand was crazy but his touch weakened me. When my body wasn't on fire, his jealousy angered me. But right now, it turned me on!

To know he wanted me to the point that he would probably kill over me drove my sexual desire for him to new heights. My pussy moistened and I got the unexplainable urge to feel him inside of my every hole. I wanted him to do things to me that I'd never dreamt of doing before.

"Choppa, I'll never look at any other man but you!" My body forced the words out of my mouth.

"You better mean that shit, shorty." He bit into my shoulder blade as his fingers stroked my wet petals.

I called on Jesus to forgive me for the nasty things I wanted Choppa to do to me.

Going blind with desire, I reached behind me and grabbed ahold of that shaft like it was my salvation. Stroking every hard inch if it, I closed my eyes and bit down on my lip.

"Please, don't make me wait," I begged like a nympho.

Choppa spun me around and lifted my hands above my head. He lowered his mouth to my breasts and ravished it. I wiggled out of my panties, kicking those bad boys across the floor. "Come and get your pussy, boo." I said.

Choppa stepped back and looked me up and down, hungrily. His eyes were filled with beastly desire and his dick stood straight up, with a curve.

I saw his eyes roam down my body and rest on my kitty kat. Then something in his expression changed drastically. "Get up on the counter and spread your legs."

"Bae, what's wrong?" I asked.

"Just do what I said." This was an order, and it carried with it no sexual tone.

Confused, I did as he demanded.

"Choppa, what's wrong?" My voice quivered.

"Open your legs. I need to see your pussy."

I didn't understand why but I had nothing to hide so I widened my legs. I saw his brows knit together and his top lip curl under.

"Why the fuck is your pussy shaved?"

"Huh?" I looked down between my legs to inspect myself.

"You hadn't shaved before you went home. Why would you need to shave your pussy to go to a muthafuckin' funeral?"

"Choppa, are you serious?" I was offended.

"As a heart attack!" He spat.

And just that quickly, our mood was lost. Choppa's dick had deflated and my juices had dried up. He straightened up his clothes and stormed out of the bathroom, leaving me confused, angry and crying.

I spent the first night in my new house alone in bed, hugging my pillow and wondering if my man, who slept downstairs on the couch, was bipolar.

As the morning sun parted my blinds, I felt the inclination to pack my clothes and return the house key to him. I loved Choppa but his suspicions were too much to bear.

Leave him now.

I wanted to follow my first mind and run but my heart overruled my common sense, and I stayed.

Chapter 48
Julz

"Five—Four—Three—Two—One, Happy New Year's!" Me, Choppa and Justus chorused as we brought in 2016 in the comfort of our home.

"Happy New Year's, baby!" I repeated before I gave Choppa tongue, ending it with a peck on the lips before I bent down and addressed Justus. "And Happy New Year's to you, mama's prince." I gave him a kiss on the lips and hugged him tightly.

"Julz, cut that incest shit out." He pulled me away from him. "He's too old to be kissing you in the mouth. You're his mama not his girl!" Choppa lectured for the umpteenth time.

Justus cut his eyes at Choppa and I did the same. "*Incest?* You're being preposterous. Besides, he's still a baby in my eyes." I squeezed at Justus' jaw, squishing the plumpness of them.

"A'ight, well, I'ma put it to you like this. You're either his woman or mine. You decide."

"Really, Choppa?" I tilted my head in awe of his bogus ultimatum.

"Shouldn't be that hard, if you ask me." Sarcasm dripped from his voice.

"Choppa, I'm *your* woman and *his* mother. There's no choice to be made because the love I give you two are different."

"Act like you know, then. Real talk, let this be the last time you kiss your five year old in the damn mouth." He plopped down on the sofa. "*Shit's ridiculous!*" he mumbled audibly.

He couldn't be more right about that. He was beyond ridiculous when it came to me. However, I just shook my head and let out a sigh. *Boy, you need help.*

Putting my focus back on Justus, I made him an offer. "If you promise not to be a Grinch come morning when it's time to wake up and head out, you can stay up as long as you like, watching TV in your room."

"Yea, I promise." He stuck his pinkie finger out. I latched mine around his, went in to give him a kiss but I felt Choppa's hot stare on the side of my face, so, instead of kissing my son I gave him an awkward smile.

Justus took off running upstairs to his room and I sat down in the oversized chair adjacent to where Choppa sat.

"Why you over there?" he questioned the moment I coiled my feet under my body.

"No reason." I lied. Truth was I didn't like how he made everything so damn uncomfortable these days.

As far back as Tyriq and especially since my visit home for the funeral months ago, Choppa had been insanely jealous over every little thing, causing strains in all of my relationships, including the one with my son.

The last conversation I had with Marcel made me question my parental skills. After the unwarranted beating Choppa gave him, he claimed my allowing a maniac like that into my home around our son made me unfit to be a mother and he'd do everything in his power to get full custody of him. I must admit I lost sleep over his promise to take Justus away from me but not enough to voice my concerns to Choppa. I didn't want to relay the message to him because I feared he'd eradicate the threat of a custodial battle by eliminating Marcel altogether.

The whole KiKi situation distorted Precious and Fat-Fat's view of my relationship with Choppa. They didn't understand how I could remain with him, considering they linked Essence's death to him. And it didn't matter how many times I tried negotiating a different perspective, they'd stood in protest of it.

"Had Choppa known we were going out there to beat her ass, he would have stopped it, hands down!" I argued.

"Had you known about this KiKi bitch and their involvement from jump, you wouldn't have fucked with him and Essence would still be here." Precious made clear and Fat-Fat amen'd.

From their vantage point, I agreed. But at the end of the day, fault could be placed at all of our feet. We brought the drama to KiKi and she answered with a very unexpected deadly response. One that I'd regret for the rest of my life.

It had been months since I heard Tyriq's voice, and Justus would occasionally ask about him, but I knew that Choppa would act a whole fool if I so much as entertained the thought of my son spending time with Tyriq, who Choppa despised.

If that wasn't bad enough, now he was manipulating the way I showed my own boy affection.

It don't make no damn sense!

I gave Choppa the side eye. Sometimes I could not understand that man. He could be so gentle, loving, kind-hearted and attentive, and then the simplest thing could set him off.

Like the time several weeks ago when I decided to wake him up with a smile on his face.

Choppa had been in the streets for three days in a row. When he came home I could tell by the look on his face that his chosen lifestyle was beginning to stress him out.

I watched him for a minute, wondering what was on his mind. One thing he never did was discuss his business with me. I was perceptive enough to gather that he probably sold drugs but he didn't bring any to the house and whenever he came out of the streets, he left the streets out there.

But tonight I could tell that something was the matter. I sat up and scooted close to him wrapping my arms around him. "You wanna talk about it?" I offered a listening ear.

Choppa flashed a little smile. "Nah, shorty, everything is cool. Thanks, tho', you're a nigga's rider." He leaned in and gave me a kiss. "Go on back to bed, you gotta get up early in the morning."

As the day was dawning, I wanted to ease a little of my man's worry before I started my day.

I pulled the cover down and slid my hand in his boxers. I felt him get heavy in my hand as I trailed kisses down his chest and stomach, and stroked his dick. For some strange reason, Choppa hadn't ever asked me to give him head. I had wondered about that, but hadn't brought it up yet. I kind of figured that I must've given him the wrong impression that I didn't do that.

Well, this morning I planned to wake him up with that beautiful, long, dark meat in my mouth. I would go all out by swallowing his babies and, in the moment, his mind would find peace from whatever had his mood so sullen.

I released his dick from its restraints and slowly circled the huge head with my tongue. "Ummm!" I moaned as he grew stiffer in my hand.

Inch by inch, I took him deeper into the warm and wet cavern of my mouth. His chocolate stick tasted delicious. I gently rubbed his balls while slurping loudly.

"Why you doing this?" he said.

The question surprised me but it was his voice that left me confused. He sounded like a little boy.

I stopped for a split second but when he went quiet, I told myself that maybe my ears had played a trick on me. After all, he was asleep. Even I sounded different when I first woke up.

Continuing with my mission to have my man awake with his dick in his woman's mouth, I slowly licked up and down Choppa's length. My pussy moistened as I felt his nuts filling up. I wasn't really a shallower but Choppa had done more than enough for me to deserve my tonsils.

My head started bobbing up and down in a sync with the stroke of my hand. I let spit run from my mouth and I used it as lubricant to make the strokes feel better to him.

I smiled inwardly when he stirred awake, and I stepped my game up. "Good morning, bae. Do you like to wake up to some good head?" I bobbed up and down faster, taking him to the back of my throat.

I felt him grab my hair and wrap it around his hand. I closed my eyes and relaxed my throat muscles more, in preparation for him to ram me with all that dick. But what he did next totally caught me off guard.

"Get your ass up here! What, you a ho now?" He yanked me by the hair, pulling me up from between his legs.

"Owwww! Choppa, why you do that?" I looked at him with my arms spread out in confusion.

"You're my woman, not a ho! Hoes and thots suck dick. Fuck is wrong with you?" He looked like he had lost all respect for me.

I watched him get up out of bed, go in the bathroom and slam the door. Twenty minutes later, when he came out, he was back to being a sweetheart.

When I brought up the incident a day later, Choppa said, "Shorty, let's not talk about."

So, we didn't.

Recalling that now, I became even more confused about some of his likes and dislikes, and especially his unfounded suspicions and jealousies.

Gurl, no man is perfect.

"Come over here and watch this movie with me." He patted his thigh and I got up to sit across his lap, like he wanted.

Choppa affectionately held me close to him and I swear it felt as if all of his shortcomings shrunk under the guise of his touch. I loved him, there was no denying that. I just had a hard time swallowing who he became when he was convinced something foul was happening under his nose.

I typically brushed off his accusations because they were baseless but they were annoying as hell, no lie. I reminded myself that the first year was the most trying because couples still needed to feel their way, but something was telling me that Choppa just wanted things *his* way!

"You're comfortable, baby?" He snuggled me into his chest.

I kissed his neck. "There's no better place than right here."

He smiled at me, twisted his head to press his lips against my nose. "I love you, shorty. I put that on everything."

"I love you, too, Choppa." I did with my whole heart but I wasn't oblivious. I knew something had to give.

Ca$h & Coffee

Chapter 49
Choppa
Three days later

Justus was upstairs in bed, sick with a cold. Julz and I were downstairs in the den, watching Monday Night Football. My Cleveland Browns was playing her New Orleans Saints and shorty was doing a lot of pop-pin' because Drew Brees was lighting the Browns' defense up. The Saints led 28-3 and it was only the second quarter.

"Who dat!" she screamed when Cleveland's quarterback threw his second interception of the game.

I smiled happily because, really, it was the first time I had seen shorty truly enjoy herself since the day Essence died. Yet, and still, I couldn't swallow the smack down her team was applying to mine.

"Man, they need to get rid of that sorry ass white boy we got at quarterback! I can throw a goddam bowling ball better than he just threw that stupid ass pass!" I picked up a pillow off of the couch where we were sitting and slung it across the room in frustration.

"Ooh, somebody is big mad," she teased.

"Real talk, shorty, this my last year rooting for these sorry mutha-fuckas. They probably can't even beat a high school team." I kicked the bottom of the table as the Saints made a field goal right before halftime, increasing their lead to 31-3.

Disgusted, I sat up and grabbed a couple of barbeque wings off of the platter that Julz had prepared and washed them down with a Hei-neken.

While I was stuffing my face, shorty was staring at the screen of her phone, laughing. "Levon Tranay and Raychelle is cray cray," she said.

I had heard her mention the names of her friends from New Orleans before so I recognized them. "You must be on Facebook," I guessed.

"Yep, and they're going in on your Browns. Levon Tranay just said, 'Tell your man his *Clowns* are getting fucked with no grease.'"

"Oh, yeah? Lemme see what they talm 'bout?" I didn't have a Fa-cebook page myself because, to me, all of that social media shit was for women and lame ass niggas. I was too busy stacking old dead white men to waste time on that.

Julz held her phone out to me. "Read the comments, bae, they're talking real bad about your team." The smirk on her face told me she had been talking smack on there, too.

I tapped on the appropriate comments and started reading what people were saying. Saints' fans were talking a whole bunch of trash because they were winning. "I bet all these muthafuckas be quiet as a mouse when y'all getting y'all ass kicked."

As I continued to read the comments, a new one popped up. The name attached to it immediately caught my attention. *Tyriq Theriot.*

Keeping my composure, I looked up at Julz. "Baby, you mind getting your man another beer?"

"I sure don't." She got right up and headed to the kitchen.

I looked back down at the screen and went to Julz' home page. From there I tapped myself into her messages and began scrolling down. I only had to scroll past two recent messages from females to get to what I suspected I would find.

The third most recent message in her box was from that bitch nigga, Tyriq, and it was dated yesterday. My face balled into a frown and my hand shook with brewing rage, as I opened the message and began reading.

It didn't take long to scroll up and see that Julz had been keeping in touch with that nigga for months!

A few days after I made Julz change her phone number, Tyriq's message read: *Damn, love, I can't believe you let that insecure ass nigga put you on lock like that. If he can't respect that you have friends, something is seriously wrong with dude. It don't matter, though, you gonna always be my round, ya heard me.*

Her response was right underneath that.

Julz: *Ikr. But it's best that we communicate on here. I don't want y'all to end up killing each other. And if you need to see me and Justus you can meet us by any of my girls.*

Tyriq: *That's what's up. I love you anyway and I don't care what you think, that shit ain't gonna last. A man gotta allow his woman to breathe or she'll suffocate. #RNS*

Julz: *I hear you.*

Tyriq: *No, you don't, son. I love you, anyway, big head.*

Julz: *Boy, you can't talk about nobody's head. LOL. I love you too.*

Another message from him read: *Julz, you know I love you with my whole chest but I'm kinda mad at you for still fucking with that nigga after what happened to Essence. No matter how you flip that shit, love, he has to share some of the blame. I wanted to talk to you about that at the funeral but you were too messed up. But now I ain't keeping quiet, you need to cut that nigga off. For Essence, ya heard me.*

Julz: *Riq, please don't do that to me! I'm already tormenting myself back and forth about this enough. I honestly don't know what to do. Some days I tell myself I should leave him. Other days, I feel that he's not to blame. Please, Riq, I don't need you judging me right now. I already have Precious doing that, and Fat-Fat won't hardly answer my calls.*

I didn't have to read no further!

Julz came back into the den carrying two Heinekens. She placed one on the table and handed the other one to me. "Here you go, bae. Is halftime over?" She sat down beside me on the couch and glanced up at the flat screen on the wall.

I took a swig of beer and sat it down on the table beside the other bottle. *"Slick ass bitch!"* I uttered.

"What you say, bae?" Julz turned to look at me and saw the expression on my face. "Is something wrong, boo?"

"Nah, I'm good. But let me ask you something..."

"Okay."

"When's the last time you heard from ya boy?"

"Who?"

"Shorty, you know who the fuck I'm talm 'bout!" I stood up with her phone behind my back.

"No, I don't. But if you're referring to Marcel, he called to speak with Justus the other day. Why? Is there a problem?" A look of confusion covered her whole face. She just didn't know, shit was 'bout to get real.

"Fuck, Marcel! I'm talm 'bout Tyriq. When's the last time you heard from him." I grabbed the beer by the bottleneck and turned it up, draining it.

"I haven't talked to Tyriq at all, not since I changed my number," she lied effortlessly.

"Come again!" I gritted. "You gon' sit there and lie to me?"

"Choppa, I'm not lying!" She had the muthafuckin' nerve to sound offended.

I brought her phone from behind my back and tossed it in her lap. It was still on her Facebook message from Tyriq.

When she looked at the screen and saw she was busted, I saw her whole expression change. She opened her mouth to explain but the words never made it out.

"You lying, bitch!" I threw the beer bottle against the far wall. It shattered and fell to the floor. I stepped closer to Julz, grabbed her by the hair with one hand and slapped the fuck out of her with the other.

Whap!

She looked at me, stunned.

Her hands went to the side of her face and tears spilled from her eyes. "You hit me," she uttered in disbelief.

"You muthafuckin' right, I did! You telling that nigga you're thinking about leaving me, huh?"

Whap! Whap!

I knocked her onto her ass. "All this time, I'm taking care of you and another nigga's seed, and you're plotting to leave me?" The thought of that made me see red!

I took a step forward and Julz scooted back.

"Choppa, baby, please let me explain," she cried. "It was after my best friend's funeral and I was so confused."

"Nah, you wasn't confused. You meant that shit! You just stayed because you need a nigga."

"That's not true! I stayed because I love you."

When she said that fuck shit, I went into a rage. All I could see was the message where she told Tyriq the same muthafuckin' thing—she loved him, too.

I caught up to her. Reaching down, I grabbed her around the neck and started choking her. "Bitch, you told that bitch ass nigga the same thing! You love me and him? Huh, bitch?" I shook her like a dust mop.

She clawed at my hands tryna pry them from around her neck but I would not let go.

"Choppa. I. Can't. Breath." She managed to cough out.

"Ask me if I give a fuck! You wanna play with my heart? I'll kill your dirty ass!" I tightened my fingers and squeezed harder.

In desperation, she clawed at my face, drawing blood.

"Aww fuck!" I spat when her nails dug into my left eye. I jerked my head to the side and let go of her neck.

Julz laid on the floor, coughing violently for a few minutes. When she refilled her lungs with air, she climbed to her feet. Crying, she picked up the closest thing to her, which was a bowl I used to keep my personal weed in. "I hate you!" She hurled the crystalline bowl at me and started sobbing.

I ducked left and the bowl missed my head by inches. It crashed to the floor but remained in one piece. "Oh, you hate me but you love that nigga." I spat. "What, he fuck you better than me?"

"I'm leaving!" Her face was wet with tears but so was my heart. So, I didn't feel no mercy.

"You damn right you're leaving—*on a muthafuckin' stretcher!*"

In two long strides, I blocked her path. When she went to step around me, I grabbed her by the back of the hair and snatched her back. "Let go of me!" she yelled.

When I looked in her face, all I saw was an ungrateful, lying bitch, who had probably fucked Tyriq and her baby daddy behind my back. I balled my fist up and punched her dead in her deceitful mouth!

Wham!

I let her hair go and she crumpled to the floor.

Standing over her, I spat, "Now you're about to see the beast in me! See, I know what your muthafuckin' problem is! You too fuckin' pretty, so I'ma fix that shit."

I reached down and grabbed her by the collar and drug her through two rooms to reach the kitchen. There, I snatched open the door of the dishwasher and grabbed a knife.

357

Julz looked woozy from the punch. She was crying and mumbling through her busted lip, then her eyes widened with fear when she saw the knife in my hand.

"No, Choppa! Please!"

"I ain't even tryna hear that shit!" I grabbed a handful of her hair and chopped it off. "I'ma see if that nigga want a bald headed bitch!" I twisted another handful around my fist and hacked it off.

"Oh, God!" she cried.

"Don't call on *him* now. Did you call on God when you was dissing me to that bitch nigga Tyriq?"

"I wasn't doing that!" she wailed and then started tryna fight back.

I let go of her hair and allowed her to climb to her feet. She swung and hit me in the mouth but that shit was nothin'. I smiled. "Not only do you fuck around behind my back, you think you can go toe to toe with a nigga. A'ight, bitch, now I'ma beat you to a pulp!"

I drew my fist back and slammed it into her face. Julz fell against the stove and more blood ran from her mouth. I didn't feel sorry for her, though. *Hell no!* Not after reading that fuck shit she had messaged back and forth with her little cuddy buddy!

They were playing me for a fool.

And for that, she had to be taught a lesson!

Chapter 50
Julz

"Please don't hit me no more! Please!" I used my hands to shield my-self as I begged for his wrath to come to an end, but he didn't put a stop to his malice until he delivered one last blow to my head.

Whap!

From the corner of my eye, I saw him stoop down to my level as I lay balled in a knot on the kitchen floor. "Now tell me you're sorry."

I didn't even have time to process how this muthafucka was crazy as hell if he thought I would apologize for anything, but fear propelled my speech. "I'm sorry, Choppa."

"Sorry for what?"

I didn't do shit wrong but I knew the tune he wanted me to dance to, so I danced. "For messaging Tyriq."

"And?"

"And for lying about it."

"And what else?" He sought out a confession but I didn't do shit.

I grabbed at my side in agony from when Choppa kicked me as I scooted away slowly. "I didn't do anything else."

His grimace was so tight it transformed his look totally. "You still wanna lie to me, like you didn't fuck them niggas? You think I'm stu-pid? You think I can't see through your games? I done been with a hundred hoes who tried the same punk shit you're doing. You ain't no muthafuckin' different! You wanna fuck behind my back? Okay, I'ma give your ass what a trifling ho deserves!"

I shook my head rapidly as fear enveloped my face. Trying to ap-peal to his caring side, I softened my voice and sweetened my look, if that was at all possible. "Bae, noooooo. I never! I have no reason to be with anyone when I have you." Now it was time to take responsibility for something so he didn't accuse me of saying what he wanted to hear. "And I was wrong for communicating with Tyriq. I'll never do that shit again. Not through Facebook, phone calls, texts, letters, anything!" I apologized again although I felt I was the one who deserved an apol-ogy.

He then stood to his feet and brought me with him. I flinched and that angered him. "Fuck you jumping for? If I wanted to haul off and stomp yo ass some mo', I would'na stopped." Spit flew from his mouth to my face but I refused to wipe it off.

I tried to relax a bit as he stared me down but my body trembled uncontrollably. No man had ever put his hands on me before and I didn't know what to expect next. But I said the only two words I assumed a man with a compulsion to control wanted to hear.

"I'm sorry." The more I said it was the more I realized how truly sorry I was.

I was sorry for not adhering to the signs because they were there all along. I had mistaken his possession for assuredness. *"I own you! You're mines! You belong to me!"* I foolishly thought he was simply being boastful about his love for me but in truth he was just stating ownership.

Damn! How could I be so blind? In that moment, I wanted to cry, not only for me, but for my son. Thank God the commotion didn't disturb him from his sleep. The last thing I would ever want is for my son to see his mama being abused. He'd carry that image for the rest of his life.

Choppa looked at me despicably, so I repeated myself. I needed him to take my plea seriously and not start his rampage again. "I'm so sorry. Please forgive me."

"Yea, I bet you are sorry now. You thought you were fuckin' with one of those weak niggas you're used to? But I'm cut from a different cloth. I don't take no shit from muthafuckas out there," he pointed at the wall, "and I damn sure don't take no shit off of *my* woman." He stabbed his finger into my chest plate.

"And you shouldn't." I agreed. I couldn't beat him, so I had to join him. "But, bae, it's not what you think. You should know I would never do that to you. Never, ever, would I cheat." Tears poured from my puffy eyes.

Suddenly, he looked at me tenderly. That frightened me more than the menacing look his face housed a second ago because it proved his actions were bigger than him having a fucked up attitude. He wasn't working with a full deck.

"Fuck!" He ran his hand over the botched up hair cut he gave me. Then, he gingerly touched my swollen face.

"Owe!" I winced.

Choppa stared at me for a long moment without saying a word. I feared he was deciding my fate and the decision wouldn't be a pretty one. I started to plead for his mercy but my plea wasn't needed.

Choppa let out a long sigh. "Ah, man! Why you make do that? Fuck I hurt you like this?"

Are those tears I see in his eyes? I couldn't believe it!

He shook his head as he looked around at the bloody mess he caused. "Julz," he touched my cheek and I cringed, "I can't love a woman I can't trust. I would never do no shit like this if you didn't give me a reason. My word was to love you, only. I promised you that, and I upheld it. And your love and loyalty was to me, above all, including your shorty. What am I s'pose to think when you talking to a nigga behind my back?"

"I was wrong but I swear to you I wasn't trying to cheat," I said pliantly.

He sucked in a deep breath and then let it out slowly. "A'ight. Don't you ever lie to me again. And don't ever let nan muthafucka talk against me. I'm your man, your homie, your friend—all of that. You don't need no other nigga's friendship. You remember that and an episode like this will never happen again. You understand me?"

I shook my head *yes* but I couldn't fathom a word he was saying. It was all Greek to me. How the hell did he expect for me to love him knowing he was capable of such viciousness?

"I understand."

He examined the visible knots on my forehead, rubbing them gently. "I hate that I had to do this shit to you but sometimes a nigga gotta let his woman know not to fuck with his heart. Do you hear me?"

"Yes."

"Good. So you're gonna delete any social page you have and I trust I don't have to second guess you handling that business, right?"

"I don't need it. I'll deactivate them." I was willing to agree to any term he issued if it meant he'd go to his corner and I could go to mine.

"A'ight. Go wash up, shorty, and come to bed." He headed out of the kitchen and I walked in tow so I didn't stir any insecurity in him with my lingering behind.

Once in the bathroom and behind closed doors, I spent some time looking at myself in the mirror, sobbing shamefully, before I got into the tub.

Out of the frying pan and into the fire, I thought.

Tonight, Choppa made Marcel, at his worst, appear like sunshine and rainbows by comparison.

You've put up with your share of shit from men but abuse isn't going to be added to the list. Get your son and get the fuck from 'round him. What happened once can and will happen again, I told myself.

An hour in the bathroom was more than enough time for me to conclude that I needed to feign forgiveness to appease the moment before I left like a thief in the night.

I climbed in bed where Choppa awaited me, praying he wouldn't touch me in no way, shape or form. I didn't believe I had enough theater in me to act like I could tolerate his touches.

Luckily for me, he only spooned me. That was hard to stomach but at least it wasn't sex.

Choppa fell asleep easily. Me? Not at all. I simply stared at the digital clock on the nightstand, abiding my time.

I didn't have a foolproof plan but I knew whatever I did, it would begin once Choppa was in the dead of his sleep.

Three hours passed and he was completely knocked out. It was then I made my move from under him and out of the bed. I cautiously tiptoed over to my purse. After I grabbed it, I headed out of the room discreetly, ignoring the terrible aches and pains that shot through my battered body.

My heart raced and a lump formed in my throat as I made my way into Justus' room. I was so nervous I was having difficulty breathing.

I sat on his bed and shook him softly. "Wake up, baby. Wake up."

He stirred for a minute before he groggily spoke. "Huh?"

"Shhh! Don't talk. Just get up. We gotta go."

Justus sat up and I rushed a pair of tennis onto his feet and stuffed him inside of his coat. Grabbing his backpack and a luggage from his closet, I began filling it with as much clothes and shoes as possible.

From there, I stood him to his feet, demanding he wake up fully so he could walk on his own.

"Mam—"

I cupped my hand over his mouth quickly. "I told you to be quiet. Don't pout. Don't do nothing but walk. Silently."

Justus was disoriented but he didn't buck my orders.

We walked soundlessly through the house, stopping in the laundry room. I then grabbed dirty clothes of mine from the hamper as I didn't want to risk taking any from our closet and waking the sleeping monster.

With Justus and some of our things, we headed to the front door to leave. To my right, I spotted one of my coats on the rack along with a fitted cap belonging to Choppa. I grabbed them both and threw them on. I didn't have on any shoes but it wasn't worth going back into our room to get a pair.

I eased the door open and then closed it in the same manner.

The four a.m. air was chilly and the overall pain I was in was pronunciated the more my body shivered from the cold wind encircling me.

I quickened my step and virtually dragged my baby behind me. We walked down the street and around a corner before I pulled out my cell phone and called Precious. She didn't answer. I called Fat-Fat but she didn't answer either.

"Shit!" I cursed below my breath.

"Mama, I'm sleepy." Justus was having a mild tantrum.

"I know, honey. I know. Just hold on."

Electing not to continue ringing their phones back to back, I called an Uber driver, giving them the address of the house we stood nearby. After securing a ride, I bit the bullet and lifted my son in my arms, silently apologizing to him.

Twenty minutes later, a silver Taurus pulled up and I hurriedly ran over to it, throwing my luggage into the backseat and sliding myself and Justus in behind it.

"Good morning," he spoke. "Where to?"

"Good morning," I replied, giving him the address afterwards.

Thirty minutes later, we pulled up in front of Fat-Fat's. Although we hadn't been talking much lately, her house was the closest and deep down I knew she wouldn't turn me away. The friendship could be rocky all day but our sisterhood remained solid.

I paid the gentleman who looked at me oddly. No doubt he was probably creating a scenario in his mind as to why a battered looking woman was fleeing at this time of the morning but he remained mute.

"Thank you," I said as I exited his car.

He pulled off and I urgently knocked on the door of Fat-Fat's town-home apartment.

It took a good five minutes before I saw her bedroom light come alive. A minute later, I heard her call out. "Who is it?"

"It's me. Julz and Justus." Her front porch's light illuminated her doorstep.

Then the chain could be heard flying off of the housing bracket along with the turn of her deadbolt.

As she opened her door, I heard her say. "What brings you by at this hour?" I lifted my head while removing my hat, so I didn't have to explain. Her eyes watered instantly. She grabbed my luggage and ushered me in. "Aww, baby, come inside."

Fat-Fat took Justus off of my hands and brought him upstairs into her guest bedroom, laying him to back to sleep.

A few short minutes later, her steps could be heard stampeding down her stairs. She ran over to me, where I stood, and hugged me tightly. Her embrace ached me but I dealt with it because her comfort was worth it.

She fingered the choppy lengths of my short and uneven hair as she caressed the side of my face. Tears coated her cheeks but she neglected to wipe them as she focused on me.

"Tell me what happened?" Fat-Fat's voice croaked of pain.

"Where do I start?" I shook my head, questioning rhetorically.

She hunched her shoulders. "Wherever you want. From the beginning if you need to."

Restraining Order

Fat-Fat held and squeezed my hand, conveying her care. I took a deep inhale and from there, I opened up, revealing things I once only shared with Essence, while she was alive, where it concerned Choppa.

By the time we finished talking, hours later, it was daylight outside.

"Wow! I didn't know you were having to deal with all that. Why didn't you tell me this sooner?"

"Ever since Essence died, you've pulled back, sis."

"I know but I wouldn't have turned my back on you had I known this. You gotta believe that."

"I know but I distanced myself after a while as well, so it's not all on you." I sighed heavily. "What am I gonna do? I can't go back to him and Lord only knows what he'll do when he awakes and finds out that we're not there."

"First thing first, I'm going to give you something of mine to put on and we're going down to the police station to press charges against him, have him arrested and file a restraining order. Once he's in custody we'll get all of your shit out of there and you'll come stay with me."

Press charges? Restraining Order? Those words alarmed me the moment they left her lips. "I don't think I can do that. I don't want to get him in trouble. I just want to be free of him."

"No, no, baby. He needs to know there are consequences to his actions. Cowards like him think they can manipulate a woman's silence by striking fear into their hearts. Well, fuck that! Have you seen yourself, sweetie? He doesn't give a damn about you and that's obvious. He's not only put hands on you but also Marcel. Not to mention he threatened Tyriq's life and I still hold him accountable for Essence's death. He's unstable, sis. You need to get an order of protection so if he violates, the law is on your side."

I started bouncing my knee and shaking so bad my voice began to tremble. "I'm scared. I'm so fuckin' scared!"

Fat-Fat wrapped her arm around me. "I know you are, which is all the more reason we need to do this and now!"

There goes my babyyyyy...

Hearing Choppa's ringtone caused me to jump out of my skin. "Oh, God! That's him." Tears pushed from my eyes. "Should I answer?"

"No. Don't answer. Matter of fact, cut your ringer off so his repeat calls don't give you an anxiety attack." She must have seen my nerves getting the better of me.

I knew that would piss him off for certain but I gathered my absence already secured his rage. So, I did as she suggested and powered my phone off.

Standing up from the sofa, we headed upstairs to get dressed and ready to set in motion what would alter my life as I've known it over these seven months.

Fat-Fat touched me on the arm, getting my attention. "You're doing the right thing, Julz."

"Yea?" I questioned because my intuition was telling me very differently. I swallowed hard and then went on to further ask. "Then why do I feel no good will come from this?"

Chapter 51
Choppa

After everything I did for her, she had me locked up! Dirty ass bitch! That's all that kept running through my mind as I sat in the holding cell.

The po's had come to the crib and arrested me two days ago, charging me with domestic violence. By policy, I had to remain in jail 72 hours before I could be bonded out. It was supposed to give a nigga time to cool off but as the final 24 hours ticked away excruciatingly slow, all that time did was increase my anger.

I had already kicked a nigga's ass in the holding cell because he tried to boar hog the phone. And I was close to fuckin' up another one when a guard called my name letting me know I was being released.

A half hour later I walked out of jail with a muthafuckin' restraining order in hand.

"You see this fuck shit?" I tossed the papers in Pop's lap as soon as we got in his car. "Like that's supposed to keep me off of that ass."

"Big bruh, I know you're gonna do what you're gonna do, but if you want my advice I think you should just let Julz go on her way. Real talk, you got too much to lose."

I looked at him like he was a traitor. "Youngin, when I ask for your advice, that's when you give it! Until then, stay in your lane."

"You're right, handle your biz," he backed down.

Pop started the engine, put the car in gear and we drove off. He went in his coat pocket and passed me a blunt. I fired it up and welcomed it to my lips.

After getting my head clear, I said, "So, what's been going on out here?"

"Business is good but your homies still stepping on our toes. I had a few words with Cardale the other day at the mall. Straight up, I was 'bout to blaze that ass but there were too many people around."

I saw the anger in Pop's face. "Don't worry, that nigga is on borrowed time. I'm not playing no more games. I'm crushing any and everybody that test our G! Now they're about to see why they call me Choppa." The bullshit with Julz had me in a murderous mode.

Pop dropped me off at the crib where I took a long bath to get the smell of jail off of me. Going through my phone, I saw I had mad missed calls and messages. Most were business related but a dozen, or so, were from KiKi.

I called and talked to her for more than an hour. She told me how much she missed me and I promised to visit her soon. But, really, my mind was on Julz.

A nigga couldn't eat or sleep. As the days passed by, I started missing her like crazy. Some days I would regret what I'd done to her and other days I would be boiling with anger, thinking she was somewhere laid up with her baby daddy or, maybe, Tyriq.

Both scenarios drove me violently insane. To make matters worse she had changed her phone number. But I knew how to reach her.

Kim Marie placed the call to Julz' job, while I quietly remained on a third line listening to their conversation.

"Hello?"

"Hey, Julz, this is Kim Marie. How are you?"

"Hi. I'm doing okay."

"Uh, I'm sure you know who I'm calling for. He just wants a chance to tell you he's sorry."

"Goodbye."

"Hold up, shorty," I spoke up. "You ain't even gotta do it like that."

"Choppa, by contacting me through a third party or otherwise you're in violation of the restraining order you were served. Please don't attempt to reach me again or I'll report it to the authorities," Julz said dispassionately as fuck.

I took a deep breath to control the anger that threatened to spew out. "Oh, that's how you're playing it? You put those white folks in our business already, now you're threatening to do it again?"

"Goodbye, Choppa!" Her tone carried no sign of the love she had claimed to have for me.

"Shorty, you'll do me like that?" I asked, allowing the hurt I felt to carry with my voice.

"Don't you dare! Look what you did to me!" she snapped.

Her clicking the fuck out was alright, though. At least she was still on the line.

"Baby, I'm so sorry. I've never done anything like that before. I was hurt and angry, and I just lost it. C'mon, boo, you know if I was in my right mind, I would've never done no foul shit like that to you. Don't you know that?"

"No! I only know what you did do."

"Let me make it up to you. Please, shorty, a nigga miss you so bad. I promise, I'll never even raise my voice at you again," I shamelessly begged.

"No, Choppa. Please don't call me again." She hung up in my face.

I sat there staring at my phone. My heart was shattered inside my chest.

"Do you want me to try to call her back?" Kim Marie's voice trickled through the haze.

"Yeah." I took a drink from the half gallon bottle of gin that sat on the table in front of me. Julz' office line rang over and over again with no answer. "Just hang up."

Kim Marie disconnected the call and clicked back over to my line. "You okay?" she asked.

I didn't even try to hide my pain. "Nah, but it's all good. Tell Pop I'ma fuck with him later."

"Okay, don't do nothing crazy. No woman in the world is worth that. You're a boss, bitches fall at your feet," she said.

"Facts!" I uttered. But I knew that no other woman on God's green earth could take Julz' place in my heart.

Every day after that, for two straight weeks, I sent flowers and balloons to Julz' job and each day she refused to accept them. Desperate to see her, I took to staking out her job and following her home from work.

During that third week, I observed her having lunch with Tyriq. *I oughta run up in there and leave them both slumped over the table.*

I was halfway out of my whip when I got a call from Cross. Reluctantly, I answered.

"Yeah."

"What's going on down there? I've had this shipment waiting for you for almost two weeks."

"Yeah, I know. Give me a few more days and I'll get with you. I'm having a few problems," I said.

Cross was talking so much I almost missed Julz and Tyriq exiting the restaurant. By the time I noticed them, Julz was getting in her rental and that nigga was pulling off in his ride.

"Yo, don't panic I'll be up there this weekend," I promised Cross.

He hung up and I trained my eyes on Julz taillights as the sky suddenly opened up and rain began coming down in sheets.

Following her without being seen was easy. I was skilled in stalking my prey, while she obviously had let her guards down.

I remained several cars behind her as she drove to her girl Fat-Fat's house. *After all of this shit, the bitch still fuckin' with that nigga!* By now my anger at seeing her with Tyriq was thicker than any stress I'd ever encountered. *This bitch ain't gon' learn!*

The darkened sky and the heavy rain gave cover to my presence as I turned onto Fat-Fat's street just seconds after her. She turned into the apartment complex and parked in front of her girl's building.

I parked a few doors down, and I was outta my whip in a nanosecond, banger out and ready to blow her deceitful head off.

Ignoring the rain, I crept up behind her as she was leaning into the backseat to get something, probably an umbrella. In one swift motion, I grabbed her around the neck and put my steel to the back of her head. She tried to scream but I applied pressure to her windpipe with my forearm, cutting off her words.

"Scream and you'll never see your son again!" I threatened as I kicked her door shut, drug her to my car and forced her inside.

Before going around to the driver's side, I placed a pair of plastic handcuffs around her wrists to limit her movement.

"Choppa, why are you doing this?" she cried as I slid behind the wheel and drove off.

She was shaking badly when I glanced over in the passenger seat at her. But in my blind rage, I didn't give two fucks.

"You can run, shorty, but you can't hide. And ain't no nigga or piece of paper in this world can protect you." I pulled the restraining order out of my pocket and tossed it in her lap. "Like I told you, you belong to *me!*"

370

Whap!
I backhanded her so hard her head hit the window.

"Say your prayers, baby girl," I advised in an ominous tone. "I been planning this shit for weeks."

Chapter 52
Julz

The BMW came to a sudden stop at the curb of an eerie, dark road. He yanked the gear in park and stared straight ahead. The vein on the side of his temple pulsated with hot anger that terrified me to no end. In the passenger seat, I was shaking frenziedly as I looked out of the window, too afraid to look at him. The sky was as dark as his mood and even though the heater was on full blast, inside of the car felt as cold as that muthafucka's heart.

Raindrops drummed on the windshield in an ominous symphony that matched the tears cascading down my battered face dripping onto my torn, bloodied blouse.

The fact that he wasn't talking didn't bode well for me at all. I could somewhat gauge the level of his anger when he was going off, spewing deathly threats and unfounded accusations. But when he was quiet like this, I had no idea what he would do. The only thing I was absolutely certain of was that he was going to punish me severely—death was not out of the question.

Out of the corner of my eye, I saw him pull his gun out of his waist and place it in his lap. At the sight of it, I became terrified. My heart pounded hard in my chest and pee ran down my leg.

He's going to kill me this time, I feared. *How could he claim to love me so much yet treat me so foul?*

Filled with fright, I began rocking back and forth.

Lord, if you get me out of this safely tonight, I promise to move far away from him, I silently prayed as my body trembled all over.

I jumped when I felt him touch my face. "Baby gurl, look at me," he said with a gentleness that belied the cruel monster he could become in the blink of an eye.

I didn't want to look at that bastard but I knew better than to defy him. Slowly, I turned my head in his direction. He cut the dome light on in the car and locked eyes with me. Stroking my face with the back of his hand, he asked, "Why you trembling? Are you afraid of me?"

I didn't know whether to answer honestly or lie. Either response could incur his wrath, so I decided to just keep quiet. But that was a mistake. "Fuck you gon' do, ignore me?" he growled.

"No," I replied meekly, casting my eyes downward.

"Answer me, then," he demanded. "Are you afraid of me?"

"Yes," I admitted in a voice barely above a whisper.

His response came with lightning quickness.

Whap!

I hadn't even seen him raise his hand but the stinging sensation on the side of my face and the taste of fresh blood in my mouth confirmed why my ears were now ringing.

"Bitch, you ain't scared of me," he spat. "Because if you were, you wouldn't keep tryin' a nigga like you be doing. Would you?"

"No. And I'm sorry," I apologized, though I hadn't done a damn thing but try to get far away from his crazy, jealous and controlling ass. Lord, he was nothing like the man I had fell in love with.

He smiled triumphantly. "Give your nigga a kiss and tell me that you belong to me."

I leaned over and offered him my lips. He covered my mouth with his and slid his tongue inside.

I couldn't help recalling a time not long ago when his kiss ignited a fire in my body that only his insatiable sexual appetite could quench, but now it felt like a serpent was slithering around in my mouth.

I forced the bile back down my throat and pretended to enjoy our lip lock. I didn't dare break the kiss until he pulled back first. "I belong to you," I said perfunctorily.

He lifted the gun from his lap and placed the tip of the cold steel against my forehead. "Say that shit like you mean it or I'll blow your brains outta ya muthafuckin' head!" he threatened.

His tone was as menacing as the weapon he held to my head. "Baby, I belong to you. Forever," I said.

"That's my gurl," he smiled. "Damn, I love you, bae. So much that I'll murder your ass if you ever try to leave me again. You understand me?" He lowered the gun from my forehead to my mouth and forced it inside. I gagged as he shoved it to the back of my throat. "You know, a few years ago I killed a bitch who looked just like you," he taunted.

I didn't know if it was true but I didn't doubt it. He was crazy beyond definition.

"Bitch tried to cut me off. Don't ever try that shit. Because if I can't have you, nobody will. On my life, ya feel me?" His sincerity rang loudly in my ears.

"Yes," I cried.

He removed the gun from inside of my mouth and then leaned in and placed a soft kiss on my tear stained cheek. I prayed his anger had subsided and that I would live to see my son again, but the next words out of his mouth caused me to shiver all over.

"Nah, bitch, you don't really feel me," he said. "But you're about to. Get out the car. I'm 'bout to bury your ass right next to that other ho."

Choppa got out of the car and walked around to my side. As soon as he opened the door and roughly pulled me out, I screamed my head off.

"Help! Please, somebody help me!"

He looked at me and grinned. "If a tree falls in the middle of the forest, does anybody hear it?"

Oh, Lord! This muthafucka is psychotic! I'm going to die!

"Choppa, baby, please. This is your shorty, don't do this to me," I appealed desperately.

"Bitch, don't talk to me!"

"But, bae, I have a child who needs me."

"Your boy, Tyriq, can finish raising him."

"Choppa, Tyriq isn't my boy. He's nothing but a friend. You're my everything." I begged and pleaded for my life.

Choppa didn't respond and he ignored my loud screams as he drug me by the arm up into some dark woods.

Frightened beyond words, I tried to fall to the ground to keep him from pulling me further into the woods but he was relentless. He put his arms underneath my arm pits and drug me through the rain and the dense foliage. My heels left a long track in the muddied ground as I scuffled and fought to prevent him from succeeding.

The cuffs around my wrists cut deep into my skin, almost cutting off the circulation of blood. My voice was fading fast from the loud screaming and my vision was blurred by my tears.

Finally, Choppa released me. I laid on the ground crying and shaking as he stood over me breathing heavily, saying nothing.

After a minute or two, he pulled his cell phone out and turned on the built-in flashlight. The bright beam lit up the small area. Fear choked off my breath when I saw a shallow, empty grave to the right of where I lay. Lying on the ground next to it was a shovel, which told me that this crazy muthafucka had already planned my death.

Panic set in, causing me to gulp for air.

"How do you wanna die, shorty, fast or slow?" He taunted me.

I didn't want to die all.

"Choppa, please don't do this!"

"If you don't wanna die, tell me the truth. Admit that you slept with that nigga. I already know the truth so ain't no sense in continuing to lie. Just admit it and we'll work it out. But if you lie to me again, I'ma bury you alive." His voice was so callous.

I hadn't even thought about sleeping with another man since we'd met but telling him that might get me killed. *Just tell him what he wants to hear even if it's not the truth.*

I opened my mouth to say that I had slept with Tyriq but the lie wouldn't come out. I figured if I was going to die it might as well be over the truth.

"Baby, I've never slept with any other man but you since the day I first met you. Even before that, it had been more than a year."

"You just refuse to tell the truth, don't you?" He snapped.

"I'm telling you the truth, bae," I cried.

Choppa came over and picked up the shovel. I thought about raising my foot and trying to kick him into the grave, to give myself a chance to escape. But before I could build up the courage to try it, he was again standing upright.

The rain had ceased falling from the sky and just like the instant change in the weather, his demeanor transformed as well.

Placing the shovel at my feet, Choppa sat down in the mud beside me. He looked at me with regret. "Shorty, I loved you with all my heart. You should'na done me like that." I heard tears in his voice.

"I didn't do anything, Choppa. Please believe me. I swear to you on my son's life, I have never slept with Tyriq. Matter of fact, I haven't slept with any man besides you. That's the God's honest truth, bae."

"Don't lie to me, Julz."

"I'm not, boo." My tone begged him to believe me. And it must've broken through his psyche because his look softened.

Instead of threatening to bury me alive he asked if I still loved him.

"Yes, I still love you," I replied.

He looked deeper into my eyes as if searching them for genuineness.

Then after a long moment of silence, I saw tears fall from his eyes.

"Shorty, I done fucked everything up between us and I'm sorry for that. This shit ain't about you, it's about me. I'm just fucked up in the head."

He reached behind me and freed me from the cuffs. I rubbed my tender wrists and stood to my feet. My first instinct was to scream and run but I could sense that peril had passed.

"Choppa, you have to get yourself some help," I said.

Looking down at him, he looked pitiful.

"It don't even matter now, shorty. I've lost you forever. So, fuck it!" He pulled his gun from his waist.

"Don't say that." Tears fell for him. I couldn't help it.

"Go on, shorty. Just leave me here."

"No!" I sat back down beside him and wrapped my arms around his shoulders. In spite of the abuse, I couldn't forget how wonderfully he had loved me most of the time. I couldn't bring myself to leave him there in the mind state he was in. "Let's go, Choppa, please."

"Nah, shorty, I'm good."

"Please, Choppa, it's cold out here." I quivered.

"Look, shorty, I wouldn't even wanna live without you. Money, cars—all that shit is nothin' if I don't have you," he said with conviction.

My heart broke for him. I didn't want to be with him anymore, I thought, but I surely didn't want him to hurt himself.

"Choppa—"

"Don't worry about me, baby gurl. Like I said, I'm good. But check this out, I got money stashed at the condo. A whole lot." He told me where the safe was and he gave me the combination to the lock.

None of it registered in my mind. I didn't want his money, I wanted him to live. "Please get help. Do that for me." I pleaded with him.

"Nah, I'm good." He lifted his arm and stuck the gun to the roof of his mouth.

"No, Choppa!" I cried.

My heart settled a tiny bit when he removed the gun from his mouth. It appeared he heeded my petition to put a stop to the madness but then panic set in again when he placed the barrel to the side of his head.

"It's over, shorty. I love you."

Boom!

"Nooooo!" I screamed.

To be continued...
<u>Restraining Order 2: The Finale</u>
Available Now!

TORN BETWEEN TWO
By **Coffee**
LAY IT DOWN **III**
By **Jamaica**
BLOOD OF A BOSS **IV**
By **Askari**
BRIDE OF A HUSTLA **III**
By **Destiny Skai**
WHEN A GOOD GIRL GOES BAD **II**
By **Adrienne**
LOVE & CHASIN' PAPER **II**
By **Qay Crockett**
THE HEART OF A GANGSTA **II**
By **Jerry Jackson**
TO DIE IN VAIN **II**
By **ASAD**
THE BOSS MAN'S DAUGHTERS **II**
By **Aryanna**

Available Now
RESTRAING ORDER **I & II**
By **CA$H & Coffee**

LOVE KNOWS NO BOUNDARIES **I II & III**

By **Coffee**

LAY IT DOWN **I & II**

LAST OF A DYING BREED

By **Jamaica**

PUSH IT TO THE LIMIT

By **Bre' Hayes**

BLOOD OF A BOSS **I II & III**

By **Askari**

THE STREETS BLEED MURDER **I, II & III**

THE HEART OF A GANGSTA

By **Jerry Jackson**

CUM FOR ME

An **LDP Erotica Collaboration**

BRIDE OF A HUSTLA **I & II**

By **Destiny Skai**

WHEN A GOOD GIRL GOES BAD

By **Adrienne**

A GANGSTER'S REVENGE **I II III & IV**

THE BOSS MAN'S DAUGHTERS

A SAVAGE LOVE **I & II**

By **Aryanna**

WHAT ABOUT US **I & II**

NEVER LOVE AGAIN

THUG ADDICTION

By **Kim Kaye**

THE KING CARTEL **I, II & III**

By **Frank Gresham**

THESE NIGGAS AIN'T LOYAL **I, II & III**

By **Nikki Tee**

GANGSTA SHYT **I II &III**

By **CATO**

THE ULTIMATE BETRAYAL

By **Phoenix**

DON'T FU#K WITH MY HEART **I & II**

By **Linnea**

BOSS'N UP **I & II**

By **Royal Nicole**

I LOVE YOU TO DEATH

By Destiny J

I RIDE FOR MY HITTA

I STILL RIDE FOR MY HITTA

By **Misty Holt**

LOVE & CHASIN' PAPER

By **Qay Crockett**

TO DIE IN VAIN

By **ASAD**

Ca$h & Coffee

<u>BOOKS BY LDP'S CEO, CA$H</u>

<u>TRUST IN NO MAN</u>

<u>TRUST IN NO MAN 2</u>

<u>TRUST IN NO MAN 3</u>

<u>BONDED BY BLOOD</u>

<u>IN LOVE WITH A CONVICT</u>

<u>SHORTY GOT A THUG</u>

<u>THUGS CRY</u>

<u>THUGS CRY 2</u>

<u>TRUST NO BITCH</u>

<u>TRUST NO BITCH 2</u>

<u>TRUST NO BITCH 3</u>

<u>TIL MY CASKET DROPS</u>

<u>RESTRAINING ORDER</u>

<u>RESTRAINING ORDER 2</u>

<u>Coming Soon</u>
THUGS CRY 3
BONDED BY BLOOD 2
BOW DOWN TO MY GANGSTA

Stay Connected with Us!

Text **LOCKDOWN** to 22828 to stay up-to-date with new releases, sneak peaks, contests and more...

Thank You!

Made in the USA
Columbia, SC
03 December 2021

50342297R00211